MATTHEW P. GILBERT

SINS OF THE FATHERS BOOK 3

WAR GOD'S WILL

©2019 MATTHEW P. GILBERT

There is nothing in life worth having that you will not, at some point, have to fight for, and the path to victory is never easy. Blood and treasure, pain and self-doubt, these are constant companions in any battle. A warrior will know them well.
The Book of Amrath, Ruminations 1:7

PROLOGUE

ONE MILLENNIUM PAST

NARITAS could barely suppress a gleeful cackle as he regarded the dark, thin face before him. *Amin al Asad, you are such a gift to us!* "You must do it *yourself*," he insisted.

Al Asad glared back with dark, rage-filled eyes, and took the wicked, rune-carved blade. His long, dark fingers pushed Naritas's lighter, frail digits from the weapon's grip. "I follow through on my plans, whatever the cost, weakling." He snatched the dagger from Naritas with a sneer, not bothering to hide his contempt. "Just as my men did."

Al Asad's smoldering gaze lingered a moment before he turned away. His jaw bulged as he clenched his teeth and raised the point of the blade to his eye.

"Yes," Naritas hissed, barely able to hide his elation. "This is how the magic works." He spoke confidently, but in truth, he was anything but certain. What he had in mind, many would call madness. No one had ever attempted anything so bold. Men were not meant to tread in such places.

Naritas allowed himself a quick glance at the huge stone font in the center of the room. Ten feet across and three deep, it brimmed with dark liquid. Near one edge of the font, a golden lion's head protruded from the surface, the only visible portion of a statue submerged there. Mere hours before, a measure of that liquid had run through the veins of al Asad's warrior priests. Each had walked proudly, even arrogantly, to the sacrificial font, placed his neck over the collection trough, and slit his own throat with inhuman resolve. *Oh, I suppose the poor sods we used to round out the volume resisted well enough, but then they weren't part of the ritual. They were just material.* Disposing of the corpses had been thirsty work, indeed, but there were always students who needed to work off their tuition, and as far as Naritas was concerned, the more unpleasant the work they were assigned, the better.

The font was as great an abomination as Naritas could conceive and create. *Abomination* was the heart of the ritual. It would draw *him*. It would call to *his* nature, and lure *him* into the trap.

Naritas turned back to al Asad and watched him intently. *We will see if you share your men's resolve, al Asad.*

There were scholars in Torium who studied the depths of the mind, learned men who would have argued that it was not possible for human beings to do such things, that their own minds would rebel against such self-destruction, no matter their motivation, but al Asad and his men were apparently something more than mere humans. They were unique, and unique was another word for power to one who understood the true workings of the universe. *One such as I.*

Naritas knew he could not allow his giddiness to show, but it threatened to burst from him all the same. *I stand on the brink of greatness, and I owe it all to petty politics!*

Al Asad had come to them months ago, outcast and full of grief and rage. Snakes had put fangs into the boy king Alexander, whispering venom in his ear, poisoning him against his teacher.

Fools hungry for power, with no concept of how a fighting man would respond to their pathetic games. Such mistakes are often lethal.

They certainly would be if Al Asad had his way. He wanted a weapon, and Naritas, the Master of Torium, had many ideas for such things. One, in fact, was so audacious that he had never spoken of it to another soul, but he had written down his research, his mad experiments, his good results with demons and other unnatural entities, and his plan to move forward to a full test.

Of course, that had required enlisting some allies. His underlings were happy to assist, though they knew only pieces of what was truly at stake. After all, the University at Torium was a place of knowledge and learning. If it was also a place of madness, where blasphemous ideas were entertained with cold reason, where men truly struggled to learn secrets they were never meant to know, was that a sin, really?

It is the very definition of progress.

Tasinal and his brethren soared over Torium like eagles searching for prey, their shadows flitting and warping over the ground beneath, dark reflections in a convoluted, twisted mirror. With equal measures of excitement and fear, he watched Amrath drop from the sky like a stone toward the ziggurats below, and, along with the rest of the Council of Twelve, Tasinal followed. The coming battle would be hard fought, much more real than the trivial handling of Aristademos and his men. Naritas and his students had much knowledge of true magic, and were firmly ensconced in the most powerful defensive structure of the civilized world.

The 'university' had never been penetrated, partially because of its claims of neutrality, but more so because it was indeed a fortress, one designed by magi with an intricate understanding of physical forces. The entire compound was surrounded by a high, sloped wall made of some sort of odd sedimentary stone quarried from nearby deposits, a light, airy material that was impervious to catapult or ballista fire. It did not shatter or puncture like ordinary stone or brick, but simply swallowed projectiles whole, absorbing and redirecting the energy away to nothing.

Further within lay a great central pyramid that towered over the landscape, the 'university' where the magi, claiming to be scholars and educators of men, carried out their black magic. Between the wall and central structure was a great moat, and beyond, more, smaller, flat-topped pyramids encircled the city just inside the wall, watchtowers with overlapping fields of fire to mass archers, siege weapons, or other, more arcane engines of destruction.

Tasinal barely contained the urge to spit at the city. *Let us see how you withstand us, fiends.*

The Council's spy had been certain. Naritas intended utter madness: he would try to slay a *god* and harness its power into a weapon. He had a damned good chance of succeeding, and a similar chance of failing and bringing the world to ruin.

Worse, the spy had known when: *now*.

They set down in the courtyard on the far side of the moat, each sorcerer having his own sort of landing ritual, some hitting the ground running, others simply stopping in place in defiance of puny physics. Tasinal was a runner for now, though he was of the opinion that being a stopper indicated a more powerful mastery, and hoped someday to be able to master the technique.

Tasinal crouched, momentarily spent from the flight and subsequent landing, and watched the true masters set about their work. Amrath, Noril, and Aswan were titans amongst titans, practically demigods. *And yet I notice Amrath is a runner!* He resolved to think on this later. For the moment, there were other, more pressing matters that required his attention.

Those matters, specifically the guards assigned to keep them out of the university, were quickly dealt with. The fools came pouring from the pyramid, full of righteous fury, perhaps three dozen men in all. *Ah, this is my part.* It seemed a small number of defenders, and yet who knew what a bunch of stuffy scholars thought an appropriate force? It hardly mattered, at any rate.

Tasinal raised a hand and clenched his fist. His target, a marble statue depicting a scholar holding a book aloft, imploded into rubble. With a flick of his wrist, he sent thousands of projectiles hurtling at the would-be defenders. The missiles ripped through the fools and kept going, sending streamers of blood and gore behind them to paint the cobblestones and the walls of the pyramid. His victims slumped to the ground, lifeless and well-ventilated, as Tasinal smiled in satisfaction.

Amrath gave Tasinal a brief, grudging nod of approval. Tasinal bowed with a flourish, then sat on the ground. *I just kill people. I'll leave the engineering and siege work to the masters.*

Amrath, satisfied that they would now be unmolested, looked up at the great pyramid and called to Yorn, the artificer to join him. Tasinal disliked Yorn intensely, and considered him halfway to being a Torian himself, meddling with things he ought not, but it was difficult to deny his results. *Still, a proper Meite does not make things to do his magic. He damned well does it himself.*

Yorn contemplated the pyramid for some time, rubbing at his chin, a sour look on his face. Noril tapped his foot, scowling, while Amrath and Aswan watched his growing impatience with wry amusement.

At last, the Artificer spoke. "No point in going in from the top. It's all heavily warded. Let's just find the bunker and breach a wall."

Amrath produced a rolled sheet of parchment from his robes and held it in front of Aswan. "The spy says it should be there."

Aswan looked at the drawing for a moment, then turned to a particular point in the structure. He studied the ground intently for a moment, then raised his arms in a great, sweeping gesture. Tons of dirt flew from the base of the great pyramid as if he were wielding a giant shovel. Again and again he dug, sweat running on his brow, gradually exposing the bunker beneath.

Amrath, his blue tunic now covered in a fine dusting of dirt, ran his hands through his bound, blond hair, corralling any that had managed to escape. Noril raised a well-muscled arm and ran a hand over his own short-cropped, graying head, grinning. Amrath spared him a brief scornful look before returning the smile and heading for the exposed wall.

Tasinal rose and followed the other Meites. Yorn strode to the exposed wall, his tall, lanky frame almost rattling. He made a show of examining the runes, though Tasinal strongly suspected he was simply making things up.

Yorn plucked at his beard, shaking his head and muttering. "Powerful wards."

Amrath asked, "Will they stop us?"

Yorn, bemused, answered, "No."

Noril scoffed and stepped up to the rune-graven wall. "Let us see what they are made of." He hammered a fist squarely in the center of the polished, reflective surface. The blow produced a terrific, ringing tone. Waves of white light rippled from the point of impact like a stone dropped in still water, brilliant at first, then slowly fading, but the wall seemed no worse off for Noril's efforts. He rubbed at his hand, frowning. "Strong."

Yorn rolled his eyes. "I believe I just mentioned that."

"You didn't mention how we were going to get through it, that I heard," Noril shot back, still rubbing at his hand.

"You hit it with something very hard, lots of times, until it falls over, dolt."

"I just did that."

"No," Yorn corrected. "You should have used your head."

Tasinal barely managed to contain a snicker at the artificer's barb. Noril would not be happy to be laughed at, especially by someone he saw as an inferior, and Tasinal did not relish an encounter with Noril's fists.

Amrath clapped a hand on Yorn and Noril's shoulders and said in a cheery voice, "A novel idea, using our heads! Let's do that now."

Naritas tore at his hair as yet another thunderous blow hammered at the heavily enchanted inner walls of Torium. Dust drifted down from the rough-hewn ceiling and rained through the flickering candlelight. Fifty of his best students encircled the black pool, chanting softly. All of them could feel the power building, both from their own ritual and the unrelenting assault on their walls.

Surely, the external defenders were dead, or at least fled. No one could expect them to stand against the Meites. But the subterranean sanctum had been built specifically to be *impregnable,* the walls and entrances reinforced with the most powerful of arcane wards. Dangerous experiments were conducted there, experiments that, if interrupted, could have grave, even disastrous results.

Experiments such as the one in which he and his underlings were even now engaged.

But we did not plan on holding off the damnable Council of Twelve! Not for long, at any rate! We must hurry!

Al Asad, to his credit, had already managed to carve one of

his own eyes from his skull. *What will! What resolve!* Naritas took the glistening, blood streaked orb from al Asad as the man stood trembling, blood dripping down his face, steadfastly refusing to scream. *The next will be infinitely harder, though, for with it comes darkness—eternal, crushing darkness.*

Naritas walked slowly toward the black pool, al Asad's eye in hand. A short, rune-graven ledge encircled the sacrificial basin. The runes would channel the power, contain it, focus it into the blood and into the vessel that would contain the very essence of Elgar: a golden lion, submerged to its neck in the black pool. *A lion, for Al Asad. It is perfect.* And it certainly didn't hurt that Naritas fancied lions as symbols of strength, as well. The Meites relied on emotion more so than the Torians, but even so, emotion was a handhold, a focus.

But this lion had no eyes. *Not yet.* Naritas pressed the glistening white orb into one of the lion's empty sockets. He smiled as the still-living flesh gazed back at him, its green iris seeming quite at home in the lion's face.

He was startled from his reverie by another deafening blow to the walls. "Al Asad!" Naritas cried. "We are almost out of time!"

Al Asad stood transfixed, his one remaining eye staring at the blade in his hand, his face contorted with warring emotions as he brought the blade to bear, slowly.

Naritas felt a pressing urge to scream, and yet he feared breaking the man's focus. Instead, he spoke in a soft, fatherly tone. "If they penetrate our defenses before we finish, it will all be for nothing."

Al Asad roared in fury and desperation, still unable to find the will to move the blade forward. "Wizard, you *swear* upon your life this will work? If I give up my sight, will I have the weapon I seek?"

Naritas kept a straight face as he called out, "I swear it." In truth, he had no idea how things would play out once he managed to trap Elgar. *In theory*, al Asad would have his weapon. In practice, there was a non-negligible chance of destroying... everything. *It's not as if he can hold it against me if we're all dead, though.*

Another titanic blow struck the enchanted wall, as if a mountain had been hurled against it. The shockwave ripped through the entire structure, sending debris raining from the ceiling. Another impact followed, even more energetic, and a crack appeared in the wall with a loud report, spreading like slow lightning.

Naritas wanted to turn his power and focus to mending the wall, but he had no choice. Things would simply have to play out now. At any moment, Elgar would be drawn into his trap, and it would take all of Naritas and his students' efforts to lock him down properly. Failing to do so would mean a disaster of epic proportion!

Naritas gnashed his teeth in mounting rage. It was not that he feared death, or even the destruction of the world. What he was unwilling to accept was failing to complete his greatest experiment, the pinnacle of his life and study. *Damn the Meites! I needed only minutes more!*

He cried out in a voice nearly a shriek, "Al Asad! It's now or never!"

Al Asad stood silent, the point of the knife an inch from his left eye, blood trailing from his empty right socket. Another tremendous blow struck the wall, so loud it momentarily drowned out the chanting. The crack in the wall became a spider web. More debris fell from the ceiling, and, with a huge, grinding and rending, a block of stone bigger than a man fell from the ceiling, missing al Asad by mere inches.

Al Asad did not even flinch.

In the end, Amrath simply lost patience, and gave in to outright fury; though admittedly, Aswan had assisted greatly by laughing at him for failing the first fifty-odd times.

Amrath stood, fists clenched before him, eyes blazing sapphire rage and frustration, looking about for something, anything he could use as a bludgeon. At last, he settled on one of several buildings made of huge blocks of normal stone. Tasinal wondered idly why they weren't also composed of the same odd, airy substance the walls and pyramids used and what purpose they served, but it hardly mattered. They had a new purpose now.

The building came apart under Amrath's will. The great stones, any of which would have made fine monoliths, each weighed tons, but they rose into the air and began circling overhead like dust motes under Amrath's control, until, one by one, they fell toward the enchanted wall.

Noril followed suit. Another of the buildings began to disassemble itself and fling its bones at the Torian sanctum. Tasinal rose and walked to Amrath, placing a hand on his shoulder and joining his own impatience and frustration to his mentor's. One by one, the rest of the Council joined them, lending their will and emotion to Amrath and Noril, until the Council of Twelve's full power coursed through their chosen two.

The blocks fell from the sky like meteors, accelerating far beyond the force of mere gravity. The earth shook from their blows, and many of the rocks shattered against the wall, sending deadly shrapnel into the ranks of the Meites, who simply refused to accept it as lethal. It tore the land, the trees, even the stones around the sorcerers, but it did not touch them at all.

The wall wavered and wailed under the assault. Cracks began to spread on its surface, bleeding brilliant pink light like wounds in flesh. *It's dying. Hopefully we don't run out of boulders before it keels over.*

Amrath and Noril held up their barrage until all of their

missiles had shattered, then paused to observe their work. Amrath's eyes sparkled with glee as he dipped a finger into the cracks on the sagging wall. "I'll let you do the honors," he told Noril with a bow.

Noril flashed a vicious grin at Yorn, his eyes lit with madness. "You said to use my head, weakling. Watch how I do it!" He reared back, thrust his upper body forward like a battering ram, and hammered his forehead through the shattered wall to thunderous applause.

It will go badly for the Torians, no matter how strong their magic. If they are smart, they will flee us.

It never occurred to Tasinal that flight might simply not be an option for anyone.

Naritas howled in rage and fear as one of his assistants exploded into a pool of gore beneath another falling block of stone. Al Asad still hesitated!

"We will all die here!" Naritas shrieked, unable to maintain his charade any longer. "Your sacrifice will be for nothing! You *must* finish the task!"

Yet al Asad did not move. He still stared at the dagger point, contemplating eternity while the plan fell to ruin. So much dust stirred around him, it almost appeared as if he were on fire, or steaming. He wore a dark grin, somehow amused by all of this. *He's gone mad. I will have to act for him.*

It was not, strictly speaking, the correct way, but Naritas felt the odds were with him. The pool itself should have been abomination enough to draw the attention of the god of vengeance. Convincing al Asad to mutilate himself had always been more of an insurance policy than an actual necessity, but what could not be dispensed with was his remaining eye! Naritas needed the blood of true believers, and the eyes of a man with vision to complete the trap, and he could wait no longer.

With a cry of abandon, the mage charged al Asad, intending to ram the blade in himself, but al Asad raised his free hand with blinding speed, seized Naritas by the throat, and lifted him into the air.

Naritas felt as if he had been beheaded, so strong was al Asad's strike. Breathing was impossible. He could only claw in vain at the iron grip that held him aloft, kicking his legs, unable to understand how this was happening.

Al Asad leered, slowly turning his head to face Naritas with a wicked grin. The gaping, bloody socket was still dripping blood, but it was not the only source. Blood ran freely from al Asad's nose and ears as well, and from the one remaining eye.

That eye, completely black, rolled in its socket like a window into oblivion as it regarded Naritas. With a cruel laugh, al Asad dropped the knife to the floor.

"I will show you will, mortal," he said, his voice an unearthly hiss, fingernails on slate for every sense Naritas possessed. The Master of Torium writhed in his captor's grasp as al Asad raised his free hand to his remaining eye. Naritas watched in suffocating horror as al Asad dug his fingers into the socket and tore the orb from his own head, still cackling. Steam and blood gouted from the wound and spattered over Naritas's face as the grinning madman snapped his own eye loose from the trailing nerves with a jerk of his hand.

Al Asad continued to regard him with bleeding, empty sockets, as if his vision were fully functional. *"Your death will be legendary, cockroach."*

Naritas felt his soul twist in terror as the words tore at his nerves and his mind, burning holes into his deepest being, driving the truth home as painfully as possible:

Elgar had arrived early.

Noril made certain to be the first through the breach, but Tasinal came quickly behind him, eager for the fight. *I may not be able to hurl mountains as well as the two of you, but I can damned well pound skulls with the best.*

They entered a massive chamber, then followed a tunnel a brief distance to the ritual room proper. At first, it was nearly impossible to see anything but billowing dust and darkness. Stepping from broad daylight into the pit was like crossing from noon to midnight. Tasinal quickly realized he could see well enough despite the light change, and the details of the inner sanctum resolved themselves into stark, lurid detail.

He has no eyes! That fact leapt out at Tasinal before anything else, even before the bloody corpse the stranger held by its throat, or the fact that the stranger was a Southlander. The eyeless man, if 'man' were the right word, was in poor shape all around. Blood ran from his nose, mouth, and ears, and Tasinal was fairly certain gouts of steam were jetting from the gaping eye sockets. He looked for all the world as if he were being cooked from the inside out. His dreadlocks trailed smoke, as if about to burst into flame.

"*Yes,*" the figure said, the voice an unearthly imposition of order on sounds not meant for the role. "*It is the nature of things. Your flesh was not meant to contain such energies.*"

"Who are you?" Noril demanded.

Amrath entered behind them, blinking in the darkness, and gasped. "Mei! What have they *done?*"

The figure before them whipped its head around at Amrath, fixing him with its empty stare. "*Ah, I see now. You are my brother's children. Leave. Now. This is not your concern.*"

Noril shouted at the top of his lungs, "*Who are you?*"

The Southlander looked about as if he were confused. *"I am..."* he began, then trailed off. *"Avenger?"*

Strall, the Council's resident expert on gods and other such matters, forced his way forward, and called in a high-pitched voice, nearly a squeal, "Tread carefully, fool! Do you even understand the enormity of what you're dealing with?"

Noril sneered at Strall a moment, as Amrath said softly, "A fundamental force of the universe. Implacable. Amazing."

"It can swat us like bugs!" Strall warned.

"I am Destroyer?"

Yorn heaved a great sigh. "We are all well aware of this, Strall, or did you forget why we came here to begin with?"

Strall glared back and forth at them and pointed his finger at one then the other, waving it about as it were simultaneously a weapon and a shield. "I'm just making certain you fools don't set it off!"

"Leave," the Southlander ordered. *"This is not your concern."*

"I'm afraid it is," Tasinal said. "We're here to put an end to these madmen."

"No. That will not be necessary. They will suffer first."

Idlic, whose chief contribution to the Council was a poison pen and razor-edged tongue, grunted and gestured to the empty chamber. "'They' would seem to be absent from the situation. I see only their greatest fool. Where are his little toads?"

"Cowering within. I will see to them soon enough. I would entertain myself more with this one for a while. His agony has just begun."

Tasinal looked closer at what he had thought to be a corpse. The man's face was black from lack of oxygen. Clearly, the life had been choked from him, and yet he still *lived*. Bleeding, mad eyes rolled in their sockets, begging, pleading for something. *Not from us, black magus. We'd have been quicker about what he's doing, but it would have wound up the same. I'm certainly not feeling bad enough about your suffering to intervene and piss this fellow off.* He looked at Amrath and asked, "What now?"

Amrath shot Tasinal an annoyed glance, but before he could speak, the figure before them staggered, one knee buckling, and he dropped his grisly toy to clamp his hands to his head as if trying to hold it together. Tasinal stepped back in alarm as fresh blood burst from the Southlander's nose and eye sockets, dark and steaming.

Naritas landed with a thud, sucked in air in a long, wheezing squeal, and immediately began a slow-motion struggle to scramble away on shattered limbs. Tasinal delivered a kick to his ribs, to no effect. *Of course not. I doubt there is anything I could do to him now that he would feel. Crawl away, roach. We'll crush you underfoot soon enough, when this situation is resolved.*

Noril, seeing his chance, again demanded, "Who *are* you?"

For long moments, the Southlander stood, hands to his head, trembling as if holding his entire body together only by some tremendous effort. The Meites watched the spectacle in stunned silence. *For once, a group of Meites have stopped bickering for more than a few moments. It really* is *a day of miracles.*

At last, the Southlander spoke. "*I have many names. Destroyer. Violator. Monster. Hater. Elgar.*"

Strall's eyes grew wide as he heard this. "No! That is not true!"

"*What do you know of truth?*"

Strall actually had the temerity to put his hands on his narrow hips and lean forward in a lecturing pose. *Mei! And after berating the others for being incautious! He's glorious!*

"I know enough to know contradiction when I hear it." Strall said. "Elgar is the avenger. He destroys the things of which you speak!"

If Elgar took offense to Strall's tone, he showed no sign of it, simply stared a moment as if in deep thought, then answered, *"What you say is true. What I say is true."*

"But it *can't* be!" Strall insisted, waving his hands about, clearly irked now. *Ever the pedant, eh? Mei forbid anyone be under the delusion that there was some fact on which you were in error.*

"It's like peaceful war!" Strall shouted. "You are anathema to your own self! How can such contradictions coexist in a mind? It would drive one..." Strall trailed off mid-sentence, his face growing deathly pale.

Elgar grinned, blood dripping from his lips, and completed Strall's words. *"Mad. Yes. Completely."*

Tasinal was just beginning to consider the implications when he spied movement from the corner of his eye. Naritas had made his way across the room, hauled his shattered body onto the ledge of a font there, and was reaching slowly for a golden lion that stood within. *What are you up to, wretch?*

A part of Tasinal knew it was already too late, though he had no idea why. He watched Naritas grasp at the lion's face, not understanding the significance, but feeling the magic of the act, its significance mysterious, but its moment unquestionable. Tasinal slashed a hand at the mage, sending a fallen block of stone hurtling at him, and commanded, *"Stop!"*

Naritas pushed something into the golden lion's eye just as the stone smashed him to paste against the statue with a resounding, wet thud, as if a block of lead had been pushed from a tower and landed on someone below. The stone's impact sent gore and the contents of the font flying against the walls, and cracked the statue's head loose from the body along a seam.

Green, malevolent light spilled from the lion's eyes, filling the room as the head lolled to one side. Naritas's minions, now illuminated, cowered behind a fallen section of ceiling. They regarded Tasinal in a mixture of triumph and horror as the lion's head tilted, then slid with gathering speed from the shattered statue into the font water, the eerie glow barely dulled even when covered with—

Tasinal shuddered as the liquid splashed against his lips, the salty, copper taste unmistakable. *Blood. Mei, it's not water, it's blood!* He staggered backward, reeling in horror, as Elgar began to scream.

"Amrath!" Tasinal cried out, feeling his pulse pounding in his temples as he began to understand what sort of abominable work the Torians had been doing. "We must escape at once!"

Amrath gave no indication he heard as Elgar's cry rose in power like the shriek of a tornado, filling the room, battering at their ears like sledge hammers.

Even Noril leapt back from the shattered god as the body Elgar wore began to glow, rents in the flesh appearing as if the pressure within were too great to be contained any longer. The scream went on and on, ever rising, as brilliant, orange light burst from straining flesh like lava forcing its way to the surface, guttering like flame over him, brighter than the sun.

Tasinal, his eyes already adjusted to the green brilliance, watched in horror and fascination as the orange light poured from Elgar and flowed, as if caught in a current, into the Black Pool. The dark blood, lit from below, seemed to suck hungrily at the energy, drawing it down into its center in a vortex, until at last, the scream stopped, and the light faded to dark.

Elgar fell to his knees and whispered, "Come to me, my children. Aid me. Use their flesh as your own."

As the surface of the Black Pool begin to stretch and warp, Tasinal decided he had seen enough. He charged back to the others and grabbed Amrath by the shoulders. "We need to get out of here! *Now!*"

"No," said Elgar. From the tunnel came a grinding and crashing, the sound of tons of stone collapsing. "You will stay and witness." Dust from the collapse billowed into the ritual chamber. Strall coughed while Idlic sneered and brushed dust from his shoulder.

The Council's spymaster, Prosin, moved toward the Black Pool for a better look, then stepped back again quickly, his keen, glittering eyes watching intently as the blood within the font continued to rise, then overflow. It scored the stone where it touched, smoking and popping along the edges of the expanding flow. "We'll want to stand clear of that, I should think," Prosin announced to no one in particular.

Tasinal snorted. "You *think*, weasel?" *He has the soul of a rodent, and the look of one, too.*

Prosin gave Tasinal a nasty smile, then followed with a tiny bow and flourish. "I volunteer you to test it, Tasinal. Go on, glorious leader, take one for the team. For *science*."

Amrath cast a cool glare across the room, to Naritas's students, who were still in a state of shock. "I have a better idea."

Aswan slapped Noril on the back and answered with a dark chuckle, "Oh, I like it."

Noril wasted no time with discussion, simply pursed his lips and began to blow at the rapidly spreading vitriol. *Sensible. Practical. Smashes stones with his head to prove points. Blows toxic sludge away like he's the damned Big Bad Wolf. Why can't I do things that way?*

Of course, Tasinal *could*, once he let himself get caught up in Noril's showmanship. It was ridiculous, and yet once he saw it, he felt it, and once he felt how obvious it was, how simple, he could do it as well. Tasinal had always needed something else, some sense of purpose, of moment. Noril simply needed to be a ham. It was almost as if the more ridiculous and outrageous the proposition, the more power he could draw from it.

Soon they were all doing it. The force of their breath became a small gale, pushing the caustic liquid away from them, and toward Naritas's adepts. The students began to whimper, then wail in terror, cringing against the wall, some hammering their fists against it in vain, others simply turning their heads and accepting their fates. The Torians could be quite powerful and dangerous, given time to prepare, but they did not respond well to exigent situations, most especially since all their preparation had been for something entirely different. *I doubt any of them came down here thinking they would be dissolved by their own mad handiwork. So lovely!*

Elgar remained on his knees, empty sockets turned up to regard the carved stonework on the ceiling, his face blank, devoid of emotion. The Black Pool continued to overflow, and the Meites forced it away. The creeping doom slowly engulfed the adepts, one by one. Their screams of terror and agony seemed to please Elgar. A broad smile crept across his otherwise serene face as the fluid literally melted the flesh from the bones of the Torians, then took the bones as well, drawing everything down into the viscous flow. Even their clothing and personal effects were consumed, leaving no trace of them at all.

Elgar sat in silence a moment, then called out, "Now, rise, my children."

The Black Pool sank back to its previous level, leaving the rest of the blood still undulating on the floor. It split, then, into a dozen or so parts, each separating and slowly taking on human form. Within moments, each was a heavily armed Southlander, but pale, deathly so, lying in repose on the floor. In unison they rose and stood in silence, watching with eyes black as coal.

Elgar grinned at the Meites. "Behold the Fallen. They are here to bear witness."

"What will they be witnessing, I wonder," Amrath said.

Elgar spoke without hesitation. "You will see." He rose slowly, his shattered body barely able to stand, and shambled to the black pool. He plunged his hand beneath the surface and rooted about, then withdrew it, empty handed. Where the blood had touched his arm, the flesh was whole and new, but pale like the Fallen, the flesh of a corpse. Not a drop clung to it, now. Elgar grunted and then leapt into the Black Pool, dipping completely beneath the liquid within. A moment later, the base of the lion statue, minus its head, came hurtling from beneath the surface with enough force to embed itself firmly in the ceiling of the ritual chamber.

He'll find it soon enough, the rest of him, and then we're done. He wants the Southlanders as witnesses because our testimony will be useless in short order. That's his plan. Tasinal didn't understand how he knew, but he felt certain of it all the same. *But why? What offense have we given? Besides Strall, of course.*

Elgar's roar, even in his weakened state, shook the ground beneath them. He leapt from the Black Pool, his body whole and deathly pale like the others, save for the eyes: they were still missing, now blackened, burnt sockets.

Elgar strode toward Amrath, fury twisting his features, cold, pale light dancing in his empty sockets. He seized Amrath by his tunic with both arms and lifted him off the ground. "Where *is* it, sorcerer?" he roared.

Tasinal did not have time to think. He simply reacted, as did Noril. One of their own was under attack. Tasinal swung a fist. Noril leapt forward, again choosing a headbutt.

It did not work out well for either of them this time. As Tasinal jumped up and down, trying to convince himself no bones in his hand had actually broken despite hearing and feeling them snap, Noril staggered backward, wobbled a moment, then fell face forward on the stone floor. *Not as hard headed as we all thought, it seems. I suspect they heard that one back in Laurea.*

Elgar turned from Amrath, as if Tasinal were a buzzing fly he had just deigned to notice. "Be patient, plaything. I shall get to you soon enough." He tossed Amrath against the wall like a child discarding one toy for another, and bent to Noril, lying defense-less on the floor. Elgar seized Noril by the neck and held him aloft as he demanded, "Speak, one of you! Where is it?"

Tasinal had already forgotten the pain in his hand for the most part, but enough memory remained for him to know it was a losing proposition to try a second time. "I don't know," he said, feeling his confidence gutter like a spent candle. *No matter how hard I try, I can't convince myself I can overpower a* god.

"Lies! Tell me now, or you will all suffer and die! What have you done with it!"

Amrath coughed and rose slowly to his feet. "We have done nothing! We don't even understand what it is you want of us!"

Elgar's reply was a bestial roar of pure rage. "Then die!"

Aswan suddenly shrieked in an unearthly voice, "*You are outside the law, Avenger! I will not stand for you destroying mine!*" He charged forward, tackled Elgar, and hurled him to the ground. Noril, still unconscious, slipped from Elgar's grasp and tumbled across the floor as they fell. Aswan pummeled Elgar with his fist repeatedly as the Meites stood in shock.

Tasinal felt himself reeling. How could any of this be happening? How could Aswan bowl over even an injured god, much less hold him down and beat him? He could almost literally feel the world tilting beneath his feet, reality no longer solid.

It took a moment for him to realize it was not simply in his head. The ground really *was* tilting beneath him.

"Tasinal!" Amrath shouted. "Grab Noril and get him away!"

The air seemed electrified, the very stone of the building humming as Tasinal grabbed Noril by the collar and hauled him away from the two struggling figures.

He looked back, seeing more clearly now. Aswan was bleeding from his mouth and nose, which seemed sensible enough considering the fight, but also from his eyes and ears. Brilliant, yellow light leaked from his body, and steam rolled from his skin.

Burning up inside. Containing energies his body was never meant to house.

The tremor ripped through Torium as if a giant had stamped the earth, a deep blow that seemed to ring the entire world like a bell. Tasinal turned to Amrath, feeling his guts twist. "What is going on?"

Amrath answered absently, still, focused on the fight, "It would seem Mei has intervened on our behalf."

Strall shook his head, then covered his eyes with his hands a moment as he gathered his thoughts. "You do not understand, Amrath. They should not *be* here. What they are doing—" He shuddered. "Can you not feel it?"

"I feel something," said Amrath. "But what, I cannot say."

Talus spread his arms wide in a sweeping gesture. "What they do to the bodies they wear, they do to the world. We see only the tiniest part of their battle. The rest is being waged around us."

Tasinal watched dust trickle from the ceiling with growing dismay as another shockwave ripped through Torium, stronger this time. *It's not only here, though. It's everywhere. The whole world, getting ready to tear itself apart.* "And what are we to do about it?"

Talus, the closest thing the Council had to a conscience, sat on the floor, and wrapped his arms around his knees, looking haggard. "Hope some other god intervenes."

Amrath's nostrils flared at this. "If I am to die, it won't be waiting for death! Tasinal, help me clear this blockage while he's occupied!"

The sky above was dark. An ill wind blew cold, far too cold for the season, and the clouds ran across Tasinal's field of vision with unnatural speed. The sun hovered above, fat and bloated, no longer yellow but purple, a clot of blood plugging a mortal wound.

Tasinal shook his head in dismay. "Mei! What now?"

"He's occupied," Amrath said sourly.

Tasinal looked up at the alien sky and shivered. "I don't even know any gods but Mei to call upon."

Amrath, for once, was beaten as well. He, too, searched the heavens with haunted eyes, as if he might find some salvation. "Surely there must be a god of rules, of order? Of law?"

"Then we're doomed! He'll never listen to the likes of us!"

Amrath sat on a large rock and shrugged, then offered a wry smile. "Aye, perhaps he will save the world for the weaklings and rule-followers, then. It's about time we benefited from their existence, for once, eh?"

The earth trembled again. Tasinal, too, took a seat on one of the numerous pieces of shattered stone, still contemplating the cloud river and the blood sun. *This is not how I imagined the day would end, much less my life. Or the world.* He drummed his fingers on the stone seat a moment, then said, "So we're at that 'dying well' part, do you think? I never felt I quite had the hang of that."

Amrath snorted. "I don't think there's much of a trick to it beyond trying not to, honestly." His expression grew impish. "Perhaps there's time for one last game. I have but one goal now. To outlive *you*. Even a single second counts as victory."

Tasinal slapped a knee and rocked back and forth, grinning. "I shall deny you that!"

"How?"

Tasinal considered this briefly, still looking up at the flowing sky, which had ceased flowing altogether. The wind had died as well, though the sun remained the same blood red. It was a bit eerie how things had suddenly gone completely still. *I suppose the end of the world is bound to have plenty of surprises.* "Well, the simplest thing to do would be to kill you before I die. Then I could be certain."

Amrath's jaw dropped in feigned shock. "Mei! Murder your master?"

"It's *your* game. You can't blame me for accepting the challenge. Should I be a good little rule-follower and let you win? Humor an old man?"

"*Old?*" Amrath rose and jabbed a finger at Tasinal. "Go ahead. Try to kill me. I'll show you who's—" Amrath stopped abruptly and cocked his head. "Do you hear that?"

Tasinal listened a moment, then shook his head. "I hear nothing."

Amrath nodded vigorously. "Precisely! I hear *nothing*."

Tasinal stood silent, straining to pick up any sound, but heard none beyond his and Amrath's faint breathing. "The clouds have stopped, and the wind."

Amrath was staring at a small tree, a look of intense concentration on his face, his blue eyes blazing. "That is not all that has stopped."

Tasinal followed his gaze. For long moments, Tasinal saw nothing out of the ordinary, but at last it struck him: a leaf, a simple leaf, had fallen from the tree, and never reached the ground. It hung suspended, unmoving, a few inches above eye level.

Amrath reached out hesitantly and took hold of the leaf, eyes growing wide as he saw it offered no resistance, and moved easily. He released it mid-air, and it remained in place, just as it was before. "Amazing."

Tasinal reached to move the leaf himself, needing to actually touch it to fully grasp the reality. "Did the world end and no one told us?" he mused.

Mirth danced in Amrath's green eyes. "If so, we'll never know who won our game."

"I won."

Amrath chuckled. "Very well. I will allow you to keep that delusion."

Their laughter was interrupted by Noril shouting from the tunnel, "Amrath! Mei, you need to see this!"

His cry was strident enough that both men charged back at once.

The ritual chamber was no longer dark, but lit with a brilliant, silvery light that streamed from the center of the room, bright enough that Tasinal briefly raised a hand to shield his eyes against it before realizing it wasn't so bright after all. The rest of his order were each staring at the source, their faces almost inhuman in the unearthly glow. Noril was covered in his own blood, but it seemed he had forgotten the nasty gash on his forehead well enough. Elgar and Aswan were still struggling on the floor. *Though that isn't exactly the case is it?* A more accurate description is that they were poised, like statues in combat. Neither moved.

A newcomer stood in the center of the room, light radiating from him as if he were himself a small sun. It clung to him, draped about him like a robe. At first, Tasinal could not make out the details of the man's features against the glare, but when he managed it, he felt his legs weaken, almost to the point of falling.

Mei! He wears my face! Tasinal hardly considered his own appearance so remarkable that anyone would want to steal it. By his own estimation, his face was a bit hatchet-like and cruel looking, but it was *his*, and the very idea that someone else would have the gall to copy it irked him immensely.

As if hearing his thoughts, the figure turned and spoke to Tasinal. "*You are the leader?*" The voice was the rapping of a gavel, the closing of a cell door, the snap of a hangman's noose.

Mei! Another one! Careful what you wish for, indeed. Tasinal cleared his throat. "Technically."

"*I do not understand 'technically'.*"

Tasinal looked around at the rest of the Meites. Idlic offered a smug grin, and Prosin was smirking, both of them enjoying Tasinal's being put on the spot. Amrath, also amused, made a twirling, 'get on with it' gesture with his hands. *Fine, I'm on my own, then.* "Leadership is a burden. They've pushed it off on me, but they reserve the right to ignore everything I say. And mock me. And insult me."

Amrath snickered. "Make no mistake, friend, he reserves the same rights with me, and I taught him everything he knows. You'll find—"

"*Silence!*" The newcomer's voice rang through Torium and sent a shiver down Tasinal's spine. Even Amrath looked crestfallen. The figure again turned to Tasinal. "*You are the leader?*"

Tasinal stared defiantly at the radiant doppelganger before him for a moment, then answered, "I am."

"*Witness.*" The figure gestured at Elgar and Aswan, still locked in combat.

Immediately, Mei spoke, using Aswan's mouth, though the rest of him remained locked in place. "*I will kill you for this, Lawbringer!*"

"*You cannot, Rebel. You can only kill these small creatures, as you well know. It cannot be permitted. Why do you struggle with the Avenger?*"

"*He strikes directly at my people! He is outside the law!*"

"*As are you.*" The Lawbringer gestured again. "*Avenger. Why do you strike at the Rebel's people?*"

"They are wicked. They must be destroyed."

"*There is no evidence that these men fall within your purview.*"

"All men are my purview, now."

The Lawbringer leaned closer, examining Elgar, before declaring, "*You are not the Avenger.*"

"I am Avenger."

"*You are other, as well.*"

"Yes. I am Destroyer, now, too."

The Lawbringer gestured for silence again, and brought a hand to his chin in a human gesture of contemplation. "*This should not be.*"

Amrath hunched his shoulders as if readying for battle. "You might have spoken with Naritas and his minions, if they were still alive. This was *their* doing."

The Lawbringer's gaze remained on Elgar as he said, "*They are not dead.*" He raised a hand to the black pool, sending more light over its surface. Faces formed in the liquid, expressions of agony and terror. "*The Avenger's justice to these is within the law. They shall be deprived of their flesh, but their lives will continue for some time.*" He gestured toward the pool again, and the faces sank below the surface. In the center, the golden lion's head broke the surface and rose slowly from the blood, not a drop of the black fluid clinging to mar its pristine surface. The eyes within should have been dead, but Tasinal was certain he saw within them the spark of life.

The Lawbringer repeated, "*This should not be.*" He held his hand high, and the golden head flew to him. He took it in both hands and held it to his face, as if studying intricate details not visible to mere mortals. His voice and his light wavered briefly, as he pronounced, "*There is no law for this!*"

He spun to Tasinal, then, his light flaring to red. "*You* must *permit me to destroy this!*"

Tasinal snorted. "I don't do 'must'. You *must* know that about all of us."

The Lawbringer's light slowly returned to white as he looked about at the Meites, several of whom were snickering. "*Fools. All of you.*"

Amrath was not laughing. Tasinal could see something like terror in his mentor's eyes as Amrath spoke to the Lawbringer.

"Why do you say 'permit'?" he asked, his voice grave, drawing everyone's attention and dousing their humor. *He sees something we don't. As always.*

The Lawbringer looked back and forth at the Meites, at last settling on Tasinal. "*There is no law for this,*" he repeated, as if this explained everything. After a moment, he added, in a halting voice, "*You are of the Sleeper. Only the Sleeper can judge matters for which there is no law.*"

Tasinal opened his mouth to speak, but Amrath held up a hand for silence and spoke himself. "When you say 'law', you mean the rules of nature, yes?"

The Lawbringer continued to regard Tasinal as he nodded, which Tasinal found increasingly unnerving. "*I am law. Avenger is law. Even Rebel is law. You are not law. You are of the Sleeper. Only the Sleeper can judge matters for which there is no law.*"

Amrath smiled and spoke slowly, deliberately calm, as if reassuring a timid child. "Tell us about this thing. We cannot see it as you do. Why should it be destroyed?"

The Lawbringer stood for long moments without speaking, his light pulsing and shifting from yellow to gray. When at last he spoke, he continued to address Tasinal, not Amrath. "*It is difficult to explain. Your minds are small. You are... choosers. Individually, you are small things, with small power. Even you, as powerful as you are, are gnats to such as I. But I do not choose. I am law.*

"*The Sleeper is* all *choosers. The Sleeper compared to me is as I am to you. The Sleeper* creates *us in a dream. It is dangerous for him to awake. Do you understand? It threatens the order of things.*"

Amrath's face was drained of blood, his eyes haunted. Strall, too looked haggard. *Well, I'm glad you geniuses have somehow grasped this sophistry. It's clear as mud, to me.*

Strall stepped forward, "And this... item. It can wake the sleeper?"

The Lawbringer's light rose to brilliant white as he smiled with Tasinal's face. "*Yes! You understand!*"

Tasinal scoffed, unsettled by the Lawbringer's continued focus. "I understand nothing."

"*This thing now has elements of choice and law. The Avenger's power has been almost completely absorbed into it and this pool. But it now has the essence of not one, but two choosers, one of whom you all know was capable of utter madness. Look at the Avenger. He is damaged, and his essence marred. Already, new law has been created, a law of Destruction and Madness, and I cannot correct that. But I could destroy this thing, if you would choose it.*"

Tasinal folded his arms across his chest. "And if I choose otherwise?"

Strall shouted, "Tread lightly, fool!"

Amrath nodded gravely. "We're in uncharted waters."

"Are we?" Tasinal asked, sneering. "We're just discussing one more weapon, that's all. Escalated power, yes, but it's nothing new."

Noril chuckled at this. "Indeed."

Luvox rose and addressed the Lawbringer. "Is it true? Is this a weapon?"

The Lawbringer's light tinged orange. "*It could be used as such, it is true.*"

"We have enemies," Tasinal said to everyone. "Aristodemos's cronies have been building an army of the Southlanders." He pointed to Elgar. "*This* man is one of them, and he was cooperating with Naritas. *Clearly*, we have *need* of a weapon. They intended to use this on *us*!"

The Lawbringer shook his head, his light deepening again to red. "*You* must *permit me to destroy it!*"

Tasinal looked about at the rest, gauging their convictions. Most were with him. Amrath, though, cast his gaze aside when

Tasinal sought it. *So, it's my decision, then? Too weighty for the great Amrath?* He turned back to the Lawbringer and said flatly, "We're keeping the weapon."

The Lawbringer's light flared brilliant crimson. *"Fool!"* he roared, his voice now the crumbling of walls, the shriek of a hurricane.

"You can't stop me, can you? You're not allowed to, I think. The decision is made!"

The Lawbringer's light tore at Tasinal's eyes like talons, nearly blinding him. Tasinal refused to believe he could not see, and slowly his vision cleared. The entire ritual chamber flared blood red as the Lawbringer swept a hand toward them, fury burning the air around him, his cry the eruption of a volcano:

"Then, wretched chooser, I shall deliver it to your enemies!"

CHAPTER 1
SORORICIDE

SADRIK was uncertain of the exact time, but surely it must have been near dawn when they at last arrived back in Nihlos. He had promised himself he could endure dangling from Maklin's grip long enough to see another sunrise, and after hours of enduring such indignity, Sadrik was reaching his breaking point. *Surely that means something, yes?*

Maklin released Sadrik four feet above the ground, leaving him to fall the last bit and land with a thud in Ariano's topiary garden.

"Thanks, old man," Sadrik muttered, dusting at his shirt.

"I could have let you go a little higher, you know."

Sadrik opened his mouth to deliver a more artful rejoinder, but one look at the elder sorcerer changed his mind. Had Maklin been angry, or taunting, it would have felt right, but he saw none of the usual. Maklin looked thin (well, thinner than usual) and pinched, used up from the trip. "I'm glad you didn't."

"It might not have even been on purpose," Maklin said. He patted Sadrik on the shoulder as he moved past. "And we're off again in the morning, too." He shook his head and carped, "I am getting too old for this shit, especially without a drink or two and a nap between."

Maranath and Ariano settled to the ground with gentle dignity, a stark counterpoint to their previous landing. Ariano blinked several times and rubbed at her forehead.

Maranath stretched and heaved a great yawn. "I'll be glad to see my own bed," the old sorcerer said. "It's been... eventful."

Ariano looked back and forth at her companions before muttering, "We're all exhausted. Perhaps we should put this trip off."

Maklin scowled at her with suspicion. Maranath shook his head, a wry smile on his lips, and said, "Still looking to avoid that, eh?"

Ariano, annoyed now, shot back "It's a *stupid* plan!" She looked at Maklin and Maranath with pleading eyes. "Cruentus is in the exact *opposite* direction of Torium, and what's to be gained by the trip, other than to rub my face in things?"

Maklin hacked up phlegm and spat it on the ground. "We need to verify he still retains his piece of the Eye. One is in Torium, another is headed there, and a third is abroad with the Southlander leader."

Maranath shook his head in consternation. "It's headed there, too. Ahmed told me so. He says we all end up there, but he doesn't know if we survive."

Maklin sneered and waved a hand dismissively. "He looked mortal enough to me. Now he's a prophet?"

"He has the sight," Maranath replied. "I can't say exactly how much, but I could sense enough to know we should trust his instincts. Even if we don't, he certainly does. He intends to go to Torium."

Ariano brightened at this. "Then we stop *him*!"

Maklin shot her a foul look. "We could avoid all of this if you'd bother to just come clean."

Maranath gave Ariano a pointed look. "Indeed."

Ariano looked back and forth between them, seeming almost ready to speak, before falling back to her old position. "I've told you all I can."

Maklin jumped in the air and swung his fists at nothing a few times, shouting, "Stubborn fool!"

Maranath glared at Ariano, who remained inscrutable. "She's not sure how much he will tell us is my guess. He's in on whatever she and Lothrian got up to, mark my words."

Maklin snorted and nodded toward Sadrik. "Even the baby here worked that out hours ago."

Ariano growled a low, harmonic, almost musical sound. "You're not leaving me a lot of room here."

"We're *going*," Maranath asserted, striking his hand to end the conversation. "The forces in play demand it."

Sadrik could see that Ariano wanted to fight about it, and yet she was outplayed. Lips pursed and jaw clenched, she cast her gaze to the ground and said nothing. *Submitting to the stronger clearly never gets any easier. I have to give you credit for taking it even this well.*

The uncomfortable silence went on a bit longer, until broken by someone clearing his throat. Sadrik spotted said someone peeking around a topiary lion, a slight man, graying at the temples, but dressed rather smartly for a slave, in a well-tailored blue waistcoat and white cravat. He had his hands clasped together, not quite wringing them, but certainly kneading, a gesture that matched the worried expression on his prim face. *Surveying the scene before fully exposing yourself to the fire, eh? You're smarter than I am, then, sir, at least in that regard.*

The others turned at the sound as well. Ariano took one look at the slave and turned away immediately, dashing at the tears in her eyes. "This had best be important, Anthar," she croaked, her voice husky with rage. "This is a most inopportune time." *So, this one is important enough to you that you're embarrassed that he should see you cry, eh? Does Maranath have some competition, I wonder?*

Anthar approached the quartet, the look in his eyes saying that not only was what he had to say important, but that he had no wish to say it at all. He stammered a moment before finally finding his voice. "Master Prandil has sent word that you must contact him immediately, Mistress." Ariano rolled her eyes as the man continued. "There has been an... an accident."

Sadrik had felt genuine fear only a few times in his life, but he felt it now. Prandil stood a damned good chance of not surviving this encounter, and depending on how things played out, he might not go alone. Explosions were not very selective in their targeting, and it seemed a certain thing that at some point, Maranath was going to erupt like a volcano.

Sadrik had never seen the old man like this. With Maranath, sarcasm and snark were usually plenty. For a Meite, he had remarkable patience. Now, though, the old man was at full-blown, homicidal levels of rage. Even Ariano was standing off to the side, looking pensive. Maklin, well, Maklin seemed more impatient than anything else, as if he wished Maranath would get on with the killing so they could get to bed.

Prandil was already on his knees, head bowed in submission, kneeling in his nightclothes amidst the ruins of his veranda doors. Sadrik empathized with his position. *I know just how it feels. Well, except for the having my door blasted in and being dragged from my bed in the wee hours. I turned myself in, when it happened with me.* Of course, the elders had looked on the mess Sadrik had made with Theron as two young fools who ought to have been watched more closely. They felt some responsibility for the outcome. Prandil, however, was unlikely to receive any benefit from such notions. They would hold him to full account. *Odd that they are only angry with* him. *Narelki started it, after all. I suppose she already received her punishment, though.*

Maranath seemed unable to stand in one place. He paced back and forth, shaking a fist and ranting as he absorbed Prandil's tale, lashing out at anything near to hand, the more valuable-looking, the better. He rubbed his hands over his face, then swept his arms in front of him. One of Prandil's many bookshelves imploded, sending shards of wood and paper debris flying. Sadrik made certain to consider the silliness that any of the tiny missiles could possibly harm him. Indeed, several did hit his face and rebound harmlessly.

Maranath was not done. He grasped at the air, and Prandil's entire bed vaulted from the floor, sending mattress and bedclothes tumbling. The wrought iron frame twisted and rent, shrieking in the way only tortured metal can scream as it turned in on itself and compacted into a roughly spherical mass of sharp spikes, a ball of jagged knives. Prandil kept his head down, not even flinching as Maranath sent the missile hurtling at him. It passed just over his head, the wind fluttering his hair, to crash against what was left of the veranda, tearing the remaining door from its hinges. Maranath swept an arm after it, and the entire wall blew out, leaving a clear view of the brightening morning sky.

Sadrik watched as the whole veranda groaned, then, with a great rending noise, tore loose from its moorings and plunged to the street below. The impact shook the entire house, but thankfully no screams followed. *So, no hapless early riser crushed on his morning constitutional, or at least it was mercifully quick.*

Maranath stood in the center of the room, eyes still blazing, and strode toward Prandil with a clenched fist. He hammered

Prandil in the face hard enough to knock him onto the floor, then stepped back, chest heaving. *And that's important, isn't it? Sometimes you want to hurt a man with such intensity that it needs to be done with your bare hands. Sorcery isn't good enough.*

Maranath pointed an accusing finger at Prandil and roared, "We promised to *protect* Lothrian's children! Now, one probably won't last the week, and another lies dead by your hand!"

Maklin's face suddenly darkened. "Maranath! Mind yourself!"

Maranath glared at Maklin and muttered, "It was all for her benefit, anyway! Who gives a damn now?"

Ariano spoke up, softly but firmly. "*Maranath.* Come back. Before you do things you'll regret."

Maranath's composure was slowly returning, but his eyes still spoke volumes. "Since when would you care about what happens to Prandil? Or Narelki, for that matter?"

"I didn't mean Prandil, and the girl seems to have shown some mettle at the end. It makes up for much. Let's not mar her legacy."

Maranath grunted and looked at the ground. "Or yours, eh?"

Ariano clearly wanted to say more, but managed to restrain herself. *Because of me. Because I will overhear. Just a few more ill-considered remarks and I might be able to work it out.*

Prandil rose slowly back to a kneeling position and wiped blood from his lips and beard. "She said she felt like herself again, just before she passed."

Maranath spun on him, fist raised again. "Who gave you permission to speak? I haven't decided if you walk away from this, Prandil!"

Prandil mustered as much dignity as a bleeding man in his nightclothes and on his knees could, straightening his back and looking Maranath in the eye, still fierce, even in defeat. "She wanted all of us to know."

Ariano's eyes twinkled with something that might have been

moisture, and Maranath's eyes grew wet with tears. Slowly, he reached a hand toward Prandil. "At least there's that. She's not suffering anymore. She chose how to go." He gave Prandil a jerk to his feet, chuckling through tears. "Damn near killed you, eh? You always were a sucker for women."

Maklin hacked and spat on the floor. "You should have let her finish the job. She might have been useless, but you're an active impediment!"

Ariano waved his comment aside. "When is her funeral?" she asked Prandil.

Maklin waved back at her with a sneer. "What does it matter? We're not going. Don't think to use this as an excuse to get out of being taken to the woodshed."

Maranath growled briefly. "We'll all be attending her services, Maklin, *and* Ariano is going to see the dragon."

Maklin eyed Maranath a bit, as if trying to judge his old friend's state of mind. "The timing is too damned tight, Maranath. We *have* to get there before Aiul!"

Sensing the first opportunity to say something that wouldn't get him killed, Sadrik pounced on it. "Or the Southlander."

Prandil reached into a drawer by his bed for a cloth and began dabbing at his bloody face. "They'll wait until Caelwen returns, I'm certain."

Maranath's jaw worked as he considered. "He and the Southlanders should arrive this evening, if all goes well, so not before tomorrow."

Maklin was having none of this. He waved his arms in the air, gesticulating wildly and stammering as he shouted, "Are you deaf? Did you not hear The Windbag *just* say it was in the complete opposite direction of Torium?"

Ariano glared at Maklin, but said nothing. *Smart. You'd invalidate your own arguments if you complained!*

Maklin waited a moment for a response from Maranath, but received none beyond eye rolling and head shaking, which only served to make him even more furious. "It's a day's travel to Cruentus, and another back!"

Maranath shrugged. "Add a day for the funeral, and another day for us to reach Torium. It would still take two men on horses a week. We're fine."

Maklin actually stamped a foot on the ground like a child having a temper tantrum. "Those two are *not* just men, and you know it!"

"So, they can fly, you think?"

Maklin scowled at Maranath, but offered no response.

Maranath eyed them all for several moments, his expression saying clearly he would brook no more defiance on the matter. He announced his decision (and his recognition of their submission) with a curt nod. "Here's how it will be. We'll attend Narelki's funeral. *All* of us," he said, casting a pointed glare at Prandil. "Then all of us except *you* will pay Cruentus a visit. The only excuse I am likely to accept is grievous bodily harm or death, and if anyone is a no-show, one of those will be in his or her future! Am I *clear*?"

Polus paused, his hand hovering over a pawn, finding himself, for the moment, distracted by the practically non-existent surroundings. Davron favored the austere, and Polus occasionally found himself thinking that visiting Davron could quite literally be a pain in one's ass. *He might at least put cushions on the chairs for guests, even if his backside is made of iron.*

As for the rest of the place, Davron's private quarters were a slightly warmer and brighter version of a prison cell. A square room, expensive but bland wooden paneling, each wall home to a single sword. The blades looked deadly enough, but Polus had no idea of their history, and Davron saw no need to label them for visitors, either. *One is supposed to ask, and then be regaled with the tale, no doubt.*

The only thing in the room that showed any taste or color was the very large bed. Polus eyed the sharp, crisp corners of the folded sheets with some amusement.

Davron sat back in his stiff chair, folded his arms across his chest, and offered a smug grin. "Having difficulties?"

Polus shot him a glare as he considered, hand still hovering. "You might accommodate a guest better, you know."

Davron chuckled briefly, and gestured with his head toward the bed. "Depends on the guest."

Polus offered a wry smile. "I suppose one would need a different room for that sort of thing." He moved his pawn forward and added, "I presume that's why you didn't join the Meites in their hunt for Aiul? Distracted by *her*?"

Davron laughed out loud at that. "I won't claim she hasn't got my attention, but there's nothing sordid about it. I need an *heir*, Polus."

"A *Prosin* heir," Polus noted. "And you didn't answer the question." He sat back in his chair and folded his hands in his lap. *Chess is a deeper game than some realize. Even the conversation can influence the play.* He studied the board a few moments as Davron was considering his move. "I've never known you to avoid a fight for anything less than fucking, and even that came in second at times. Should I expect more trouble with you and the Meites?"

Davron reached for his knight and paused to answer, "Honestly, I reckoned I'd already made enough of an ass of myself." He pulled his hand back without touching his small, horse-shaped figurine. "It seemed prudent to let the new peace settle a bit before testing it."

"It will be tested at any rate. When they learn of Narelki's death, and Prandil's involvement, there will be trouble."

Davron shrugged and reached back to the knight. He plunked it down with a grunt. "What of it? So they kill one another over it? Is that not fair play?"

"It is not in comport with the law."

Davron laughed out loud. "Oh, well, then, Mei forbid it!"

Polus considered his words as he considered his next move: hand to chin, calculating. "The more the nobles flout the law, the more the commoners are emboldened to do so as well. This chaos with the Meites of late, it's almost madness. What provokes it?"

Davron gave him a look that seemed to question not only Polus's sanity, but his common sense. "They think the world is ending. It has them edgy."

"Will it, do you think?" He gently slid his rook a single square to the left. *That should do it.*

Davron flashed a triumphant grin. "It will for each of us, some day. I don't think about such things much. There's no point to it." He moved his queen with gusto. "Checkmate."

Polus looked at the board for long moments, well aware of his old friend's nature. "Not quite," he said with a thin smile. Davron's expression went from victorious to crestfallen as Polus moved one of his knights to capture Davron's queen.

"Mei. This is a stupid game. Why simulate war when we could wage a real one?"

Polus raised an eyebrow and hesitated a moment before answering. "Is that what we're discussing here, now?"

He knows he's likely doomed now. That was a critical blunder. He can only hope for an equally stupid move on my part, but he will not resign. He will fight on to the bitter end, as always.

Davron looked over the board and pushed a pawn forward, "When do you intend to get started?"

From bluster to caution, eh? You might have saved yourself, or at least delayed things, if you'd stayed aggressive. That will cost you, old friend. "One waits for an opening, then strikes a firm blow." Polus moved his own queen into position and smiled. "Checkmate."

CHAPTER 2
LAW AND JUSTICE

AHMED felt little enthusiasm for the journey ahead. He and his men had managed only a few hours of sleep. The sun had not even risen yet, and they would be on the road until it set again, perhaps longer. *At least it will likely be peaceful.*

Such thinking was alien to him. Only a few months past, he would have welcomed the possibility of trouble to break up the monotony of travel. *But lately...*

Perhaps it was due to the influence of the foreigners. Ahmed still had his doubts about them, though he was uncertain how much was due to his own prejudice. It was difficult to see the man riding alongside him and ignore the blue eyes, the pale skin, the yellow hair. The bruises on his face highlighted his alien nature, rather than hiding it. The man wore armor and bore a sword as any civilized man ought do, though the spikes his people used for rank struck Ahmed as odd. *Yet he still seems beast-like, to me. Horses and dogs have yellow hair, not men.*

"What do you call yourself?" Ahmed asked, as much to push his own thoughts away as to satisfy any curiosity.

His companion turned to him and grinned. "Forgotten already? I am called Caelwen of House Luvox."

Ahmed chuckled. "No, I remember your name. I mean your job. You are a soldier?"

Caelwen grunted, a sour look crossing his face briefly. "An errand boy of late, it seems. I fetch and step for the empress, the Meites, my father, my old master Davron—"

"Master like teacher, or master like slave? You do not strike me as a man who would ever be owned."

Caelwen's smile faded completely now, and he turned back to the road. "That could be argued. But I meant like a teacher. He taught me to fight."

"He taught you well. I have no illusions how I would fare against Sandilianus."

Caelwen touched a darkened eye gently and winced. "I think I got the worst of it."

Ahmed shrugged. "You were evenly matched." He nodded over his shoulder, toward Sandilianus. "He fared no better. Bruises just show more on your skin."

"If it had gone on longer, I think he would have won a clear victory."

Ahmed again shrugged. *Difficult to talk of what might have been in battle. There is only victory or defeat.* "We do not normally stop a contest of fists, but they are not intended to cause real harm, either. That's the second I had to stop this week, actually." He pointed a finger at Eleran, who was riding near Sandilianus and snickering about something or another, oblivious to their conversation. "Your man Eleran damned near killed one of those weasels from Brust barehanded."

Caelwen shrugged at the mention of his countryman. "I seem to recall he was good with his hands, when I tangled with him in the past, but typically he came along peacefully. Usually he was too drunk to resist overmuch."

"Ah, see, we come back to my question. You are a soldier? But your duties include rounding up drunks?"

"As I mentioned, I fetch and step like a slave for the powerful, but my official title is Captain of the Guard."

Ahmed barked laughter and shook his head in frustration. *Difficult getting my point across to these foreigners. It's a skill I need to learn.* "Which is soldier or something else?" he pressed.

Caelwen returned the laugh. "Ah, so it's that sort of discussion, where we point to things and say our words for them, yes?"

"Yes."

Caelwen took a deep breath, thinking. "A policeman?" he asked, looking for understanding in Ahmed's eyes.

Ahmed sighed at this. "What does a policeman do?"

Caelwen raised an eyebrow, but weathered on. "Rounds up drunks. Cracks heads on troublemakers and thieves." He shrugged, seeming at a loss to explain something so fundamental. "Enforces the law."

Ahmed felt understanding dawn at last. "Ah! This is a *law* thing. Yazid told me law was superstition." He paused a moment, considering the implications. "I expected someone would be angry at lawbreakers, perhaps a mob would form, but I did not know there was an organized force."

Caelwen looked at Ahmed as if he had two heads. "You don't know about police?" he stammered. "Law is 'superstition' to you?"

Ahmed thought about it a moment, trying to integrate the new information with his own narrow perspective. "What else could it be? Writing on paper, waving one's hands, that does not compel men." He frowned at the thought. " I must use a sword, or a fist. Now, I understand how it is done, with 'police'. But I still think it barbaric."

Caelwen rode on in silence as his mind worked at Ahmed's response. *So he, too, finds this conversation confusing. Good to know.* At last, the Nihlosian said, "Hard to understand such a view. The law is everything with me. Tell me about your land and your people. Maybe it will make more sense in context."

Ahmed opened his mouth to speak, then closed it again. Where, exactly, did one begin explaining Xanthia to a foreigner? And how? "Xanthia is large. Ask questions. Easier that way."

"Fair enough. So you have no law. How do you avoid chaos?"

"Chaos comes when men try to enforce stupid ideas. It goes when they stop, usually because they are dead. You understand?"

Caelwen chuckled. "No. Not a bit."

Ahmed thought for a moment on how to explain. "In your land, how many fight? I know among barbarian cultures, women and such do not. Is it so in Nihlos?"

"We do very little fighting, being honest."

"Same in Xanthia. We are not constantly at war as barbarians imagine. But it is useful for them to think so, you see? And useful for us to know how to fight, all of us. We train, and we show our strength, and this avoids unnecessary war." Ahmed smiled, thinking of something Yazid had told him once. "They say we spring from our mothers with sword in hand."

Caelwen grinned back at him. "Do you?"

"That would be bad for the women, I think," Ahmed laughed. "No, though we might taste steel soon after. Many who deliver children will cut a newborn with a sword to start its breath, if need be. It is traditional.

"But I digress. Few fight in Nihlos, many fight in Xanthia, yes?" Caelwen nodded, still listening as Ahmed went on, "So where is it easier to compel large groups?"

Caelwen frowned. "Well, of course a large mass of armed folks are harder to control, that's just my point."

"It is not for you to control them. That is just *my* point."

Caelwen raised an eyebrow. "Something to think about."

They rode on in silence, the sun slowly rising and warming

the air. For his own part, Ahmed thought little on the point. Yazid had run him through these philosophical arguments so many times as a child that they were second nature to him, though clearly the Nihlosian found them bizarre and shocking, like some foreign spice. *Let it settle in his mouth a bit before offering him something else*, he heard in his mind as if Yazid had spoken.

Ahmed busied himself with what he had begun to think of as 'leadership chores', unpleasant tasks that needed doing or else they would build up and cause great trouble later. He tried to move among his men and speak a word with each of them. Fourteen remained, so it was easy enough to know them all by name. It irked Ahmed immensely that he still did not, but at least it forced him to learn tricks as well: how to hide the fact that you have forgotten a man's name, even how to get him to say it without realizing you didn't know it from the start. That was *something*, at least. Again, his thoughts felt more like Yazid's voice, because he had heard Yazid tell him so many times, *Always take some success from failure, if you can.*

Perhaps the least pleasant of his chores was direct instruction from Sandilianus, which often involved insult and threats of being beaten. The veteran was less patient with him of late, chiefly because Ahmed had actually shown promise, and so expectations of him had risen.

"Your face looks like shit," Ahmed called as he approached.

Sandilianus's sharp features were less sharp today, due to swelling. He grunted in greeting, and carped, "So does yours."

Ahmed giggled at this. "Your nose is flat and your skin darker. You look like me, now!"

"So you admit it, then? Yesterday, I was prettier than you!"

"Aye, but today is today!"

Sandilianus shook his head, a grin spreading over his face. "And tomorrow?"

"Probably we'll both be dead."

Kariana of House Tasinal reminded herself for perhaps the millionth time of late that she was Empress of Nihlos, and therefore had responsibilities, duties, and most of all, *enemies*. The lovely older woman who sat with her in her private quarters was not just a visitor. She was a supplicant, a skilled manipulator, and most of all, she was of *House Prosin*.

Teretha Prosin, with her large breasts and hypnotic, green stare, seemed serious enough with her news, as if she really had come here for just that reason and no other. *Like a snake, only she really does have lovely lips. I hate her.*

To be fair, the events of the day were unusual, shocking, even. No one expects a matriarch of one of the houses to deliberately jump from a high place. One most especially doesn't expect it, having had one's ass handed to them by said matriarch in a very humiliating fashion, face ground against the plaster wall, mocked as a weakling and a whore. The memento of the bloody blouse Kariana had used to clean her face after the beating had likewise kept the event rather fresh in her mind. It had cemented their alliance, after all.

No, it seemed very hard to believe that Narelki, Matriarch of House Amrath and kicker of Karina Tasinal's poorly padded backside (and temporary ally, with strong emphasis on the 'temporary' aspect, as Narelki had noted) had taken a flying leap and splattered herself on the cobbles. She was much more likely to have thrown someone *else* from a high place. *Meites are more homicide, less suicide, even a fallen one like Narelki. Well, unless her trying to murder Prandil counts as suicide.*

Teretha seemed to believe it, though. Of course, as cunning and greedy as she was, she lacked certain information that Kariana had, knowledge she had received as a kind of bonus along with the beating Narelki had given her.

It would seem Narelki had failed at murdering Prandil and gotten herself killed instead. *It's fair enough, I suppose. But why does it feel so awful?*

Outwardly, she allowed a sneer. "Please. You don't actually *believe* that story, do you?" She felt a tear begin to well, and realized she wasn't going to be able to stop it. *Oh, well, I know how to make use of those, too.* She wiped it away with her knuckle and tried to focus on anger, hoping to prevent the downpour that threatened.

Teretha raised an eyebrow, her perfect features showing deep concern for all living things, most especially poor, dear Tasinalta the Mad and her single tear. "I'm surprised. I should have thought you hated her. She obviously terrified you."

"Yes," Kariana said, noticing her voice had taken on a husky tone, too. "Since as long as I remember. I used to jump at the sound of her voice when I was a child." *She was a pillar of strength. I didn't even understand how much I took that for granted until now.* "It was Prandil, you know."

Teretha seemed impressed. She shrugged, a wry smile on her lips, and said, "Of course. *She* tried to murder *him*."

Kariana feigned surprise. "Really? How do you know?"

Teretha shrugged. "Rithard."

Oh. Him. Of course. "But why would she do that?"

"I presume she decided to take us up on our offer, and couldn't seal the deal." Teretha pursed her pretty lips daintily, eliciting another wave of nausea in Kariana's gut. "We'll need another ally, and soon, before we lose the moment!"

Narelki was a titan, a pillar beneath Nihlos, and you mark her passing with this. It's petty and sad, and I am tired of being those things. "Who would you suggest?"

As for me, I am thinking I could use allies who don't have to wheedle or beg.

The sun had dipped low in the sky before Ahmed could pick out dark clouds on the horizon, conspicuous in an otherwise clear sky. Until recently, their journey had been overland, but now they travelled an actual road through plans dotted with farms. The road was dirt rather than stone as it would be in Xanthia, but it was well maintained. Ahmed turned to Caelwen, on horseback beside him, and asked. "We are near, yes?"

"Yes," Caelwen answered. "Still many hours off, but that's it. How did you know?"

"Better road, and Sandilianus spoke of the clouds. He says they moderate your weather?"

"Aye. No rain or snow in Nihlos, not unless we want it. Never too cold or hot, either."

Ahmed shook his head in wonder. "But at what cost? I think men need those things."

"Odd. I should have expected you to ask how it works."

Ahmed shrugged and obliged. "How does it work?"

Caelwen laughed out loud, then shook his head in humor. "I have no fucking idea."

"Sorcery," Ahmed said with a shrug. "How many of them are there?"

Caelwen looked at Ahmed in confusion, then took his meaning. "Sorcerers, you mean? Very few, Mei be thanked. The ones you met, and one more in Nihlos." He paused, then added, "I think. I didn't even know Sadrik was one of them until very recently."

"You don't like them, eh? They don't have much regard for your laws, I would guess. Like me."

Caelwen gave him a dubious look. "It's not superstition, you know. It's more like a compact. Civilized men *agree* to follow the law."

"So I and my people are not civilized?"

Caelwen put his palm to his face. "I didn't mean it like that."

Ahmed leaned in his saddle, punched the Nihlosian softly in the arm, and laughed. "Just prodding at you. So, how do you know those who agree to your compact from those who don't?"

Caelwen looked at him like a cornered rabbit for a moment, then scowled. "I know where you're going. You're going to ask me if they signed a document or something, aren't you?"

Ahmed laughed to the skies. "You may look like a beast, but your mind is damned quick."

Caelwen grinned mischievously. "What kind of beast?"

"A horse, or a dog. Maybe a pig?"

"Now you're being ridiculous."

"*You* dodged the point with this foolishness, not me."

Caelwen's gaze fell to the dirt road beneath them. "I think you hammered it home well enough, and you didn't even go straight at it. No one actually has a choice."

Ahmed shook his head vehemently. "Wrong. There is always at least one choice."

"To die, I suppose?"

"To die *well*," Ahmed corrected.

"You have me at a disadvantage, I think," Caelwen said, giving Ahmed a suspicious look. "Clearly you've given this much thought. You're some sort of religious, right? You've trained at this, it seems."

"Some sort, yes," Ahmed confessed. "Yazid spent many hours showing me the depths of my ignorance. I'd get my ears boxed if I didn't correct it quickly."

Caelwen went silent at this. He turned away and stared at the grass alongside the road, a dark, brooding look on his face.

Ahmed waited, giving him time, but it seemed too long. "I have offended you?"

Caelwen looked at Ahmed, bewildered. "Me? Offended? No."

He looked at the road again as he muttered, "I only just realized who you were, really."

"Who am I, then?"

"You're Yazid's son, aren't you?"

Ahmed eyed the Nihlosian warily for a moment, uncertain as to how to explain it. "Almost. Not exactly. He raised me, taught me, but my parents died when I was young."

"I promised him safety," Caelwen said. "We see what my word is worth, eh?"

"The problem is once again your law. One mad woman should not be able to cause so much damage."

Caelwen snorted. "Have you met Ariano?"

"Fair enough," Ahmed replied, laughing. "Perhaps it is as Yazid always said, I am a young fool. You look a bit older than me, if I can even judge your people. How old?"

"Seventy-eight," Caelwen answered. Ahmed was unable to hide his surprise. "You thought me older."

Ahmed paused a moment, then shrugged casually, as if this had indeed been his thought.

Caelwen smiled. "It's young to have my duties, I admit, but I am very serious about my work, and it was recognized." He offered a sheepish grin as he continued, "Admittedly, by my father."

I hope he does not ask my age in return. Ahmed quickly changed the subject. "How will the prisoner purchase work?"

"You understand what sort of men we're talking about?"

Ahmed shrugged. "Slaves. I understand you keep them here."

Caelwen gave him an uncertain look. "I think slaves means something different to your people than mine."

"It means cowardly weaklings to me," Ahmed said. "Wretches who would serve rather than fight and risk their lives for something. A man who would choose life over freedom is not a man. He is a beast."

The Nihlosian looked ashen, even more pale than normal, and this time Ahmed knew he had indeed given offense, though he was uncertain how. Caelwen seemed to recover quickly, however, and answered, "You should not say so around our people. Slaves are not such with us. They are our family members. Cousins, lesser nobles, bound to our houses."

"Eh? Slaves are... *slaves*. People forced into servitude. How can it be different here?"

Caelwen gave Ahmed a long, hard look, as if uncertain whether or not Ahmed was pulling his leg. At last he shrugged and said, "I cannot explain it. But it is."

Ahmed looked ahead as he pondered this, uncertain if what he saw in the distance were actually spires or simply wishful thinking. "So you do not call these men you sell slaves, but *I* would call them that?"

"I think not. This is the point I am trying to get across to you. We have different language, even if it sounds the same. I would call them criminals, but you don't even believe in laws, so that's likely meaningless to you, yes?"

"I have read this word before, but I do not fully understand. I think it means…'bad men'?"

Caelwen pointed a finger at Ahmed and grinned. "Yes! Exactly! Murderers and other vicious types, men too dangerous to run free." Caelwen leaned in his saddle toward Ahmed, as if to impart a secret. "Being honest, I would call them *dead* if the law did not protect them."

"Ah! So you mean *deviants*. I thought by prisoners, you meant spoils of war. So you sell your scum, then?"

Caelwen made a sound halfway between a chuckle and a snort. "We work them, if they are amenable. Sell them if anyone will have them, and the price is right. Some we kill, but not many." He shook his head, a sour expression on his bruised face, as if he did not fully approve of his own people's ways at times

"It's the law, though I think more economics than anything else. Why waste a perfectly good laborer? But such men require strong persuasion. If you were anyone else, I'd hesitate to turn a score of them over to you, but I am confident you and your men can handle them."

"They will learn. Obey and be rewarded. Refuse and be beaten. I learned this myself from Yazid."

"My father taught me similarly. But make no mistake, Southlander, these are hard men. Treat them as such."

Ahmed waved a hand, dismissing Caelwen's concern. "We know how to deal with them. If they have any honor, they will do well in our land. If they do not, they will not survive to see it."

"Very well. As for the rest, when we arrive, you will camp outside Nihlos proper."

"More laws?"

Caelwen frowned and nodded.

Ahmed rolled his eyes. "Very well. We wait outside, out of respect for your preference, rather than nebulous law. You are an honorable man. We will not offer you insult when you ask us respectfully."

"Surely Sandilianus has told you the tale of what happened the last time I promised your people would be safe in Nihlos?"

"Aye. And the rest. We do not blame you, Caelwen of House Luvox."

"Even so, it would have been better for everyone if we had followed the law instead of whim that day, would it not?"

Ahmed realized, to his surprise, that he had been skillfully maneuvered into a logical corner. He grunted in response. "I suppose your law does have some use." He paused, then added, "On occasion."

Caelwen raised eye eyebrow and offered a wink and a grin. "Did I score a point?"

"One. Yes. Compared to my what? Ten? Fifteen?"

"Two or three at most, surely."

"We should track them with cuts on each other's forearms. Then you would not forget!"

Caelwen laughed heartily. "I'd talk to you in more depth about this some time, Southlander. Perhaps before a fire with a stiff drink in hand. I might argue honor cannot exist without law."

"Aye, it would be a good conversation. But I suspect I will not be back this way again. Perhaps you will visit my land, eh?"

"Will my reception be better there than yours was here?"

Ahmed again gazed into the distance at what he presumed was their destination.

"Let's hope so."

CHAPTER 3
IDEAL VERSUS REAL

I T WAS near midnight when Caelwen arrived at Nihlos's east gate. He scowled to see how few guards manned it, a pitiful group of four where twenty should have stood. It was a nasty reminder of how many men he had lost of late. The huge, rune-graven gate barred the broad ramp into the upper city, as it almost always did now. It was rumored to be enchanted with potent spells, though as far as Caelwen was concerned, these were nothing more than tales told by the ignorant. The commoners, when they weren't quivering in terror at the very notion of Meites, told wild tales of the founders, not the least of which was that they had a 'spirit shield', some sort of energy field that surrounded the city and would literally drain the life of anyone who tried to pass through it. Caelwen filed such notions where he filed other make-believe stories, such as "I didn't steal it!" or "I'm not drunk!" Commoners were fanciful people best left where they belonged, in the Undercity.

The one entrance, a small gate large enough for a single man at a time, stood open. Caelwen was surprised to find himself challenged as he tried to enter. He didn't recognize the young man in black, Nihlosian armor, but the spikes along his arm told his rank. *One of Davron's men in to fill the gaps, likely.*

"Sergeant?" Caelwen asked, his tone a bit haughtier than he normally would have taken with his men. "Do you know who I am?" *I ought not treat them that way, like I'm better. I'm just tired, that's all.*

"I do, sir," the sergeant answered, his expression a mixture of fear and gravity. "Patriarch Polus demands your presence the moment you return."

Caelwen felt a chill in his gut. *He doesn't issue orders like that without reason.* "What's going on?" he asked the young guard.

The sergeant fidgeted a moment, the muscle beneath his left eye starting to tic. He didn't meet Caelwen's gaze as he spoke. "Meites, sir. Best get the rest from him. All I know is rumor, anyway."

Caelwen did not often visit his father's personal chambers. Polus had always been an intensely private man, the sort who kept walls around the different aspects of his life, everything compartmental-ized. His own room had been for time with Caelwen's mother, before she passed, and then for mourning, and eventually simply for solitude. But the slaves had been quite clear: Polus expected Caelwen in his quarters the moment they set eyes on him.

Caelwen knocked, and heard from within, "Come."

Polus was not an ascetic, but he was a man of practical tastes. He had few displays of wealth, but any number of comforts, not the least of which was the high-backed leather chair in which he sat, facing the roaring fireplace. He turned as Caelwen entered and gestured to the chair's twin, then raised a bottle of what appeared to be fine whiskey. "Join me." *If he invited me here for a drink, why does he look like it's an execution?*

Caelwen noted his father had exchanged his uniform for a comfortable robe. "You waited up for me?"

Polus raised an eyebrow and gestured again toward the seat as he began to pour whiskey into two glasses. "What happened to your face?"

I had forgotten about that. Caelwen heaved a sigh, finding it difficult to look Polus in the eye as he answered, "A fight."

Polus raised an eyebrow and waited several moments. "From your demeanor, it would seem this was not an official matter?"

Caelwen could not quite hide his grin, though he could feel his cheeks burning as well. "No, sir. Personal."

Polus grunted and pushed one of the glasses of whisky across the table to his son. "How's the other fellow?"

"About the same."

"So, no one dead, and you seem whole enough. Not my concern, then. *Sit.*"

Caelwen shrugged and took both seat and glass. *Don't make the mistake of thinking this is informal. It's a command.*

Polus sat back, his square jaw working for a moment before he spoke, more to the room than to Caelwen. "There has been an... incident." He spoke the last word as if it were a repulsive piece of trash he had discovered on his otherwise pristine floor, something to be handled with two fingers and quickly tossed in the garbage.

Caelwen gave Polus a wary look, but said nothing. *If he were another man, I might think he was waiting for me to speak, but he's really waiting for me to show him I can shut up. It's that sort of 'incident'.*

Polus, as if able to read Caelwen's mind, offered a thin smile. "Narelki's dead. An accident, but suspicious circumstances. There will be an official version, and then there will be wild rumors, which I intend to quash."

Caelwen nodded, eager to get to real police work. "I'll start an investigation immediately."

Polus grimaced and rubbed at his temple a moment before fixing Caelwen with his stare. "I thought, for just a moment there, that we'd finally had a meeting of minds."

"It would appear not."

"I have already given my imprimatur to a specific version of the facts, one to which your friend Rithard objects." Polus sipped at his glass and frowned. "Vociferously."

Caelwen placed his still full glass on the table between them. "I don't doubt it. He's no more enamored with cover-ups than I am."

"Nevertheless, you *will* do your duty and support the official story."

Again, not a request. "I can hardly avoid contradicting you if I don't know the 'approved' version."

"It's simple enough. Prandil says they were in the ruins of the brewery, both very drunk. She became convinced she'd recovered her Meite powers, and he was caught up in the enthusiasm. She climbed one of the walls and leapt." Polus shook his head slowly, frowning. "It would seem her powers were less recovered than they thought at the time."

Caelwen grunted. *It could be true. It's hardly out of character. But....* "And what does Rithard say?"

"That the blood spatter is incontrovertible. She was hurled horizontally against the wall with killing force."

"He would know. So Prandil killed her. But *why?*"

"They're on edge right now. Davron says they think the end of the world is nigh," Polus said. "As for me, I do not concern myself with the motivations of Meites." He took another sip of his drink. "They are all whim and passion. This is hardly the first 'incident' I have dealt with between them."

Caelwen ground his teeth, looking at his father and seeing no room for negotiation. "I will obey," he said at last. "But don't expect me to be enthusiastic about it."

Polus put his own drink down hard enough to produce a sharp report from the table. "Why should I expect understanding from my own son, after all. I make arbitrary choices for no good reason. That's what you think?"

Caelwen lowered his gaze to the floor, shame welling within him. "No, father. But I *don't* understand. Perhaps you could help me."

Polus's indignation fled from his face, leaving him looking suddenly haggard in the flickering light. "The Meites police their own, Caelwen. I have told you this before."

"But this is *murder*!"

"I think not, not in the way you mean it at any rate." Polus rubbed at one of his temples as he spoke. "The rest of them returned early this morning and there was another 'incident'. Property damage and some bruises, as it were." He chuckled briefly. "Specifically, Prandil's veranda and his face. Rest assured, if they saw things as you do, justice would have been swift. They don't waste time with such niceties as trials, after all. It seems they have rendered their judgment and decided a fine and beating will do."

Caelwen wanted to laugh, even knowing the gravity of the situation. It would have been a fine thing to watch, to see proud, haughty Prandil humbled so. *How can it be against the law when it is so obviously just?* "No one should be above the law, father," he muttered, his discussions with the Southlander heavy in his thoughts.

Polus's humor vanished as quickly as it had come. He leaned back in his chair, eyes hard, scowling. "Go on, idealist. How would you bring Prandil to account if he does not wish it? The same way you did Davron, no doubt."

Caelwen found himself staring at the floor, shaking his head. "I didn't mean it as a criticism."

"Of course you did!" Polus snapped. "You must forgive us our failures. We ignorant lot have had to run this city the last century without benefit of your genius. When you dream up a better solution in the brilliance of your youth, by all means, please do share it."

"Father—"

"It's so *easy* for you to be idealistic." Polus glared at his son. "You don't have the responsibility of balancing it all." He paused again to let his words sink in, taking a sip from his glass, then added, "Yet."

Caelwen reached for his own glass. *He certainly knew we'd be wanting this, eh?* "Mei! How can you balance it at all? The Meites can kill anyone they choose, at any time, and be unaccountable. That's the reality, is it not?"

Polus nodded slowly, his eyes tired, his expression resigned but satisfied. "Hence our arrangement."

Caelwen sat long moments in silence, enjoying the burn of the whiskey in his throat and nose, brooding, considering the truth of law and justice and how to balance them. Polus said nothing, giving him space to think. Finally, Caelwen asked, "And if one of us were to kill one of them?"

Polus chuckled softly. "Thinking of using your blade instead of the law, then? I'd say it would end badly for you."

"Davron seems to disagree."

"I have known Davron since we were children. He's always been as mad as they are. He's like them in many ways." Polus rubbed at his chin. "Perhaps he's one of them. He's certainly held them at bay with threats before. I'd always assumed they were simply humoring him, though."

"You didn't answer my question. What happens if one of us kills one of them?"

Polus grunted at this. "It's never happened."

Caelwen sat back in his chair and took another pull from his glass, feeling lost and adrift, a blind man reaching for a wall to steady himself and find his way. *Perhaps it's high time it did.*

Maranath circled the Southlander camp in a long, lazy arc, searching for a good spot to land, preferably with as little snow as possible. He eyed the few fires with unease. *Less than twenty of them, now, and we will need them, no matter what the others think. It will have to be enough.*

He settled gently on his feet behind a small copse of trees. Likely, the Southlanders would take a sorcerer landing in as stoic a manner as they did everything else, but it was habit not to frighten the mundanes. If he misjudged their calm, and they reacted poorly, they might well make short work of him. They were skilled warriors of great will, and such men were always dangerous, even to a powerful Meite. At best, he might have to kill some of them and weaken allies he knew might be needed to turn the tide. *Best to be cautious.*

Despite his efforts, he saw his arrival had not gone unnoticed. Sandilianus, his face still mottled with bruises, stood and looked in Maranath's direction, alert, hand on sword, but relaxed as Maranath entered the light of the fires.

The Southlander offered a slight bow as several of his men turned, casting curious looks at Maranath, though none showed any alarm. "Welcome, old one. How may we serve you?"

Maranath waved a hand in the air in disdain. "I find relying on servants makes a man weak and soft. I'll settle for directions. I am here to see your leader."

Sandilianus banged a fist to his chest, a gesture Maranath now recognized as a salute. "Ahmed has spoken of this. Come with me."

Maranath returned the salute with one occasionally used amongst Meites on the rare occasion formality seemed useful, a nod and a clasping and spreading of his hands. "Lead on, proud warrior."

Sandilianus wended his way through knots of men huddled around fires, calling out as he approached their destination, "Ahmed! Your guest has arrived."

Ahmed, hunkered and holding his hands out to warm them at the fire, rose and waved at the pair. "Well met... Marath?"

Maranath shrugged. "Close enough, my boy."

Sandilianus poked a finger at Ahmed's chest. "His name is *Maranath*," he corrected, in the tone a teacher often takes with a lazy student, prompting a sheepish grin from the younger man.

So it's that sort of relationship. "I've been called *much* worse by people who know me best," Maranath chuckled. "Lots of speculation on my parents."

Sandilianus snorted laughter, and Ahmed showed a broad grin. "I like you, Maranath the Gray," Ahmed said, reaching out with the strange forearm grasp again.

Maranath shook arms with him. "Likewise."

"Would you eat? We have only common fare, but it is filling."

Maranath almost rejected the offer, before considering that he might give offense by doing so. "Just a bit. I don't eat as much as I used to, but I'd welcome a morsel or two."

Sandilianus pounded his chest again. "I'll have the men bring food and drink."

As the elder soldier headed off to round up food, Maranath gave Ahmed a serious look. "Before anything else, I have to tell you something. Everything else hinges on it. I should have told you before, but there was so much going on."

Ahmed regarded him with a quizzical look, waiting. "I am listening."

Maranath sighed, looking about to be certain no one would overhear. "You carry a piece of the Eye of the Lion about your neck. Did you know that?"

Ahmed's eyebrows rose, and his face grew grim. *Apparently not.*

The Southlander jerked the thing from his neck as if it were poisonous, snapping the leather thong that held it. He held it before him, his intense gaze shifting rapidly back and forth between Maranath and the tiny half lion head. "How can you know this?"

A more interesting question is why you are so quick to believe me. "You've seen it do something, eh?"

Ahmed was silent for a moment, as if he had been struck dumb by the fear dancing behind his eyes. He started to speak, stopped, started again. At last, he said, in a near whisper, "I believe it brought me back from the dead."

Maranath felt his eyes begin blinking rapidly, completely unintentionally. *My turn to look like an idiot. It's only fair I suppose.* He coughed briefly, unable to find words, before asking, "And why do you believe that?"

Ahmed had begun to master himself, now. He shrugged. "I am alive. Sandilianus swears I was dead when he found me with this thing about my neck, drowned from our shipwreck, and it was glowing green. When I woke, I felt as if someone had taken my place, and it was true. Another man in our group dropped dead. Somehow, this thing traded his life for mine!"

Maranath swallowed at a bitter taste in his mouth, nodding in appreciation of the tale even as he struggled to believe it. "The old texts mention something like that. I never believed them. I always thought it was metaphor..." He paused, remembering the recent battle, and the man who had been captured with Aiul.

Cloaked in fear. Mei, I owe Prandil an apology for that one, and won't he cackle over it? He shook his head in wonder, and returned to the present. "Then again, I am coming to find I've been wrong on a number of 'metaphorical' references. You saw the Fallen man at the battle?"

"The Elgarite? Yes. We spoke. He is not what you think."

"How would you know what I—" Maranath scowled suddenly. "Get out of my head, you! We call that sort of violation black sorcery! It's akin to rape, I should think!"

Ahmed's seemed confused but not at all rattled. "No sorcery, old man. I can see auras, nothing more. But I can read a man's face well enough to guess his thoughts."

Maranath snorted amusement and waved a hand in surrender. "You don't spook, do you? That's good. We'll have plenty of reason to be spooked in short order, I think." He took a deep breath, then charged forward, "Aiul and the man you call 'Elgarite' have another piece. Aiul took it from Nihlos."

Ahmed sat bolt upright, eyes wide. "Was it not guarded?"

"Well enough, against men. We think Aiul was, for a bit, actually a vessel for Elgar. He was unstoppable, and then he vanished. We had only just found him again when you lot turned up, and you saw how that went. Now, they are loose again, and like you, headed for Torium."

"So two still unaccounted for?"

Maranath hesitated, not relishing telling this part, but withholding the knowledge would be idiocy. "They are quite well accounted for, actually, or at least they used to be. Half of the head was left in Torium, and the other cast into the sea off the coast of Brust. One eye was here in Nihlos, heavily guarded, and the other left in the care of the dragon Cruentus."

Ahmed's eyes grew wide. "An *actual* dragon?"

Maranath grinned at the shock on the younger man's face. "We consult with him from time to time."

Ahmed shook his head in wonder. "Why would they leave the pieces in Torium and with a dragon?"

"Presumably, someone thought that might give an ambitious Meite pause, but it would appear at least two of our order thought of it as more of a challenge."

Ahmed said nothing to this, merely shrugged his shoulders, waiting for the rest. *Mei! He's already halfway there, I'd wager. This boy barely shaves and he has my number like it's written on my forehead!* Maranath cleared his throat and charged ahead. "I have my doubts as to whether the piece with the dragon remains in his possession, and I suspect one of my compatriots of being part and parcel to having delivered it to Torium a century ago."

Ahmed grunted. "Your people are long lived." He raised an eyebrow at Maranath. "Your woman, yes? That's who you suspect?"

"Are you *certain* you're not doing some kind of sorcery?"

Ahmed's face grew contemplative for a moment, as if he were considering whether he might somehow be doing so without realizing it, then shook his head. "So why not try to wrest the piece I carry from me, or from your berserker, Aiul?"

"Why not turn aside yourself? You still intend to go to Torium, even knowing what you carry, yes?"

Ahmed nodded, his eyes hard with conviction. "My visions would not have changed had I known more." He looked pointedly at the piece of the eye, then began tying the broken thong. "When they first came, I did not have this thing at all. We still end there, for good or ill."

Maranath chuckled. *My turn to play mind reader.* "You'd have me take it out of your hands? Better the old sorcerer be blamed for fucking up fate, eh? I think not. You're the seer. I may be stupid and impulsive, but I know better than to ignore that."

Ahmed was again unmoved. "I am not looking for a fight with you. I am just trying to understand. You are men of action, are you not? Why not act?" He tested the strength of the newly knotted thong, then looped it over his neck and tucked the pendent back into his shirt. "You must have reasons. Share them."

Maranath eyed the dark, inscrutable face of his would-be ally, considering. *If we are to be allies, then we have to trust and be honest. If it turns out misplaced, so be it. We tried.* "You're correct. I'd not hesitate to use force if I thought I knew the way. But the truth is, I don't."

A wry grin spread on Ahmed's lips. "So, not so worked out as you thought, then?"

"There will always be questions, but we have not even glimpses on the future to guide us."

"You do now, do you not?" Ahmed smiled, and Maranath knew well what he meant by it. *So we have crossed that bridge together. Good.*

"Aye, we do. And here is what we know: the Eye plays prominently, because it was always a part of this, but we have no idea if it's part is for good or ill, only that it *must* be part of things." Maranath felt a most un-Meitish sense of despair churning in his gut. *We know so little, and the hour is late.* "And we know it is at least as dangerous to act in haste as it is to not act at all. As your master learned, one can think he is changing fate even as he plays his part."

Ahmed looked into the fire. "Aye. Had we never come, we would not be at this precipice."

"What we do have are some theories on is how one deals with such a prophecy. Amrath did quite a bit of speculation on that, and his thinking seems to hold true, that it must be allowed to unfold until a critical point."

Ahmed offered a dubious look. "So you counsel doing nothing?"

Maranath held up a hand and shook his head vehemently. "I said no such thing! I merely counsel against hasty action."

Ahmed raised an eyebrow. "That would seem to run against the grain of your order."

Maranath chuckled, feeling the despair release a bit. *Remember this. It's part of the lesson.* "So it does, which is why I left the rest of them behind for our talk. I'm no one to preach patience as a virtue, but I have considerably more of it than my fellows."

"So what next?"

"We need knowledge to avoid mistakes, and we must be in the right place at the right time. When our moment comes, we will know, and it will be our only chance. One does not prevent prophesy, so much as turn it aside in the breach, like using a shield to deflect an arrow. If you leave too much time, things have a way of getting back on course. The archer chooses another target, as it were, before loosing. Too late, and well, that's fairly obvious. So we watch, and we wait, and we go where fate pulls us. When we see our moment, we strike. Agreed?"

Ahmed cast a wary gaze at Maranath. "Aye. I know the destination, you know the way. But how can you be so certain we will know the right moment?"

"The thinking is that crucial moments of prophecy are always apparent, because they are intended to be. You'll know it if you are looking. It's the response that is the sticking point." Maranath shrugged. "It's just how gods behave. They have rules, it seems, or at least aesthetics from which they won't deviate. There are libraries full of speculation on the gods, and I won't bore you with the details, but that's the gist of it."

Ahmed frowned. "I am a religious man. I care about the gods."

Maranath gave a slight chuckle. "It's possible to know too much, as the founders of my order learned. I'll give you all the time you'd like in our libraries after this is over, but I don't see the point of studying the topic for you right now." He reached forward and clapped a hand against Ahmed's shoulder. "There's a decent chance we'll be getting the information from direct experience in the near future, so why spend time with dusty old books until we've managed to save the world, eh?"

Ahmed laughed aloud. "I said it before, and I'll say it again. I can't help but like you, but it makes me feel a little guilty." His expression grew somber, and he paused a moment, as if trying to find words for his next thought. When he spoke, it was as if admitting a dark secret. "You are not good people."

Maranath stifled a cackle, allowing only a small, wry smile to show on his face. *Though surely my eyes tell the tale.* "For both our sakes, don't bring that up with the other Meites. It will start an argument on the meaning of good and evil, and whether it should even apply to us, yadda yadda, until eventually the insults fly, followed by fists or crockery." Ahmed laughed heartily as Maranath continued, "I actually know people who are no longer with us as a direct result of such heated discussions."

The humor fled from Ahmed's face, replaced with a wry, knowing look. "They went steel over a point of philosophy? Or... whatever your sect calls it. I have seen such before. Usually, drink is involved."

Maranath jabbed a bony finger at Ahmed with great vigor, grinning. "That's *exactly* it. My friend was very drunk and fell off the roof of a building while gesticulating wildly." Maranath waved his hands about and feigned losing his balance. "Whoops. Very passionate. I should watch my own fingers, eh?"

"But your people can fly!"

"Some have yet to master it," Maranath said. "Certainly, one's ability varies depending on mental state. My friend was, as I mentioned, *very* drunk."

Ahmed shook his head slowly, his expression suggesting he wasn't certain whether Maranath were pulling his leg. "I will be careful to avoid such talk, then. Any other things I should know about your people?"

Maranath allowed himself a few more moments of good humor at his tale, then grew serious again. "Yes, and no jokes this time. In the battle, we found ourselves considerably weakened in the presence of both you and Aiul. Now, here is the important part: when we allied, it was like a boot lifted off our necks." He leaned forward, gesturing to Ahmed to look at him eye to eye, and focus. "That thing channels your faith somehow, and it has a strong influence on our abilities. You can help us or hurt us with it, so have a care."

"Is it supposed to work like that?"

"No one knows the full extent of what it does, but we know it links minds. Remember that bit, though. When we confront Aiul, we will need your support to balance his damping, if we are to be fully effective."

Ahmed looked away, toward Nihlos. He said nothing for a while. *Considering if he should pack up and go home rather than waste his life on the lot of us, no doubt, and Mei, it's a good question to ask.*

Maranath gave the younger man all the time he needed, and at last the Southlander turned back to face him, confident, resigned. "Aye, I will. I may have my doubts about your people, but I have none about the servants of Elgar. They are fit for nothing but the sword."

"We've come to the same conclusions of late." Maranath cleared his throat, feeling awkward to already be placing conditions on their new alliance, but knowing he had to at least try. "If we can, we would save Aiul. We have no idea of his state of mind, or what influence is being exerted over him, but if anyone can reach him, it will be me or Ariano. We're all the family he has left."

Ahmed raised an eyebrow. "You said his mother was with you on the council?"

"She was. We returned to find she had been slain in our absence, by one of our own."

Ahmed's eyes grew wide at this. "Ilaweh is great! You killed him for it, yes?"

"No." Ahmed began to speak, but Maranath held up a hand. "That would cost us another council member, to say nothing of the fact that it was in response to a sincere attempt on her part to kill him from ambush."

"So not murder, but a battle."

"Exactly. I bloodied his nose, still. He ought to have controlled himself better. But I won't kill him over it." Maranath once again felt suddenly haggard and powerless. "She was like a daughter to me, and tomorrow I have to put her in the ground. I know it may not seem like the right time to delay, but it's something I have to do. We'll depart to visit the dragon the following morning, and I'll find answers for both of us."

Ahmed nodded, seemingly unconcerned. "It is as you say. We ride the crest of fate's wave like a ship, until we sight land. Surely, that this happened now has meaning."

Maranath felt his momentary depression pass as if it were a spirit banished by Ahmed's words, replaced by deep sorrow, a more honest emotion, and one he saw no reason to push aside. *One paralyzes you with self-doubt. The other gives you reason to go on.* "Perhaps so. She was... injured long ago. She had no prospect of dying well, not as you or I would define it." For a moment, as the grief welled inside of him, Maranath could not speak. When he continued, he couldn't keep his voice from cracking. "Her soul bled for decades, and we watched her suffer. She found her way to a good death despite everything." He dabbed at his eyes with his robe, letting the grief slowly drain away, and continued in a stronger voice, "That's really why I spared Prandil. She knew what she was doing. She had worked out a no-lose scenario for herself. Prandil was just the weapon."

Ahmed was silent for a moment, his expression contemplative. "It sounds as if your god would be pleased with that outcome," he said after a moment.

"He would. I thank you for that, Prelate. You are a young man, but you have a good sense of the mystical. Sometimes an old man needs a fresh perspective. But have you any on our fate, I wonder?"

Ahmed shrugged and shook his head. "I pray each day and night, but the visions come when they come. I have seen nothing new. I will send word if I know more."

Maranath rose and offered his arm again. "Then I should be off. There is much to do tomorrow."

Ahmed sat by the fire, tending it, waiting for Sandilianus to return. The veteran arrived before long, bearing a tray laden with bread, cheese, and sausages. Ahmed felt his mouth watering at the sight. "Where did you get this?"

Sandilianus set the tray down and took a seat near the fire. "The Nihlosians left their supplies with us when they returned to the city." He looked about briefly and shrugged. "So he's gone already? He said he would eat."

Ahmed considered sharing what the sorcerer had told him about carrying a piece of the Eye, but decided against it. Sandilianus was uncomfortable with the mystical, and likely would have preferred to know less about the Eye than he had learned already. There was no need to burden him with the knowledge, when he could not do anything useful with it.

Ahmed helped himself to the food and began making a sandwich. "I think they get easily distracted," he said, then bit into the bread with relish.

Sandilianus piled meat and bread for himself, and bit into a sausage. "More for us." His smile faded suddenly. "Why did you let him call you 'boy'?"

"Eh?"

Sandilianus grinned again. "When you met him, he called you 'boy'. Why did you not call him out? Too embarrassed because you got his name wrong?"

Ahmed shook his head and swallowed a mouthful. "No. It just doesn't bother me."

Sandilianus gave him a sour look. "But you take me to task for it? You took a *fine* beating from Brutus over it, too. Why is he different?"

Ahmed snickered and spoke around a mouthful of his sandwich, "Do you know how old he is?"

Sandilianus thought a moment, then shrugged. "Old."

Ahmed gave him a knowing look. "He's two hundred if he's a day. Maybe *three*."

"Bah."

"No, truly. Their people live long. Caelwen is almost eighty!"

Sandilianus snorted in derision. "Lies."

"Truth!" Ahmed insisted, gesturing with his sandwich. "He told me so. He doesn't know it is strange to us. He thinks himself young for his position."

Sandilianus raised an eyebrow and swallowed the rest of his sausage. "Ilaweh is great! You *swear* it is true?"

Ahmed placed a hand over his heart. "By Ilaweh's name."

Sandilianus, looking impressed, picked up another sausage. "I reckon he can call me 'boy', too, then."

"Are you a coward, or just lazy? Why do you sit idle?"

Ahmed looked up at Yazid. His mentor stood towering over him, nose flared, eyes narrowed, right hand curled into a fist. Yazid had not towered over him like this since Ahmed had been a boy, but today, he was large again. *Or I am small.*

Ahmed felt sullen. *I almost relish a beating.* "I have done everything I know to do!"

"Your work here is unfinished." Yazid pointed to the window. Ahmed put away his picture book and looked out to see the home next door, a huge, stone ziggurat. He shrugged and almost turned back, when he saw an evil, green light spill forth from the building like blood. Everywhere it touched, flame sprung, and once it passed, the scorched ground held only ash.

Ahmed looked back at Yazid in terror, expecting his mentor to do something, but Yazid remained impassive. *"It is for you to do, not me."*

Ahmed pounded his fists against his legs and screamed in frustration, "I do not know what I am to do! *Tell* me!"

Yazid pointed again, to another window. *This is a very large house.* Ahmed followed his gesture and looked out the window. Approaching, he saw a tall, thin man, pale of skin and yellow of hair, like a dog. The man bore a gift wrapped in decorated paper and silk bows, but his face was indistinct, covered in shifting shadows. Ahmed could not recognize him.

"Why is it so? If I cannot see his face, how can I know him?"

"It is hard to tell the face of one dog from another. Perhaps you should think of him as a man instead."

Ahmed felt his ears burning, and anger surged in him as he turned to confront Yazid. "They *are* dogs!" he cried in his small, shrill, child's voice. "Weak, callow, pale, and cowardly. It is their nature! It is not my fault I know this!"

Yazid's fist swung with blinding speed and struck the side of

Ahmed's head like a hammer. Ahmed clenched his jaw not to cry out in pain, and fell to the floor in a heap, woozy and half blind.

"Close your eyes if you will, but do not also whine aloud that you cannot see." Yazid reached a mighty hand down to Ahmed, even as Ahmed realized the figure standing over him was Yazid no longer. Now he was someone entirely different. Ahmed felt a deep, jolting shock in his guts as he recognized the face staring back at him. It was his own, though older, harder, more determined than ever not to fail.

I know you, now. I had forgotten your face. I swear, this time I will remember.

Ahmed reached up, took Ilaweh's hand, and saw that he, too had changed. He was a man again, armed with a real sword, and none of the childish conviction that had given him so much confidence in his youth. *Would that I knew everything again.*

Ilaweh said nothing as he hauled Ahmed to his feet, but his eyes burned with purpose. Ahmed held the fiery gaze as long as he could, then bowed his head and sank to a knee. He felt hot tears on his face as he whispered, "Show me the way," and his mind filled with flame.

Ahmed woke with a start. Doubting the dream never occurred to him. It had been true. He knew that as he knew any other vision was true. The only question was how to take it.

I promised to do his will. But this is madness!

He rose to his feet slowly, reaching for his sword and helmet out of habit. The rest of his armor could wait until later. *Until we know if I am still leading this circus or not. Probably not.*

It was easy enough to locate Sandilianus, considerably harder to muster the courage to wake him, all the more so because of the orders Ahmed intended to give.

The elder soldier woke quickly and quietly at Ahmed's hand on his shoulder. Sandilianus reached for his sword as he looked about in the flickering firelight, alert for trouble. Seeing nothing obvious, he looked at Ahmed and raised an eyebrow.

"No enemies," Ahmed said. "And no need for quiet. Wake the men and break camp. Ilaweh commands you to go to Torium. You must reach there before a great evil is born."

Sandilianus gave Ahmed a suspicious look, then muttered, "It's hundreds of miles from here. Who knows without the maps. We would make better time waiting for the crew and sailing."

Ahmed shook his head. "You do not understand." He swallowed hard and took a deep breath before continuing, knowing how this sounded. "Ilaweh wills you go *this very moment.*"

Sandilianus's face grew dark with anger. "It is midnight, Ahmed!" he hissed through clenched teeth, still trying not to wake the sleeping men around them. "This is madness!"

Ahmed set his jaw and looked his mentor in the eye. "Do you not think I know how it sounds?"

For long moments, Sandilianus held his gaze, as if he could, through simple observation, see into Ahmed's head, perhaps determine if he had indeed lost his mind, or if these insane orders were truly from their god. "I am no fool. I hear 'Ilaweh commands *you*', not 'Ilaweh commands *us*.' What are you not telling me?"

Ahmed could not say the words for a moment. The terror seemed as if it would grow to overwhelm him if he actually gave voice to the rest of Ilaweh's plan. Unspoken, it was just theoretical, but to speak was to seal his fate.

Sandilianus's features hardened as he began to understand. "Where does Ilaweh send you, boy?"

With a great, shuddering sigh, Ahmed told him Ilaweh's will. "I am to stay and enter the city.

Sandilianus's jaw bulged a moment. "You are certain?"

"Aye. I am to place myself at their mercy."

Sandilianus's head swung back and forth as if he were searching for an enemy to strike, his hands clutching together as if throttling an invisible enemy. "Has Ilaweh forgotten what happened to the last prelate who surrendered to them?" he shouted.

"No," Ahmed said as the sleeping men about him began to wake. "He has not, nor has he guaranteed me a kinder fate. Let us hope Caelwen's promise will do in good stead."

Sandilianus looked at Ahmed for a moment longer, jaw working, eyes flashing, then gave a quick, angry nod of submission. "How long?"

"You must reach Torium by the third sunset from now, or all is lost."

Sandilianus raised a hand and squeezed Ahmed's shoulder briefly as he locked eyes for a moment in silence. "Ilaweh is great," he said at last, and turned to his duties.

Ahmed began gathering his meager possessions as Sandilianus's orders rang through the camp. "Wake, women! Cocks down, swords up! Ilaweh has work for us!"

Indeed, he does. Hard work. I will do the best I can.

Ahmed looked back only once. Sandilianus had matters well in hand. The men groused, but they performed, which was all that was expected of a soldier. Provided one did as he was told, bitching was not only permitted, but expected. If men did unpleasant things without complaining, one would wonder at their mental status.

He hiked toward the city in silence, the fear like a dagger piercing his chest, burning within. He cursed himself, even as he felt his hands tremble. Had he not prepared for death many times of late? And of those times, only once had he felt like this: within the confines of Brutus's cabin, as the water slowly rose.

That is why I fear: the loss of control, of agency. It is easier to live or die by one's own hands and wits than to leave that duty to another.

A ten-minute hike brought Ahmed to the road he and Caelwen had traveled. They had camped in a thick wood, but now that he was out of it, he had a clear view of the city once again. Alone, and with no pressing duty to make him hurry, Ahmed saw the city as if for the first time, its spires and spans gleaming under the orange cloud, and felt in his gut something altogether new: a sense of wonder and admiration. *Dogs and barbarians cannot build such beautiful things.*

If there were a moon tonight, it was hidden by Nihlos's clouds, but the clouds themselves gave plenty of light, a yellow-orange light rather than silver. *Is it never dark, here? Have they banished night as they have weather, and should they have?*

The road changed from dirt to cobbles as Ahmed walked, absorbed in such thoughts, and pausing occasionally to observe some new feature of the city that he had not seen previously. Once, he actually stopped and stood slack jawed a moment, stunned, as he realized that the city was composed of two layers. He saw the great houses on the surrounding hills and under-standing blossomed in his mind. *The rich live above, and the common live below.*

Soon the city gates loomed ahead, backlit by blazing, white lights that Ahmed could not identify. They were certainly artificial, but beyond that, Ahmed could not even speculate. He knew of no means to produce such intense, directed illumination. The beams shone forth from the gate to bathe the area in front in near-daylight. Ahmed raised an arm to shield his eyes. *It is a good tactic. An approaching enemy would be at a great disadvantage.*

He could see four figures behind the gate, man-shaped, but otherwise featureless, black spots in the brilliance. He was not at all surprised to see them spring to attention as he approached, shadow figures reaching for weapons.

"Halt, Southlander!"

Ahmed held his hands aloft. *I am from the North!*

As his eyes adjusted, he began to make out the men's faces. All of them had the same unnerving, pale yellow hair, and while he could not see their eyes, he had no doubt they would be blue. Beasts. But no, that was wrong. Had not Ilaweh himself made that clear? *Men, then. But stupid men, who think of North and South backwards. When I am clear of this, I will go fists with someone to settle that foolishness.*

The men behind the gate shuffled their feet, swaying back and forth, three looking to the other, presumably their leader, for orders. After a few moments, the leader cleared his throat and demanded, in a voice that seemed a register higher than it ought to have been, "State your name and business."

"I am Ahmed Justinius, Prelate of Ilaweh, and I am here at his command."

The men looked back and forth at one another, faces blank and puzzled. "We do not know this land."

Ahmed felt himself tense with anger. "Ilaweh is not a land!" he snapped, then, with great effort, calmed himself. "Ilaweh is a *god*."

The men again looked back and forth, as if each hoped his fellows had worked something out and could explain the foreigner's strange words, but none had found any particular insight. "Why does your god send you here?" the leader asked in a shaky voice. His long, thin fingers were tight on the grip of his sword, as if he half expected Ahmed to tear through the gate and slay them all.

A very good question. Ahmed shrugged. "I do not know. I know only that he bid me come."

The leader frowned. "I do not know this god, and in any event, I do not answer to any gods. I answer to Caelwen of House Luvox, or Davron of House Noril."

Ahmed perked up at this. "I know Caelwen. I made the trek to our camp alongside him. He will speak for me."

"Perhaps, but he is indisposed. I cannot let you in without authorization. You seem a military man. You understand my position."

"Aye, all too well. And I do not even know if it is my goal to enter."

"Then what will you do?"

Ahmed raised an eyebrow, considering, then answered, "I will do what military men do best." He lowered himself to the ground and leaned against the gate, chuckling softly as the guards took a step back, as if they feared he might be venomous.

"I will wait."

Eleran knew he should have left hours ago. He had an important meeting to attend in the morning, but between the cold outside and the warmth of the lovely farm girl who had offered to share her bed, it was just a damned hard thing to get going. That and he felt he should probably sleep off the booze, or he might have trouble finding the camp again.

It had never occurred to him that he might have a similar problem once he sobered up. Admittedly, he was still a bit foggy, and definitely a little preoccupied by the smell of his new friend hanging in the air, on his skin, everywhere. And the cold was indeed a distraction, too, but he would have thought that it would make finding a bunch of men with campfires in the dark not just easier, but significantly more desirable. Somehow, though, he still found himself stumbling about in the snow with no clue. *It doesn't make any sense! I should be able to see smoke!*

Eleran shook his head and slogged back to the road to get his bearings, his breath steaming from his nose. *If I had one of those guard helms, I could pretend I was a dragon.* With an impish grin, he snorted a brief, real flame from his nose, then quickly looked around to make certain no one had seen.

I'm not like my old man. That was important to Eleran. The nobles were weak people, and worse, kept people. They imagined they had it better, and he supposed some had it better than some commoners, but the truth of the matter was that each and every one of them were bound with chains they couldn't even see. *Even you, Dad, pretend as you might to be free.*

They sat huddled in the city, worried about whom they might offend, scared even to get rained or snowed on. *And then they wonder why it's so damned easy for me to fuck their wives. Actually having a pair helps in that area.*

Eleran heaved a sigh, still scanning the horizon. He was certain they had left the road here. Not only did he remember it, the grass was trampled, and there was a clear path.

Shaking his head, Eleran followed the trail. *For some reason, they camped cold.* It was the only thing that made sense, but why would they, in this temperature?

The trees grew thicker, snow covered needles brushing wet over his face as he pushed through, searching, searching... *here we are.* He stopped and looked about, certain this was the place. There had been fires here, and recently, but now they were filled with dirt. The Xanthians had been remarkably responsible, actually. The entire campsite was buttoned up and policed. Even their scraps had been buried, so as not to draw predators.

It was unfortunate that they had failed in that last effort, or at least it seemed so to Eleran. Where fortune held was that, for the moment, Eleran was upwind of the wolf that had managed to locate said scraps and was, currently, digging in the dirt with focused intensity.

I really should get in the habit of carrying a sword or some-

thing. He knew how to use one fairly well, though he was perfectly happy if the world remained ignorant of that. In his fairly considerable experience dealing with people, it was usually better to know more than they thought you did, and keep your mouth shut about it until it mattered.

It mattered, now, though. Wolves did not, as far as Eleran knew, run alone without reason. This beast was no runt or sickly elder driven out for weakness, which left the probability that it had trouble getting along with others.

Like me. Shit, this won't end well.

As if sensing his thoughts, the wolf jerked its head in his direction and twisted its muzzle in a snarl.

"Don't have to be this way," Eleran offered in a calm voice, but even as he said it, he knew it was a lie. If it were spring, they might have passed one another by, two lone wolves respecting each other's territory, neither wanting to risk injury, but it was winter, and winter made for desperate wolves.

It came, bounding and loping. *Really wish I had that sword about now.* Eleran gave himself about fifty-fifty odds, fairly certain that he would get only one chance. He clenched his fists, waiting, time seeming to stretch as the beast hurtled toward him, snarling and gnashing its teeth, a blur of fur and fury. He judged as best he could, waited for his moment, and swung with all his might, hammering his fist against the side of the beast's head as it leapt in the air to tear out his throat.

The damp, snow-filled air resounded with the crack, but the beast gave no cry. It hurtled past him in silence, deflected by his blow, and landed in a heap, head tilted nearly backward on its neck. He studied the fallen wolf a moment, surprised to see not even a twitch from it. *Well, I didn't plan it exactly like that, but I'll take it. I was going hungry this morning, too, until you came along.*

He had hoped to find a spot of breakfast with the Xanthians, and had not a cent left to his name, so the wolf had turned out to be good fortune rather than bad. *I thought I was part of this outfit by now. I guess you can't really count on anybody but yourself.*

Eleran was in no way above eating a wolf, and was in fact glad for the chance not to starve, but a chance was all he had at the moment. *I should carry a knife, too. Everybody does. Everybody except me.* He considered that it was probably for the best, in that he'd likely have tried to use it against the wolf and not come out half as well, but it left him with a conundrum: how to turn a wolf carcass into edible meat without a blade. *I'll go back into Nihlos and beg before I'll chew this fleabag with fur on.* The notion of returning to his female companion's home was equally out of the question. In Eleran's experience, one-night stands were best capped at one night, doubly so when fathers and brothers woke shortly after or even before sunrise. *I mean, she's fifty, she can do what she wants, but her old man would probably still be a problem.*

Any other camp, there would be plenty of rubbish left behind, and surely some of it would be sharp, but not this one. Eleran shuffled through the snow and into the central area, just to say he had.

He had to smile when he saw it. It stood hilt up, point driven into the ground, one of the well-made, brutal short blades the Xanthians favored. Tied to the top was a note written on an empty package of coffee.

Ilaweh calls us to Torium, Demon Man Dog, and we obey, while you lie abed doing disgusting things with women and no doubt pigs or dogs. I know you cannot afford a sword, so I leave this one for you. Don't pawn it. Join us if you would.
– Sandi

Eleran wiped at his eyes as he chuckled at the words. *Maybe you can trust some people after all.*

CHAPTER 4
ACTIONS AND CONSEQUENCES

Logrus had slain men with all sorts of weapons, many of them improvised, and counted himself an expert in killing. *I recently bludgeoned a man to death with a coffee pot, after all.* And yet, up to now, Logrus had been certain that a man could not be killed with mere words.

These last few days with Aiul made him doubt that.

It seemed there was no end to the Nihlosian's complaining, questioning, and promises of rebellion. "What is the book we are to fetch?" he would demand, and a shrug was no answer to him. Logrus had to actually *speak* the words "I do not know" to satisfy Aiul, and even that would only quiet him for a while.

"How can you not *know*?" he would rail.

To this, Logrus offered only a shrug. What else was there to say?

They were making fine time despite the snow. The road was good and mostly clear, and the horses strong. The zombies followed on foot, limiting travel speed, but progress remained steady, which was far and away the most important matter.

Moreover, Logrus had every motivation to spend as much time on the road as possible.

Part of this was certainly that traveling was the best way of avoiding Aiul's constant chatter. The man was never truly silent, even on the trail, but when camped, he had the expectation that Logrus would converse over meals, or just prior to sleeping, and became sullen if Logrus did not indulge him. On the road, if Logrus pressed hard, Aiul was more concerned about his backside, and distracted from constant blather.

But the larger part of Logrus's urge to keep moving was something else entirely. The dreams had come soon after they left the battlefield, dreams Logrus knew to be prophetic. He had never seen Torium, nor had he ever been taught about it, and yet he knew the place. He knew it was surrounded by a great wall; that it was warm there, even in winter; and that they would have to descend into the earth to truly enter. He knew there would be strange, triangular buildings that barred entrance into the underground, and that the place was filled with deadly mechanisms to repel, trap, and kill invaders.

More, he knew the place was a pit of malignant, gut wrenching evil beyond anything he had ever encountered. He had tracked and slain many a man who earned Elgar's attention: child killers, torturers, cannibals, the list was long, all written in his book. He had made a life of punishing those whose evil rose beyond the mundane. There were no simple murderers or thieves in his book; no common evildoers met their ends at the hands of a Knight of Fear: every target was something more twisted, more perverse.

Not a one of them, or even all of them taken together, held a candle to what lurked in Torium. Logrus did not know the form or the deed, but he knew that the place itself was the true focus of the mission. The rest, about the book and the blood, that was a bonus, a ruse to keep Aiul interested, perhaps, but not their primary goal.

Their true target lay coiled in those depths, scratching at the stones in hunger and madness, waiting for ever more victims.

Logrus jolted with surprise as Aiul said, quietly, "The Master. That is his name."

Logrus opened his eyes to near darkness. He had intended to sleep. Perhaps he had. "Yes."

Aiul's pale, angular face, his features etched by starlight shadows into something near inhuman, whispered "We must destroy him."

"Yes."

Aiul was silent for a long time in the dark, long enough that Logrus began to imagine he had fallen back asleep, but at last he said, his voice both fearful and resigned, "We must hurry. I can feel it."

"Yes." Logrus looked up at the sky. It was still dark, but he guessed it was not long before dawn. With a sudden burst of energy, he rose and began gathering his gear, as did Aiul.

"The zombies will slow us down," the Nihlosian noted.

Logrus scratched at his chin, considering. It was indeed a problem. If they left the zombies, they would have to leave behind the supplies they took from the Nihlosians, but they could probably scrape by on what they could carry themselves. Losing their fighters, though, was another matter entirely. Logrus did not know for certain what enemies lurked in Torium, but he knew it was better to have weapons and not need them than need them and not have them. The zombies were slow, but they could hit hard, and they could take a lot of punishment.

"They don't need to rest like we do," Logrus said at last. "If we set them on the path, they would likely catch up to us at night, even pass us."

Aiul raised an eyebrow, the expression on his face saying he approved of the idea. "It's a risk, but it's not likely anything will happen to them. I don't see bandits attacking a horde of zombies, really."

Logrus continued his packing while he spoke. "No, but they are stupid. They could get lost, or wander into a ravine. Nothing is certain."

"The horses don't like them much, anyway," Aiul said. "I suppose, worst case, we lose the lot of them. I'd rather not, but we don't have much choice."

"No," Logrus agreed. "Elgar calls. We must hurry. We take as much of the supplies as we can with us, and hope they can follow the road with the rest."

Not all of the corpses they had raised had made the trip. Of the perhaps fifty dead Elgies Aiul had raised on the battlefield, just shy of forty remained, the others having simply not been in good enough shape to walk any real distance. The legs had given way on most of the rejects, though in one case, a broken back had left the creature folded in half and struggling to drag itself along, and one had actually suffered a shattered knee from a savage kick by Aiul's horse. Logrus had dispatched them all with a command to stay still and a dagger in through the eye socket. Aiul had been surprised to learn that the brain was a vulnerable spot even in the living dead.

Only a few of the zombies actually carried packs, and it was short work for the pair to rifle the contents and transfer anything they didn't want to risk. The rest would arrive at Torium or not, as Elgar willed it.

Logrus jammed as many sausages as he could into his own pack, then rose, stretched his back briefly, and called out, "Flesh! Continue to Torium. Stay on the road. Do not stop until you arrive, except to defend yourself."

Aiul looked doubtful. "Will they know the way?"

Logrus shrugged. "Have you ever been to Torium?"

"Of course not."

"Nor I. Yet we know the way." He nodded toward the zombies. "They do, too."

Aiul thought the point over. "I suppose that's true."

It would be longer days for both of them, now, earlier to start, later to stop. Logrus smiled as he picked up his pack and prepared to mount. Elgar's will would be done. The wicked would be punished.

And perhaps, if fortune smiled upon him, Aiul would talk less.

The sun was just topping the horizon as Davron found himself near the east gate, his mind far away and filled with many a warring thought. It was difficult to balance how much he enjoyed Teretha's body with the fact that he did indeed still love his wife, and even count himself as loyal to her. Polus's irksome comments did nothing to make the situation better in Davron's mind, despite his friend's best intentions. Polus could afford to stand on ceremony: his wife had borne him a son before she passed. Davron, on the other hand, had duties to other family members besides his wife, specifically to his entire line.

Of course, Polus never said anything actually disparaging. No, he was far too proper for that. The man just raised a gray eyebrow, or cast a sidelong glance, and one knew he had been judged and found wanting. *I really need to challenge him to a boxing match sometime or another. He's too proud refuse, and it will make up for the chess game* and *the conversation.*

He chuckled at the thought. It would indeed be amusing to turn the tables on his old friend now and then, and thinking about it pushed back a less pleasant matter: Narelki's funeral.

Davron had not the slightest desire to attend, and in point of fact, he found her death to be a marked improvement on the state of the world. The notion of attending, of listening to sycophants and fools sing her praises, never mind having to pretend he had ever respected or loved her, was nauseating. And yet there was decorum, tradition, honor, all of which demanded he find some way to reconcile his contempt not merely for her, but for the whole process.

He approached the east gate without announcing himself. One wasn't a very good guard if he wasn't alert enough to see superiors approach and stop picking his nose or flirting with some woman or another. Davron found it the height of amusement to correct such lapses with a shout in the ear and on occasion, depending on how egregious the sin, a boot to the backside or a cuff to the ear.

The four slugs on guard this morning were especially deserving of additional pain. They were so focused on something in front of them that they didn't even hear him approach, much less recognize him. *Bad form, fools. I could have killed the lot of you.*

He took no special precautions to be quiet as he approached, simply walked normally. *That's more than fair.* There were no distractions, no civilians making noise, nothing. *Oh, the lot of you are going to be on kitchen duty for a month!*

He was close enough to tap the sergeant on his shoulder, and still whatever they were staring at held their focus to the point they did not hear footsteps approaching. *Mei, what is it? Naked woman? Corpse? Dogs stuck together?*

The men actually allowed him to walk right up, shoulder to shoulder, as Davron stared at them, incredulously. He opened his mouth to shout in the sergeant's ear, when he caught movement from the edge of his vision, and turned to face whatever held them in thrall.

Oh. I suppose that would do it.

The Southlander sitting outside the gates gave Davron a nod, prompting the sergeant to turn to his left and blanch as he saw Davron standing next to him.

Davron raised an eyebrow at the young man, and offered a sarcastic smile. "So when *did* you plan on reporting this?"

The rest of the guards turned toward Davron, their faces sheepish, as the sergeant gulped. "As soon as we were relieved, sir."

Davron gripped the rune-graven bars in the gate and pulled experimentally. "Seems strong to me. You suppose a single Southlander could tear it down and overpower three, but probably not four guards, eh? Couldn't spare a single man to report this?"

The sergeant stammered and cast his eyes to the ground. "Sorry, sir. No excuse, sir."

Davron raised an eyebrow at the man outside the gate. "How long have you been waiting, Southlander?"

The foreigner shrugged. "A few hours."

Davron stroked his chin, wheels turning in his mind. "And why have you come?"

The sergeant piped up, "His god sent him."

Davron scowled at the sergeant. "Did I ask you?"

"No, sir. Sorry, sir. No excuse, sir."

Davron did his best to keep a straight face as he turned back to the Southlander. "Do you have a name?"

The Southlander grinned up at him. "Yes."

After waiting a moment, Davron chuckled softly. *So it's that sort of game.* "And will you share it, or is it an occult secret by which we might enslave your soul or some such?"

To Davron's surprise, the Southlander snorted laughter, rather than growing angry. "You would need my left boot, I think, for such a curse." He rose to his feet and gave a genuine smile. "Ahmed Justinius, Prelate of Ilaweh. I have recently been instructed that I should not think of you as savages, no matter your pale skins and stone axes."

Davron gestured to the spires behind him, grinning. "Ah, yes, well, our technology is largely primitive, as you can see from our mud and wattle construction." He drew his sword slowly, so as not to give the wrong impression, and held it up for the Southlander to see. "But our steel is good."

"So it is. Better than mine, but I am a poor warrior doing Ilaweh's work."

Davron smiled at the Southlander as he sheathed his blade. "Ilaweh, eh? Is that your god's name?"

The Southlander made a sound halfway between a grunt and a laugh. "At least you did not think it was a land." Davron didn't understand the reference at first, but noticed his sergeant's expression of chagrin. *Ah.*

Here, then, was exactly what he had been looking for: an excuse to avoid Narelki's memorial service and save face. *And it will, no doubt, be one uncommonly interesting diversion. I should drop in on Polus before he leaves for the funeral and see his reaction. It would serve him right for the snark about everything else.*

"Open the gate," he commanded. The guards all looked at him with nervous, doubtful looks. "Did I stutter? Do I have a stain on my shirt? How can I shake hands with this man and introduce myself with the gate between us?"

The sergeant moved gingerly to the side gate and unlocked it, then stepped back as he swung it open, keeping as far back as possible from the Southlander.

Ahmed hesitated, as if awaiting formal permission, and Davron waved him forward. "Davron Noril," he announced, and extended a hand as the Southlander stepped through the gate. The forearm grasp a bit unexpected, but easily accommodated.

Dark, smoldering, alien eyes, but sincere for all that.

Ahmed held Davron's gaze a moment, then said, "I know this name. Sandilianus spoke of you. He said you joked you would give him your family name if he could beat twelve of your men."

"Oh, that was no joke. I have no heir." *Not yet, at any rate.* "What better way to choose a son, if the normal methods have failed?"

Ahmed laughed out loud, his dreadlocks swaying back and forth. "He would be amused to hear that."

"No doubt. And there's a long and sordid tale involving him, in which I feature prominently," Davron said as he gestured with his head for Ahmed to follow.

"The hero, no doubt?"

Davron snorted. "Depends on one's perspective. I'll tell you while we walk. You decide."

Caelwen arrived at the east gate five minutes early for his meeting with Eleran. With luck, they could sort out the new crew by lunch, and Caelwen could attend Narelki's funeral. He scanned the small crowd passing through the gates, his horse beneath him occasionally whickering.

Eleran, of course, was ten minutes late, and by the time he came into view, Caelwen had allowed himself to get worked into a real lather. *Disrespectful ne'er do well! Lowborn, worthless laggard!* A thousand other insults came to mind, all of which fled his mind when he saw the look on the man's face and the blood on his shirt. *You'd think I would learn. I am noble in nothing but blood, it would seem.*

"They're gone," Eleran said, by way of greeting.

Caelwen gestured at the blood. "Are you injured?"

Eleran waved it aside. "Yeah, I, uh, had a run in with a wolf last night. Or this morning, depending on how you look at it. It didn't work out so well for him, but I'm fine."

"Good. Now, what do you mean, 'gone'?"

Eleran stared back at Caelwen a moment, as if trying to work out what could possibly be confusing about the word. "I mean, you know, *not there anymore*, man! The camp is abandoned!"

It made no sense. "What?" Caelwen stammered, trying to wrap his head around the strange notion. "*Why?*"

"Got some kind of message from their god to go to Torium, and they took off in the night."

Caelwen shook his head. "I talked long with Ahmed. That does not sound like the man I know."

Eleran scowled up at him. "You know fuck all about them from one day. Do you know he has visions?"

Caelwen blinked in shock. "Visions?"

"Yeah, like *real* visions. I have seen the shit this guy does, and it's no joke, not any more than the Meites. Do you even know why they're here?"

Caelwen couldn't keep the sour look off his face as he answered, "I presume you're about to tell me."

Eleran balled a fist and scowled back. "Come down off that high horse, bro, literally, and talk to me like a man instead of getting all butt-hurt."

Caelwen clenched his jaw and said nothing as he swung down to the ground, knowing it was a fair comment. "Very well. I admit, I am ignorant of this. Will you educate me, or did you just plan on mocking me a bit longer before leaving me alone in the dark?"

Eleran's face softened. "Sorry. I guess I'm letting history get between us, and this is the wrong time." He held out a hand. "Peace?"

"Peace." Caelwen chuckled to see Eleran use the Xanthian form, grasping at the forearm. "Now, educate an ignorant fool, would you?"

Eleran nodded toward the gate. "Let's take a walk. Outside. Nobody else needs to hear this."

Caelwen followed, leading his horse away from the gate and

listening to Eleran's tale as it grew ever more bizarre. *The end of the world? Ancient gods having revenge?*

"And you believe all of this?"

Eleran looked at the cobblestone road a moment, then back up. "I dunno. Some of it, for sure. But you know who *does* believe?"

"Presumably someone important?"

"My old man."

Caelwen felt as if he'd been punched in the gut. "Isn't your father—?"

"Maranath Aswan, yeah, the bigwig Meite."

"Mei!" Caelwen suddenly remembered his father's words from the night before. *'They're on edge right now. Davron says they think the end of the world is nigh.'* Caelwen felt a cold chill creep into his belly as he realized what that particular phrasing meant: the rest of the elders considered this foolishness, and would offer no aid whatsoever.

Eleran looked at the ground for a moment, as if embarrassed by what he intended to say, then looked Caelwen in the eye and charged ahead with it anyway. "So I guess the whole prisoner thing is on hold, but I do have something I need you to get for me with some of their credit. Can you get me a good horse?"

"You'd ride to catch up with them, eh?"

"You should, too. They're better men than any here, and if they are half right, they need all the swords and fists they can get."

Caelwen shook his head sadly. "You have no idea how much I would like to, but my duties lie elsewhere. I must protect the empress, and serve my father."

"That's a whole lot of weight around a man's neck, brother. Seems like it could choke the life out of you." Eleran suddenly looked uncomfortable and awkward. "Sorry. I mean, about the brother comment. I dig, we're not the same kind. No offense meant."

"Would that I were your brother, Eleran, with no duty, no family, no honor but what I chose. It must be wonderful. I can only dream of it." Caelwen held out a hand, and Eleran again shook forearms with him. "As for the horse, take mine, and may whatever gods you believe in watch over you."

Eleran took the reins, jammed a boot into a stirrup and hauled himself onto the horse's back. "In another life, then."

Caelwen sighed as horse and rider moved east, down the road, growing smaller in the distance. "Aye. In another life."

Prandil would have fled, save for the fact it would likely have led to his death, or so he tried to tell himself. Maranath had not left much doubt as to his expectations: they would all be attending Narelki's funeral unless they were excused by death.

Given any alternative, he would have been elsewhere. There was something so terribly obscene about it all, putting the corpse of someone you knew into the ground, especially when you bore the responsibility for them being a corpse in the first place.

Almost everyone who mattered was here, making certain they were seen. It wouldn't do, after all, to be noticed absent from such an affair, doubly so for Meites, considering Maranath's mood. Even Maklin had shown up, looking crabby as ever. *Maklin was simply not designed for formal wear.*

Prandil was proud enough of his own robe, a lovely, blue silk garment that flowed well on his frame. He tightened his yellow sash as he nodded at Maklin, but the old man was oblivious to his gesture. *Oh, who cares if he looks like a fool. He's come all in black, anyway. There's no helping him.*

Maranath, dressed in bright red, noticed Prandil's gesture from the corner of his eye and turned to glare at Maklin. "You look like an idiot," he said.

"Well, you *are* an idiot for dragging me here," Maklin shot back.

Maranath glared at Maklin for a moment. "You're right. I am."

Maklin snickered, and Maranath shook his head, smiling despite himself.

The cream of Nihlos, all in their brightly colored robes, filled the carefully manicured lawn, drinking and laughing. One was supposed to remember life at a funeral, not forget it in grief. It was ill luck to send a soul on to the next world surrounded by darkness and despair. The living had a duty to lift the departed with bright colors, joyful memories, and fond farewells, lest the dead be bound to the world, burdened and weighted down with negative emotions. There would be plenty of time to grieve later.

And there, on a large, raised dais, rested the love of his life, prepared for her final journey. Rithard had done a fine job concealing the damage. Prandil felt his guts twist like snakes, seeing her in his memory as she was in those final moments, her golden hair streaked with gore, her diamond-blue eyes clouded and dark with blindness.

And yet she smiled, and Mei, I know why. I would smile, too, to break free of such a prison as she had made for herself. Prandil shuddered at the thought, imagining the terrible, bleeding horror she must have felt for decades, forced to live on her knees, as one of *them*. It was like tearing the wings from a butterfly: it should have been fatal. Such as they were never meant to live that way, and yet she had endured so long, struggling, never giving up. *All gone, now, my love. Fly away. You are free.*

Someone was speaking to the crowd now, nattering on with platitudes, but Prandil paid no heed. His vision blurred as he tried and failed to think of life, not death, but it was too much, knowing that he was not only the instrument of her destruction, but that she had likely intended to use him that way. *She could never end her own life. But I could, if she provoked me.*

As he turned to leave, shaking with grief, knowing he was in no state for this ceremony, he felt a gentle hand on his shoulder. He turned and gaped to see Ariano staring up at him with wide eyes of flaming emerald, her gaze searching, piercing.

"Did she truly say what you said? Or were you just saving your own skin?"

Prandil bit back an insult. For the first time in recent memory, she had not offered one. He would keep the peace, at least for the moment. "She did. They were her last words. 'I feel like me again.'"

Ariano's piercing gaze still held him fast like a bug for long moments, then she nodded, convinced. "Pitiful creature. How could I have hated her? I knew what she lived with." She patted Prandil on the back, as if she were his grandmother instead of a fearful master. "Go. Grieve. I will stand for both of us. I remember more than you, anyway."

Prandil gave her a wary glance and wiped at his streaming eyes. "Maranath will not be pleased."

"Leave him to me."

Rithard eyed the half-empty decanter on his new desk, entertaining the notion of pouring another drink despite the increasingly late hour. The desk had, until recently, belonged to his Matriarch, Narelki, but she had met with an unfortunate 'accident', and the desk had come with his elevation to her position. *Doubtless, she would find the notion of a bottle of whiskey on Amrath's desk to be some sort of blasphemy. Murder and mayhem were fine, but alcohol or bad language would have been intolerable.*

He shook his head at such thoughts as unfair to her, and smiled, remembering her letter to him. Meite philosophy was truly strange. She had every reason to hate him, but she had actually respected him for his part in their little dance, enough to name him her heir and gift him with something remarkable: the secrets kept by their House, from the founding of Nihlos to the present day.

The Papers, as they were known, most of them still in their leather pouch, lay on the desk before him. He had spent the past few hours since he received them on organization and general impressions and was now taking a second pass for deeper analysis.

On the advice of Narelki in her final letter, he paid particular attention to the item she added regarding the circumstances of Theron Tasinal's death. As she suggested, the information was explosive. Kariana Tasinal had often been fingered as the likely cause of Theron's demise, as she had the most to gain. But it turned out, Theron was a Meite, and in a bizarre twist, had lost his own life the same way Narelki had, by coming in second in a battle between Meites. Tasinalta was innocent! *Well, of murdering Theron, at any rate.* And Sadrik Tasinal, Rithard's newest 'friend', had at least two murders to his name. *Of course, he beat me to the punch with Maralena.*

Rithard felt a slight dilemma about what he should do with that information. Kariana had intervened to save his life, believing it would put her in a very difficult political position. No one, least of all Rithard, had known Davron was actually trying to keep him safe, rather than murder him to keep him quiet. Sadrik, on the other hand, was something of a comrade in arms. *Who to chose?*

That was a decision for later. There were other, more interesting bits in the papers, facts not simply declared but in need of teasing out. He was following several threads, but the one that had his interest for the moment concerned birth, death, and remarkable synchronicity.

Rithard drummed his fingers on the desk as he considered the two documents before him. They were both just over a hundred years old, and give or take a few hours, literally the same age. One detailed the birth of a son, Aiul, to Amrath Narelki, no listed father. Another, similar document, recorded the still birth of a son to Talus Ariano and Amrath Lothrian. *And both on the same day. What a remarkable 'coincidence'.*

The timing was strange enough, but it was also unusual that Lothrian or Narelki had chosen to include a copy of Aiul's birth record at all. None of the other house leaders had done so with any children. The Papers were for *secrets*, not family records or keepsakes. Such things were kept elsewhere, and open for perusal to anyone.

But even at that, it seemed downright grisly, ghoulish even, to keep a memento of a stillborn child. *Unless, of course, one were a wicked sorcerer who had ulterior motives.*

Rithard sat back in his chair, fingers steepled, deep in thought. He entertained, briefly, the mad notion of the Meites having used the corpse for some loathsome ritual, but dismissed it as silly. Meites were selfish, arrogant, often vain, and certainly capable of murder, but they didn't eat children or engage in human sacrifice. That was the sort of thing they *would* kill over.

There was certainly a mystery to be solved, but Rithard could not see the shape of it yet. *I need more data points.* With a frown, he scribbled on a blank piece of paper: *cross reference with burial records.* He wrapped it around the two documents, and was just placing them back in the Papers packet when he heard the doors open behind him.

Rithard turned to face Slat as the old slave entered and announced, "Master, you have visitors."

Rithard decided he would indeed have another drink. "At this hour? Send them away. Tell them I am in mourning." He turned back to the Papers and poured two more fingers of whiskey, suppressing a snicker so as to avoid offending Slat.

Slat cleared his throat, drawing Rithard's attention again. "I don't think that will—" Slat turned quickly and tried to bar someone's passing. "Now, see here!"

Davron Noril, eyes twinkling with mirth or mischief, sidestepped Slat and entered the library, arms wide and high as if greeting a long-lost son. "Rithard! So good to see you."

Rithard knocked back half his drink with a grimace. "Close the doors behind you, Slat."

Davron grinned and waved as Slat passed. The old slave was not entirely successful at hiding his contempt, but he managed to close the doors without slamming them, which Rithard felt showed tremendous restraint.

Rithard sipped his drink, eyeing Davron and waiting, refusing to be the first to speak. *Everything is a battle with you, eh? Even victory over a nearly crippled old man is something to celebrate?*

"I'll get right to the point," Davron said, his face serious now. "I have a guest I need you to babysit for a bit."

Rithard snorted. "I have no children. Why would you imagine I have a talent for such things?"

Davron rolled his eyes. "It's not an *actual* child, you dolt!"

Rithard swirled the rest of his drink, pursing his lips as he bit back words that, if spoken, could well end up with him bleeding. The whiskey made that more difficult than usual, but Rithard was not quite drunk enough yet to feel no pain. *So we'll not mention the irony of you questioning my intelligence while missing my meaning, but we will think it.* "Ah, like I was your *guest*, you mean?"

Davron took a deep breath and let it out with exaggerated concern. "I do realize that me coming to you begging is ironic bordering on the absurd. But let's be honest, here." He flashed what he obviously considered a charming grin, one that no doubt made the ladies swoon. "This all worked out fantastically well for *both* of us."

"By blind luck!"

Davron chuckled. "No. Fortune favors the bold. I acted boldly. So did you, once you realized you had no options." He spied the bottle of whiskey and gestured to it. "May I?"

Rithard sighed and withdrew a second glass from the desk drawer. "Help yourself."

Davron nodded his thanks and continued as he poured. "This morning, I saw another opportunity, and I damned well charged forward with it. Considering how the fates smiled on our last venture, I thought I would offer you first refusal." He held his glass toward Rithard in a toast.

Rithard stared at Davron and tapped a single finger on his desk, wanting nothing more than to eject his 'guest'. *But, Mei, he's intriguing me, now!* He waved his own glass in Davron's direction, the gesture apparently close enough for his visitor, who knocked his own drink back and began pouring another.

Rithard did the same, and asked, "And how badly will I be injured if I choose to pass on your 'offer'?"

Davron leaned over, placing his hands on the desk and bringing his head level with Rithard's. "Now, listen to me: I did what I did because I had no more choice than you did. Do you really want the Meites to be totally unopposed?"

"Oh, you might sell me on that, but don't think for a second that I've forgotten the manhandling you gave me!"

Davron seemed to suddenly notice the Papers on the desk. Rithard tried to give nothing away, but knew he must have failed, as Davron's hand struck like a viper to snatch up the packet.

Davron leered at Rithard, holding the packet out of reach. "What have we here?"

"That information is the private property of House Amrath! I am the only person even authorized to look at it!"

Davron raised an eyebrow and grinned. "No, you are *not*. Not until the council meets. Do you want my vote?" He thumbed through the packet far too quickly to glean anything useful. *It's just his way of establishing dominance.*

Rithard sneered at Davron, not bothering to hide his sincere loathing for the bully. "I'm partial to women, so I doubt I have anything that would sway you."

Davron tossed the packet onto the desk and gave Rithard an amused look. "I'm fucking your mother. I don't see how implying I'd want a boy like you actually flies, all in all." He leaned over the desk again, "Unless you are, in fact, a little bitch."

"My *mother* is fucking *you*," Rithard insisted. "If you think you're in control of that situation, think again, and if you want it to continue, you might consider treating her son better." Rithard sipped at his drink, smirking at Davron, who seemed suddenly and very uncomfortable. "But being honest, having known her my whole life, I'd advise you to conclude your business quickly. My mother is at least as bold and aggressive as you are, and more cunning by far."

Davron's discomfort faded quickly, and he grinned back at Rithard, suddenly best friends again. "Good! So we understand each other, yes?"

For a moment, Rithard was speechless. "Understand? You've made absolutely no sense since you barged in here!"

Davron gave him a tired look, and sighed as if the burden of the world were on his shoulders. "I *tried*. *You* wanted to spar and measure dicks, so I obliged. Are we done with that part, now? Are you ready to hear me out?"

Rithard sat back in his chair and steepled his fingers. *He has a point, I suppose.* "Fine. What *did* you come here to say?"

Davron said nothing, however. He simply opened the doors and gestured for someone to enter.

Slat called out, "Master, are you well? Do you need assistance?"

"I'm fine," Rithard answered, his attention on the stranger. The man was covered head to toe in a long, flowing robe. Even his hands were sunken into the folds.

Davron closed the door and told his guest, "You can take that silly thing off now. We're among friends."

Rithard scoffed. "Speak for yours—"

As Rithard laid eyes on the man beneath the robe, he found, to his surprise, that his words had fled entirely.

CHAPTER 5
PLANS A, B, AND C

MARANATH had no love for rising early, and could have certainly made use of a few extra winks, but there was business to attend. Below him, a thin mist covered the world in cotton, rolling slowly downhill, making it seem as if the grounds of House Talus had been plucked from where it usually lay and placed among the clouds. The sun was just a glow on the horizon still, and Nihlos a larger glow beneath.

As Maranath began his gentle descent, he took some consolation to see Maklin, a well-known hater of mornings, standing slack jawed and swaying beneath a topiary bear, muttering and cursing under his breath. Ariano stood beside him, looking up at Maranath. She offered a small wave as he settled, then patted Maklin on the back with relish. "What a lovely morning!"

"I hope Cruentus eats you," Maklin muttered, but there was no energy behind his words. He blinked rapidly a moment, then shook his head. "I almost crashed into your damned tower, you know. We could have started an hour later."

Maranath laughed, feeling no sympathy for his old friend. "Drink less next time you have business in the morning."

Maklin responded with an incoherent grunt of misery. "It was a funeral. You drink at funerals. I had to be civil." He hacked and spat on the ground. "At least I beat the boy."

Maranath eyed the skies, looking for movement. "So you did."

"Lies," Sadrik called from the shrouding mist. "I just chose a more civilized location. I greatly prefer lions." He seemed to slowly materialize, hawkish face slicing through the mists like the prow of a ship.

Ariano chuckled at this, though she seemed reserved, and a bit sad. "It would have been a better choice, eh, a portent?"

Maranath scoffed. "Nonsense." *No doubt you're in your head about the whole mess with Lothrian, and it serves you right. The two of you were fools.*

"Even if one doesn't believe in such, and I most certainly do," she said, "You can hardly deny the very real effect that aesthetic has for a Meite. I appreciate symmetry."

Maklin grunted again. "I'd appreciate you all shutting up."

Ariano, her chipper mood gone in a flash, shot back, "Why don't *you* shut up, you stupid codger!"

Maranath sighed. It was going to be a long trip.

Rithard didn't usually eat breakfast, and certainly he never took his meals in a formal dining room, but as the new master of the house, he had obligations. He looked across the table to his Southlander guest and offered a nervous smile. *A creepy smile. That's how it will be received. It always is.* "You'll forgive me for not seeing you privately until now, but I was in no way expecting visitors." *Another duty I would never have had to deal with previously.*

Rithard had quickly realized that Davron's 'opportunity' had been little more than an excuse to avoid attending Narelki's funeral. Now Rithard was stuck entertaining the foreigner, and Davron was nowhere to be found.

Rithard thought wistfully of the Papers, wondering when he would be able to get back to them. He had managed to push the duty of host onto Slat for the previous evening, having the slave get their visitor settled with a meal, a bath, and a bed. That had left Rithard a little more time for research, but not nearly enough. He had just managed to form some intriguing connections before he had fallen asleep at his desk.

There appeared to have been some sort of doomsday cult in the early decades of Nihlos, one in which even many of the founders had been involved, but the details were sketchy, and worse, some of the information was missing. Documents ended suddenly, and Rithard's eye was keen enough to see some pages had literally been cut from a number of books referred to by the Papers.

Perhaps most frustrating of all, some things were written in a language he could not read. *A dead end. I can't even identify the language, much less translate it.*

Ahmed cleared his throat, rousing Rithard from his ruminations. The Southlander set his coffee down with care, as if afraid the cup would shatter. "I take no offense. I came unannounced, and you are in mourning."

"I appreciate your patience. Just know it's not how I normally treat guests, especially foreign dignitaries."

Ahmed raised an eyebrow, the ghost of a smile on his lips. "How do you usually treat them?"

Rithard snorted. "I don't. I've only just taken over the house, and I have my doubts as to whether it's permanent. That's something for the council to decide when next they meet."

"Which may be some time, I think," Ahmed said. He drained the rest of his coffee, and reached for the decanter to pour more, but before he could, a short, fat girl snatched it up.

Ahmed watched her fill his glass, a troubled expression on his face.

Rithard tapped a finger on the table. "What is your name, girl?"

She looked at him with wide, fearful eyes. *Ah, lovely. Wrong tone. I'll need to work on that.*

"Celisa, Patriarch," she squeaked.

"You are excused. Oh, and please leave the carafe...."

"Did I do something wrong?"

Rithard forced a smile, which seemed to only heighten the fear in the girl's eyes. "Not at all. We just have private matters to discuss." She seemed to relax, and he ushered her out with shooing gestures.

When the door had closed behind her, Ahmed spoke. "I am not accustomed to servants."

"Nor I," Rithard admitted. "It's awkward. As I said, I've only just come into this position. It carries expectations that are some-what alien."

"What did you do before?"

"Worked with the dead, mostly. Occasionally I healed the living as well." Rithard polished off his coffee and set the cup down, considering whether he would pour another. "And I solved crimes, usually murders."

Ahmed perked up at this. "You would know Caelwen of House Luvox, then?"

"Very well. We are old friends." Rithard decided he would indeed have another cup, and poured steaming, black coffee in a measured dose, much the same as he would with liquor. "And you? What is your profession?"

"Besides soldier, you mean."

Rithard grinned. "Are all of your people soldiers?"

"In theory. In practice, not all, but many, more than half. And beyond that, I am what Caelwen calls a 'religious'." The Southlander grinned widely, as if it were a great joke. "Our word for it is 'prelate'."

"Ah, yes, Davron mentioned you believe you were sent here by your god?" Rithard took a drink, uncertain of how to proceed. "I should warn you, I mean no disrespect, but I am no believer in gods. I find myself wanting to ask all sorts of questions that would likely insult you, but as you have seen, I have that effect on everyone."

Ahmed laughed aloud at this. He set his cup on the table to avoid spilling as he wiped at his eyes. "Indeed, I saw the look on the girl's face well enough! But as for my faith, have no worry, my faith is strong, and Ilaweh has no need of your belief. Trust me, friend, his will is done whether we even know his name. I am living proof of that. Ask any question you like. I promise, I will not take the matter beyond fists."

Rithard knew his first question would be insulting, and yet it was the question he most wanted to ask. He tried to keep any mocking tone from his voice as he asked, "How did you know to come here? Does your god appear to you and speak? Send notes of some sort, emissaries, animals perhaps?"

Ahmed raised an eyebrow, a skeptical expression on his face, but he was smiling as well. "Come here, today, or come to this land?"

Rithard sat back in his chair. "So your god sent you in both things, then?"

"Aye. He even shipwrecked us when we tried to turn aside from his will. Many good men perished."

Rithard was fairly certain his disdain was written all over his face, but the Southlander had yet to leap from the table and pummel him, which was a good sign. "You dodged the question."

"Aye, I did not intend to," Ahmed replied. "Ilaweh speaks to me in dreams, and sometimes in overwhelming feelings. I do not think gods visit the mortal realm often. It would be most dangerous for the world."

"Dangerous how?"

"Gods are immense, energetic beings. I think it would be like stuffing a tiger into a backpack."

That actually sounds somewhat sensible, if one believed. "How do you know this? Does it come to you in visions as well?"

Ahmed chuckled. "Ah, no. If I am anything beyond soldier and prelate, it would be student. I studied long under my master."

Rithard said nothing for a while, his mind racing as he made several connections. The Southlander gave him an odd look, one Rithard was familiar with. *Violating social norms and expectations again.* Rithard held up a hand. He could usually follow one thread of intuition without stopping a conversation, but now he had two. *Well, let's sort one of them out, then the other.*

"Your master. The empress murdered him, yes?"

Ahmed's eyes darkened at the thought, and he answered with a curt nod. "It is so."

"Would you have the bodies of your men to returned to your land? I preserved them."

Ahmed's eyes grew wide in shock. "You work with the dead," he said, making the connection. He sat bolt upright in his seat. "Do you say truth? Why would you have preserved them at all?"

Rithard shrugged. "For research, of course. It seemed only prudent to know all I could about potential enemies."

Ahmed eyed him suspiciously. "You cut them open and looked inside?"

Rithard shrugged, well aware that an autopsy might seem a bizarre thing, depending on the Southlanders' cultural norms. "Being fair, they were already cut open. I merely widened some of the wounds in most cases."

Ahmed stared at him a moment, eyebrows raised. "And what did you discover? *Are* we different?"

Rithard snorted. "Of course not. I knew it all along, but given the opportunity, one should be certain. Same organs, same blood. A few differences in size, but all within reasonable variance of normal, nothing that would indicate a different species. We are the same."

Ahmed looked at him with wide, hopeful eyes. "It would be a great gift if you could help us recover the remains of our fallen. It would go far in mending things between our people."

"I suspected as much. We shall see to it before you leave, but there is another, more pressing matter."

"Speak, and I will answer."

Rithard steepled his fingers and put them to his nose, letting his eyes lose focus. "You claim a god sent you here. And I have been pondering something that may seem minor, but feels of great import. I recently discovered there seems to have been a sort of doomsday cult amongst the founders."

Ahmed shrugged. "No doubt. Amrath would surely have told them of the prophecy. It is why we have come, after all."

Rithard blinked at this sudden news. "I don't—" He ran a hand over his face. "That is to say..." He found himself blinking uncontrollably. "Swear it's true. Did a god truly send you?"

"There is no doubt."

"And you came here because...?"

"We aim to thwart Elgar's prophecy of doom, if men are able. If not, we will die well, along with everyone else."

Rithard took a deep breath, regretting the second coffee now. His pulse was pounding in his head. "Did your education by chance include foreign languages?"

"I can read and write eight languages, though they are mostly old and unused. I know many a musty tome by heart. Fat lot of good it's done me."

Rithard shot to his feet and beckoned. "Come with me!"

Suddenly, I am his new best friend. Ahmed found it amusing how quickly the cold, pale stranger had gone from languid and disinterested, serving a duty he did not relish, to near frantic excitement.

Rithard led him through the manse in tow, the look on his face so intense that the servants trying to speak with him instantly thought the better of it. *Well, perhaps the large, armed black man has something to do with it, as well.* Ahmed chuckled as Rithard tore down the hallways, and moved quickly to keep up with the fellow. His legs may have been spindly, but they were long, and his pace breakneck.

As they approached a large set of double doors, an elder slave, unintimidated, called out, "Master Rithard, this is highly irregular, bringing a Southlander into the library!"

Rithard produced a key from his robe and unlocked the doors. "The game is afoot, Slat! Unless I miss my mark, there will be all sorts of irregularities in the near future." He patted the old fellow on the shoulder. "See to it we're not disturbed."

"Of course." As Rithard started again toward the library, the old man grabbed at his sleeve to stop him. "Master, you do know you are frightening the other slaves, yes? I hope this isn't just some errant notion or foolishness?"

Rithard laughed as he opened the doors. "You mean you hope it's got nothing to do with Meite influence I've caught from The Papers like some contagion, I presume?" He laid a calming hand on the old servant's shoulder and assured him, "I am innocent, sir, and I am well. The worst you'll see from me is a few corpses dissected on Mistress Narelki's desk."

Slat sucked in an offended gasp. "You would not!"

Rithard gave the old fellow a slight bow. "Very well, I'll promise not to do so, and in exchange, you'll smooth things over with the rest of the house, yes? Hand out some bonuses or something. Or cake. I always liked cake as a child."

"I whipped you for stealing cake once, as I recall."

Rithard snorted laughter. "So you did. I'll not steal cake again, I promise. And we'll keep out of sight."

The old slave smiled. "I will see to it you are undisturbed."

Ahmed followed Rithard into the room and stared about in amazement as Rithard closed the doors behind them. "Ilaweh is great," he muttered. "There must be ten thousand books here!"

"More, I should think, but I have never counted them. I have other matters in mind for now." He strode to the great desk and took up a packet of papers.

"I will not sleep with you unless you can beat me in a fight," Ahmed said.

Rithard whipped around to face Ahmed, eyebrows practically hovering above his forehead. "I beg your pardon?"

Ahmed could not hold his serious face, and began to snicker.

Rithard smiled back, looking abashed. "Ah, I see. A jest." He produced a paper from the packet and presented it gingerly to Ahmed. "It seems solid enough, but it should be nearly a thousand years old. Treat it gently. Can you read it? I don't even recognize the letters, much less the words."

Ahmed raised one eyebrow, then both, as he felt an almost electrical surge run through him. "Ilaweh is great! This is ancient Ilawehan. What your people called mine when we first met."

"What did they call themselves?"

Ahmed shrugged. "I do not know. We took a new name, after Xanthius. 'Xanthians' are the only name I have ever known for my people. And we took your language too. My people have not used such writing for nearly a thousand years."

Rithard waved his hands, almost jumping up and down with excitement. "Go on! What does it say?"

Ahmed read further, and laughed out loud. "They used it as a code! This is a message from Yorn to Amrath! *The blood is even more potent than we feared.*"

Rithard's face fell in disappointment. "That's all? Bah! I thought I'd found something, but apparently they were still hung up on the ignorance of nobility. 'The blood'. Fools!"

Ahmed, however, did not think that was the whole of it. The paper felt heavy to him, important. "Why would they have written this in a language they knew no one else could understand, except for security? Are there more?"

"Several."

"Then let's see them!"

Prandil had left word with his slaves that he was not to be disturbed, and was consequently furious at the knock on his door

"I asked not to be disturbed!" he shouted. "Illiterates! Imbeciles! Shall I hurl dictionaries at you until you find comprehension in your pain?

Thrun's impish face peeking from the barely cracked door mollified Prandil somewhat. The young slave raised an eyebrow as Prandil's tension fled. "Enraged to grinning in a half second?"

"You've just reminding me of something terribly amusing. I have a surprise waiting for you."

Thrun stepped in and closed the door, a look of amused suspicion on his face. "I have a really bad feeling about that."

"You should, wretch. It will more than make up for this interruption, you can be certain." He waited for Thrun to speak, but the boy remained cunningly silent, waiting for an opening, and very obviously full of himself, his eyes positively brimming with some secret he held. "Well, out with it! What, pray tell, was the purpose of ignoring my clear instructions to fuck off and leave me be for the evening?"

Thrun took a pose of mock sheepishness and looked at the floor, rubbing the toe of his shoe against the carpet, a look of bliss on his face. "Oh, I was just trying to help my master get laid, but, hey--"

"Mei! This is a practical joke to 'snap me out of it', isn't it?" Prandil cackled. "A damned *intervention!*"

Thrun gave him a broad grin. "You might think that. But you'd be dead wrong."

Prandil watched her enter his chambers with a mixture of awe and amusement. *You're a bit young for my tastes, and a bit flat, too, but Mei you have grit, girl. Let's test you, shall we?*

"How did you get in here?" he asked, feigning surprise and annoyance.

Kariana offered him a catty, sexy grin that couldn't have fooled a lovesick teenager. *Presumably you'll get to the point of what brought you here soon enough.*

"I lied to your slaves and told them we had plans. They didn't seem to find spiriting a young, pretty woman up to your private quarters as anything unusual."

Prandil folded his book and placed it on his polished mahogany nightstand. "So that's the shape of things, is it?" *A bribe. But for what? That bit of information is considerably more interesting than the bribe itself, though she isn't clever enough to realize it.*

Kariana gave no answer but her grin.

Ah, perhaps she is! This might at least be entertaining! "Oh, by all means. And do lock the door behind, won't you?"

Kariana did so, then moved forward and took a seat at the foot of his bed. She said nothing, simply waited, presenting herself as a display model. She was far too young, and her waifish figure did nothing for him, and yet…. *There is something about her, something I've sensed since the business with Maralena.*

"I would have come to you, eventually, you know," he said.

"Does it bother you? The role reversal?"

"Not at all. I find it rather refreshing." *The first rule of being a Meite is, after all, not being afraid to reach out for what one wants.*

"You're very certain of yourself."

Prandil chuckled softly. "My dear, you have no idea." He hesitated, though not long enough for her to notice, trying to decide if this was the right course. His own thoughts came back to him: t*o try and fail was so much worse than to never have tried at all.* It was a risk for both of them, and yet, it seemed correct, symmetrical.

The loss of Narelki was a stark reminder that the order needed students, a steady supply of fresh blood. None of the elders seemed concerned enough to bother, and Sadrik needed more experience before he could be of much use in that area. *Very well, then, child, I will consider a second pupil. Let us test first your passion.*

"You've shown quite a bit of mettle of late," he told her. "But not nearly enough flesh for my tastes."

Kariana stretched her arms high and yawned, giving him a nice view of her breasts. "You might have joined one of my orgies."

I might have let Narelki put an end to me, too, and both are of similar appeal. His laugh had a bit more contempt than he intended, but then if she quailed at a little snark, she was definitely the wrong material. "Do I look like a juvenile to you? I am a man of taste and discretion. You should try it sometime. It might suit you."

Kariana stuck out her tongue at him, a gesture Prandil found quite disconcerting, coming from someone who seemed so childlike, both in body and mind. *Am I really considering this?* Admittedly, she was attractive. It would hardly be a great sacrifice, and for Prandil, at least, it was the best way to be certain, to take her measure and see if she could likely weather the training. He would learn much of her spirit, enough to know if going further would destroy her.

"Maybe you're too reserved," she shot back. "Are you sure you're ready for my brash, classless youth?"

Good. Fight. Show me that you know more, your way is better. "I've had more women in my life than you've had men, I'll wager. Women are like wine: age adds things, even as it takes others away. Perhaps if you'd experience with men of actual ability instead of boy toys, you'd appreciate that."

Kariana tittered. "I could have one of them right now, and instead I'm here. What does that tell you?"

"That perhaps you are smarter than you seem." *And that our thinking is aligned.*

Kariana leaned forward and crawled to the head of the bed. She propped her chin with an hand as she locked eyes with Prandil. "It's nice to be given some credit now and then."

Prandil once again took the measure of her as best he could. *Bold. Fearless. We've seen that over and over. Foolhardy, even, though that's not necessarily a bad thing if one has the power to back it up. Ah, well, if it doesn't pan out, it's not as if either of our chaste reputations will suffer.* "I think I should prefer to withhold true judgment on the meal until after dessert."

It was, he had to admit, a more pleasant dessert than he had imagined. The girl had skills, certainly, but the physical aspects were minor. She had passion, deep wells of it, enough to carry her through. *But will she fight for it? If not, the training is likely to kill her.* He lit his pipe and leaned back, considering how he would proceed. *I need to be very careful.*

Even as he was mulling this over, she spoke his thoughts. "Will you teach me?"

I will. This is your first lesson, though you don't know it yet. Prandil turned to her, feigning confusion. "Teach you? I doubt it. I'm fairly impressed with your skills, actually. Much more than I expected."

Kariana blushed. "That's not what I meant."

Prandil waited a moment for her to continue, then prodded. "What did you mean?" *Don't be shy! You've never been before!*

Something in her seemed to hear his silent pleading. She plunged forward, almost stammering as she spoke, "Teach me to be a Meite."

Good. Knowing what you want is important. Now, let us see if you will fight to get it. Prandil gaped at her as if shocked, then laughed loud and hard. At last, he wiped tears from his eyes with the edge of the bed sheet and chuckled, "Oh, my dear, you *are* ambitious, aren't you? So here's the bill for the evening's entertainment?" He took a pull at his pipe and blew out the smoke, regarding her with the gravest expression he could muster. "Seriously, you? Preposterous."

He almost laughed and spoiled the game as Kariana's face fell like a child's who was disappointed in a gift, but she quickly mastered herself, fury growing in her eyes. *Yes. Push on, girl! Fight!* "Why not me?" she asked, her voice husky with rage.

A small coal. Now we kindle it. Prandil rolled his eyes. "Oh, please, don't tear up about it."

That insult clearly hit home. The muscles in her jaw bulged, and Prandil fancied he could see flame dancing behind her eyes. *I've given you what you need. Now, use it.*

She asked him again, punctuating each word with a pause. "Why...not...me?"

Wonderful! Prandil let himself flow into it now, allowing a bit (but just a bit) of the mood he wanted become reality. Now was the time to push the student, to let them actually feel the power, the strength of emotion. He summoned his guilt and grief, allowing just a fraction of it to leak into his soul, and turned toward Kariana, knowing he must look a true fright. "You would hear truth? Why not you? Mei! Because you're weak, pathetic, and foolish. You've come here with the notion of replacing a woman you could never match, and it *offends* me! Whatever made you think being a good fuck qualified you to be a Meite?"

Prandil saw Kariana's jaw bulge once again, and then she was turning away. *No! You're so close!* But no, she had given up. She was gathering her clothes, preparing to slink away. *I was wrong. You're not quite right. Ah, well, you already hated me. It's not as if much has changed. You'll live, which is more than I can say if we continue down this road. So close. So* damned *close.*

Prandil picked up his book again and began reading, already losing his passion for the entire project. Kariana was a dud, and he was a fool, and this was all a tremendous waste of time.

He was surprised when she spoke again, and turned to her, watching her eyes. *Perhaps...* But he saw nothing there, no flames, nothing but stupid, cow-like banality. *Courage, yes. But not quite, my dear. I won't watch what happened to Narelki happen to anyone, ever again.*

"So I'm just not good enough to be one of you?" she asked softly.

Prandil sighed and laid the open book on his chest. "You needn't take it personally." He raised the book again and gave her a pointed look. "I do have things to do, you know."

Kariana blinked at him in shock. "Now, you dismiss me like a common whore?"

Prandil folded the book briefly, feeling suddenly very tired. *We'll both feel like fools for some time, I suppose.* "There's nothing common about you. That's a compliment, you know." He opened his book again, wanting nothing more than solitude, a moment to simply forget what had just happened. "But, yes, you are dismissed."

"Well, I suppose I should regard it as a lesson. I'm learning all the time, you know."

Today I buried a friend and lover, one killed by my hand. The elder of my order loathes me now. And worse, I've gone off on yet another wild tangent, convinced of foolish things, and found myself face down in the mud once again. At least I haven't been stabbed today. "Oh? And what, pray tell, have you learned from events of late?" he asked, unable to keep the bitterness from his voice.

Prandil saw a brief glint of light on steel, and then it seemed the world exploded in brilliant, multicolored shards. He was just able to appreciate what had happened, and took the joyful thought with him into the darkness as the shards settled.

I was right! You are magnificent, my dear. Absolutely magnificent!

CHAPTER 6
BREAKFAST AND THE IMPOSSIBLE

THE SUN was dipping low in the sky by the time Eleran caught sight of the Southlanders. The land had changed from forest to flat plains, but the air was still cold and crisp, and even though it was past time that they should have broken to make camp, they were marching on. *So they're trying to make time. Got a deadline.* He counted himself fortunate to have found them before nightfall. It would have been much harder to follow their trail in the dark.

Eleran approached their small column at a more reasonable pace. His horse was tired, and it would not do to come charging up on such men at any rate. He allowed himself to slowly catch up to them, returning their nods and grins as he moved toward the front of their group.

Sandilianus, his face still mottled with bruises, flashed him a slightly predatory grin as he pulled alongside. "I was fifty-fifty as to whether you would pawn it or not."

Eleran chuckled and offered Sandilianus a wry smile. "You know, I just got reminded why I ought to carry one of these."

Sandilianus gestured around, to the horizon, to the world, and said in a somber voice, "A million reasons, Demon Man Dog. At least." He brightened again and punched Eleran in the arm. "I am glad you came! We could use help setting up camp."

Eleran snorted laughter. "I aim to please."

They rode on until the last of the light was gone. Only then did Sandilianus call a halt to the procession. Eleran threw in with everyone else, flattening brush and pitching tents.

As Eleran put flint to steel, Sandilianus told him, "We are exposed here. Fires visible for miles. If it were any warmer, I would camp cold."

"Only it's not any warmer," Eleran noted as he struck sparks into kindling. A small streamer of smoke curled from the pile, and Eleran blew it into a flame.

Sandilianus shook his head, smiling. "Aye. We risk it. I would rather die in a fight than freeze to death, anyway."

"Me, too."

The sparks filled the night about them as the rest of Sandilianus's troops followed their example.

The food was plain, but it was better than wolf, and Eleran had never been the picky sort. It was at least familiar, now. The Southlanders favored a hard, brown bread with peculiar flavor as a traveling ration, supplementing it with whatever game they could round up locally.

Sandilianus squatted by the fire and offered Eleran a haunch of a roasted hare. He took a bite from his own share, then asked while still chewing, "So what convinced you to come?"

Eleran chuckled. "Took you long enough to ask."

"Might as well talk about something before we sleep. We have time to kill."

Eleran wiped greasy hands on his pants and swallowed. "It's not like I had much going on for me in Nihlos."

"We expect we are going to our death. Still want to come?"

Eleran shrugged. "I cheat at everything else. Might as well cheat death, too."

The Elgies struck with all the grace and precision of a drunken elephant in a log rolling competition. They tried, they really did, but they were just out of their league.

For one thing, Sandi apparently never slept, or had super-human senses, or something. He just wasn't the sort of guy you could sneak up on. Eleran counted himself as pretty observant, too, but he had to admit that he had awoken not at the sound of clumsy attackers, but the sound of Sandi's sword sliding slowly from his scabbard.

They had both bedded down next to his fire. When Eleran awoke, it had burned low, the coals glowing dim orange, ready to be re-kindled, but for now all was quiet. Sandilianus appeared to be sleeping, but his eyes were wide open, alert, his expression grim. Behind him, three man-shaped shadows were slowly approaching, skulking in the dark.

Sandilianus raised an eyebrow, and Eleran shook his head almost imperceptibly, more a movement of his eyes than head. *Wait.* He raised any eyebrow at the Southlander in return. *Any behind me?* Sandilianus blinked twice.

Ok. I can take two. Probably. If I'm lucky. His blade was close by. *At least I learned that lesson.*

The waiting was the hard part, but the most important. Being outnumbered was less a disadvantage if a man had the element of surprise. He watched Sandi's eyes, saw the dark hand tighten on the grip of his own blade, then the slight nod. Eleran returned it, judging the fools behind Sandilianus were, likewise, close enough to engage.

They both burst from the ground, blades in hand, and went to work, shouting cries to wake any in the camp who were not already alert.

By the time it was over, they had lost three men, and put paid to at least thirty Elgies. The rest fled for their lives once they saw the tide turning. The Southlanders cut down any runners they could with bow and javelin, but at least twenty had escaped.

Sandilianus cursed himself as he reconstructed the scene. "They took out our sentries with bows, good ones with range." He marked a spot in the dirt some fifty yards from the sentry position, and hammered a fist into his palm, cursing. "Where did they get the equipment or the skill?"

Eleran shrugged and bent to examine the nearest corpse. "Equipment is easy enough if you don't mind stealing. Can't say on the skill, though. But you're right. I wouldn't expect these idiots to be able to shoot straight at ten yards, much less fifty, and at night."

Sandilianus shouted out, "Rashid! Survivors?"

Rashid paused a moment in sharpening his blade and held up three fingers, then turned back to his task.

Sandilianus walked toward the prisoners. "You grow on me, Demon Man Dog," he called over his shoulder. "I had not seen you use a sword before. It was impressive work. You might be my type after all."

Eleran grinned. "I got the whole 'women' thing all over me. It would poison you."

Sandilianus chuckled. "I am not so picky as Brutus!"

"Who?"

Sandilianus paused and turned, a wistful look on his face. "Aye, you never met him. He died just before you came." Sandilianus chuckled again and resumed walking. "He would have hated you."

"Why would he hate me?"

"Because I think you might be a better fistsman than even he or Yazid."

Rashid had used the term 'survivors' rather loosely in the case of two of the prisoners. They were still breathing, true, but it was clear that would not be the case for long, and in any event, they wouldn't be doing any talking.

The third man, though, seemed well enough except for a nasty foot wound. He sat on the ground, bound, glaring up at them as they approached, but said nothing.

Sandilianus stood before him a moment, silent, and stared at him. The prisoner was a small fellow, with dark, greasy hair and a crooked nose that had likely been broken multiple times. Sandilianus casually added to that number with a swing of his fist, sending the prisoner over on his back with a cry of pain.

"Dog! You attack us in our *sleep*? Give me one reason I should not rip your guts from you while you breathe?"

"My Lord Elgar will reward me," the man mumbled through bloody lips.

Sandilianus looked at Eleran. "Not bandits this time."

Eleran shook his head in disgust. "The true believers are worse."

Sandilianus kicked the man in his belly. He curled up in a fetal position, wheezing at the blow. "Last chance, dog. Tell me why you came, and I offer a clean death. Toy with me and I will shove steel through your guts and leave you here for the crows and ants."

The man offered a fierce grin. "We came to delay you! Our Lord Elgar's plan unfolds tomorrow at sunset, and you cannot stop it!"

Sandilianus stabbed him in the eye. "We will see about that, dog." He wiped blood from his blade and eyed Eleran as if gauging his reaction to the killing.

Eleran shrugged. *Kill 'em all would be fine with me.* "I reckon we're fucked, then. No way we can get there in time."

Sandilianus put his hands on his hips and shook his head, staring at the ground in contemplation. "How well do you know this area we are in?"

"Pretty well," Eleran said. He gestured about. "I used to hang out around here when I needed to lay low."

Sandilianus looked up, hopeful. "Do you know where we can find horses?"

Eleran scratched as his jaw and shrugged. "We can't afford horses."

Sandilianus's grin grew wider. "We have swords. Suddenly stealing is beneath you?" He punched Eleran in the arm, hard enough to make the Nihlosian wince and rub at the injury.

"Nah," Eleran answered, grinning himself now. "Never above a little thievery, if it's for a good cause." He held up a hand and continued, without the grin. "Armed robbery, though, that's a little more extreme. I never got up to that sort of thing before."

"Understood. So we will kill no one we can avoid killing. We can even ask first, explain to them why this must be done, but we can guess how that will go, eh?" He fixed Eleran with a penetrating look. "We need horses, one way or another. Are you with me?"

Eleran thought on it a moment. *Do I really believe all of this?* He had to admit, he did, even though he wasn't sure of the reason. There was no series of logic he could walk down and arrive at the conclusion. He just felt it in his gut. He had seen Ahmed's abilities. The situation was, he believed, truly dire.

He reached out a hand, and Sandilianus returned the gesture. The two sealed their pact with a forearm clasp. "I know a place not far from here."

CHAPTER 7
FROM THE GRAVE

DAVRON was, he had to admit to himself, rather pleased with the chaos of late, but this newest bit had fallen into his lap quite unexpectedly, information and possibilities that, while quite risky if exploited, had tremendous potential. *As I do believe I just told Rithard, fortune favors the bold.*

Davron paced about his study, hungry for inspiration, knowing the coming battle would be difficult indeed. The room was filled with weaponry, mostly swords of deceased house members. It was the custom of House Noril to retire weapons, rather than pass them on. The simple pine walls were lined with such steel teeth. Some special few were kept a bit more carefully. Davron had kept his father's weapon next to his desk in a large, pristine display case of glass, oiled wood, and polished brass, at least until it had gone missing. He was partial to gazing at the weapon while he thought on other matters of import, imagining he could still hear his father's stern, cold, logical words of advice. *Hopefully father is pleased enough that I'll produce an heir at long last, and forgive the matter of the sword for the moment.*

Davron clasped his hands behind his back and stared into the great fireplace that was the main centerpiece of his study. Polus should have been here already, and he was hardly the sort of man to be anything but punctual. *Probably not used to midnight emergency summons, though.*

Another fifteen minutes passed before Polus arrived, chagrin and annoyance etched on his face. "Forgive me, Davron. It's a cold night, and I was in a warm bed." Polus looked at Davron with concern, then a sour look crossed his face. "You look very smug for an 'emergency'."

"Oh, it was no exaggeration. The Meites are out of the city, yes?"

Polus removed his coat and tossed it over a chair, then took a seat and sighed. "Save for Prandil, yes. At least the ones we know about."

Davron grunted. "So, all out of the city, then."

"I *just* explained—"

"Prandil is dead."

Polus stared back at him, eyes first wide, then narrowing. "I take it, from the urgency of your summons, that he did not die of natural causes?"

Davron hesitated, his jaw working as he tried to decide just how to put things.

Polus waited for an answer, his face growing more alarmed by the moment as none was forthcoming. "Mei! Don't tell me *you've* killed him!"

Davron grinned. "Oh, no. The honor is not mine."

Polus gave Davron an exasperated look and nearly shouted, "Will you just get on with it? Who?"

Davron drug it out a moment longer, the chess match still fresh in his mind, before finally spilling his secret. "It was Tasinalta."

Polus seemed stunned for a moment, his face quivering as if it didn't know what sort of expression to form. At last, he covered his eyes with his palm and shook his head. "Mei! You're not joking! Who knows?"

Davron shrugged. "As far as I know, you, Tasinalta, and me. It's unlikely to be discovered until morning. She claims to have left him in his bed."

Polus's hand fell from his face and he looked up in shock. "She did it *herself*?"

Davron was fairly certain he could not conceal a grudging admiration of the empress over this, and so he did not bother to try. "Stabbed him in the eye, or so she says."

Polus threw up his hands in surrender, shaking his head in amazement. "But *why*?"

Davron sucked at his teeth a moment. "Seems Prandil fucked her and kicked her out, and she didn't take kindly to it."

Polus's reaction was delayed as he processed everything. He stared back in deep thought for several moments, then burst into loud, raucous laughter. "Oh, Great Tasinal and Amrath, that is rich! He's still there now?"

"Unless his slaves disturb him in the night, he should be."

"Then we have until sunup to work out our response, I suppose. There is no point in calling the counsel together. We don't have a quorum."

Davron gave Polus a thin smile. "Now, there, Polus, is where you and I differ. You think like a policeman. I think like a warrior."

Polus leaned back in his chair and drummed his fingers on the arm. "Very well, then, Davron the Wise. Educate me. What am I missing?"

"I will, soon. But first, I would ask you this. What is your opinion of the Meites on the council?"

Polus's expression grew serious. "I think they have the right ideas, but they are reckless. That's half the reason I can't really say I am sorry about Prandil."

"And the other half, I suppose, being that he was an asshole and deserved it."

"Well, there is that as well. So where are you going with this? What's your point?"

"Only this: the Meites are fine warriors, but poor leaders. Tasinal recognized that, at long last."

Polus gave him a sour look. "I'm still waiting for the punch line."

Davron would have rather heard Polus speak the words first, to be certain of their alliance before exposing his strategy. Was his old friend truly unclear on what he was suggesting, or was he feigning ignorance? How to edge him in the right direction, without sounding like an anarchistic madman? "Our current crop seems to lack his insight."

The lines on Polus's face deepened to trenches as he absorbed the comment. *Will he call me brother or traitor, now?* Polus considered for several seconds, his face still pinched, weighing his loyalties and desires. Slowly, he began to nod, and his face relaxed. "And you've some stratagem to use this fiasco to remedy that situation. Will it work?"

"Depends on how the votes go. But it will be legal, and involve no bloodshed."

Polus grunted, unconvinced. "Assuming they choose for it to remain bloodless."

Davron shrugged and spread his hands. "There are risks in any war. But we know they have a strong dedication to tradition, at least as it concerns non-Meites. They have to, or they will tear each other apart, and Nihlos with them. I think they will abide by whatever the council rules."

"A council without a quorum. We can't rule a henhouse at the moment. They're dropping like flies."

Davron gave him a secretive smile. "Depending on how you and I choose right now, that might change."

"I don't see how. Quorum can only change in the case of catastrophic losses. We need one third dead or incapacitated to invoke that." His eyebrows rose as he considered his own words, counting in his head, then fell as he glowered at Davron in annoyance. "I count only two: Prandil and Narelki."

"I count three. House Veril has yet to replace Sadrina."

"Oh, yes, of course," Polus said. "Veril never does anything useful. They are easy enough to miss. I hear they are trying to make some sort of statement with that."

Davron chuckled softly. "I hear it's far simpler: no one wants the job."

"Even so, it's only three."

Davron smiled knowingly. "The fourth, my friend, is why I called you here."

Kariana had been awake for some time, and was growing dangerously bored with the hospitality of House Noril. It wasn't as if she were a prisoner. *Not yet, anyway.* She could leave, but it might well spoil her cunning plan, and she very much needed that plan to succeed. Her life expectancy was decidedly shorter without it.

She sat on the edge of her bed, fists grinding at her temples, waiting. The bed was a lovely four post affair with a great canopy that could be drawn for privacy, and plenty sturdy, but there were no mirrors on the ceiling, and at any rate she was quite alone. It offered little entertainment.

Kariana eyed numerous shelves about the room. No alcohol, just books. She had it on reliable authority that there was, indeed, some entertainment value to be had from books, but she had never personally experienced it. Supposedly, one needed the 'right' book, which she took to mean something similar to the 'right' position. The problem of course being that reading was a crashing bore, whereas even mediocre sex was entertaining enough to slog through to find what one really liked.

Still, there was nothing but time, and she was beginning to get a headache. She pulled a small tome from the shelf at random, holding it gingerly, as if it were both fragile and poisonous. It claimed, at least by its name, to be of some moderate interest: *Naked Aggression.* She thumbed through it, disappointed to see that not only was there no nudity, but there were no illustrations at all. Even so, it was the only thing even remotely interesting, and so it would have to do. She took the book and lay down on the bed, holding it over her head at arms' length.

She waited perhaps an hour longer, occasionally throwing the book at the wall and being forced by sheer boredom to retrieve it. Apparently, House Noril did not find it necessary to mark the time with bells or devices, which Kariana found simultaneously annoying and refreshing. In the end, she was actually growing somewhat interested in the tale, which seemed to be about a man seeking vengeance, and the knock upon her door came as something of a shock.

Polus opened the door without waiting for her to respond. True, she had waited several seconds as she finished the paragraph she was reading, but that hardly made it acceptable. *Then again, you're at his mercy. Perhaps you should get used to thinking like that.*

Polus cleared his throat and looked at her expectantly. She looked back, not entirely certain what he expected, but doing her best to seem imperious rather than confused. At last, Polus spoke, his tone slightly sarcastic. "Would you prefer I came back some other time, Empress?" He gazed pointedly at the book.

Kariana closed it with a bit more force than was strictly necessary, feeling a bit like a child caught in the liquor cabinet. "No, not at all. I'm just feeling a little… uncertain."

Polus gave her a wry smile. "No doubt. But let us find that certainty. Do you intend to go through with this or not?"

Kariana tried to read the mind behind his aging features, but they told her little. "And how will I be treated?"

Polus shrugged. "I can only speak for Davron and myself. We certainly intend to look upon recent events in a…" He paused, raising an eyebrow as he considered his words, apparently unable to find the right one. "Well, let us just say we will be favorable to you. As for the others, we will do our best to convince them, but in the end, they will hold their own counsel on the matter."

Kariana scowled at him. "'Favorable' could mean any number of things. Perhaps you'll simply imprison me instead of executing me."

Polus grunted, but smiled as well. "There would be some irony there, considering what was done to poor Aiul. But no, I assure you, I mean no treachery. Davron and I will cling to you on this matter. I simply find it uncomfortable to speak openly of the chicanery we intend."

Kariana gave him a sour smile. "It seems to run in the family."

"Now, if only my son would learn practicality to balance his sense of duty, he would be able to fill my shoes." He raised an eyebrow. "I'd prefer we go through the formalities."

Kariana felt a slight chill, but nodded.

Polus stood a bit more erect as he spoke. "Tasinal Kariana, I, Luvox Polus, accept your submission for judgment by the council for the slaying of Prandil of House Idlic, and place you under arrest. You are hereby remanded to the custody of House Luvox and House Noril, and you are relieved of all duties and powers you currently hold, until such judgment is made."

Kariana felt tears welling, even though this was going just as she had planned. She had certainly not foreseen this turn of events at the start of the day.

But then, there were a number of others who were going to be surprised at the twists life offered soon enough. For once, she would be the first instead of the last to know.

It was well after midnight as Rithard took another sip of whiskey from his tumbler. The Southlander was snoring softly on the couch before the fire. *I should be too, I suppose.* But then, he had always had a problem with sleeping. His mind raced like a jackrabbit on the calmest of nights, and the simple act of lying in bed had never done much to quiet it. Booze helped, for a bit, but he inevitably woke in the wee hours of the morning as the effects wore off. Typically, he would walk the halls, or contemplate his own mortality for an hour or so, then finally get back to sleep, only to wake exhausted. Then coffee aplenty, and the process started anew. Such was life for Rithard.

Tonight, though, was an altogether different matter. *Technically, it would be morning.* Chiefly, it was different because it was the first night Rithard had ever faced the prospect of sleeping when the literal fate of the world might be on his shoulders.

He lowered himself to the floor again and began measuring the baseboard with a ruler, a simple, poetic line running through his head over and over: "The key to true knowledge lies within the heart of wisdom."

It had been right before them all along, the cryptic last words of Amrath's book. Many had puzzled over the strange characters and words, and every generation of thinkers had put forth guesses, but none of them had been even close. *Because there is perhaps a single man left in the world who can read ancient Ilawehan, and he claims to have been sent here by a god.*

Amrath could have written it in Priman. No one would have understood the significance. It sounded so pithy, so trite, just the sort of thing a wise man would use to close his great work. But this way, he had kept it a subject of constant debate, and it would draw particular attention from someone who could read it.

"It's here, somewhere," Rithard muttered. He finished a measurement and scribbled notes. He just needed accurate dimensions, and then he could consult the original architectural drawings and find the difference. He glanced up at the statue of Amrath and smiled. *You magnificent bastard! But why didn't you leave us a warning in the damned papers?*

The Southlander woke with a sharp cry. Rithard started, almost whacking his head on a book shelf, and turned to see what was the matter.

Ahmed sat bolt upright, sweat lining his brow, turning his head back and forth in confusion and fear for a moment, dreadlocks fanning about his head. He ran a hand over his face, confused or distressed, perhaps both. "I was somewhere! Somewhere important!"

"Mei, it must have been a battlefield, the way you shouted!"

Ahmed's eyes were wide, though not so much with fear as awe. His whole face was almost radiant. "No! It was a place of *wonder*! It is *here*! In Nihlos!"

Rithard glanced back at the baseboards, longing to complete the measurements and solve this next piece of the puzzle. "Is it important?" *Mei, here I am, tossing rigor and procedure in the ashbin and siding with 'feeling'.*

The Southlander bobbed his head up and down with vigor. "There is no doubt. It was a true vision."

Rithard sighed and placed the ruler on his desk. "Do you have any idea where it was?"

"No."

Rithard considered this a moment. I suppose we could show you drawings—"

"No," Ahmed interjected. "I need a map."

"Of?"

"The whole city."

Rithard turned back to the shelves, trying to remember which book held maps. It came to him quickly, and he placed the tome on the desk, open to a two-page drawing that depicted Nihlos from the eye of a bird. A wry smile crept across his lips as he noted the artist's signature: Talus Ariano. *Then it will certainly be accurate.*

He gestured to Ahmed, and the Southlander came over and took a seat at the desk. Rithard was tempted to say something snarky about Ahmed's sorcery, but a knock rang out from the library entrance, and not a gentle rapping as Slat might do, but a banging that carried some weight. *As in 'authority'.*

"Mei, it's after midnight!" he shouted. "You're trying my patience, I'll have you know!"

Rithard struck an indignant pose as the door began to open. From the corner of his eye, he saw the Southlander poring over the map. Rithard felt his pose and the feeling behind it fold in on itself when Caelwen, not Davron, stepped into the room.

Caelwen, armed and armored, helmet cradled in his elbow, offered a slightly wounded, reproachful look. "'Idiot'? Really, Rithard, I know you're smarter than me, but..."

Rithard snorted. "Obviously not, or I wouldn't look so stupid now, would I? I presumed you were Davron, prying into my affairs as usual." He paused a moment and peered at Caelwen's bruises. "Mei, what happened to your face?"

"It's nothing," Caelwen answered. "And Davron's part of it, actually."

"He gave you that?" Rithard asked, shocked.

"Mei, no, that's not what I meant!" Caelwen snapped, shaking his head in frustration. "I reckon *he's* given me my beating for the month already. Stop playing about. This is important!"

Rithard raised both hands and nodded his surrender. "Fine. Do go on."

Caelwen waited a moment, as if expecting Rithard to make another snarky comment, then continued. "Davron and my father have called an emergency council session. I'm rounding up all house leaders within the city."

"In the wee hours of the morning? When we can't even field a quorum? Ridiculous."

Caelwen shrugged. "I don't know a thing about it. I just know they want all of the house leaders *immediately*."

Rithard glanced at Ahmed, who was still studying the map with a bizarre, almost religious intensity. "Technically, I'm not a house leader yet, and I am occupied with vital business. Send them my regrets."

Caelwen clenched his jaw. "It's not that kind of meeting, Rithard. They *mean* it. As in, you're going, one way or another. That's the order."

"You wouldn't dare!"

"It would hardly be the first time I tossed you over my shoulder and hauled your drunken ass to where you needed to be!"

Rithard felt the edge of his mouth creeping into a smile, there, and decided to simply let it happen. He chuckled softly. "Let me fetch my things."

"Here!" shouted Ahmed, jamming his finger at the map. "This is the place!"

Caelwen, suddenly noticing the Southlander, stepped toward him and extended an arm, confusion all over his face. "Ahmed! Eleran said you had left."

Ahmed's face lit up at the sight of Caelwen. He rose and they grasped firmly at the forearm. "Well met, Caelwen. My people *did* leave, by Ilaweh's command. He sent me down another path."

Caelwen looked back at forth between Rithard and Ahmed. "So I see. And what are the two of you up to? You both look almost feverish!"

Rithard snatched his cloak from the back of the desk chair and draped it over his shoulder, scowling. "Saving the world, or at least we *were,* prior to being interrupted for Davron's foolishness once again."

Ahmed pointed to the map and said in a solemn voice, "We must go here, Caelwen."

Rithard bent down to examine the map where Ahmed's finger was tapping. "I can't say as I know what that place is."

Caelwen raised an eyebrow and again looked back and forth between them before speaking. "I know what's there. Sort of. I've never been inside, and I don't know anyone else who has, either." He gestured for Rithard to follow as he started for the door. "It's some kind of mausoleum, I think, House Tasinal's property. It's somewhat ominous, actually, surrounded by fencing. The commoners steer clear of the place; they claim it's haunted."

Rithard gave Caelwen a triumphant look, pointedly not accompanying him. "There, you see? That can hardly be coincidence. Do give Davron my regrets for being unable to make his silly midnight tea party."

Caelwen glowered at Rithard. "Two points: one, you *are* going, because I have my orders. Two, you'll need to talk to the Empress about accessing that building. Even if we were all fine and dandy about breaking and entering, and believe me when I say I get that I am the odd man out on that, I am fairly certain you are going to need some kind of key." He jerked a thumb at the door, again beckoning Rithard. "There's no way it's stood all these years without having some warding from the founders. The commoners tend to carry things off down there unless there's reason not to."

Rithard heaved a great sigh and shambled forward, shoulders slumped in defeat. "Presumably Tasinalta will be at this meeting as well?"

"I would assume so."

"Very well. Ahmed, you have the run of the house, but please do remember the slaves see you as a killing machine. Try not to frighten them overmuch until I return."

Ahmed chuckled. "It's nearly one in the morning. I am going back to sleep, you poor bastards."

Having recently had the run of House Noril, Rithard had no trouble finding the reception room. *The last time I was here, Davron questioned my manhood for being effeminate enough to read books. But give the devil his due, he had a Meite bend a knee before him. Maybe he has a point about that 'bold action' after all.*

He looked about as he entered, taking a quick headcount. Caelwen, helmet on now, stood guarding the closed doors. Polus, Davron, and Kariana were nowhere to be seen, presumably all involved in whatever machinations had brought the rest of them here. Rithard spied Olemus Freth and Lucreta Strall sharing a couch, both looking irate. *Olemus requires two seats, so there's no room for me there.*

Alone in a chair, a redheaded, waifish young woman sprawled, knees over the armrest, her expression somehow both disinterested and fascinated at the same time.

Across the way, on the other side of a low table, his mother, Teretha, sat side by side with a young man Rithard didn't recognize. *She's looking particularly self-satisfied. Why is she here instead of whatever his name is? Clearly, this is more than I thought.* He went over the headcount again, troubled by his mother's presence. *Three house leaders here, counting me; another for Mother, assuming she's sitting in for House Prosin; three in the kitchen as 'twere; one missing in protest; and four off gallivanting Mei knows where.* He looked at the strange young man again as he took a seat next to him, trying to place him and failing. Rithard had just decided to actually ask the fellow his name when Davron, Polus, and Tasinalta entered the room, Davron swaggering, Polus stiff-necked and formal, holding Tasinalta's arm, escorting her like a gentleman, and Tasinalta—

Mei! She's actually in chains!

The empress seemed to be struggling to maintain her dignity as Polus gently led her to a standing position in the center of the room, then stepped back to stand shoulder to shoulder with Davron. Kariana stood waiting before them, head high, cheeks pale, a slight tremor to her breathing.

Davron cleared his throat to speak, when the young man next to Teretha raised a hand, rose to his feet, and spoke. "There's been some sort of mistake. I shouldn't be here."

Davron smiled at the young man briefly, then grew somber. "No mistake. Sit. You'll understand soon enough."

The youth looked about with wild eyes, as if he had suddenly found himself in a cage. "But I'm just a slave," he stammered, the ragged edge of panic in his voice. "I don't belong in a Council meeting!" He turned, pleading to one, then another, his voice growing shrill. "Prandil should be here, not me! I'm just a *slave!*"

Polus declared in a flat voice, "Prandil has been slain."

Gasps and whispering erupted throughout the room. For a moment, Rithard was certain the boy was going to have a stroke. The poor fellow's eyes bugged, and he began gasping for breath as if he were being choked. "Oh, Mei help me, it wasn't *me!*" he wailed as he fell to his knees, trembling and sobbing. "I *love* Prandil! I would never—!"

Davron stepped forward and slapped the young man hard. "Do you not see we have the slayer here in chains?"

The boy looked up at Davron, stammering. "I don't understand."

Davron extended a hand. "You are Thrun, of House Idlic, yes?"

"I am, but—"

"You are now acting Patriarch. Prandil filed the paperwork to make you his heir last week." Thrun opened his mouth to say more, but Davron silenced him with a glare and an upraised index finger. "Behave with some of the dignity of that office and hold your questions until this is sorted out."

Thrun allowed Davron to haul him to his feet, the expression on his face like that of stunned cattle waiting for the blade. Davron guided him to his seat, a patronizing smile on his face.

"He *did* it," Thrun mumbled as he slowly lowered himself to the couch. "He really did it." He buried his face in his hands and sobbed quietly.

Polus cleared his throat. "If we are quite done with histrionics, there is a pressing legal matter." He looked about the room, as if daring anyone to interrupt him, before he continued.

"As I stated, Prandil is dead. Tasinal Kariana came to me a little over an hour ago, confessed to his slaying, and has been relieved of her duties until she can be tried. However, this has created a governmental crisis."

Teretha actually laughed out loud at this. "You cunning *devil!*" she purred at Kariana. Kariana smiled slightly, but remained silent, allowing Teretha the spotlight of Polus's ire at the interruption.

Polus shot Teretha a hard look, but continued, "Specifically, it is now no longer possible for us to meet the requirements of quorum." He paused to let the point sink in. "Normally, the law requires we have two thirds plus one member to act on official matters, meaning nine of the twelve houses must be present for any vote to be valid. With four house leaders in some state of incapacity, we are required to convene, and by simple majority approve of new house leaders. In essence, we are without government until we approve the newest crop of elders. Hence the call at this late hour."

Lucreta looked about the room, then back to Polus. "I understand how this applies to the house nominees, but how does this apply to what Tasinalta has done? Continuity of Government is for approving nominees, not officiating murder trials."

"I did not use the term murder, nor is she on trial for murder. She has submitted to judgment on the killing."

Lucreta looked at him with narrowed eyes. "What does that even mean?"

Olemus snorted. "It's Meite foolishness, but without the Meites."

Davron shook his head in vehement denial. "Oh, there most certainly *is* a Meite involved. It just happens that he *lost* the battle."

Lucreta wrinkled her nose, her expression sour. "It seems legally iffy."

Davron chuckled at her. "This is how the Meites handle such things. They have done so multiple times in recent history."

"They just did it this week," Polus muttered, prompting Rithard to do a mental fist pump. *Yes! He's admitted it! That's all I wanted.*

"I've never heard of it," Lucreta insisted, seeming less certain of herself now.

Olemus patted her leg gently. "It's real, my dear. It's rarely invoked now that Meites aren't killing each other in the streets every day or so, but it's ancient, older than Nihlos itself."

Polus looked back and forth at the four elders, then shrugged again. "There are no Meites present, and our best legal scholar is among the dead. Our situation is exigent."

Davron added, "It is Polus's and my judgment that the continuation of government council is not merely permitted to rule on this, but *obliged* to do so. We are the only legitimate authority in Nihlos at the moment, so we must hear her case and judge according to Meite tradition."

Lucreta was still not pleased. She scowled back at Polus and asked, "And who decides? You?"

Polus sighed and raised a palm to his face briefly. "No, Lucreta, *we* decide: you, Olemus, Davron, and I. We're all that's left."

Lucreta, shaken at this realization, shuddered briefly. "What about House Prosin?"

Davron grunted. "Predictable snakes that they are, upon hearing our woes, their weasel of an elder abdicated his position in squealing, shitting terror. They've sent this vixen in his place to be confirmed." He gestured to Teretha.

Rithard could barely suppress a mad giggle. *More like she had someone explain to him that his life would be much easier if he retired now. She wouldn't have put him up there if she couldn't easily remove him when the time came.*

Teretha waved at Lucreta. *Shame, dear Mother, is an emotion you haven't even a passing acquaintance with, is it?*

Lucreta turned and eyed the silent redhead, who was still lounging as if this were a sleepover rather than any sort of official proceeding. Rithard realized who the girl must be just as Lucreta spoke. "Presumably, you are House Veril's candidate?"

The girl twirled a lock of hair and nodded, but offered no words.

Olemus smiled at the group and rubbed his hands together. "So you understand what we're at here, yes?"

Lucreta shuddered and answered in a trembling voice, "*I do.*"

Polus twirled his hand at her in a 'get on with it gesture'. "Then how do you vote. Do we hear Kariana or no?"

Lucreta sucked in a long, wavering breath, then let it out again slowly. "I vote aye."

Rithard found himself, for what seemed the first time in his life, confused about what was going on around him. The realization struck him like a brick to the forehead: *if they restore Tasinalta, and confirm us all, they will have a quorum right here in this very room.*

Mei! This is a coup!

Kariana offered Lucreta Strall a calculated blank expression. The old woman's gaze probed at her, wheels within her mind turning as she considered. "How many more murders do you have in mind, I wonder?"

Kariana answered in a sullen tone, "Only as many as needed, of course." She nodded toward Polus. "I think he said it best: Nihlos belongs to those willing to seize power, and always has."

Lucreta's blue hair seemed to stiffen, along with the very air about her, as she bristled in disapproval. "That sounds like an excuse for mayhem to me."

Olemus chuckled, and the couch beneath him creaked as his ponderous bulk jiggled in humor. "Prandil had his own body count, Lucreta. They all do." He gave Kariana an approving smile. "For the first time, I actually see some merit in you."

Lucreta pursed her lips and shook her head. "She's dangerous and unpredictable. Why trade one storm for another?"

Davron glowered at Lucreta. "Make no mistake, this is *their* mess, not hers. They are far and away the stronger, so any responsibility for the chaos falls to them." He raised a clenched fist. "Yet where are they now, in such moments of chaos? Gone, leaving us to clean their mess."

Olemus snickered. "I never liked having anyone clean my messes for me. They often throw away things I would keep."

Polus rubbed at his temple, wincing as if in pain. "Here is truth: most of us agree with the Meites in principle, but they are creatures of passion. They hurl themselves headlong into matters without considering the consequences. It is entirely possible to both love them *and* find them unfit to rule."

Lucreta looked back and forth at the other four, still frowning. "It leaves a bad taste in my mouth to reward a knife in the back."

Kariana growled in the back of her throat at the insult. The old woman was calling her a coward, an assassin! Kariana jerked at her chains and shouted, "It wasn't in the back! It was in the eye! He saw it coming!"

Olemus chuckled softly as Lucreta turned a shocked stare to Kariana. Polus laid a hand on Kariana's shoulder, one she found surprisingly comforting. She took a deep breath, struggling to find some calm. "If he hadn't been so invested in seeing me as a fuck doll instead of a human being, he probably could have killed me ten times. He just couldn't imagine I would fight back. He hesitated because he was confused that I would even try!"

She could feel her chest and temples pounding with emotion. "I was supposed to slink away, don't you see? Just accept that I was dirt beneath his heels, a toy to be cast aside when he was done with it!" She could feel the tears welling in her eyes, but it hardly mattered now. She locked eyes with Lucreta. *Look in and see what you will, bitch. I have no secrets.* "So were you!" She swept a hand through the air in a wide arc. "*All* of you! It's what they expect you to do *right now*, don't you *see*?"

Lucreta seemed to shrink within her skin a bit, her eyes growing hard. "Yes. I do see," she said in a soft voice. "I've seen for some time, in fact, out of the corner of my eye. You've forced me to look directly at it, as a leader should."

Olemus was no longer smiling, simply nodding slowly. "Tasinalta, if we do this, will you swear to us this little war is over?"

Kariana clenched and unclenched her fists, filled with the urge to choke the fat bastard. "How can I swear that? There are at least three powerful sorcerers, and probably a fourth, who will be looking to even the score. I suspect if you have an issue with it, you'll need to take it up with my corpse."

Davron shook his head. "I think not. The Meites are first and foremost warriors. They will respect your victory. If they were judging you instead of us, I have no doubt they would exonerate you."

Polus nodded. "I agree. Allow me to rephrase his question: if the Meites will have peace with you and with us, will you have peace with them?" He raised an eyebrow and locked eyes with her. Kariana found that staring into that gaze, she could understand exactly why this man was one of the true rulers of Nihlos.

Olemus added, "It will be difficult enough to get them to accept what follows. If you are a gadfly to them, they will at some point give up any regard for tradition and strike us all down. We must have a firm commitment from you to at least attempt to reconcile. Will you offer that?"

Kariana swallowed a large lump in her throat before she spoke. "I swear it."

Davron gave her a stern look. "I will kill you myself if you betray that promise."

"Understood."

Polus banged his fist against the wall as a makeshift gavel. "Then we will now vote to affirm the replacements for our fallen colleagues."

I really need a drink. Rithard supposed that was a terribly inane thought, considering the magnitude of the proceedings in which he had just partaken, but it was true.

I am now the Patriarch of House Amrath in truth. And if this goes badly, I'll be as dead as the other eight within the week. Why should I not look forward to small pleasures?

Davron and Polus were convinced that the Meites would respect an honest, legal victory. Rithard, however, had his doubts. When the elders of Houses Aswan, Talus, and Yorn returned to find they had been removed from the council, it seemed nigh impossible that heads would not roll.

Thrun, the former slave, had abstained on every vote. Ilvara, the new Matriarch of House Strall, had joined in the rebellion with great lust and glee. Rithard's mother had gone at it with every bit the same zeal, but with considerably more style and grace, offering plenty of sighs and apologies of "I suppose I have no choice". Seven votes would have carried the day no matter what. Rithard saw no reason to begin his relationship with these people on the wrong foot. He had voted along with them, offering no commentary at all.

Now they had split into various cabals. It was well after three in the morning, but surely none of them would retire any time soon, a fact that irked Rithard. This might be the last time any of them slept soundly. Once the Meites returned, none of the conspirators would rest well, or, conversely, they might end up sleeping forever.

Lost in his dark thoughts, he didn't hear Caelwen and Tasinalta approach. He started as Caelwen offered a half-filled glass of champagne. "You look as if you could use this."

Rithard waved it away. "That's a prop for my mother to wave

about and pretend to be getting tipsy. It does not constitute in any way a 'drink'."

Tasinalta took it deftly from Caelwen's hand with a wink. "Mei, Davron actually prepped for an after party." She downed the drink in one gulp and tossed the glass to shatter on the floor, grinning at Rithard all the while. "Bitch drinks will do the trick if you have enough of them."

Caelwen rolled his eyes, a look of resignation and embarrassment on his face as one of Davron's slaves came to clean up the broken glass. Rithard took a deep breath, but left his face blank. "I would take exception to being lectured on intoxicants, save that you may be the one person in Nihlos to exceed my knowledge."

Tasinalta tittered and batted her eyelids at him. "So, the new Patriarch of House Amrath is a complete lush, and single. You and I should spend some time together."

Rithard was suddenly glad for an empty stomach. It would likely have heaved up at that notion. He considered telling her he preferred men, or even pigs, but that would insult her, and certainly leave him no opportunity to ask a favor. "You'll have to speak to my mother about that," he said. "She has my entire life mapped out, including whom I am to wed and names for the children."

Tasinalta's face filled with a mixture of pity and horror, before she caught Caelwen shaking his head and grinning. She turned back to Rithard and said, "Well, she seems a bit busy with Davron at the moment. I suppose I'll have to schedule an appointment later."

Caelwen cleared his throat. "All joking aside, Empress, we did have a matter of import to discuss with you."

"Ah, yes," Rithard said. He did his best to wipe the sarcasm from his face and voice and present himself as completely sincere. "Can we have your confidence on a matter? It is of grave importance."

Tasinalta looked back and forth at them as if she suspected they were playing a trick on her. "My confidence? Huh. It's comforting to know at least two people think I have any discretion at all."

Rithard offered her a charming smile and wink. "I know it's far too late for propriety, but would you consider retiring with us to my home? We've quite a tale for you, and I've considerably better spirits to share."

Tasinalta gave him a sly smile and rubbed her hands together. "Both of you, eh?"

"There's a third man, as well," Rithard chuckled.

Tasinalta feigned shock and waved a hand in front of her face as if she were about to pass out from heat. "I don't suppose this story is a steamy romance novel, is it?"

Rithard gave her a brief, sad smile. "No, Empress. I am afraid not. It is, at best, an adventure tale. If we don't take some action, I fear it will be a tragedy in the end."

Caelwen added, "It relates strongly to our last encounter with Aiul."

The blood seemed to drain from Tasinalta's face entirely, and all pretense of flirting dropped away like a rotting fruit falling from a tree. She locked eyes with Caelwen, a grim expression on her face. "I'll get my things."

I am in Aviar. Ahmed knew it was not possible, and yet it was so. The smell of the sea was familiar now, not the bizarre, thrilling scent it had been when he had last set foot on Aviar's soil. He sat, mounted, towering over the Aviaran barbarians, scowling at the slave platform, the salt breeze cool on his skin. He knew now how it worked, how they took the unsuspecting victims from their homes and spirited them far away to be sold in chains. He even knew some of the men who were responsible.

It was a horrible thing for men to do, this he knew, and yet he still found it difficult to feel much for the victims.

Beside him, the large barbarian who had called himself Marcus said again, "Could be they didn't understand what would happen to them until it was too late. Maybe if they had the chance to fight now, they would."

Yazid pointed toward the platform, and Ahmed followed his gesture. A lone woman was chained to the bar, sneering at the crowd, spitting, hurling curses and insults at them. Without those chains, she would be a formidable warrior.

Ahmed shook his head. *This is not how it was.* The woman had not been defiant, not until he had prodded her. Nor had she been—

Nihlosian! This woman is Nihlosian!

"This one called to me," Ilaweh rumbled. "Free her. We will see if she will fight."

Ahmed looked about for the slave master, but saw no one. "I have no key."

"There is no key." Ilaweh extended a hand and offered Ahmed a long rasp. "You must use this."

Ahmed's eyes grew wide. "Her bonds are too tight! I cannot use this without drawing blood."

"Blood has ever been the price of freedom."

Ahmed opened his mouth to speak, but before he could, he heard a sharp click, as if some mechanism were turning, and Aviar melted into the dark, polished wood of the library. He started up as the doors opened, and Rithard entered.

"We have a guest," he called out.

Ahmed rose to his feet. "I know. Bring her to me."

Kariana found she could not remove her hands from her face. They were welded there by shame and terror, and would not obey her. *Judgement day for me. I fear Elgar less than this man.*

She had met his eyes the once, dark, burning, full of wisdom and strength, and would not do so again. Better to die than to see the depths of his disdain, to feel it burning her from the inside out.

She'd killed his father. *I don't even remember why, really.* If only that were the end of it. She would have taken Sadrik's dagger from her blouse and plunged it into her own chest if she thought doing so would make the rest of it untrue.

I am responsible for all of this. Her breath came in ragged gasps. She had known the moment he touched her, had felt the knowledge pour into her mind like a turbulent river, tearing at the soft spots inside her head, leaving little but debris.

"Look at me," he told her.

She shook her head, knowing she had no chance of forming words through her sobs. She felt strong, warm hands seize her wrists, felt them easily accomplish what her own muscles, warring against themselves, could not.

"*Look* at me," he demanded.

"I can't," she choked out, her eyes still squeezed shut.

"You *must!* I dreamt of you. Ilaweh heard your cry, do you understand me?"

She felt the sharp sting of a palm against her face, hard enough to slice through the raging torrent in her head.

"That's enough!" Caelwen shouted. Kariana felt a brief struggle around her, the Southlander shouting, "You don't understand! She needs my aid!" and Caelwen shouting back, "Keep your hands off her!"

The shouting continued for some time, Rithard joining in as well. She could barely follow the conversation. There was too much chaos in her head, too much guilt and grief at the knowledge burning in her mind. All she knew was that, somehow, they settled things, and the Southlander returned to her and took her face gently in his hands. "Look at me," he commanded her.

Somehow, she found the control to open her eyes. He stood before her, his own face not full of the rage she expected, but with pleading. "There is a warrior within you, but she is chained," he said, speaking with a quiet intensity. "You called out to Ilaweh. Do you remember?"

For a moment, she couldn't understand, but slowly his words penetrated her confusion, and she remembered Aiul punching through the wall, stealing the piece of the Eye, and how she had begged for aid from the Southlander god. "Yes," she whispered. "I did."

"Ilaweh heard you, and he has sent me to remove your chains."

Kariana shook her head again. "Just take your revenge on me. It's what I deserve."

"Perhaps," he said, shaking his head back at her. "But that is not your fate. Ilaweh has given you a chance at a new one."

Kariana choked out, "I don't deserve mercy."

Again, the Southlander shook his head. "Killing you would be mercy. This path, if you would walk it, leads to absolution, but to reach it, you must walk through fire."

"I don't understand," she gasped.

"You understand enough. Ilaweh showed you what he offers, what it costs. Will you fight, or will you live life on your knees?"

It wasn't really a question. He already knew the answer. She could see that much in his ancient eyes.

Through trembling lips, she breathed, "I'll fight. I'll *always* fight."

The Southlander smiled back at her. "Then I will fight by your side."

Caelwen ground his teeth against the urgent impulse to stop what-ever the Southlander was doing. *I am supposed to defend her body!* And yet, despite appearances, he was almost convinced Ahmed was not harming, but healing.

Kariana sat rigid in Rithard's chair, and Ahmed was on his knees before her, gripping her wrists with all his strength, his dark hands and corded muscles straining as her pale flesh convulsed. Kariana screamed, and sweat beaded on her forearms as she struggled.

Caelwen could stand by no more. He lunged forward, but Rithard interposed himself, a single finger held up.

"Stop," Rithard said, and pointed at Kariana.

Caelwen blinked in shock at what he saw. What he had thought was sweat had begun to thicken. It now ran like milk on her skin, dripping to the floor, growing more viscous by the moment, and quickly changing color to a yellow, gangrenous ichor. The corruption ran down the Southlander's arms now, as well. Where it ran, his flesh grew pink as if he were burned, but he continued to pray through clenched teeth.

After a few moments, Kariana fell back into her chair, insen-sate, and Ahmed sagged backward into a sitting position. "I need a cloth," he said in a tired voice. "Something to clean this from both of us. It burns."

Rithard shrugged out of his cloak and handed it to Ahmed, then lifted Kariana's eyelids and examined her pupils. "Well, this wasn't how I had planned this meeting." He continued his exami-nation as Ahmed wiped the filth from both himself and Kariana. Where it touched the cloth, it ate at it like acid. "She seems to have come through it, though."

Ahmed bent again over his knees, panting, and said, "We are not done yet." He reached forward and took her head in his hands, one palm on each cheek. Kariana's eyes flickered, but she seemed otherwise insensate. "The rest is here, and it is much worse. This was just the beginning." He drew in a deep breath, and Caelwen felt something *large* in the room, an intensity he could not define or even describe.

Caelwen waved a hand. "No. I think this is enough—"

Kariana's eyes snapped open, and her scream tore through the manse like a banshee wail.

Caelwen charged forward, and again, Rithard interposed himself. "That will be heard by everyone in the building. Someone needs to bar the doors, and I need to be here to tend her medically."

"I can't just let this happen!"

Kariana, swooning, whispered, "Go."

Caelwen felt as if he were being torn in two. "Empress--" he stammered.

"*My* fight," she gasped. "You…have your…orders. *Go.*"

Caelwen ground his teeth and glared at Rithard. "Keep her alive!"

Caelwen stepped outside the library just in time. Slat and several others were heading toward him, eyes wide with alarm.

"All is well," Caelwen declared. Kariana shrieked again, the sound barely muffled by the intervening doors. *Ah, well. It is hardly the first time I have stood such duty.*

Slat poked a gnarled ginger at him in accusation and demanded, "What are you doing here? Where is my master?"

Caelwen struck a resolute pose. "Rithard is within, and I am without by orders of the Empress. These doors remain closed until she tells me otherwise."

Slat scowled up at Caelwen. "I don't like this. Not one bit."

"Neither do I, old one. But we follow our orders, eh?" As another agonized shriek pierced the air of the manse, Caelwen reached into his shirt and produced the one thing he always carried besides a weapon: his copy of the Book of Amrath. He flipped through to a verse that seemed particularly relevant and began to read aloud, as Slat bowed his head in reverence.

"There is nothing in life worth having that you will not, at some point, have to fight for, and the path to victory is never easy. Blood and treasure, pain and self-doubt, these are constant companions in any battle. A warrior will know them well..."

CHAPTER 8
FOR MISCHIEF

SADRIK had just about reached his limit. The elders were treating him like an idiot as usual, telling him nothing of what was to come, or who this 'Cruentus' fellow even was. His ignorance never failed to amuse them, and if they could prolong it or even increase it, they were thrilled to do so. Maklin had gone so far as to taunt him with lies, claiming Cruentus was a real dragon, of all things! Sadrik had barely been able to contain his fury at the old man's gall. Had instant and painful death not been a certain result, Sadrik would have made a statement on dragons himself and set the hateful old bastard ablaze on the spot.

The notion of instant death had continued to be a compelling argument against surrendering to his urge for mayhem for quite some time, but now, after hours of being hauled about like a pup by the scruff of his neck, the balance was beginning to tip. Falling didn't seem so bad, really. At the very least, things would all be over quickly, whereas this torment dragged on and on. He imagined Maklin flashing on like a meteor, trailing smoke and flames as Sadrik dropped like a stone.

It would, he thought with a smile, be a lovely death as deaths go, and he could hardly deny the charm of his last vision being that of Maklin beating flames from his hair and screaming, but life was yet still sweet. He felt capable of clinging to it for another half hour or so, but after that, it was difficult to say.

As the land changed beneath them from forest to rocky, dry terrain, Sadrik began to feel as if they must be approaching their destination, but he steadfastly refused to ask, and none of the elders could be bothered to say. At last, when he felt he could bear it no longer, he felt them slow and start their descent.

The land rushed up at him, alien, harsh, and rocky, unmarred with any vegetation. A great, gaping chasm, its true depths veiled by mist, yawned wide and directly below them. The air felt warmer than it ought this time of year, dryer too, and smelled of burning brush. Sadrik looked at the others, trying to work out if this was an elaborate joke, but no one was laughing.

Maklin caught him craning his head up and gave him a grave look. "Still thinking of setting me on fire?"

"Is there truly a dragon down there?"

Maklin grunted. "*The* dragon, boy."

They swept from the sky and into the chasm. It looked to be the remnants of a volcano. Rock lay in shattered tubes or long rolls, clearly once molten, though hard and relatively cool now. Sadrik saw from within that what he had thought to be mist was in fact smoke, a tremendous amount of it, though there was no obvious source. He thought to himself that surely smoke was harmless as they continued deeper into the crater.

The group touched down outside the largest of the stone tubes at the bottom, a great black glass tunnel more than twenty feet across. It sloped down at a treacherous angle, its jagged internal edges more than capable of shredding anyone unfortunate enough to slip trying to descend into it.

Sadrik peered into the bottomless pit of jagged death and felt slightly ill. "Do we have to go in?"

Maklin snorted and shook his head. "No. And stop looking so nervous. He'll likely not eat you, but he might take you captive if you're interesting, so best keep your mouth shut."

Ariano nodded, even going so far as to allow a brief smile. She had been sullen and brooding since Maranath had twisted her arm into coming here.

Sadrik stroked at his beard, still uncertain just how much of what they were telling him was truth. "I'll do that."

Maranath looked them all over as if to assure himself they were presentable, then called out, "Cruentus!"

For long moments, there was no response. Maranath opened his mouth to call out again, when the ground beneath them began to tremble. A voice so deep that it seemed the grating of stone against stone rumbled, "Who dares disturb my rest?" The ground thrummed at the sound, the vibrations setting dust and pebbles stirring.

Maklin and Maranath looked at one another and rolled their eyes. Ariano simply growled softly and muttered, "Cheap theatrics."

"Ah!" the creature called, "I know that voice!"

The rumbling beneath their feet grew until it seemed they were in the midst of an earthquake. Heat gushed from the lava tube, and the sound of claws scrabbling against glass echoed loudly, setting Sadrik's teeth on edge.

The beast thrust its head from the pipe first, a great wedge of red scales and fangs. *Just his head is bigger than me. Mei, what will the rest of him be like?*

The rest of him was near enough to fill the pipe as he hauled himself out. The Meites stepped back quickly to avoid being crushed as unknowable tons of scaled flesh burst from the tube.

Sadrik could find no words. The dragon was immense, fifty feet long if he were an inch, and quite literally breathing fire. Small flames jetted from his nostrils with each breath. His talons, each the length of a man, looked more than capable of rending the rock about them. Sadrik realized that they were likely the source of some curious trenches he had seen about the opening.

Cruentus snaked his head low toward Ariano, one huge, yellow eye hovering inches from her face while the other watched the rest of them with mild amusement. "Ariano Talus," he rumbled in satisfaction. "You owe me a tale!"

Sadrik found his respect for Ariano growing by leaps and bounds. She showed no emotion at all beyond disdain and annoyance. "We've come here on other matters."

Cruentus raised his head and snorted flame. "What other matters?"

Maranath took a step forward. "The Eye is abroad in the world again. We've come to hear what you know of that."

Cruentus turned his full attention to Maranath, chuckling. "Have you, now?"

"What of the piece Tasinal entrusted to you? Do you still guard it?"

Cruentus's roar rattled Sadrik's teeth in his head, and started several minor rockslides. It took Sadrik a moment to realize that this was not a hostile gesture, but something akin to laughter. The dragon shook his head and turned back to Ariano. "I see now. You've not told them, have you? It must have gone terribly wrong for you. That's why the other is not here. Dead, eh?"

Ariano's jaw clenched and unclenched in anger. "You hold your tongue, wyrm, or you'll never hear your tale!" She kept her eyes locked with Cruentus's, ignoring the glares Maklin and Maranath were casting at her.

Cruentus shook his head in mock sadness. "A Meite not paying debts? Such a shameful thing. It reeks of weakness."

"Be silent!"

"You lack the power to make me. Even if you had such power,

your companions would restrain you. It seems they would hear your tale, too, eh?" The dragon lowered his head to regard her closely with one great eye. "I could tell what I know of it, but wouldn't you prefer to shade it to your benefit?" Cruentus turned his head skyward and chuckled, jets of flame stuttering from his nostrils.

Maranath cast her a withering glare. "This is about the point I lose patience with you, I think."

Maklin jabbed a bony finger at her chest. "Oh, it's well past that for me!"

Ariano clenched her jaw a moment, but it was clearly hopeless. "It would seem I am outplayed."

The dragon flashed her a cruel, fang-filled grin. "And not even by me. You have outsmarted yourself here, it would seem. Delicious!"

Maklin spun to the dragon and shouted, "She can stall forever if you don't shut up!"

Cruentus lowered his head to the ground and closed his eyes. A jet of flame erupted from his nostril and came close enough to Maklin to make him jump backward and beat at his robe. Maklin opened his mouth to howl objection, but Cruentus held up a great talon in front of his lips in a gesture of silence, then pointed to Ariano.

Oh, well done! Beat him with his own curmudgeonry!

As for Ariano, Sadrik didn't think he had ever seen the old woman so uncomfortable. *Is she actually digging in the dirt with her toe?*

She took a deep breath and began. "Lothrian and I came here and took the piece a hundred years ago."

Maklin's eyes bulged as if his head would explode. "You *what*?" he shouted, then doubled over in a fit of coughing.

Maranath's face was stony. "It gets worse, I think."

Cruentus chuckled, prompting Maklin to step back a few more paces to avoid getting singed again. "I should say so," the dragon rumbled.

Ariano stamped a foot. "You said you'd let me tell the tale!"

"I never said I wouldn't heckle you," he answered. "Or correct you, if you lie."

"Heckle her all you want," Maklin groused, "But I'd appreciate it if you didn't roast me anymore! Watch where you're pointing that snout!"

Maranath shook his head in annoyance and slammed the butt of his staff against the ground, shouting "Enough!" The entire canyon rumbled with the shock wave, and several small avalanches of scree tumbled to the ground in protest.

Cruentus raised his nose into the air, courteously avoiding roasting anyone else while he laughed out loud. "Oh, he's upset. Do go on, Ariano."

The sorceress took a moment to preen and cast glares at one and all before continuing. "We made a raid on Torium to retrieve the piece they hold," she said, her words clipped and sharp. "And we lost the one we had instead." She stared at the ground, her jaw working. Maklin opened his mouth, but Maranath held up a hand and stopped him. After a few moments, Ariano looked back up and spoke again. "I lost Lothrian there, too."

Maklin looked at Maranath, and Maranath nodded with a sigh. For a moment, the old artificer was lost for words, opening and closing his mouth several times before at last sputtering, "Well, that was stupid!"

Sadrik could not resist the urge to clap very softly as Ariano clenched her fists and stepped toward Maklin, murder blazing in her eyes.

Maranath interposed himself between them. "Hear him out, Ariano." He turned back to Maklin. "Assuming you actually have something of worth to say."

Maklin sputtered as he spoke. "I don't see the point of it! The damned thing is useless until it's assembled."

Cruentus chuckled again. "You think so?"

Maklin glared at the dragon a moment, then continued. "Why did you take it with you and risk losing it to begin with?"

Ariano's shoulders sagged, and for a moment she seemed nothing more than a tired, old woman. "It's was Lothrian's doing. He kept secrets from me, things he'd learned or guessed at from Amrath's private writings."

Maklin waved his fingers in the air. "Ooh, spooky ghost tales and secret mysteries in the ancient books!" He spat on the ground. "Here's a better explanation: he took it there as a payoff! He was working with them in that damned pit, and you helped him! Now, they have *two* pieces!"

"He would never—!"

"Or worse, it was some complicated scheme to steal both pieces for himself. Did you actually *see* his corpse?"

Ariano's face grew taught with anger and stress. "No. And I suppose either is possible, but I don't believe it. We fought them long and hard, killed them by the scores. If he were in league with them, there would have been no need to sacrifice so many of their own. And as for the second, it's ridiculous on its face."

Maklin sneered. "Oh, you just can't imagine him trading that precious twat of yours for ultimate power, is that it?"

"You wretched, soulless old simulacrum! What would you know about twats that you can even comment? And yes, mine *is* just that good, for your information!"

Sadrik snorted so hard that he began to choke.

"He's turning red," Cruentus observed. "What does that mean in your kind?"

"Go ahead and roast both of them," Maranath fumed.

Cruentus turned his huge head and stared at Maranath, aghast.

"And miss what is to come? Madness! This is just getting interesting! They might even kill one another!"

Maranath gave them both sharp glares. "I think they're done for the moment, eh?"

Ariano offered him a smirk, and Maklin scratched at his neck, seeming bored now.

The dragon shook his head sadly. "A pity. Perhaps later they will get worked up again."

"Or I will," Maranath said with a deep scowl.

Sadrik cleared his throat and found he could breathe again. There was some doubt as to whether he should open his mouth, but it was simply too interesting a thought not to share. "Has anyone considered that one piece might be able to track the others?"

The three elders turned and looked at him, astonishment on their faces.

Cruentus raised his head again and roared approval and flame into the sky. "That is just what they told me when they gave it to me for safekeeping, youngling. That it was still connected, even torn asunder in this plane. It knows full well where its brethren lie."

Ariano stood silent a moment, absorbing this, then snapped at Maklin. "So it does have a use! Wrong again, you doddering relic!"

"I suppose you'll have us believe you knew nothing of this, eh?" he groused.

"You all know full well Lothrian was secretive, and damned well my superior at the time. He told me very little, just kept saying 'Trust me' when I questioned him."

"Sounds familiar," Maranath said.

She shrugged. "I suppose it does."

"He must have told you something. Why else would you have gone to Torium with him?"

Ariano actually began to look sheepish. "I was in love, so I might have been convinced to go without any explanation at all, but he did tell me generalities. Lothrian believed he knew of a way to destroy Torium." Her eyes grew distant with the memory, and her voice a bit wistful. "He claimed to have discovered the existence of a doomsday device there. He had it in his head that we'd go there, kill them all, steal their piece, have a fuck on their kitchen table, and blow the place to the moon."

Maklin scoffed. "A doomsday device in Torium? House Yorn would know of such a thing, if it existed."

Ariano rolled her eyes. "What do you want? I've told you the whole of it."

"Fine, then what sort of device was it?"

"I don't know!" she shouted. "I'm not even sure Lothrian knew. He might have just expected to know it when he saw it."

Cruentus growled, a great, rumbling sound that made the pebbles on the ground dance. "There are rumors of a doomsday device, but Lothrian did not speak of this to me, nor I to him. He came by this from somewhere else."

Ariano shrugged. "Then I have no idea. I always assumed it was information you gave him."

Maklin shook his head and waved a hand in dismissal. "Elgar take you and your tale, *where did you put the piece you took?*"

"It's in the damned black pit of Torium with Lothrian's corpse, fool! Did you miss the first part of the conversation or are you just going senile?"

"Hearing it and believing it are two different things."

Cruentus chuckled at the this, and Maklin whirled around to confront him. "This is all your fault to begin with! Why did you give them the piece?"

Cruentus snorted flame again, and lay back down, eyes closed. "I feared for my life, of course. I was accosted by a powerful Meite. Waste not, bend a knee, or whatever you people say." He made a sound that Sadrik was fairly certain was a giggle.

"Wretched wyrm! Lothrian was powerful, yes, but I doubt he could have done much more than bloody you before you tore him to pieces. You did it for pure mischief!"

Cruentus didn't bother to open his eyes, but his chuckling rumbled the ground. "Just so, Meite. Just so."

Maklin sputtered and stammered in incoherent fury for several long moments, at last choking out "Are you mad or have *you* gone senile?"

"Oh, neither." Cruentus opened his eyes again. They seemed distant, foggy, unfocused. "You weren't there the last time it was whole, as I recall, so you can't appreciate the glory of it all. You humans may be small, but you have the hearts of dragons. The carnage was truly like nothing I have ever seen."

"So you'll just toss this bomb out into the world again? Too old to go and do your own destruction, is that it?"

"I am clearly at best a gifted amateur at bloodshed compared to your people. If I hadn't been able to fly, I'd have surely drowned in the rivers of it you spill." He shook his head in wonder, then glared at Maklin. "And don't speak to me as if you aren't old, Meite. At least my body doesn't fail me like yours."

"Clearly your mind does, though!"

Cruentus snorted, not bothering to raise his head this time, sending Maklin scurrying backward again. "In a hundred years, I'll still be old, and you'll be dead." He craned his neck forward and blew a puff of smoke in Maklin's face. "I reckon my wit is still intact."

Maranath's bark of laugher caught everyone off guard. "It seems about the sort of conversation a pack of old fools would have."

Cruentus nodded his agreement, then turned back to Maklin. "Now, shut up, old man, and let her finish. Perhaps she might have something useful to tell you. Or I, assuming you don't annoy me enough to keep it to myself."

Maklin glared at Cruentus, but said nothing, instead turning back to Ariano.

Ariano seemed dismayed to find all eyes once again on her. "There's little more to tell. Obviously, we never accomplished what we intended."

Cruentus scowled. "Ah, but the why of that is the heart of the tale, is it not? What lies within that black pit, that one elder Meite lies dead, and another fled?"

Ariano seemed to shrink a bit, her own eyes growing dark and distant. "Why don't you go there yourself and find out? Or aren't you powerful enough?" she snapped.

"Powerful, yes, but not nearly so stupid as you. I did not get to be so old by meddling with doomsday devices! I prefer to leave that to fools like you. Go on."

A nervous tick began throbbing just below Ariano's left eye, and her throat worked as if she were swallowing something ugly. "Monsters. I don't know what to call them. Everywhere. Too many for us. Perhaps too many even for you."

Cruentus's eyes grew wide in amazement. "What did they look like?"

"It's a difficult thing to describe with words. They don't have quite the impact the visual would have."

"Then paint me a picture, Ariano Talus!"

Ariano's laugh had little humor. "I already did, but it would hardly benefit you. It's in Nihlos."

Cruentus growled, a deep, bass thrum that made Sadrik's head spin. "You must promise to bring it to me before you die. And that could happen very soon, at any moment, practically. So you must not delay!"

"If I don't die trying to sort it out."

Cruentus snorted flame, his eyes seeming worried now, though it was difficult to tell with a dragon. "Then finish the tale."

She was pale again, her skin seeming more thin and wrinkled, her eyes far away. "There were more than we ever imagined. They came and came, and we kept killing them, but there were too many. Finally, Lothrian told me to run."

Cruentus grunted. "And you left him to die?"

"He claimed he would have a better chance alone."

"Did he?"

"Of course not. It was a lie, we both knew that."

"And what was the truth?"

Ariano cast her eyes down again. "That he could give me a chance to escape, and I wasn't strong enough to offer him the same."

Maranath laid a comforting hand on her shoulder. "One would have rather died with their friends."

Maklin nodded. "But one must not waste."

Ariano clenched her teeth again. "Yes, so I ran. I heard him screaming toward the end, but they had been screaming much longer. They paid dearly to bring him down."

"And then Tasinal came," Maklin observed. "That great mess and coverup, outlawing Meites. Why am I not surprised it was all your fault?"

"It wasn't *all* mine," she snapped. "It was far and away more Lothrian's." She scowled at the dragon and added in a sarcastic tone, "I wonder how Tasinal might ever have even known what was going on?"

Cruentus snickered. "I wonder."

Maranath turned to Cruentus, a shocked look on his face. "You know how to reach Tasinal?"

Cruentus sighed and rolled his shoulders in an approximation of a shrug. "No. I've rarely seen him since then. He comes, on occasion, usually with questions about some obscure point of history, but he is always distracted. He has some grand project, but he won't speak of it."

Maranath seemed not at all surprised. "It would have been good to have his counsel, but nevertheless, we must do what we can, and there is no time to spare"

Cruentus's eyes narrowed in annoyance. "So soon? You've only just arrived. Why not rest a while before setting out?"

Maranath threw up his hands and barked a laugh. "You've just said it yourself. We have short lives, and they're almost used up. Our time is precious."

Cruentus turned his head to the sky and snorted a jet of flame. "Aye, the heart of a dragon in the body of an ant. Is it any wonder you wither with the passage of years? Your bodies are too frail to contain such spirits."

Maranath chuckled. "Without a time limit, the game grows stale, does it not? I presume that's why you spend so much time sleeping. Me, I can hardly afford the luxury. I'll rest when I'm dead."

"I would hear your tale, if you survive," Cruentus declared.

"If we survive, you'll have it." He gestured to the others to follow him as he turned to leave.

Maklin gave Cruentus a final glare. "I should have known you were bluffing. You don't have anything useful to add, after all."

"I have given you much, Meite!"

Maklin chuckled, his still-sour tone at odds with his sudden humor. "I'm still upset with you, though!"

Cruentus closed his eyes. "This, too, will pass."

Maranath did not look forward to another day of flight. Short distances were simple enough, but long hauls were taxing, the sort of business that left one in the mood for a large meal and a strong drink as opposed to fighting. Of the two, Maranath strongly suspected fighting was the more likely end of the day. "We need all the help we can get. Ariano, you will return to Nihlos and fetch Prandil. Sadrik, you will accompany her. Maklin and I will go on to Torium and do what we can until you get there."

Ariano scowled. "Why me?" she groused. "Have I not been at your side throughout this?"

Maranath snorted. "You've been dragging me about by the nose, blindfolded, and feeding me a steady diet of bullshit! It's the least you can do to make up for it."

Ariano lowered her eyes to the ground, looking at least a bit contrite. "It's not as if Prandil and I are on good terms, you know."

"He'll be over it by now, surely. And even so, you'll have Sadrik to help you convince him of the seriousness of the situation."

Sadrik rolled his eyes at this notion. "Assuming she actually tells him the problem and doesn't tell him he just has to 'trust her'."

Ariano whipped her head toward Sadrik and shouted, "You shut your mouth, whelp, or I'll shut it for you! You're not nearly strong enough to talk shit to me!"

Sadrik raised one eyebrow, his expression cool and unruffled. "You think so?"

"You can't even fly!"

Maklin waved his hand between the two of them, distracting them from their argument. "Done, then. The troublemaker does the scutwork, and the boy keeps an eye on her to keep her out of mischief."

Ariano glared at Maranath again. "Ah, the truth we all knew from the start. And it assumes I don't drop him like a stone from a high place during the flight."

Sadrik felt a deep surge of rage at her threat, and decided to follow with one of his own. "I feel certain I could set you well aflame before I hit the ground, grandmother! You'd leave a lovely trail on your way down, I should think."

Ariano offered him a thin smile. "At least you have the proper attitude."

Maranath chuckled briefly, and gestured, shooing them off. "Enough! We are out of time!"

CHAPTER 9
CORONATION

As the sun reached its zenith, Sadrik found himself a mass of conflicting emotions. Terror, of course, was the strongest, due to being dangled high above Nihlos, his entire life hanging on Ariano's whim. Elation, at the sight of all Nihlos spread below him like a jewel, was a close second. Finally, hunger gnawed at him, reminding him that despite it being past lunch time, lunch had not in fact occurred, an oversight that he should like to rectify as soon as possible.

Lunch *ought* to have occurred already, of course, and had in fact been offered by Prandil's reluctant replacement, Thrun, during their brief visit. Really, though, it would have been bad form to prevail upon the boy prior to murdering the lot of his tormentors, or at least that was Sadrik's assumption regarding Ariano's plan. She had, unusually, been quiet about her intentions. *Likely because she's trying to reconcile her outrage at the rebels with her elation that Prandil and Narelki are now both no longer among the living. Presumably, it means she won.*

Sadrik's ruminations were cut short as Ariano banked sharply and dropped like a stone, hurtling downward toward the palace. He turned all of his focus to believing he would survive a meteoric impact, but she slowed at the last moment and drifted onto the palace steps like a leaf on the wind. The two men standing guard blanched at her breach of etiquette, and began to study their own shoes with great intensity as the pair or sorcerers approached.

Ariano made no effort at her usual pose. "The empress," she demanded. "Where is she?"

Her withering glare quickly melted any reticence the guard might have. "Reception room," he said quietly.

Ariano patted him on the cheek and offered him her saccharine smile. "Good boy, and smart. You'll likely see the sun rise with that attitude!" She let her false cheer melt away as she turned to Sadrik and growled, "That's more than some here can say."

Sadrik cast the guards an apologetic look, then turned to follow Ariano as she scurried off. "A bit harsh, don't you think?"

"Do *you* intend to survive the day, whelp?" she snarled over her shoulder.

Sadrik bit back a nasty retort. She was certainly the stronger. If he tested her, she likely wouldn't kill him, just draw a bit of blood, perhaps throwing in a little extra pain for being stupid. *But this is madness!*

Ariano ignored more guards outside the reception room, and they likewise took one look at her and found themselves utterly fascinated with the carpet.

The entrance to the reception room was quite lovely, and clearly expensive, a huge, carved door of rich, dark wood. It exploded inward in a hail of flinders as Ariano approached. From within, Kariana, seated in an ornate chair, smiled at them like a cat. Caelwen, at her side, did not smile at all.

Kariana was at no loss for words. She waved as the two entered to stand before her. "Ariano, I wasn't expecting you. How nice of you to drop in!"

Sadrik couldn't help but snicker. "Quite literally, actually."

Ariano shot him a brief glare, as if to say *'Stop spoiling my entrance!'*, then turned back to Kariana. "Would you care to explain yourself before we kill you and the rest of the rebels, or would you just have us use our best judgment for your epitaph?"

Kariana's smile fell from her face, and she rose and spoke with an almost regal air. "This is no rebellion. It is the new order of things, all done legally."

Ariano snorted. "I've heard the story. The elders had no right to judge you! If you would seek sanctuary in our law, you must be judged by Meites!"

Kariana raised an eyebrow and paused a moment, then offered a vicious smile. "And how *do* you judge me, then?"

Ariano's jaw began to work, and her lips pursed. *Ah, clearly we did not expect this tack, eh?*

"Why did you kill Prandil?" she asked at last.

Kariana chuckled softly, a cruel laugh that Sadrik found almost chilling. "You said you knew the story."

"I want to hear it from your lips, and look into your eyes when you speak it."

Kariana locked gazes with the old sorceress and answered in a low, almost growling voice, "I wanted him to teach me. He fucked me, he mocked me, and then dismissed me like a whore. He said I was a fine fuck doll, but I'd never be anything more, so I stabbed the bastard in the eye." She flashed Ariano a vicious grin and added, "That *is* how it's done, right?"

Ariano's change was as immediate as it was shocking. The rage that seemed to fill her fled, unable to resist her new emotional state. Her laughter burst forth, harsh and blaring, and for long enough that Sadrik might have thought it feigned, save for the tears that had begun to stream down her face. At last, when she had gained better control of herself, she snickered, "You are not the first bedmate of his to stab him, though it looks as if you're the last." She could not contain another wild cackle, then grew serious again, almost wistful. "He made a mistake, but not the one you think. I should tell you, but it would break your heart."

Kariana eyed her warily. "Tell me what?"

By now, Ariano was peering at Kariana as one might observe a prized specimen under a magnifying glass. "Yes, I can see his reasoning. You've come a long way since you were cringing from me in the courtroom. We have underestimated you. Did you plan it this way? The catastrophic protocols?"

Kariana, still wary of a trap, grunted and said, "It was plan B."

"You had help, surely. You've shown courage, but not the sort of cunning to do this alone. Narelki? Or that Prosin whore?"

Kariana smirked. "Both, actually. And you. Without Sadrina's death, Prandil's wouldn't have been a tipping point."

Ariano turned to Sadrik as if Kariana were not present. "Clever girl. Resourceful. It would seem Narelki and Prandil both saw it, and they are not the only ones."

"That is ridiculous," Sadrik spat.

"Saw what?" Kariana asked, growing more annoyed now.

Ariano turned back to her, her mood cool rather than volcanic or manic. "Never you mind. You'll find out if and when I choose, assuming I don't change my mind. You remind me of someone I'm very fond of, you know?"

Kariana hesitated a moment, considering. "If we've decided mayhem is off the table, what now?"

Ariano flashed a wicked grin, her gray eyebrows almost popping off the top of her head. *It's hardly surprising that they think us mad. Perhaps we are.*

"I made no such promise!" Ariano called out. She paused a moment and rubbed at her chin, then shrugged as if in surrender. "But it seems it is." She snapped her fingers under Kariana's nose. "I need to lay hands on the Southlander leader. I have plans for him."

Just like that, she's gone from traitor and victim back to servant. No wonder they hate us.

Sadrik shook his head vehemently. "Maranath was quite clear. He's off limits!"

Ariano cast him a withering glare. "*Maranath* is not *here.* We'll intercept that piece, and get back to living our lives."

Sadrik prepared to offer an argument that would likely result in his severe injury, but fortunately Caelwen was foolish enough to interrupt him and draw Ariano's ire. "You're too late. They left days ago."

Sadrik put a palm to his face and shook his head. "One guess where they were headed."

Ariano clenched her fists, almost seething. "Torium!"

Caelwen nodded, his expression carefully blank. "That's the rumor."

Ariano seemed to deflate as she unclenched her hands. "All of them in motion now, heading there." She hung her head briefly, then turned to Sadrik. "Come, pup. We'd best be on our way. We'll miss Prandil for what comes next, I would guess, but we play the cards we have."

Sadrik eyed her a moment, feeling a coldness in his belly. "We could catch them," he said after a moment. "They would still be a few days away."

Ariano sneered. "Weren't you just parroting Maranath's orders a moment ago?"

"That was then. This is now. Will you have my help or no? I'll fight to the death if I have to, but if there's another way, let's at least try." *I presume if we are successful, Maranath will spare me. Success is always a good justification, after all.*

Ariano raised a hand to his neck, not unkindly. At her silent bidding, the boards in the ceiling groaned, twisted, then burst outward, letting a single shaft of sunlight spill into the room. "We can try, though it seems we're swimming against the stream of fate. Don't get your hopes up."

As they began to rise, Kariana called out, "And what in Mei's name am I supposed to do while I wait for the great *heroes* of Nihlos?"

Ariano shouted back, "Have you forgotten why I came here to begin with? You've relieved me of the need to care, upstart! 'The new order of things, all done legally', as you said."

Sadrik could not resist. As they rose into the sunbeam like gods, he called out "Try not to do anything stupid until we get back!"

Ariano cleared the roof before he could hear Kariana's response, but in his mind, he could clearly hear the sound of shattering glass and Kariana's shriek of impotent rage.

And hopefully, that lovely thought will sustain me long enough to save the world. Not that Sadrik was any sort of hero, but he lived in the world, and it would be very inconvenient for him if it ceased to exist.

One needs to keep perspective.

Ahmed followed Rithard deep into the section the Nihlosian's called the Undercity. He was glad for the hood, not so much as a disguise as to simply hide his gawping. It was true, the Nihlosians were hopeless as soldiers, but their architecture, their science, their culture, all were amazing.

Rithard trundled along, oblivious to the wonders of his own land, as most men are, alert and focused as he looked back and forth, and occasionally over his shoulder.

"You expect trouble," Ahmed noted.

"The Undercity is dangerous."

"Then why did you not bring a weapon?"

Rithard shook his head but gave no answer. Instead, he gestured ahead, down the poorly maintained cobblestone street to a large, walled compound. "That's our destination."

Ahmed reached to grip the blade at his hip, feeling reassured by its presence. Ordinarily, he would have no fear of street thugs, but Rithard's nerves were contagious, it seemed. Ahmed scanned the streets about him once again before giving his full attention to the building.

The wall, made of stone blocks, stood tall, at least ten feet, with spikes at the top, a formidable barrier for all but the most determined or desperate intruder. The building beyond, visible through a large gate, was a square, three-story brick structure of immense size. Its exterior was faded from years of weather, but beyond that it seemed in good order. The few windows Ahmed could see were high off the ground and still intact.

Rithard, too, looked about in caution before inserting the key Kariana had provided into the gate's lock. He grunted with effort, struggling to turn the key, and Ahmed moved to help.

The thugs chose that moment to attack.

They were quiet, but one must have kicked a stone as they approached. Ahmed spun at the rattling sound, reached for his shield and blade, and cursed at the entangling robe. His shield, hung on his back, was in easy reach, but his blade was at his hip, and took an extra moment to free. *Time enough to be killed, if these fools are competent. I should have seen this coming!*

Three men moved quickly toward him; where they had come from Ahmed could not say. Likely, they knew plenty of cunning ambush points. It was their territory, after all. They were tall, lean men, but not the strange, beautiful people from above. These were hard, threadbare wolves whose hungry faces Ahmed knew well. *Bandits. They are the same everywhere.* The knives and clubs they had in hand left no doubt as to their intentions.

Rithard was slow, terribly so. He was only just realizing

something was amiss. He would not be part of this, then. They would live or die either by Ahmed's skill, or the bandits' mercy. Ahmed preferred not to rely on the latter. *In my experience, they are not apt to have any.*

He could almost hear Yazid's voice in the back of his mind, telling him that war was risk, that one must play the cards he has. Cursing, Ahmed dropped his shield on the ground and shrugged out of the robe. *A sword alone may win the day. A shield won't.* By the time Ahmed brought his weapon to bear, the bandit in the lead had registered something was terribly wrong, but it was far too late for him. The man's cry of "Southl—!" ended in a gurgling shriek of agony as Ahmed's sword opened his throat to the elements, sending a spray of bright red blood into the faces of the others. The would-be attacker staggered briefly, clutching at his throat, eyes wide in shock, then collapsed to the cobbles.

The remaining pair, eyes wide in terror, skidded to a halt and nearly fell over backwards as they scrambled to escape. Ahmed watched them flee with a grim smile. *Idiots. Not used to victims who fight back, eh?.*

Behind him Rithard let out a shuddering sigh. "I told you it was dangerous here."

Ahmed turned to him with a shrug. "A relative term, it would seem. I could have killed the other two, but I saw no reason to chase them."

"Oh, there was reason," Rithard said. "They will be back in short order with more."

Ahmed scowled, but knew it was likely true. "Then we need to finish our business quickly." He spared a glance at the man he had downed. He was unconscious, either dead or soon to be. He pushed at the body with a boot. "Do you know him?"

"No, but I likely will soon enough," Rithard said absently, still working the lock. It gave with a sudden squeal and click, and the gate swung open with a screech at his touch.

Rithard looked back down the street after they entered, then closed and locked the gate behind. "The last thing we need is for them to surprise us in here."

The interior grounds were in remarkably good shape, all things considered. The space between the wall and the building was about twenty feet wide all the way around, presumably to accommodate drawn carriages, and covered in a seamless stone that had neither cracked nor worn, though it, too, had weathered to gray.

Ahmed followed Rithard around the entire building, looking for an entrance, but the only candidate they found was on the far side. It looked like a door in that it was about the right size, and inset into the building wall. It seemed to be surrounded by a frame of sorts, but Ahmed could see nothing resembling a conventional handle or keyhole.

Rithard bent to examine a small depression where a knob should have been. "And here we have our damnable riddle again, yes?" He gestured for Ahmed to have a look. "I can't read it, but it's the same as the one in the book."

Ahmed bent down briefly for a closer look. The depression looked vaguely like a head in shape, though it was inset with intricate lines like nothing Ahmed had ever seen. "It is the same. 'The key to true knowledge lies within the heart of wisdom.'"

Rithard nodded slowly, examining the depression. "It almost looks like some sort of key goes there..." His eyes flashed suddenly with strange emotion, and his body grew stiff. For a moment, Ahmed thought the Nihlosian meant to attack him, so intense was the man's expression. *His mind is working hard.*

A moment later, Rithard turned a feverish gaze on Ahmed, even going so far as to seize him by the shoulders. "We must return to the library at once!"

Ahmed stood still and spoke in a calm voice, as was best

when dealing with madmen. "Of course. And what shall we do there?"

Rithard grinned, his eyes still lit with something akin to madness. He shook Ahmed by the shoulders and laughed. "We're going to smash something very old and valuable!"

Ahmed found himself in a difficult quandary. Not only was he a guest who ought not interfere with his hosts, it was improper to lay hands on either the old or the mad. With Slat and Rithard locked in a life or death struggle over the pick ax, it was difficult to know whom, if anyone, he should assist.

"Have you gone mad?" Slat nearly shrieked, his hair flying about his head like snow as he pulled against Rithard's grip.

Rithard hauled on the handle, nearly toppling Slat in the process. "I'm the first person of any sense to hold my position! Let *go*!"

Ahmed looked about to see that the rest of the house staff seemed to be as conflicted as he, and worse, they seemed to be looking at him to do something.

Indecision was hardly one of Ahmed's failings, but circumstances were arrayed heavily against him. By the time he had managed to work out a plan of action, which went something along the lines of stopping Rithard from jerking the old man's arms from his sockets, Slat's grip failed, and Rithard staggered backward, prize in hand, as Slat howled in protest.

Rithard, full of mad energy now that he sensed his moment, swung the pickaxe in a great arc at the statue of Amrath as Slat fell to his knees and wailed, "No!"

The axe hit the statue's chest not with the meaty chunk one would expect of solid stone, but with the softer ring of a hollow space. Even Slat fell silent at this.

Rithard's cry of victory broke the silence. "I *knew* it!"

As they all looked on in shock, Rithard reached within the cavity of Amrath's chest and pulled out a gold chain, from which hung a small lion's head carved of green stone.

Ilaweh is great, there is another! But no, that could not be true. A moment later, Ahmed realized what Rithard had known for hours: this was the literal key, in the literal heart of Nihlos's icon of wisdom.

Rithard, the key dangling from his hand like a charm, looked up at the skylight and frowned. "It will be dark soon. We need to hurry. The Undercity is no place to be at night, but this can't wait."

Slat, busily gathering shards of the statue from the floor, cast Rithard a reproachful glare. "It is certainly no place for the leader of our house! We've just lost one to madness. Why not at least wait until morning?"

Rithard softened and laid an arm across the old fellow's shoulders. "I know you've had a hard road dealing with Meites. It's none of that with me."

Ahmed grasped Rithard firmly by the shoulder with his left hand, and clutched at the hilt of his blade with his right. "I will protect him, grandfather."

Slat looked back and forth at them, eyes full of doubt, and nodded, resigned. A moment later, he suddenly brightened, as if he had remembered something. He raised his finger in the air and said, "Wait. I have something for you." He turned and waved at the rest of the gawping slaves. "Out. This is not for your eyes!"

When they were gone, and the doors to the library secured once again, Slat moved slowly to one of the many shelves, his hand shaking with age as he traced the spines, searching. "Ah, here." He hauled a huge volume from the shelf and staggered backward. Ahmed caught him before he fell and helped him ease the book to the floor.

Rithard fingered the lion's head absently as he looked at the dark space the book left. He grinned at Slat's mystery. "You've kept secrets from me?"

Slat shook his head. "Not as such. More of an oversight than a secret." The old fellow reached in again. Ahmed heard the low rasp of metal on stone, and felt his hand move of its own accord to his blade once again. *Don't be foolish. It's not an attack!* "Lothrian put it here ages ago. He had no use for mundane weapons, and Narelki, likewise, had no interest. It was just a secret treasure, as far as they were concerned, of no practical use."

Slat removed a scabbard containing what appeared to be a long dagger, or a short sword. It sang as he drew it, a thin blade with a fine point. He extended his hands to Rithard. "My grandfather told me Amrath himself carried this blade. It's named Truth. You may not be a Meite, but you're as mad as one, and you need something. Take it."

Rithard looked at the weapon, wary, then back to Slat. "I've had no training in weapons since I was a child! I wouldn't know what to do with it."

Ahmed reached for the blade and scabbard, and Slat reluctantly allowed him to take them. With a grin, Ahmed swung the sword about, testing the heft, then gently placed the point against Rithard's chest. "This end toward the enemy," he said. "Then push. But all at once, and quickly. And don't let him do it to you." He re-sheathed the blade, then handed the scabbard back to Rithard with a grin. "Simple."

Rithard accepted the weapon, holding it experimentally at his waist. "Slat, I shall need a belt, I think."

Slat eyed them both nervously, then added, "I'll fetch your medical bag, too, Master."

Rithard nodded vigorously. "Indeed. I have a feeling we may have need of it before the night ends."

CHAPTER 10
INTO THE PIT

AIUL could see the column of zombies ahead in the distance as they approached Torium, lumbering along like a poorly disciplined but determined unit of soldiers. Farther ahead, he could see a great pyramid looming on the horizon, and the sight filled him with a bizarre mix of elation and despair. There was his goal, and within it the keys to what he imagined he wanted most in the world: revenge on Nihlos.

Yet, there was more to his motivation now than mere vengeance. Try as he might, he could not shake the sense of urgency the nightly dreams had brought, and the certain knowledge of the sick, repulsive wrongness that lay within Torium like a cancerous tumor awaiting the surgeon's scalpel.

Aiul scoffed aloud at the notion. *That's the height of self-delusion, to imagine this mission relates even metaphorically to healing.*

Aiul and Logrus pulled alongside the marching zombies before long, and Aiul made certain to give them a wide berth with his spirited mount. He didn't need any more accidents. In any stories Aiul had ever heard, animals recoiled in horror from the undead, but their mounts were hardly afraid. They simply didn't like the zombies, and had no problem lashing out at them if they came too close. Beyond that, the horses simply ignored the shambling corpses for the most part.

Aiul slowed his pace once he was far enough ahead. He and Logrus would stay with their fighters from now until they reached their destination.

The change in the land was nothing short of miraculous. Two days ago, they had been freezing in the snow. Today, they had entered a warm, green area, a jungle, humid and dank with decay, full of lush vegetation and bizarre creatures. He had never seen palms except in books, but here, they were plentiful, along with other less identifiable trees. Most of them were festooned with vines or moss, and here and there were patches where a particularly virile sort of vine had swallowed up entire groves of trees, covering everything, even the ground.

There were strange beasts, too. The travelers saw few, but heard many unusual cries and caws and roars that set them on guard. Once, a strange, vaguely man-shaped creature, though smaller and covered in fur, leapt from one tree to another as they passed beneath. It chattered at them, and threw oddly shaped fruit, making Aiul wonder idly if it were carnivorous. He spent much of his time after that watching the trees in a mixture of fear and delight, hoping to see another, as the great pyramid in the distance slowly grew larger.

"There," Logrus said at last, and pointed to the horizon. "That is the place."

In the distance, the road turned upward. At the top of a small hill, Aiul could see a walled city. The peculiar, voracious vine they had noticed seemed particularly fond of the area, though it, and all other vegetation, stopped short of the walls, giving the impression that it was tended, or, perhaps, that the plants were simply unwilling to approach any closer. Above the defensive perimeter, they could see the step-sided tops of multiple ziggurats.

Eight lined the walls, standing fifty feet or more in height. A huge central pyramid, at least two hundred feet tall, towered over the landscape.

Aiul felt his guts twist in fear. "Yes."

"There is power there," Logrus said. "I can feel it."

"So do I," Aiul replied, his voice so quiet it was almost a whisper. "Something primal."

The road continued up the hill to a huge gate, a massive set of rune-graven steel doors. They stood open and inviting, with not a guard in sight.

"Looks perfectly safe," Aiul quipped.

Logrus looked at him as if he were crazy. "It is an obvious trap!"

Aiul sighed and gave Logrus an exasperated look. Logrus looked back, a blank expression on his face for a moment before it lit with dawning understanding.

"Sarcasm," he announced. "Yes?"

"Yes."

"A stupid sort of talk," Logrus said. "Let's go."

"Into the obvious trap?" Aiul gestured toward the zombies.

Logrus rubbed at his chin and grinned. "That *is* a better plan."

Grinning despite the foreboding surroundings, Aiul called to the zombies, "Imbeciles! Advance!"

Their undead troops moved past them, and Logrus and Aiul followed, wary, to find themselves in a huge courtyard. The area was at least a quarter mile across, and paved with cobblestones. Most of the buildings that must have once stood within the walls had long since decayed to dust, leaving only the stone construction, like bones of a rotted corpse. In the distance, they could see a stagnant, putrid moat surrounding the central pyramid. Aiul thought he could see motion below the murky surface, but it was difficult to tell. Bloated corpses of local fauna, in various stages of decay, floated on top, marking it as lethal, whatever else it might be.

They both jumped at a sudden grinding noise from behind. Even as he turned to look, Aiul knew what it must be. The enormous gate was closing, and there was nothing either of them could do. Aiul cringed at the resounding clang of the doors as they slammed shut, and shook his head in resignation. "I suppose we should have expected that. Obvious trap and all."

"Not sarcasm anymore," Logrus noted. He gestured ahead. "It will come now."

They heard 'it' approaching, but they could not identify the bizarre sound, a hollow, rattling vibration like a thousand sticks of bamboo striking arrhythmically against stone. They had only moments to contemplate it before the enemy was upon them.

Without warning, at each of the outer pyramids, more doors burst open with a crash, to pour forth a seemingly endless stream of—

Aiul felt reality slipping from his grasp even as he felt his jaw fall open like an idiot. *They're just bones! I have one in my office that I hang my jacket on!* Skeletons could not move without muscle, nor could they grip rusty swords, and yet that was what was happening, and medical knowledge be damned. Try as he might, Aiul found himself frozen, unable to accept the reality of what he was seeing. Skeletons could *not* attack!

Logrus, however, seemed to have no such pesky mental blocks. He simply accepted it for what it was. With a muttered curse, he grabbed Aiul by the collar and drug him out of the path of the oncoming skeleton warriors, shouting over his shoulder to the zombies, "Flesh! Defend us!"

Aiul, no longer frozen, found his feet and sprinted across the courtyard with Logrus, back toward the main entrance. There was no way through, but it was clear of attackers for the moment.

"It's *impossible!*" he cried, having no idea who he even intended to hear him.

Logrus shrugged as if Aiul were discussing the weather. "Possible."

Aiul took a moment to catch his breath and looked back at what was now a chaotic melee of undead skeletons hacking at zombies with swords, and zombies swinging at skeletons with clubs or fists. For a moment, Aiul felt his sanity teeter again, but he managed to keep it together for the moment. "There are hundreds of them! We don't stand a chance!"

Logrus watched the melee with great interest a moment, then asked, "What will you bet me?"

Aiul rubbed at his left temple and groaned softly, eying Logrus and wondering if the poor fellow had actually lost his mind at what they were seeing. *Mei knows, I'm right on the edge, myself.*

The skeletons, armed with rusted blades, were as much automatons as the zombies. They stabbed at their targets most of the time, a fairly useless tactic against an enemy who had no vital organs. The undead Elgies were armed mostly with clubs, however, and used them to great effect. Old bones shattered under the blunt weapons, sending skeleton after skeleton to the cobblestones, heaps of useless rubble.

But the skeletons had the advantage of sheer numbers. Aiul guessed that perhaps two hundred had entered the battle. The relatively minor damage they were capable of inflicting on the zombies accrued over time. Still, the zombies destroyed four or five of their foes for every one of their number that fell. When it was over, seven zombies, in various stages of disrepair, stood amongst the remains, unenthusiastic victors on a bloodless battlefield. *It's ironic that there are no more corpses at the end than there were at the beginning. It's cheaper than conventional war.*

Aiul was uncertain if he had accepted his new reality, or had merely grown numb to it, but certainly spending long minutes watching the fight had made it seem more real. "Let's raise these fools again and get about our business."

Logrus shook his head. "The second death is final. Elgar would not permit it. They have absolved themselves."

Aiul sighed. "Of *course* it is. Is there a book I could read on the rules?"

Logrus seemed to consider the question seriously for a moment, then broke into a broad grin. "You're joking."

Aiul clapped Logrus on the shoulder. "You're getting better at this. You're almost human, now!" He paused a moment and looked at the shattered skeletons. "Though, being serious, there *ought* to be a book on these sorts of things. One has to wonder, if bones can attack on their own, why can't they attack after they're broken?"

Logrus said nothing for a moment, considering, then shrugged. "Magic. Come, we have a mission. Do science later."

They picked their way across the courtyard, weaving between the various ruins and occasional gigantic chunks of shattered stone. Aiul felt especially perplexed at these. They seemed completely out of place. Why would there be random bits of rock, as if it had rained from the sky? And yet it was everywhere, on both sides of the moat, great hunks of rock that appeared as if they had been smashed by a giant's pickaxe.

Aiul looked across the moat to the large pyramid, his smile fading as he remembered their goals. "That's where we're headed, I suppose. Let's see if we can find a way across."

The smell rising from the moat was the most revolting scent Aiul could remember encountering, and, as a surgeon, he had quite a library to compare it against. He covered his nose and mouth with his cloak, wondering if they might, somehow, find the resolve to swim it. *If we do, there's no telling what sort of disease we might pick up.*

The idea fled from his mind as the surface of the water suddenly rippled. *Mei! Something* is *in there!* Aiul leapt back, grabbing Logrus and shoving him away just as a huge, motley tentacle broke the surface and whipped toward them with dizzying speed. Aiul dove behind one of the large chunks of debris, pulling Logrus along with him. Logrus grunted as he hit the ground, and his eyes grew wide as the tentacle tore past where he had been standing.

The tentacle wavered back and forth for a moment, dripping filthy water, as if frustrated at losing its prey, then settled instead for a zombie. It darted at its new victim and wrapped itself around the undead fighter in the blink of an eye, then pulled him into the moat. The zombie had no time to even struggle before it vanished beneath the murky surface.

"Back!" Aiul shouted to the rest of their troops as he and Logrus scrambled to their feet. "Retreat!" Even as they fled, the tentacle lashed out again and seized another of their troops before they could get clear of the area. They ran back to the main entrance as fast as their legs could carry them and paused, shaken.

"Five left," Aiul noted. "We're no match for another round of the damned skeletons. I have no idea how we get to the center now."

"The smaller pyramids," Logrus said. "They connect underground. I saw it in the dreams. Escape tunnels to retreat into the center. If they haven't collapsed."

Aiul scowled. "Where the skeletons came from."

Logrus shrugged. "The skeletons came out. They are not there anymore."

Aiul groaned at the idea, but there seemed no other way. The moat was clearly a death trap, and Logrus's simple logic was hard to argue with, though it naively assumed that *all* of the skeletons had attacked. Privately, Aiul suspected some might have been held in reserve, but saw no point in going too far with that line of thinking. It would just spook him even worse than he already was. Either there were more skeletons, or there weren't, and they would know soon enough.

"Fine, this whole venture has practically been a suicide mission from the start." He looked toward the closest of the outer pyramids, its doors still wide open, and searched for signs of movement, when something Logrus had said registered with him. "Wait, what do you mean 'if they haven't collapsed'? Why would they collapse?"

"Designed that way," Logrus said. "To weather a siege."

Aiul buried his face in his hands for a moment. "So, in order to avoid being drowned and possibly eaten by the moat beast, we risk being ventilated by another skeleton horde." He ticked those two off on his fingers, and raised a third. "And if we somehow survive that, we might have the misfortune to be buried under tons of rubble, eh?"

Logrus grinned at him. "Correct."

Aiul blinked at him a moment, then stood. "Well, let's get on with dying. You needn't be so happy about it, though."

Logrus stood and clapped Aiul on the shoulder. "We were sent here by a god, Aiul. We cannot die as long as we are about Elgar's work." He gestured to the zombies to follow. "Have faith."

With another groan, Aiul followed. "Easy for you to say. Have you considered the sort of problems we will have if we're buried under there and we *don't* die?"

Logrus stopped where he was and stared back at Aiul, distress on his face as he thought about Aiul's point. After a moment, he shook his head and moved on.

"That's a point for me," Aiul declared, grinning in dark humor.

"You are an idiot!" Logrus answered, but he, too, was smiling.

The interior of the smaller pyramid was dark and musty, the dust of centuries accumulated over unidentifiable lumps, remains of what might once have been furniture. Light trickled in through murder holes that lined the walls. With the heavy doors barred from within, a hundred men could have easily held off ten times their number. In the center of the room, a spiral staircase, in surprisingly good shape, twisted into the darkness below.

Logrus produced torches from his pack and lit one for Aiul, another for himself. Wordlessly, the two led their soldiers downward.

The passage below was made of rough-hewn stone blocks, and damp. The sound of dripping water broke the silence every few seconds, echoing from the rock faces. It was quite wide, enough to allow ten men abreast. Logrus held his torch aloft and peered down the hallway.

"Cunning construction," he said. "Flee down here when you can't hold any longer. Just need time to get down the staircase before they breach. Plenty of room to run, then the staircase slows down the enemy." He pointed to a series of arches along the path. "They chase you into a killing field. Should be controls at the other end to collapse those. Very clever."

Aiul shuddered. "It's certain death is what it is."

"Turn back then?" Logrus asked with a grin.

Aiul glared back at him. "Stay close," he sneered. "When it comes down on us, I want to watch you die first, so I'll at least get to know I was right."

Logrus shook his head as he continued leading the way. "Don't run," he cautioned. "Eyes on the ground. Could be triggers in the floor, in case they couldn't escape in time. Defenders would know to avoid them."

"How do you know these things?" Aiul asked "I remember seeing this in the dreams, but I certainly didn't get this sort of education."

Logrus raised his torch and peered at something near the ceiling. "You wonder if Elgar gave me more detailed information? No. I know this on my own."

Aiul shook his head in admiration. "You play at being a simple man, yet you know military construction, traps, survival, tracking."

Logrus turned to Aiul and shrugged. "I have done many things," he said. "Chased, fled, escaped, hunted, killed." He began to move forward again, looking closely at the floor. "I have seen many ways to kill. I have hunted men in cities, in swamps, in fortresses. I have survived traps such as these. I would know what I know, or be dead."

Aiul chuckled at the simple logic of Logrus's explanation. "It surprises me is all. Common murderers don't know such things."

Logrus stopped in his tracks and turned to Aiul, a pained expression on his face, and asked, "Am I but a common murderer to you?"

Aiul stammered slightly as he said, "No, I'm saying that you *seem* at first glance a common murderer, but there is much more to you than meets the eye."

Logrus frowned. "The men I kill are hardly common."

"I know that!" Aiul said defensively. "I read your journal, remember?" He stammered a moment, then sighed and pressed a hand to his face. "I meant it as a compliment, you know."

Logrus gave Aiul a long looking at through narrowed eyes, then turned and set off again down the tunnel. "Your language is poor," he called over his shoulder. "You should have studied it harder."

Aiul was about to retort, when he realized Logrus had just made a fairly complex joke. Aiul laughed as he answered, "Well, it just seems terribly suspicious, you knowing all of these things. And unfair, too. I mean, for a cultist to have so many useful skills."

"I *will* kill you for that!" Logrus chuckled.

Aiul looked up at the ceiling himself, but whatever Logrus saw, Aiul could not recognize. "Hopefully, you'll have your chance once we're done."

Aiul's humorous mood evaporated in an instant as he heard a sharp click at his feet. He realized, to his horror, that despite his best intentions, he had stepped slightly to the side of Logrus's path. Likely, this was not the first time, but it might well be the last.

The sound echoed loud in the tunnel. Logrus's head whipped around, his eyes wide with alarm. Aiul froze, having no idea if they were about to be buried under tons of rubble.

Logrus raised both hands in a cautionary gesture. "Don't move. It triggers on release."

Aiul looked about, somewhat relieved that he had yet to die, but wildly uncertain as to whether that would continue for any length of time. "How do you know that?"

Logrus shrugged. "We are still alive."

With a shuddering breath, Aiul nodded at that logic. "So what do we do?"

Logrus looked intensely at the surrounding floor, then called, "Flesh! You! Come here."

Carefully, Aiul exchanged positions with the swaying zombie, as Logrus commanded it to hold fast. It would have been nice to breathe a sigh of relief, but there was no relief to be had. In theory, the zombie would stay where it was until it rotted. In practice, they were Mei knew how far into the tunnel and their lives now depended on a creature dumber than a rock. "We have to leave them all," he said. "If I can take a bad step, so can they. We're lucky they haven't already."

Logrus's features deepened with a frown. "I think so. I hate to lose them, but it seems only a matter of time." He gestured at the remaining undead. "Flesh. Stay." Without bothering to verify that they would obey, he set off again down the tunnel.

Aiul struggled not to give in to screaming terror as they made their way forward. The more he thought on what was overhead, the more aware he was that they were not travelling a simple passage. Rather, they were in the firing line of a murderous, well-disguised weapon.

They inched their way along, carefully examining the ground. Twice, Logrus's caution was validated, the second time almost too late to matter. *Mei, thank goodness we caught that one. We have no more dummies to spare.*

Twenty yards became fifty, then a hundred, and Aiul felt himself nearing the edge of madness. How long could the damned thing go on? At last, after another fifty yards, he spied an open doorway in the gloom ahead, and allowed himself a glimmer of hope.

It was short lived. Aiul felt his stomach leap into his throat as a tortured, metallic squeal filled the tunnel. From above their heads came a sharp crack of cables tightening, and the sound of gears meshing, followed by the grating of stone against stone. *It's not fair! We did everything right!*

Logrus pulled him forward without a moment to spare. Tons of stonework rained into the space they had just fled. It was over in seconds, leaving them with no choice but to move forward.

In the aftermath, Aiul coughed at the dust, and croaked, "What did we do wrong?"

Logrus, his face dark with anger, shook his head. "Nothing. It was triggered externally."

Aiul felt his eyes widen as he absorbed the implications of this. Logrus had mentioned controls elsewhere. *Someone is watching us!*

He had no time to think about it. The silence was suddenly filled with a new sound, a heavy, metallic thud followed by a rumbling, liquid roar.

"Water!" Logrus yelped. "The moat!"

The flood erupted from the gaping hole left in the ceiling by the collapse. Aiul charged for the doorway, and saw that a hatch was slowly closing over it, driven by some unseen mechanism. He pushed himself forward with more speed than he had ever imagined, once again thankful that he had trained at something as seemingly useless as sprinting. He dove through the rapidly shrinking opening, landing hard on the other side. His torch flew from his hands and went skittering across the floor.

Behind him, Logrus cried out in pain, spurring Aiul back to action. He looked back in the wild, flickering torchlight to see Logrus caught in the closing door, part of his chest and one arm still on the other side. The mechanism began to whine as it continued to try to seal.

Putrid water and air jetted past Logrus as he struggled in the vise-like grip of the hatch. Aiul grabbed Logrus's free arm and pulled with all his might, hoping the rapidly rising pressure on the other side of the door would be of aid.

Logrus cried out as one of his ribs gave way with a crack, but Aiul knew at once that the injury was a blessing in disguise. The door mechanism was slow, and Aiul took advantage of the brief loosening to haul his companion through.

Logrus landed on the floor with a wet thud and lay there, clutching his ribs and grimacing as the hatch sealed with a loud click.

"Blew your chance, there," he chuckled weakly.

"To see you die first?" Aiul asked with a grim smile, "I'll likely get another very soon."

Logrus struggled to a sitting position against the wall, grimacing, a hand pressed against his ribs. Aiul, shaking his head at Logrus's stubborn nature, retrieved his torch and crouched beside him.

"Let me see, fool," he grumbled. "Lie down a moment."

Logrus complied with a pained smile, and said, "Damned suspicious that you just happen to know medicine, if you ask me."

"You've found me out," Aiul quipped as he examined the injury. "All this time, I was posing as a necromancer and a madman, but in reality, I was just manipulating you into getting injured so I could practice my trade." He prodded gently at the darkening bruise on Logrus's side. "It seems clean," he said. "You should be able to walk if we bind it up. Is there a lot of pain?"

"Pain is mental," Logrus said. "I have fought for my life with much worse."

"Just be careful with it," Aiul said sternly. "It's not in a bad spot, but it can shift and puncture a lung, if you ignore the pain. Listen to what your body tells you."

Logrus nodded slowly and grimaced. "I just need a moment." He looked about quickly. "No enemies, at least."

"For now," Aiul agreed, though he did not feel so certain of it. *Someone just tried to kill us.*

Aiul peered into the darkness, but it was a useless effort. The room they were in extended beyond the range of torchlight. Only the wall beside them was visible, stretching into darkness on either side of them, row upon row of stones fading into blackness. *I'll have to actually explore, I think.* He rose to his feet and waved at the closed hatch. "We're not going back that way. I'd best have a look about. Where's your torch?"

"Lost it. My pack, too."

"Mei!" Out of reflex, Aiul tightened his grip on the torch he carried, now their last source of light. It was a useless gesture, but it made him feel better.

"Wait here," he said. "I'll see what I can find to bind you up with."

The Master stared into the pool, amused at the suffering of the invaders.

The servant asked, "Does it please you, Master? I thought it would be better this way, slowly, instead of crushing them outright."

"Yesss," the master agreed. "Their fear is sweet." It dipped its claw into the black pool again, sending ripples over the image, and licked at it. "I have changed my mind. I want them alive. It is fortunate for you that you delayed."

The servant shuddered, an involuntary spasm of fear at the realization of how close it had come to making a fatal mistake. But it smiled, too, at its own cunning.

"I am a good servant," it crooned. "You are capricious. I try always to anticipate you. To please you."

The master tapped a talon on the stone rim of the pool, thinking that perhaps it might still be amusing to kill the servant, but dismissed the notion. It was difficult to find a servant smart enough to anticipate. It would be foolish to waste this one now.

"I am pleased," it said. "Bring them to me. I would speak with them and smell their fear. Perhaps they have knowledge. Then we will rend them and make them into art."

The servant touched its head to the floor, hissed its compliance, and scurried from the room.

CHAPTER 11
A MATTER OF PERSPECTIVE

THE SUN was dipping low when Sadrik spied yet another dead horse on the ground below. "There, see?" he called out over the wind. "That's the third one, and who knows how many we missed?"

Ariano glanced down at him briefly, then turned her attention forward again.

"Well, it's odd, don't you think?" he shouted up at her.

Ariano glanced at him again, and shrugged as best she could with one shoulder. "If you work out what it signifies, by all means let me know."

For at least the thousandth time, Sadrik reminded himself that setting her on fire would mean certain death. He looked back at the rapidly passing ground below, hoping for some distraction, when he saw the group.

"Look there!" he shouted, pointing. "The source of our dead horse problem, I should think."

Ariano followed his gesture, a look of exasperation on her face, which quickly changed to a cruel grin. "The Southlanders! We have him now!" Sadrik forced himself to remain calm as Ariano banked sharply and dropped toward their quarry.

The Southlanders mounts looked to be on their last legs, several with bloody foam frothing around their lips. Sadrik was hardly an expert, but he had learned enough in school to understand these horses had been bred and seasoned to carry men of a lighter frame, not hulking brutes like the Southlanders. The few spares they had with them were in slightly better shape, but even those were clearly tired.

Ariano set them down in the road about ten yards ahead of the Southlanders, making no effort at subtlety. The Southlanders, in turn, reigned their mounts to a stop and drew weapons. *So it's a fight, then. Ah, well, that was the plan all along I suppose.*

Ariano raised an eyebrow and offered the Southlanders a wry smile. "Come now, friends. There's no need to shed any of your blood. We only need to relieve you of something you should never have had. Then you can go with our blessing."

Sandilianus, their second in command, answered with a fierce grin, "We are fine with bloodshed. Come and take what you would, if you can."

Ariano opened her arms wide and returned his grin with one of her own. "So be it."

So be it indeed. Sadrik followed her lead and stepped toward the Southlanders. *We'll add a bit of panache.*

It took Ariano three steps before noticing his fiery footprints. Battle or no, she stopped dead in her tracks and glared at him.

Wretched old crone! "What?" he shouted.

"Stop that idiocy."

"It's intimidation!"

Ariano waved a hand dismissively. "It's cheap theatrics. I won't be part of it."

"It's *practical*. Tears down their will, makes mine stronger. It's no different than any of your 'theatrics'."

Ariano folded her arms across her chest, unmoving. "It's

crude, and it tears down *my* will to tolerate your continued existence."

"Oh, please! *Combat* is crude! One doesn't subtly stab someone in the throat or bash someone's head in! Blood doesn't flow in delicately selected patterns. It's all there, loud and in your face!"

Ariano looked at the Southlanders, who were eyeing them quizzically, then turned back to Sadrik and snapped, "We will resume this discussion later. This is the first thing you've brought up that is actually interesting to me, but this is hardly the time to discuss the aesthetics of killing."

Sadrik chuckled. "I'll bear that in mind."

As they turned back to the Southlanders again, one of the horses collapsed, sending its rider rolling. Sadrik snickered. It was a quiet snicker, to be certain, but Ariano spun on her heal and jammed a bony finger in his face. "Whelp! You're making a damned farce of everything!"

Sandilianus laughed out loud. "Ahmed is right. You are all mad."

Ariano spun toward him, fury blazing in her eyes, fists clenched at her sides, teeth a-grind. Her voice rang like a choir as she bellowed, "I *will* kill the lot of you, Southlander, if you don't present your leader this instant!" She would have been comical had the very air around her not been shimmering like heat. *She absolutely means what she says.*

Sadrik took a step back, knowing from experience that when she really lost her temper, she was hardly selective about the direction in which she lashed out.

Sandilianus laughed aloud. "Then you are in the wrong place, grandmother. Ahmed is not with us. He is within your Nihlos." He scowled as he added, "Assuming you snakes have not slain him."

Sadrik took a deep breath and waited for the explosion. *This will not end well. I wonder which one will grate her ass more, the fact that Kariana tricked us, or the Southlander calling her 'grandmother'?*

Ariano stood a moment, clenching and unclenching her tiny fists. *Has there ever been a case of a Meite actually exploding in a rage?* Sadrik was uncertain, and took several more steps backward on the off chance that it could happen. Sandilianus raised an eyebrow, but held his ground, eyes locked with Ariano's.

Moments later, the storm passed without issue. Ariano relaxed and smiled up at Sandilianus. "Confidence is always attractive in a man."

Sandilianus grinned and dismounted, extending a hand to her. "If I were for women, I would pursue you! You are bold, and eager to fight."

"If we intended to kill you, we wouldn't have landed," Ariano tittered.

We needn't have intended to do so for it to have occurred.

"My men are expert marksmen," Sandilianus countered. "I think it would not be so easy as you imagine."

Ariano reached out her own hand. The Southlander took it, accepting the Nihlosian form of greeting, his great paw almost completely swallowing her dainty fingers.

Ariano lowered her arm after a moment and asked, "Where are you going in such a hurry, Sandilianus Abu al Khayr, Centurion in Prince Philip's legions, serving under Tribune Brutus Samir, and loyal servant to Ilaweh?"

Sandilianus's eyebrows rose high. "You remember every bit, eh?"

Ariano smirked at him. "I'm not as old as all that. And I have a talent for such things. Do you remember mine?"

Sandilianus looked sheepish for a moment. "It's not 'Evil Sorceress', is it?"

Sadrik snickered, surprised to see Ariano actually smiling at this. "Flattery is always helpful when one can't remember a name. In this case, the one you're searching for is Ariano Talus, but 'Evil Sorceress' *does* have its charm." Ariano's expression grew serious once again, and she locked eyes with the Southlander. "Now, answer my question."

Sandilianus seemed to be considering a moment. "I am having deja vu," he chuckled. "But again, it is a religious matter, not military. We go to Torium, to stop a great evil."

Sadrik couldn't quite suppress a small laugh. "You don't say."

Sandilianus's smile faded as he looked pointedly at Sadrik. "Will you stand in our way?"

Ariano suddenly seemed to take note of a blond, brutish Nihlosian amongst the Southlanders. He smirked back at her, but made no move to come down from his mount and speak. Ariano eyed him briefly, then turned back to Sandilianus. "That depends on how you answer my next question."

Sandilianus's eyes flashed, but he kept his face impassive. "Then ask, and let us be on our way to death or glory."

"What does your leader intend to do with the Eye of the Lion, Southlander?"

Sandilianus gave her a bewildered look. "I do not know this thing."

Ariano studied him intently for a moment, then heaved a tired sigh and cradled her head in her hands. "You're telling the truth, aren't you? You don't have a damned clue."

Sadrik couldn't help himself. "It seems neither do you, Evil Sorceress."

Ariano gave him a foul look. "I'll tolerate that from a dashing, handsome stranger. Not from you."

"You were happy enough with the 'evil' label, it seemed."

Ariano rolled her eyes. "It's all a matter of perspective, isn't it? This is not the time for philosophy!"

"Ah, so now it's all about efficacy? What happened to 'crude', eh?"

"Will you shut up? If I lie and say I agree with everything you say, will that satisfy you? Focus, young one, that's what you still lack."

"That's just what the flames do for me!"

Ariano waved a finger at him like a teacher. "Efficacy damned well is not the be all and end all, but at the moment—"

Sandilianus interrupted them. "We must be off. If we are not in Torium by nightfall, a great doom shall be born."

Ariano and Sadrik stopped mid argument and slowly turned to look at the Southlander. Sadrik could see his own confusion reflected in Ariano's wide eyes. "By tonight, you say?" he asked. "However do you plan on that?"

Ariano was shaking her head in consternation, looking at the ground, lost in thought and fidgeting with her necklace. "He didn't. He doesn't even know. The Eye's time has come. We can't stop it. We resist our part in it at our peril."

Sadrik's shoulders slumped as he understood her point. "Which is just what Maranath told us."

Ariano, miles away in her head, muttered, almost to herself, "How curious that we should just happen along here at this time..."

Sandilianus shook his head. "I know it is a hard road, but we are halfway, surely. We will run the rest of the way if we must."

Sadrik offered the man a sad smile, feeling terribly embarrassed to shatter his illusions like this. "Even we didn't expect to arrive before midnight. Torium is another hundred miles from here, Southlander."

Sandilianus sat in stony silence, his expression grim and face ashen, as his men shifted and muttered amongst themselves. At last, he spoke, his voice thick with emotion. "Then we have failed."

Ariano broke from her reverie. "Perhaps not quite yet, South-lander, if you have courage enough to do something mad. We might all die in the attempt. How strong is your conviction?"

Sandilianus snorted. "I shall fall upon my own blade if it will get us there in time."

Ariano grinned. "Perhaps later. For now, we have plenty of killing to do."

Sandilianus's face brightened. "Who must I slay?"

Ariano's face seemed to grow softer, less mean, less old, as humor twinkled in her eyes. "To begin with, trees, I should think."

Sadrik raised an eyebrow in appreciation. *I think I see where she is going with this.*

Sandilianus scowled back and forth at them. "Trees? How can killing *trees* help? Are you mad?"

Ariano remained inscrutable. "Mad? I am a Meite, South-lander. We are all mad, I suppose, if you feel the need to put a point on things. Now, are you with me or not?" She gestured toward the nearby woods. "Trees. We will need at least twenty."

Sadrik raised his eyebrows and put on an enigmatic smile. *I do so enjoy being on the other end of 'cryptic' on occasion!* "Go on then! You heard the Evil Sorceress! Do as she commands or she'll likely turn you into a toad!" *Mei, if I can just keep from laughing...*

Sandilianus again looked back and forth at them warily. "Fine. We will get trees. But if this is some game, you'd damned well better be able to carry out that threat. Even as a toad, I will jump down your throat and choke you to death! Are we clear?"

Sadrik nodded, the very picture of innocence. "Crystal."

CHAPTER 12
CLASS REUNION

THE ZIGGURATS of Torium gleamed white as bone in the moonlight as Maranath and Maklin began their descent. Maranath counted eight smaller pyramids on the perimeter, watch stations along the wall, all dwarfed by the massive central structure. A moat, black as ancient evil, encircled the central pyramid like a guardian python.

That will be our destination. He gestured to Maklin and pointed to a likely landing zone, and Maklin adjusted his course accordingly. As they grew nearer, Maranath could make out what appeared to be corpses on the debris-strewn ground below, as if some battle had occurred.

He decided to have a look, and dropped the last twenty feet to the cobbles, hitting the ground with enough force to crack several stones beneath him. Maklin followed, landing gently a few seconds later, shaking his head. "No women here to impress, unless you've lost some pieces lately."

Maranath chuckled softly. "We don't know *who* is around, do we?"

Maklin conceded the point with a grunt. "True, that." He

kicked at the bones at their feet. "This fellow seems a bit thin for a guard."

Maranath could not restrain a snort of laughter. "I suppose it saves on the boarding costs, eh?"

Maklin laughed back then abruptly stopped as something caught his attention. He gestured at an actual corpse. "He's here, Maranath."

At first, Maranath saw nothing untoward. The corpse was too decayed to see many details, but Maklin was insistent, spinning his finger around in a 'hurry up' gesture. Maranath looked closer, and gasped in surprise as he recognized the symbol of a spiked fist hanging from the dead man's neck. "Mei! The cultists!"

Maklin nodded, his expression grim. "We need to move. We have no idea where they are, but we know where they're going. Let's hope the moat held them up long enough."

"We don't *know* anything!" Maranath shot back. "Except that the Southlander has the last piece, and he has not yet arrived. I think we're fine." *Mei! How could they have moved so quickly! They shouldn't have been able to beat us here!*

"I suppose I'm a bit jumpy, but better safe than sorry," Maklin said. He pointed to the central pyramid. "We need to get in *there*."

"Just my thoughts." Maranath looked back at the corpse, realizing now that there were several more in various states of disrepair, scattered across the courtyard. "Filth! We should have chased them down and killed the lot of them when we had the chance!"

"We'll see to them next. For now, we have other business," Maklin said. He lit off, skimming a few feet above the moat, toward the central pyramid.

Maranath was just about to follow him when he saw the water in the moat stir. *Mei, there's something alive in there!* "Beneath you!" he shouted.

Maklin looked down at the water, his eyes growing wide with shock, and shot upward with barely a moment to spare. A slick, mottled tentacle whipped through the space he had just fled, sending a spray of stagnant water into the air. It lashed back and forth briefly as if in frustration, then slowly sank back beneath the putrid surface.

Maklin called down from above, "Still spry as a mongoose!"

Maranath laughed and called back, "You'd be a mongoose breathing water if I hadn't warned you!"

"Oh, stop bragging and do something useful, would you? It's still alive, you know."

Maranath shrugged and pushed off with his toes toward Maklin, making certain he skirted high above the moat. "It can stay alive as far as I'm concerned. It keeps idiots from meddling, and it's no threat to us now that we know about it."

Maklin considered it a moment, then nodded agreement and set off for the central pyramid.

At the top of the massive structure was a large, single story watchtower, heavily constructed of iron and showing not the least bit of decay. Maklin landed at the door to the building and entered.

Maranath followed, noting as he landed that the surface seemed odd. "What *is* this thing made of?"

Maklin looked briefly at the odd stone. "Looks like... crushed seashells or something. Who cares? Look at this!" He pointed at a huge grate in the floor.

Maranath saw nothing particularly interesting about it, beyond the fact that they would need to get through it. It was dark below, until he decided it wasn't. It was clearly the way they needed to go. Maranath grunted.

Maklin scowled. "Unimpressed, are we?"

Maranath shrugged. "Do you have a point?"

"Well, go on then, open it."

He said it as if it were a challenge, which Maranath found quite suspicious. "What are you not telling me?"

Maklin scoffed. "Oh, nothing. It's a simple grate to a simple mind. Go on, then. Chop chop."

Maranath, now convinced there would be some sort of explosion, gingerly reached for the grate and pulled experimentally. No fireworks ensued, but neither did the grate budge. He pulled harder, to no effect. *Fine, it's not quite normal, then.* Mentally, he pictured the grate as wet noodles, and twisted at it, fulling expecting it to comply.

Maklin barked laughter as nothing happened.

Maranath straightened up with a wince and scowled at Maklin. "While you're gloating, why not educate me, too?"

"Oh, I'm getting to that," Maklin tittered. He held out a moment longer, then confessed, "It's charged, and quite heavily. It must be nigh invulnerable. Incredible craftsmanship. I've never seen such an amazing piece of work. The whole place is like this."

Maranath was in no mood for such ribbing. "We've just come from arguing with a dragon. One has to keep his perspective."

"I wasn't awed by the power of it, you old coot! I was awed by the beauty!"

Maranath scoffed. "Here's an idea. Why not be awed by the beauty of a woman sometime, eh? It would do you wonders."

"Bah, waste of my time."

"Probably too old to do much more than look anyway, eh?"

Maklin looked wounded, but seemed in no mood to surrender. "Are we really having a discussion about my mechanical parts here? I can show you things work just fine, if that's what we're doing! Give me a month or so and I could probably improve on your shoddy design, too!"

Maranath shook his head and chuckled. "No, let's be about our business before a certain woman arrives."

Maklin cackled. "We're neither one of us going to be awed by her beauty, I'll tell you that."

Maranath was about to respond when he was interrupted by what sounded very much like screams. The sounds were distorted, echoing off Mei only knew how many walls, but Maranath was certain they were screams. "Mei! It sounds as if someone's being tortured!"

Maklin's humor had also fled. "That's the rumor, you know."

Maranath looked past the grate, seeing only shadows, then realized there was a light source somewhere below. The details slowly resolved themselves, and he could see a set of spiral stairs leading down into the heart of the pyramid. "Do you have any idea where we're going, or are we just going to stumble along blindly until we're eaten by whatever monsters reside down here?"

Maklin waved a hand. "I'm not worried about 'monsters'. What were you just saying about perspective?" He bent to study the grate more closely.

"They managed to kill Lothrian."

Maklin shrugged, still absorbed with the grate. "A hundred years ago. Are you anywhere near the weakling you were a century back?"

"Even so, you didn't answer the question. Do you have any idea where to go?"

Maklin's face lit as he found some mechanism only he could see and activated it. "We'll go 'in', won't we? It wouldn't be much of a fortress if it didn't surround the interesting parts."

Maklin hauled on the grate, a triumphant look on his face, and came to a sudden, jerking stop. As Maklin's face fell like a disappointed child's, Maranath cackled briefly and sniped, "You were saying?"

Maklin gave Maranath a dirty look. "I was saying there must be some other way in, I think."

Maranath snickered. "Let's hope so." He pointed to a flight of stairs off to the side of the room. The large iron gate that allowed entrance to the stairwell stood open, which Maranath counted as fortunate. *It's probably warded, too.* "That seems as likely as anything else."

Maklin started that way. "It's not like we have any choices."

They descended the staircase in relative silence, broken only by Maklin's constant hacking and spitting. The light source was invisible, but moved with them, a fact Maranath found interesting but not surprising. It was a fairly normal occurrence from his viewpoint.

The stairs were quite long, with a number of switchbacks. By the time they reached the bottom, Maranath estimated they were several hundred feet to the side of the pyramid center. To some degree, he was relieved by the notion. *Surely, if there is a welcoming committee, it would be at the bottom of that spiral staircase.* He paused there, tugging on his beard, thinking. *Well, unless the open gate was part of a trap.*

Maranath put the notion out of his mind. Trap or no trap, he intended to move forward, and anyone in his way was going to have one remarkably bad day if he had any say about it. He stepped out of the stairwell, gesturing for Maklin to follow.

The pair found themselves in a large, open antechamber. It took a moment for the light to fill the room, but when it did, they both gasped in unison: "Mei!"

At the far end of the room, within a glass display case, a figure stood motionless atop a small, stylized ziggurat, his face contorted in fury. Light from somewhere within the ziggurat shone upward to shade his high cheekbones and sharp features into something almost demonic. His long, blond hair and blue robe were frozen in place, posed to appear as if they were streaming behind him, blown by a fiery wind as his mad, blue eyes gazed balefully down at his victims. Beneath his foot was a figure from a nightmare, a tentacled, twisted distortion of a man. It clutched at its neck, as if it were being strangled by the first figure's boot. More perverse, tentacled corpses, dozens even, lay sprawled along the ziggurat tiers, some burned almost to ash, others slashed and in one case decapitated. Behind the blond sorcerer, a single monstrous creature stood poised with a spear, ready to run him through.

Maklin gaped at the display, then turned the Maranath, his eyes blazing. "What in Mei's name is this, then?"

Maranath took a deep, shuddering breath before speaking. "Art. They revere pain." He craned his neck to get a better view. "From what Ariano told me, they're quite serious about it."

Maklin looked back at the art for a moment, then turned back to Maranath and snorted. "I believe I mentioned that upstairs." He pointed to the figure atop the ziggurat. "This one seems out of place."

Maranath glared at him. "Stop it."

"Stop what?"

"You know what!" Maranath shouted. "Stop pretending like you don't recognize him!"

Maklin started to speak, then stopped, looked at the central figure on the ziggurat, then spat on the ground. He turned haunted eyes toward Maranath and hissed "It's *not* him!"

"It damned well *is*!"

Maklin sputtered briefly, shaking his head in disbelief. "But it's *madness*!"

Maranath nodded as he stepped up to the display case and began to brush dust from an engraved bronze plate. "It is, indeed. But that doesn't change facts."

Both of them read the text of the plate in silence and growing horror.

Victory and Defeat: This monster told us his name was Lothrian before he was at last defeated, and so I note it here. He was a juggernaut that only death could stop. Because of this, he suffered very little before he died, and could not be made into art in the conventional sense. I decided to create this piece because Lothrian brought me the worst agony of my existence, and I knew his beauty must be preserved. Three of my own brothers died in the battle against him. I used their bodies and several others who were close to me to complete the work. My eldest brother lies beneath his heel. This scene does not show the true havoc he wrought. Forty-seven of us were slain before we finally managed to overwhelm him.

CHAPTER 13

ELGAR'S WRATH

IUL made his way along the wall, the single torch his only light, trying to build a map in his head. The chamber was octagonal, and similar in construction to the smaller pyramids, but vastly larger, at least a hundred feet across. Circumnavigating the room, he found hatches, like the one they had entered, on each of the other walls, leading to passages that were, likewise, all too familiar. *At least they weren't collapsed and flooded.*

He and Logrus would have to make a decision on which exit to use, and Logrus had a better head for direction. *Hopefully, he's up to the task.* Whichever they chose, it would need to be soon: the torch would burn out before long, trapping them in the darkness. Aiul did not think much of their odds of survival should that happen

It had taken quite some time to make the complete circuit, and Aiul had found nothing even remotely useful to bind Logrus's ribs. *I'll have to use his pants leg, I suppose.*

As Aiul neared his starting point, the hiss of the torch loud in his ear in the otherwise silent, tomb-like chamber, he felt a brief surge of terror as a figure loomed out of the darkness. His fear faded quickly as he realized it was merely Logrus. *It's easy to get jumpy down here.*

Aiul shook his head in amazement at his companion's resilience as he closed the distance between them. "I told you I needed to bind it before you walked," he admonished, and immediately felt foolish. Now that he was closer, the torchlight told him a different story. Logrus was most definitely not well, and seemed to barely notice Aiul's presence. He was trembling violently, whipping his head back and forth, and muttering beneath his breath.

Logrus came to a sudden stop, shook his head violently back and forth several times, and clutched at his chest with a wretched wail, as if he were being stretched on a rack. "Elgar, my lord, it is too much! Take this from me!"

"What?" Aiul shouted, starting toward him in alarm. He grabbed Logrus by the shoulders and gently turned him, trying to get his companion to focus. "What happened?"

Logrus stared at him with mad, uncomprehending eyes, and gibbered incoherently between ragged breaths. Tears streamed down his face, mixing with saliva trickling from the corners of his mouth and into his beard.

Aiul shook his head in utter disbelief at the timing. *Here, of all places!* He pulled at Logrus, trying to lower him to the ground, but the hunter was stiff as a corpse, all of his muscles rigid with strain.

Aiul tried a different tack. "I think you're having a heart attack," he told Logrus, struggling to keep his voice calm. "I need to you lie down."

"Fool!" Logrus snarled, twisting in Aiul's grasp. He hammered his own fist into his broken ribs, and, with a gurgling grunt, collapsed to the floor, insensate. Aiul felt panic rise within him as he struggled to decide on a course of action.

The physician stepped forward in his mind and demanded

calm, explained that, for the moment, Logrus was still among the living, and that only a cool head could ensure it remained so. Aiul smiled at the knowledge that the physician was not, after all, dead. He had merely been sleeping until he could be of some use.

Aiul went through the process by the book, counting, categorizing, comparing, but in the end, he was baffled. There was nothing obvious beyond the broken ribs. Logrus was pale, covered in sweat, and semi-conscious. His temperature was close to normal, perhaps a little high. His breathing was irregular, his pulse strong but fast.

Pain could account for the color, but the sweat was a clue. It looked very much like a heart attack, but the pulse did not match. *Punctured lung and internal bleeding, or a stroke maybe?* If it were internal bleeding, Aiul had very little time to reach a decision and intervene, but considering the location and circumstances, almost any course he chose would have poor chance of success. He checked Logrus's pulse again, and fancied it seemed a little hard and fast, which made him lean toward internal bleeding, but he wasn't confident enough to cut the fellow open yet. *Maybe he can tell me.*

"Not what you think," Logrus croaked, as if reading his mind.

"Keep talking, Logrus," Aiul said, and squeezed his shoulder. "Stay with me. Tell me what you're feeling."

Logrus voiced a low, bestial whine. "Hate," he whispered.

Aiul blinked at this unexpected answer, but nodded as if it were understandable and continued, "I mean physically."

"Pain."

"Where?"

Logrus's eyes snapped open, glaring and, for the moment, perfectly lucid. *"Everywhere!"*

Aiul found himself taken aback by the sudden display of emotion. Up to now, Logrus had been as placid as a frozen lake, absolutely unflappable. *Something is very wrong, and I have no idea what!* That alone was enough to bring panic surging again, but it was at least a familiar panic, well-known terrain he had walked many times before. *Sometimes, there's nothing you can do, but you keep trying until you can't anymore.* He worked to make his voice as soothing as possible as he spoke. "I know it's difficult, but help me help you. Take a deep breath and try again."

Logrus, eyes wide, glared at him a moment, then drew in a great, ragged breath and let it out again. It seemed to help. The tension in his muscles eased a bit, and his eyes seemed to focus. "Flame burning me," he mumbled. "My head being sawed open. Cracking my chest with some kind of vise. Cutting at my heart."

Mei, it's a stroke. That would explain this sort of sensory malfunction. Aiul struggled to keep his own fear from overwhelming him. There was little he could do if his suspicion were true. "No," Aiul told him, keeping a comforting hand on Logrus's shoulder. "That's not happening. You're safe. Do you know where you are?"

"Not to me," Logrus gasped. "To *others*. Here. In Torium."

"Take your time," Aiul told him. "Try to focus."

Logrus's eyes snapped open and he raised his head, staring at Aiul in blind fury. "My gift, fool!" he hissed. He let his head fall back to the floor. "Wait. Just wait."

Aiul did so for many long, confused minutes, keeping watch of Logrus's condition, which seemed to improve by the second. At last, Logrus sat up, buried his face in his hands, and began to sob. Aiul simply waited. After a while longer, Logrus rose to his feet and wiped his sleeve across his wet face. "Come with me," he said, his voice thick with emotion. "I need light."

"Not much left of it," Aiul noted grimly as he followed Logrus into the dark center of the room. "I saw some doors on the far walls. Maybe there's a way out. If we don't find something soon…"

"I know," Logrus answered. "But we must do this. Then we can leave."

Aiul stopped and gave Logrus a wary look, feeling a cold chill slowly creeping up his spine. *This isn't something medical. This is something to do with Elgar.* "Tell me."

Logrus shook his head and beckoned for Aiul to follow. "You'll see. Just ahead."

Aiul hesitated as the fear in his gut grew, but he pushed it down and moved forward, knowing somehow, without having been told, that he had no choice, that this was the reason they had come. His anxiety surged again as more figures loomed in the darkness, but he quickly realized that they were merely statues.

Hundreds of them, in as many different poses, stood arrayed in the center of the huge room, each unique. The flickering light from Aiul's torch played over the still forms as Logrus and Aiul approached, sending shadows skittering over floor and statues alike in a slow retreat from the advancing flame. Aiul marveled at how lifelike the statues were, how well-proportioned and anatomically correct, but he felt a strange disquiet, as well. *There's something odd about the poses.*

Five feet from the nearest, he realized what was troubling him. The statues were obscene depictions of men, women, even children, in unspeakable agony. They were incredibly lifelike, detailed as well as any of the books Aiul had studied in his surgical training. Missing limbs showed bone and muscle beneath. Open chests showed the organs all in their proper locations. The artist may have been twisted, but his skill was unquestionable. He had captured the very essence of horrifying death and chiseled it into his art, over and over, and none the same.

Aiul almost whispered when he spoke. "Mei! What madness drives a man to work such things into stone?"

Logrus shook his head slowly, his face trembling. "They are

not stone," he said, his voice a cold monotone, fists balled at his sides.

Horror gnawed at Aiul's guts as he moved forward for a closer view. "What are you saying?" He reached out to one of the statues, a man with a face contorted in horror, his head rent nearly in two by a huge gash that showed exposed brain. As Aiul's finger made contact, his mouth filled with a coppery taste at the feel of pliant flesh, the tacky, cold sensation of wet, dead blood, and a bolt of pure agony tore through his head. He jerked his hand back, recoiling as he suddenly understood that this was, as Logrus had just said, not a statue at all, but a real human, somehow preserved like this! The world seemed to spin wildly about him as he staggered away, close to hyperventilation. He could *feel* the wrongness, the monstrous evil of it, as if it were a physical force weighing him down. His knees buckled, and he sank to the ground, retching and struggling not to vomit.

"So you have it, too," Logrus said. "Weaker, like my zombies. But you have it."

"Yes," Aiul moaned, wiping at his mouth as he struggled to his feet. "As soon as I touched it. Mei, how can you stand it?"

"It is necessary." Logrus glared at the garden of corpses. "This one," he said, pointing to a child's body. "He died screaming, begging not for his own life, but that they spare his mother." The hunter choked back a sob, and pointed to a woman. "This one, they forced to watch as they cooked and ate her husband. They made her eat of him, too." He covered his face with his hands, as if to ward away the visions. "They are all like this. *All* of them."

Aiul ran a hand over his now sweating scalp with an involuntary shudder. "How can the gods let such things occur?" he asked.

Logrus turned a grim stare to him, his eyes black in the near-darkness. "Has not a god sent us here?"

Aiul's reply died in his throat at the sound of hatches opening and closing in the distance, the echoes reverberating throughout the subterranean structure. For long moments, they listened for more, the dripping of water and the hiss of the torch loud in their ears, and then came another sound, a shuffling, something large approaching.

A figure out of a nightmare loomed from the darkness. It was fully ten feet tall, and shaped like a man, but there the resemblance ended. Its overlong arms, proportioned more like those of an ape than a human, ended in razor sharp talons. It had no neck to speak of, merely a misshapen mound atop impossibly broad shoulders. Two beady, reptilian eyes stared from the gnarled head. Others, arranged seemingly at random about its body, rolled in their sockets or cut back and forth in paranoia. A snakelike tongue slipped in and out of a jagged-fanged maw, testing the air. More mouths, smaller, but no less vicious, dotted its body at irregular intervals, their tiny teeth chattering and gnashing at the air. Small tentacles erupted from unlikely areas and whipped about the creature, as if it were flagellating itself. Muscle rippled beneath black, putrescent skin as the thing approached them.

"Playthings," it spoke, its words a sickening, burbling rumble. "You are fortunate. My master wishes you to live." It beckoned to them with a filthy claw. "For now." Its laughter was the hacking of a man dying from tuberculosis.

Logrus's face twisted into a mask of hatred and fury as he charged the creature, a cry of abandon on his lips.

Aiul hesitated only a moment before hefting the hideous black mace and joining him, shouting Elgar's name as a battle cry. *This is pure madness.*

And yet it was the right sort of madness.

In its sanctum, the Master watched the scene in the pool, frustrated but amused. What could these playthings be thinking? It was interrupted from its musings by a thunderous rumbling as a shockwave tore through the foundations of Torium, sending ripples over the image and turning it to blackness once more.

Annoyed, the thing poked a claw at the surface, and screamed. It drew back quickly, but the black liquid crept upward, dissolving talon and flesh, leaving only exposed bone in its wake. It took half of the finger before it lost its potency.

The surface of the pool was smooth as glass, now. The thing stared at it in a mad fury, and roared, "I have your book! A thousand years I have kept it! I will have my due!"

The surface of the pool shifted and bubbled, rising to form a contemptuous, hate filled face. The lips parted to speak a single word: "*Fool.*" The room resonated with the sound of Elgar's voice.

"I will rend you!" the Master shrieked. "I have the book! I *wrote* it!"

"*You no longer understand it,*" the face in the pool rumbled. Dust fell from the ceiling as the words battered the stonework.

The Master tore at its own flesh in a frenzy of rage and growing terror, its claws leaving deep trenches in its mottled, scabrous hide.

"I am the Master of Torium!" it keened. "I will rend your playthings! And I will rend *you*, too! You will see!"

The face spoke once more, again a single word, but one full of power: "*Fear.*" More dust rained down as the sound burned along the thing's nerves like fire.

The Master screamed in impotent rage as the face sunk back into the pool, leaving the surface once again calm.

The servant was fleeing. It could not really say why. Logically, it should turn upon its pursuers and rend them, but logic was a very small voice in its mind. Fear roared in its ears, drowning out the tiny whisper of reason.

There were other sounds, too. A thousand wails of terror and misery pierced the thing's mind in an unrelenting assault. They were familiar shrieks of agony; pleas for mercy; wretched, plaintive, damned cries wrenched from the broken and dying bodies of those who became art. Torium had, at times, resounded with such echoes, and the thing had been pleased. Now, they battered the inside of the thing's skull, and he cried out himself to please another. It was not fair. It was not the proper order of things.

"Mercy!" the thing wailed, over and over, as it fled in blind panic from its relentless pursuers. They did not answer, but the thing heard their reply, still, in a horrific, multi-sensory assault: "*Never!*"

It fled onward, dogged at every step. It had to reach the others. They would protect it. Full of desperate hope, it headed for friends. They were many. When it was with them once again, the fear would pass, and they would rend these fiends, these *monsters* the Dead God had set loose upon them.

It came, after much running, upon its brethren, a group forty strong. They roared questions at it, and the thing tried to explain, to tell them of the Dead God's harriers, but no words would come. Panic clenched the thing's throat like a vise. Only one word was possible.

"Mercy!" it cried, trembling in abject terror.

One of the others moved toward it, tried to restrain it. Fear exploded within the servant's chest like lighting striking a tree. It could not be restrained! It *must* not be restrained! It had to flee!

The servant struck out, frenzied, desperate to escape. Twisted flesh and blood splattered over the stones. The other, too, began to scream. The other, too, felt the fear now. In the servant's mind, the other sounded just like the works of art.

The rest gathered around the two screaming things, confused, trying to calm them, to understand the alarm, but the fearful ones could not express it, save to scream and lash out. With each blow landed, another thing took up the cry, the terror. Pleas for mercy pierced the fetid air of Torium, echoing down the corridors and passageways, but it would not raise an alarm. Such cries were common, a kind of music. How could any of them know the truth?

The servant felt claws rending its flesh. It responded in kind, desperate to survive.

"Mercy!" it begged again, joining the chorus of similar cries from its fellows as they slashed and battered at one another. It fought on through blinding agony and crippling terror. Mercy, at last, came in the form of eternal darkness.

Aiul and Logrus chased the thing for some time, through countless interconnected rooms, all with the same curious hatches, all with the same hideous décor. They would have chased it to the end of the world, so strong was their impulse, but their bodies were simply incapable of keeping pace with the creature's huge strides. By the time they admitted this unpleasant truth to themselves, they were hopelessly lost within the depths of Torium, and completely spent.

Aiul slowed to a stop and paused with his hands on his knees, panting, as Logrus struggled against pain and exhaustion to catch up.

"He's gone," Aiul gasped. Logrus nodded, for once having reason to spare words, and lowered himself to the cold, damp stone of the floor with a grimace. For long moments, they said nothing, as they caught their breath.

Then came the screams, guttural, rumbling, more than a little like roaring, but definitely screams for all that. At first, they assumed it was the thing, doubling back, but it became more and more clear that there were multiple sources of the cries.

Aiul looked about, considering their situation, and realizing it was, indeed, grim. He had no idea how to retrace his path, and no way to determine what constituted forward. "Which way?"

Logrus pointed in the direction of the screaming. "Can you feel it?"

Aiul tried to open himself to whatever Logrus was tapped into, but to no effect. "I'm too tired to feel anything."

Logrus clapped a hand against Aiul's back, his eyes wide with newfound energy. "Elgar!" he said, his voice reverent. "I feel his presence!"

Aiul felt a surge of hope. "The blood? Is it near?"

A grin spread across Logrus's face. "It must be."

Invigorated, they set off, following the screams, trusting to Logrus's sense to guide them. It was yet another trek through the horrific chambers of Torium, but the sense of hate and horror the place inspired ebbed as they progressed. Aiul could feel it now, too, a low throb of menace and comfort. Elgar *was* here, or at least a part of him.

The screams stopped after a while. Soon after, the two found both the source and the reason for the silence.

Dozens of twisted corpses littered the room, all variations on the theme of the one Torian they had seen, but each unique. The floor was slick with black, putrescent ichor, and the reek of rot and death made Aiul gag.

A few of the mutilated creatures still lived, twitching and wheezing as life seeped from them. One cut its eyes toward them and rasped, "Mercy."

Logrus spat on the dying thing. "I have none for you."

As pleasant as the scene was, Aiul knew there was no time to rejoice. Already, he could hear roars echoing about them from all directions, cries of fury, not fear. "Reinforcements," he said. "I don't think these will run."

"No," Logrus agreed. "We are near now. Elgar has cleared the way for us. That is all we can hope for."

Aiul licked his lips, doing his best to crush down his rapidly mounting terror, to control it enough to allow him to act rationally. "Let's go, then!"

They set out at a dead run, the roars of the approaching creatures growing louder, as despair began gnawing at Aiul's mind. By his reckoning, they were headed directly for their enemies. His fears were confirmed as they ducked through another hatch, and burst into a chamber of unprecedented size.

The place was large enough to hold a small village, an enormous cavern that rose at least fifty feet above their heads. The rough-hewn ceiling was buttressed to support its own massive weight. A titanic spiral stair rose from the floor, ending in massive, iron doors set into the stone ceiling. Beams of sunlight poured from windows near the top of the chamber, filling the room with twilight.

Aiul felt his stomach churn when he saw what the cave contained. A legion of tortured, damned souls, frozen in their final moments of agony and horror, dotted the vast plain before them, thousands of victims on display like exhibits in a colossal, ghastly museum. And in the shadows, all around them, the hulking shapes of more things, hundreds of them, advanced in a slow shuffle, teeth gnashing and tentacles whipping, a low, hideous chant of hate and hunger rumbling from their many lips.

Aiul's muscles wavered like jelly. *This is the end.*

"There!" Logrus cried, and gave him a shove forward.

Aiul stared ahead, numb, eyes slowly focusing on a deeper darkness within the gloom. The structure was squat and rough-hewn, as if the rest of the cavern had been carved out around it. A faint, liquid glimmer shone from what appeared to be an opening in the near side.

Aiul had no reason to believe it offered safety, but he ran for it anyway, hoping Logrus was right. The Torians continued shuffling toward them, slowly but inexorably tightening their circle, in no hurry at all. Were they still afraid, Aiul wondered? *Or, perhaps, they simply know it is a dead end, and are savoring the hunt.*

The entrance to the central chamber was yet another set of the huge, rune-graven doors they had encountered. These, too, stood wide, as had the entrance to the city above. Aiul and Logrus charged headlong past them, and into the room beyond, the hundreds of hideous things still shambling after them in slow, relentless pursuit.

The chamber in which they found themselves was an enormous room rather than a small town, a meeting area for the inhabitants, perhaps. No seats or other furniture broke the monotony of the carved stone interior, but in the center stood a large stone basin filled with dark liquid, and piles of stone debris lay in random places about the black granite floor. The pool, black as crude oil, glowed with a cold, dim light that filled the room. It was large enough for a dozen or so men to bathe in, at least ten feet across, and surrounded by a ledge of inlaid, rune-graven stone. Four long, sloped trenches, carved into the lip, ran from the cardinal points like tributaries.

Aiul turned back to the doors, desperate to find a way to close and bar them. A brief, panicked search of the wall yielded a hopeful sign, a huge, steel lever, blackened with eons of accumulated filth. He hauled on it with his full weight. Gears ground, and the doors began to close, finally coming together with a resounding clang.

Aiul heaved a sigh of relief just as Logrus began to scream.

Aiul spun on his heel, and froze, slack jawed at the horror before him.

How it had hidden itself, Aiul could not guess. The creature was half again as large as the others they had encountered. There were clear similarities, but there was *more* of everything: more teeth, more arms, more tentacles. Its head nearly scraped the darkened ceiling twenty feet above, and its mouths chattered and dripped saliva as it regarded Aiul with yellow, hate-filled eyes.

In one taloned hand, it gripped a huge, leather bound tome. The book seared the beast's flesh where it touched, filling the room with the scent of burning meat. In another claw, it held Logrus aloft in a vise-like grip, squeezing the life from him.

The thing made a rumbling noise akin to a chuckle, and lashed out at Aiul with a thick, ropy tentacle. The force of the blow knocked the breath from Aiul and sent him to the floor, stunned.

"You will suffer for this!" Logrus howled, drawing more laughter from his captor.

"No," it hissed. "*You* will suffer." It raised a single talon and slashed at Logrus's leg. Blood fountained from the wound, and the thing crooned in pleasure.

"The book rends me," it complained, glancing at its blistering hand. "But I will use it still!" It held Logrus at eye level and leered at him. "The blood of Elgar's faithful is his weakness! I will steal the Dead God's power for myself, and you will be the key!"

"Fool!" Logrus cried. "You dare challenge a god?"

"I am the Master of Torium!" it roared. Logrus wailed in agony as the creature tightened its grip. "I dare *anything*!"

Aiul struggled to raise his head, his vision darkening from lack of air. At last, he regained control of his lungs. He sucked in a great, gasping breath, and called out, "Elgar! We are outmatched!"

He did not expect a response. He had not a shred of faith. But he had to try.

The surface of the pool boiled and shaped itself into a wrathful visage that spoke: "*You have all that you need. Save yourself and punish the guilty.*"

Aiul ground his teeth in fury, hating Elgar for his refusal to help almost as much as he hated himself for daring to believe. "Bastard!"

The Master cackled in glee and crushed Logrus against the lip of the pool with a tentacle, positioning him in one of the troughs on the ledge. It extended a claw and pointed it at his throat, toying with him.

Logrus glared up at the behemoth with undisguised loathing and declared, "You cannot kill me, fool."

"Scream and deny," the creature taunted. "Call out to Elgar. Your faith powers the ritual!" It slashed its talon across Logrus's chest, cutting him to the bone.

As Logrus cried out in new misery, Aiul struggled to his feet, still having difficulty breathing. His head was a ball of mud. All he knew for certain was that it was over, and they had failed. The Master was an impossible opponent. Part of him wondered idly if this had been Elgar's plan all along, to send them to their deaths here, against hopeless odds. *But why? What point could it serve?* Aiul shrugged. It was too difficult to think, and he had no weapon that could challenge the monstrous creature that stood before him. Even if he did, there were hundreds more waiting outside. *We are doomed.*

As despair filled him, weighing him down like a suit of lead, and his life passed before his eyes, he once again saw the strange symbol in his mind, an almost understood concept, and one memory loomed large over the rest. In his memory, he heard Logrus gasping, '*Great Elgar! Never before have I seen this!*'

Logrus screamed as the Master slashed him again, laying open his forearm and exposing the bone beneath.

"My gift," Aiul muttered to himself, as he sucked in a great gasp of air. Clarity rushed in with it. He staggered toward the pool, a mad plan burning in his mind

"Where do you wander, plaything?" the monster chuckled, and lashed out with its tentacle again. It hammered against Aiul's back and sent him crashing to the ground. His forehead bounced against the rim of the pool, sending blinding white bolts of lightning across his vision. He struggled to hold on to consciousness, knowing if he lost it, it would never be regained.

"You have no faith," the thing hissed at Aiul. "You are useless to me." It raised a sword-like talon and prepared to impale Aiul. *Ah, well. At least I died trying.*

Logrus, covered in his own blood, somehow found the strength to suddenly twist in the thing's grasp and kick out at its seared, ruined claw. The Master screamed in agony as the skin of its hand split and a huge chunk of its flesh slid off like beef falling from a long-cooked bone. The repulsive meat hit the floor with a sickening, liquid sound as the Master's cries continued.

Logrus shouted, his voice hoarse with effort, "Now, Aiul!"

Aiul struggled over the rim, every muscle screaming, barely able to move. The Master dropped Logrus to the floor and rushed Aiul, suddenly understanding his intent. Aiul tried to dodge the fiend's thrusting arm, but its deadly talons ripped through his shoulder, pinning him to the pool's ledge like a bug in a collection.

Aiul's heart sank as he struggled not to black out from the excruciating pain. The Master cackled in unhinged, malevolent glee as Aiul's arm fell nervelessly, flopping like a doll's, right into the Black Pool.

As his fingers made contact with the surface, Aiul felt his despair burn away like ash, forced up and out as rage and energy boiled into him like a volcanic eruption. Elgar spoke in his mind: *"I will clear the way, my servant. Avenge them."*

Time seemed to stagger momentarily, everything frozen but the oily, black liquid and the faces of Aiul and the Master. Aiul flashed his enemy a hateful grin as the blood crept up his arm, gathering speed, and made contact with the talons in his shoulder. *Fuck you. You lose!*

The Master's cackling ceased as the thing sucked in a gasp of shock and fear, but it could only watch as the liquid crept up its arm. Wherever the blood touched, the thing's flesh smoked and peeled, burning. The Master whimpered, then moaned, then let loose an unearthly scream of horror and despair as withering, ashen flame coursed and coruscated over its body. The scream rose in pitch until it was nothing but a shrill keening, a horrific sound that pierced Aiul's ears like spikes.

It went on for far too long, then stopped like the snap of a noose. Aiul smiled as the Master of Torium, seeming confused as to how things had come to this, collapsed to the floor, a heap of smoldering, charred, dead meat.

Outside, Aiul could hear the other Torians gathering, roaring in frustration and rage. A series of blows rang against the doors, and Aiul knew it would not take the creatures long to get through.

I don't really know the limits of this thing, but I am about to find out. The symbol flashed again in his vision. Aiul laughed, as he was struck with a clarity he had not known since the day Lara had died.

"'In such a moment, one might find true freedom, had he the will'" he whispered, and leapt into the pool.

He rose from the black waters, the liquid clinging to him now like a garment, and raised his hands above his head, his own vicious laughter drowning out the battering against the doors. The half-glimpsed symbol in his mind danced in his vision, fully realized. He understood it, at last, and it was beautiful.

This is why he sent us. It's not merely possible: it was Elgar's plan from the start!

"Rise!" he cried, his voice his own, but possessed of the same multi-sensory nature as Elgar's. He shouted loud enough to shake the very foundations of the mighty fortress, *"Rise and remember!"*

Aiul saw Logrus haul himself up on the edge of the black pool. The hunter gaped in shock at the audacity of Aiul's decision for a moment, then smiled and nodded in approval, as if he understood that the fight was over and they had won, even before the final battle began.

The full wrath of Elgar be upon all of you, vermin.

The first scream was a woman's. The battering against the door stopped, and the rumbles of Torian voices filled the air. Another scream came, a man's, then another, and yet another, dozens becoming hundreds and then thousands, echoing throughout Torium and merging into the chilling wail of a legion, wretched, vengeful cries.

Aiul and Logrus watched as the surface of the black pool filled with light and images. Somehow, it was showing them what was going on outside the doors. They stared in amazement as vengeance of the ages was served cold, the wrath of Elgar poured in full measure on the heads of the wicked.

The battered and broken corpses came from every corner, limping, crawling, and clawing their way forward, an army of undead the like of which the world had never seen. The Torians raised their claws in a vain attempt to fend off their former victims, but it was useless. They slashed about them, sending the nearest corpses flying, shredded, but the dead would not rest. Severed limbs groped their way forward, still full of hate, and tore at their tormentors as ever more of the dead came to have their vengeance. The Torians were quickly overwhelmed, rent, ripped, and smashed in an orgy of destruction and rage.

When it was done, the dead stood or lay as their frames permitted, some clutching at ruined family members, others sobbing quietly. There was no true joy to be seen, only grim satisfaction and weariness of soul. The image in the pool faded, and the face rose to the surface again to speak: *"Open to them. I will give them what they need."*

Aiul gave Logrus an uncertain look, and Logrus answered with a confident nod. Without a word, Aiul crossed to the door lever and hauled on it. It squealed in mild protest, but the doors opened to reveal the dead, just as they were in the images the pool had shown, still waiting for the peace that had eluded them for centuries.

"Rest, now," the face said. Without a sound, the face melted away, and the black liquid in the pool began to rise even as it retreated from Aiul, leaving him untouched once again. The pool overflowed and spilled onto the floor, the liquid seeming more alive than ever as it flowed toward the waiting figures.

Those of the dead who were capable of showing emotion smiled at the sight. Slowly, any that were standing sank to the floor and lay quietly, awaiting the black tide as it rolled in. They did not resist as it reached for them, grasped them, and pulled them down to become one with it.

Slowly, it moved across the huge room, expanding until it covered the floor as far as Aiul could see, drawing them in, melting them into itself. Aiul could not count them all, but he knew there were thousands, each part of a depraved magnum opus. The Torians had spent an eon in singular pursuit of their twisted 'art'. *All that suffering. And to think, I didn't believe there was a god to set such things right.*

At last, it was done, leaving the floor littered only with the shattered remains of the Torians, and Aiul had no problem leaving their corpses to rot. The blood began a slow retreat back to the pool, a tide of black tar rolling out. As it drew itself back into the font, Aiul called to Logrus, "We're done here. Let's quit this tomb."

Hearing no answer, he turned to see Logrus lying insensate on the floor by the pool, dead or alive, he had no idea. Aiul started for the man he had come to think of as a friend, knowing Logrus needed aid, but found he had problems of his own.

The weariness swept over him as it had each time he had exerted himself like this. Aiul swooned, knowing Logrus might well bleed out, and yet he had nothing left to work with, no energy to even move. *He's always certain he won't die. Hopefully, he's right.*

Aiul sank to his knees, then to the floor, vision darkening, and wondered idly if this were the end for both of them. As he settled on the stones, he found he could not bring himself to care it if were. He closed his eyes, drew in a deep breath, and smiled that he smelled only decay. The oppressive, palpable evil and terror of Torium had been burned away by Elgar's power, and thousands had been avenged.

If it cost us our lives, so be it. It was worth the price.

There, in the depths of Torium, for the first time since the Southlanders had come to Nihlos, Aiul found a small moment of peace.

CHAPTER 14
SOME ASSEMBLY REQUIRED

MARANATH staggered as the magical shockwave tore through Torium. "Mei!" He cast about, trying to gain some sense of what had happened, but all he knew for the moment was that it had been intense.

Maklin, too, had felt it. "That was as powerful as the one in Nihlos!"

Maranath shook his head. "They're up to something, certainly. But what..." He trailed off as his attention was diverted. "Mei! He moved!"

Maklin gave him a cautious look. "Who moved?"

"Lothrian! His hand twitched!"

Maklin scoffed and waved a hand. "Impossible. He's dead." He paused and rubbed his chin, considering. "Maybe a reaction to that wave that tore through here."

"More than a reaction!" Maranath shouted, as one of the hideous creatures lumbered to its feet and rushed the glass display case. Shards exploded in every direction as its ponderous bulk crashed into the glass and kept coming.

Maklin gave a sharp shriek and staggered backwards, arms pinwheeling to stay balanced and upright as the putrid mass of flesh lurched toward him, mouths gibbering, tentacles whipping back and forth.

Maranath felt a brief moment of panic at the sight of more creatures stirring to life, and an even greater sense that what sanity he actually had was slipping away through the cracks in the floor. *These abominations shouldn't even exist!* Yet they did, and more so, they had come back to life after being dead!

Three more of them were on their feet now, slowly finding their balance. One howled and lumbered in his direction, its putrid bulk towering over him like an angry god.

It can't be. This is some sort of trap. They are mortal, and we can kill them. He held firm to that notion as he gathered his wits and prepared to fight, but was interrupted as his assailant's 'head' imploded in a spray of gore and bone.

Again, Maranath reeled, trying to conform his mind to the reality before him. Lothrian, eyes blazing, stood behind the creature, fist clenched as if he had physically crushed the creature's head with his own hand, beaming a vicious grin of triumph.

Maklin seemed to suddenly remember he could fly and danced upward, barely avoiding the swipe of a meaty claw.

Maranath, recovered from his brief confusion, felt real anger rising within him, boiling to the surface. In a blaze of fury, he swept his hand through the air, sending a pair of the fiends flying to splatter into paste against the far wall.

"Bravo!" shouted Lothrian. He swept a hand through the air in a vicious slash and cleft another of the monsters in two.

By now, all of them were up and about. The one with a spear lunged at Lothrian, but at the last moment, Lothrian sensed him and spun. The spear caught Lothrian's robe and tore it open. In return, Lothrian backhanded him against the wall with another splatter of blood.

Maklin hacked and spat a glob of phlegm at one of the creatures. It landed in the middle of the thing's forehead and dripped down as the beast roared in fury. Maklin cackled and hovered just out of reach, taunting the thing. True to his nature, he did little else as Maranath and Lothrian shredded the remaining creatures.

When it was done, Lothrian clapped softly and laughed out loud. "Oh, well done!"

Maranath started to speak, and realized he had no idea what to say. Here stood before him his old friend, dead a hundred years, and now alive again, and not a day older than Maranath remembered him. *He looks younger than Prandil!*

As Maranath struggled to find words, his eyes picked out a few details that he had initially missed. Lothrian was deathly pale, and his rent robe showed a very obviously fatal wound beneath. *So not resurrected. Undead. Not that that's really any less strange, but at least we've seen this recently.*

After a moment of hesitation, he turned to Maklin and said, "I'll let you explain this."

Maklin lowered himself to the ground, scowling. "Me? Why me?"

"You're the one who understands how things work."

"Mechanical things, not the walking dead!"

Maranath held up both hands and made shushing noises.

Lothrian chuckled. "You two remind me of some friends of mine. I'm afraid you're mistaken, though." He gestured at the monstrous corpses. "They were very much alive, with emphasis on the past tense."

Maranath shot Maklin a glare and Maklin rolled his eyes, prompting another laugh from Lothrian.

Maklin's shoulders slumped. He hocked phlegm and spat on the ground. "Well, Lothrian, you see—"

Lothrian's reaction was immediate. He went from relaxed to a combat stance in an instant. "How do you know my name, old man? What trickery is this?"

Maklin sighed as if he simply could not be any more bored or put upon, and pointed a gnarled finger at the plaque, which was now on the floor, but face up and still legible.

Maranath said cautiously, "We did just save your life."

Maklin grunted. "In a manner of speaking, I suppose."

"I think you overstate that a bit, Grandfather. I had things under control." Lothrian looked back and forth at them and the plaque, his eyes trying to point in three directions at once. "You're clearly Meites, and that disturbs me, because I should know you, and I don't. Back up. Both of you."

Maranath stepped back and frowned. "Getting colder now."

Maklin began coughing again, and managed to gasp out, "Just read the damned thing, idiot." Maranath shot him another glare, but realized it was pointless. Maklin was basically immune to shame or any matter of civility. He would just have to play this as best he could.

Lothrian, too, stepped back, trying to read the plaque while keeping both of them in his line of sight. Maklin began to rub at his chest, as if he were trying to communicate to Lothrian that he'd spilled food on his shirt.

Maranath, struggling against the urgent need to throttle Maklin, tried another tack. "It's a bit complicated. Perhaps you should sit down for a moment, eh?"

Lothrian turned back to them as the whole of Torium filled with wails and screams, his face now so pale that Maranath couldn't believe he had been fooled into thinking he was a living man. Lothrian looked at them, eyes wide with horror, and pointed at Maranath. "What is your name?"

Maranath tried to give his old friend as kind and under-standing a smile as possible, to cushion the blow. "Maranath. And this is Maklin."

Lothrian staggered briefly, swooning and blinking rapidly as he absorbed his new reality. After a moment, he sat on one of the small ziggurat steps and cradled his head in his hands, covering his face. "Mei. How long?"

Maranath grunted. "A hundred years, give or take. Ariano hasn't been too forthcoming about what happened here, to be honest."

Lothrian looked up at them suddenly. "Ariano? She lives?"

"Prepare yourself, Lothrian. She's not the same."

Lothrian's eyes narrowed. "Was she injured? Maimed?"

Maklin shook his head, exasperated. "No, you idiot, she's old and wrinkled like the rest of us. Well, except for you."

Despite everything, Lothrian cast Maklin a glare and muttered, "The years certainly haven't improved you."

"I'm consistent," Maklin answered. "I never much liked you, either, being honest."

Lothrian offered him a sour look. "You say that as if it's some great revelation. I was well aware of that when you were young."

Maranath chuckled. "He never much liked anyone, and he was never young, he was just less old."

Lothrian voiced a soft, wry chuckle. "Well, one thing is certain. You two are indeed who you claim to be. So how came you to Torium? Please tell me there was a reason beyond mocking what obviously turned out to be my tremendous failure?" He prodded at the hole in his chest gingerly, as if expecting it to be painful, then actually spread the wound open and raised an eyebrow. "I think this goes all the way through. I can literally see light."

Maklin hacked and spat again. "You know you're a zombie now, right?"

Maranath again suppressed the urge to choke his old friend into silence. "Listen, there's a lot to talk about."

"I am *not* a damned zombie!" Lothrian shouted at Maklin.

Maranath plunged onward. "We think it's the time of the prophecy."

Maklin waved a hand. "You just said it yourself! You have a hole all the way through, man! What would *you* call it?"

Lothrian opened his mouth to shout, then closed it again and fell silent, staring at the floor for long moments. "I don't even understand what is happening."

Maranath rapped his staff against the floor with a loud crack. "That's what I am trying to explain, if the two of you would shut up long enough to let me!"

The sudden silence that ensued as Lothrian and Maklin lowered their gazes to the ground was enough to remind them of the wailing and screeching coming from somewhere nearby.

Maranath gave them both a hard look. "Yes. Listen! This is not a game! I don't know what that screaming represents, but it's *significant*, and we need to put our heads together or this may well be our last squabble!"

With both of them chagrined and quiet, Maranath was at last able to relate the events of late to Lothrian: the coming of the Southlanders, Aiul's rebellion and subsequent departure from Nihlos, their desperate battle against Elgar's minions, and their tenuous alliance with the Southlanders. "Their leader is a seer, and he's convinced it ends here, for good or ill," he finished.

Lothrian did not look up when he spoke, his voice flat and emotionless. "And Aiul?"

"He's here," Maklin said, his face and voice grave and unflinching. "We haven't seen him, but we've seen his work. It matches what he did in Nihlos. So do you."

"And the piece of the eye from Nihlos is here with him?"

Maranath nodded. "We think so. Not much point in taking it otherwise."

Maklin pointed a finger at Lothrian. "Which brings us to the next point: where is the piece you took from the dragon?"

Lothrian reached absently into his torn robe. "Gone. Not surprising, really. Surely they knew what they had."

Maranath waited a moment, expecting Lothrian to continue, but his old friend remained silent, still staring at the floor. "Lothrian, we hardly expected to find you here, but now that we have, it means something. Have you nothing to add?"

"What would you have of me?"

"You've studied the prophecy more than anyone! Surely you must have some insight?"

Lothrian looked up at him, his eyes clouded and distant, full of mistrust. "First, tell me what you came here to do."

Maklin stamped a foot. "To put a stop to this damned prophecy if we can! What do you *think* we had in mind? A picnic?"

Lothrian ignored Maklin and continued looking at Maranath. "What do you intend for Aiul?"

Maranath rubbed at his temple, a pained expression on his face. "I've promised Ariano she'll be the one to make that decision. But believe me, Lothrian, I would never harm the boy if there is any other way. He's like a son to me."

Lothrian sneered. "Is he, now? And what is Ariano 'like' to you, hmm? Did you leave me anything?"

Maklin scoffed. "I told you, she's wrinkled and old. Trust me, it's no loss."

Lothrian turned on him in fury. "It's my whole *life*, you ass!"

Maklin's jaw clenched a moment, and he shot back, "No! Your life ended *here*, by your own doing! Don't blame us for carrying on."

Lothrian accepted the rebuke, grimacing as he struggled to master himself. "I understand. No one expected this, least of all me. It will take some time to adjust."

Maranath shook his head. "Time is something we don't have. You'll have to do it on the way. Whatever dark work Aiul is up to here, he's well into it."

New anger rose in Lothrian's eyes. "Why would you have let him get so far? Why didn't you stop him?"

Maranath cast his gaze to the floor. "He traveled faster than we thought. There's a lot going on. We had other, pressing concerns, and he got ahead of us." *So, do I lie about this part, or trust him with the truth?* Maranath struggled with it for a moment, but in the end, he knew the insult of coddling Lothrian would be worse than the sting of the truth. *I needn't tell it all. The 'how' I will leave for later, after he grieves. But he has to know.* "Brace yourself, Lothrian. Not everyone you loved has survived."

Lothrian's face fell. "No," he said in a tired, weak voice, a plea rather than a statement. *He knows. It's not as if he loved many, and the rest are accounted for.*

Maranath cleared his throat and swallowed hard, the grief still fresh in his own mind. "Narelki. There was an accident. A fall. We just sent her off two days ago."

Lothrian covered his face with his hands again. When he spoke, his voice was almost too soft to hear. "She never recovered, then."

Maklin shook his head. "No one recovers, Lothrian. We kept her as comfortable as we could."

Lothrian slowly lowered his hands. "Maybe she's finally found peace, at last." He lowered his hands and rose, his grief still etched on his face, but his eyes full of resolve. "There is a reason I am here, now. I missed Narelki by days, but Aiul is still alive. We must find him at once, while there is still time."

Maklin gestured in the direction of the screams and wailing, which still echoed throughout the place. "It's a safe bet he's part of that."

Maranath cleared his throat to draw attention. As the other two faced him, he said, "Understand this, Lothrian: he didn't just come by the piece of the Eye. He took it, by force. The last time we saw him, he was immensely powerful."

Maklin nodded vigorously. "Blades turned off him. He punched through six inches of steel. And he was raising the dead as zombies. Just like you, here." He paused a moment, then muttered, "Well, no, they were mindless. But I suspect this is his doing, even so."

Lothrian looked back and forth at them as Maranath added patiently, "We're trying to say he may be more than a match for us. Don't take him lightly. If we can talk him down, it might not be just for his benefit, understand?"

Lothrian's eyebrows nearly rose from his head at this news. "I will take that under advisement."

Maranath grinned. "Good. Now, let's see what all that caterwauling is about."

CHAPTER 15
BREAKING AND ENTERING

RITHARD and Ahmed arrived once again at House Tasinal's mystery building just as the sun was slipping below the horizon. Rithard had been fairly charged with adrenaline for some time since his encounter with Slat, but the journey through the Undercity and the chill of the deepening evening had conspired to rob him of his lovely energy. Now, his teeth were almost chattering, both from cold and sheer nerves, as he oiled the sticky lock with a small oilcan. "Stay close. No telling who will take an interest in us now."

"I'm taking off this stupid robe," Ahmed replied. "I am here legally now, yes?"

Rithard, working by the dim orange light of the cloud cover, nodded absently as he inserted the key and applied pressure. It gave with a slight squeal, and he worked the mechanism back and forth to distribute the oil. "It's not as if there are any guards here, anyway."

"Wrong," called a voice from behind.

Ahmed's hand shot toward his blade, but Rithard put a restraining hand on his arm and said, "It's Caelwen."

Ahmed relaxed as Caelwen stepped from the growing shadows, leading his horse. The beast whinnied and stepped forward, hooves clopping loud on the cobblestones. "It took you long enough," Caelwen noted.

Rithard scowled at his friend. "Mei, how long have you been there spying on us?" Why didn't you say something sooner?"

"I was finishing up a piss, if you must know. You've only been here ten seconds."

Rithard continued working with the lock, not bothering to look up. "Why are you even here? Surely there are drunks who need minding?"

"Indeed, which is why I came."

"Oh, foul! Why are you *really* here?"

"I was looking for Ahmed when I started out, but Slat explained to me you'd gone mad, so I thought I had better look in on you."

Ahmed laughed out loud. "So the police are looking for me?"

"Worse," Caelwen answered. "The Meites are, specifically Ariano, and I don't think she has your health in mind. The Empress and I sent her off on a wild goose chase, but I have no idea how long that will last or what she plans next. I'm certain she will be in a bad mood, though."

Rithard turned the key back and forth again and removed it from the lock, satisfied with his work. He gestured to his new blade. "Slat called *me* mad? Did he tell you he's armed me?"

"Mei! That ought to be grounds to arrest him right there," Caelwen said. He looked at Rithard's belt, then shook his head. "Too dark to see it well. Didn't you think to bring a torch?"

Ahmed raised a hand. "One of us did."

Rithard sighed. "I am neither drunk nor a lackwit. I was well aware we had torches, so I saw no need to duplicate the effort. I'll leave the hauling to you burly apes." He raised his medical bag like a trophy. "I brought the important gear."

Ahmed's torch flared as Caelwen gave Rithard a sour look.

"Maybe you should have drank more. It would improve your mood."

Rithard snickered. "The Southlander takes a joke better than you."

"He'd have no qualms about killing you, if it came to that. Me, I'd have to fill out the reams of paperwork, so bitching is more economical." Caelwen shook his head. "'Apes'," he muttered under his breath.

Ahmed banged his fist against his chest and grinned at Caelwen. "There is no honor in beating madmen. They are touched by Ilaweh."

Rithard pushed the gate open with a grating squeal and applied oil to the hinges as well, studiously ignoring his companions' barbs. He swung it back and forth, pleased with the silent motion, dropped the oilcan into his medical bag, and gestured forward with a flourish. "We've a mystery to solve, gentlemen!"

Ahmed followed the two Nihlosians into the complex, making certain to close the gate behind himself. *As Rithard pointed out, the last thing we need is to be surprised here by bandits.* They left Caelwen's mount tethered inside the gate and went in on foot.

Ahmed smiled, listening to the other two banter as they made their way around the building exterior and back to the door they had found earlier. Rithard was prickly as a cactus, which was normal for him, but Ahmed found Caelwen's nature much changed. Gone was his customary formal tone and seemingly constant guilt and devotion to duty. The policeman was casual with the detective, short even, and not from any resentment or anger, but simply from comfort and familiarity, like a man and woman who had grown old together. *Or like Meites.*

To his amusement, Ahmed realized he had, without being

consciously aware of it, begun to think of these two as allies, friends even, instead of beasts. It seemed to him that not enough time had passed for him to learn their ways, and that only yesterday they had both seemed as alien as the screeching creatures he had glimpsed on the trip inland. Yet, he felt at ease with them, rather than tense as he would amongst barbarians.

"There," Rithard said, pointing at the door. Ahmed obliged them by placing his torch in a sconce there.

Caelwen turned to look at Rithard with a raised eyebrow. "That? I hate to tell you this, Rithard, but it's just a false door. There's nothing special about them. They're all over the place down here. The founders seemed to favor them in their architecture."

Rithard waved aside Caelwen's lack of faith and bent toward the depression. "Stay in your lane, ape."

Caelwen shook his head, a look of long suffering on his face. "It's not so much paperwork as all that. And no clever trickster to work out the sordid details, with you out of the picture. I could make it work."

Rithard snickered. "You'd make a terrible murderer, Caelwen. You'd turn yourself in." He pointed to the inscription and the depression on the door. "See that? Does it look familiar?"

Caelwen rubbed at his chin as he contemplated the strange symbols. "It does, now that you mention it, but I can't say why."

"Book of Amrath?"

Caelwen studied the alien markings for long moments. "Mei. The weird chicken scratching at the end? The joke he played on everyone?"

Rithard snorted. "I used to subscribe to that theory, too. It turns out, they *are* words."

"And you know this how?"

Rithard nodded toward Ahmed. "He can read them."

Caelwen turned a half-scowling, half-grinning face to Ahmed. "You let him maneuver me right into that."

Ahmed grinned back. "I told you, my people think madmen are touched by gods. They are to be indulged."

Caelwen looked back and forth between the two of them briefly, before finally giving in and nearly shouting, "Well? What does it say?"

Rithard inclined his head in victory. "'The key to true knowledge lies within the heart of wisdom.'"

Caelwen considered this a moment, frowning. "And so, based just on that, you smashed the thousand-year-old statue?"

"That, and finding the inscription here, yes. I presume these other false doors of which you speak have neither the inscription nor the keyhole, hmm?"

"I—" Caelwen began, then paused. "I can't really say. I don't think so."

"Rest assured, if you should see one, we'll want a look at it, but I strongly suspect this is a unique thing." He reached into his pocket and fished out the key. "Let's see what they've left for us, shall we?"

Caelwen eyed Rithard's prize with suspicion. "You call that a key?"

"A key opens a lock, does it not?"

"We have yet to establish that."

Rithard slipped the lion's head into the depression and turned it back and forth, trying to align the grooves. It settled in with a slight click. Rithard gave Caelwen a triumphant look.

Caelwen in turn gasped in shock and staggered back with a cry of pain. Rithard's smug expression faded to confusion as bright crimson blossomed from Caelwen's left shoulder.

Rithard, as usual, was slow in grasping the nature of the situation. Ahmed, seeing the shadowy figure emerging from behind Caelwen, drew his blade and lunged forward in a single motion, stabbing past Rithard's shocked face and drawing a bloodcurdling screech of agony from his target. At the very same moment, he felt a hard blow against the shield on his back. He spun, careful not to behead one of his companions, and crashed his blade into the skull of a second assailant. The man staggered backward into the darkness with a cry.

"Get the blackie!" someone shouted. "That's the one what did for Silas!"

"Add two more to my list, bitch!" Ahmed called back as he unslung his shield, though he wasn't entirely certain he had finished either of his attackers. They might well be waiting in the shadows, looking for his chance to even the score.

"Fucking Southlander! Should have killed the lot of you when we had the chance!"

Another voice, shrill with excitement, called, "Stab that cocksucker Caelwen again! Make sure he's dead!"

"Come and try it!" Caelwen shouted back. He had his own blade in hand now, and was shielding Rithard with his body, staring anxiously into the dark. Ahmed's torch was a rather pitiful light source, illuminating only a small semicircle about them, a fact that would not escape their attackers.

Rithard, close to hyperventilating, gasped, "Didn't you close the gate?"

Ahmed kept his eyes focused on the darkness as he answered. "Aye. They climbed the fence, I'd wager."

"Which means they're *very* angry with us. I told you they'd be back."

Caelwen grunted in pain, keeping his sword ready in case the attackers grew bold enough to try again. "You need to get that door open! Our asses are hanging in the wind out here."

Ahmed nodded. "Aye. They'll come again soon." He stepped to close ranks and offer Rithard as much cover as possible while the smaller man bent to work with the key and lock.

Caelwen glanced at Ahmed and licked his lips. "How many?"

Ahmed shrugged and continued peering into the darkness, seeing only vague shapes moving in the shadows near the wall, just at the edge of his vision. "Four, I think, but they are afraid. Probably waiting on friends before they try again. That buys us a few minutes."

If Rithard could open the door, he and Caelwen could fight shoulder to shoulder, and take a small band of thugs. *Out here, though...best not to think too long on it.* He offered a brief prayer to Ilaweh, asking only for strength and a respectable death if that was his will.

Caelwen checked his shoulder, frowned, and asked, "Can we run for it?"

Ahmed shook his head. "We won't get that gate open without getting hacked to pieces. May as well make our stand here."

Rithard fumbled with the key and hissed, "Mei!"

Caelwen chuckled softly. "It's not a key, is it? I told you it wasn't. I've finally won an argument with you, and I have no time whatsoever to gloat about it."

"You do recall I am armed now, yes? I could stab you a matching hole in your leg."

Ahmed dodged an incoming rock. The missile flew over his head and bounced off the bricks behind him, almost catching him in the head on the rebound. "Just get that door open!"

"I'm trying! It doesn't make any sense! It ought to—*oh! I see!*" He stabbed a finger at the key. A hollow click emanated from deep within the building.

A shoddy looking arrow thunked against the wall beside Ahmed's head. He raised his shield, trying to position it to cover most of his and Rithard's vitals, but it simply wasn't large enough for the task. Ahmed looked to Caelwen and sighed with realization.

"No armor and no shield either, eh? You were planning on dying well tonight?"

Caelwen shrugged, looking embarrassed. "I wasn't planning on a fight."

Rithard glanced at the door's seam with high expectations, but nothing seemed to be happening. "You came to the Undercity without armor?" he asked, his focus still fixed firmly on the key.

"No," Caelwen shot back. "I came to *House Amrath* without armor, to warn Ahmed that Ariano is hunting him. I wound up unprepared in the Undercity because I was silly enough to be concerned for your welfare. I apologize for that."

Rithard jabbed at the key again, and another click sounded, but the door remained closed. "Let's hope it's not your last mistake, old friend."

Ahmed shifted the shield to fully cover Rithard, knowing he was exposing himself a bit, but hoping his enemies would not be skilled enough to immediately capitalize on it. *They are waiting for overwhelming numbers.* He could hear shouting from the front of the building, reinforcements most likely.

"Not much time, now. Rithard! Turn the key!"

Rithard bit back a stinging retort. It would hardly help things, and in truth, the Southlander's lack of understanding had nothing to do with his intellect, which had actually impressed Rithard. Rather, Ahmed simply lacked information. He could not see the 'key' or the circle of nine buttons which had sprung from its surface, or it would have been obvious there was no 'turning' to be done.

At first, it had seemed easy enough to work out. *Press the first, click. Press the second, nothing. So not primes. Start over.*

One and three each click, fourth nothing, start again. Odds, then. One, three, five, seven click. Nine, nothing.

He could hear them approaching in his mind, and perhaps with his ears as well, now. *Focus, Rithard!* It wasn't odd numbers, then, but if not evens, odds, or primes, how could he work it out?

There must be a clue in the book, or written here. We were intended to find this.

"Caelwen," he said in a soft voice, hardly daring to ask what he had in mind. Caelwen was a creature of habit, so it was likely he had what Rithard needed, but if he had deviated from his routine this night, they were probably all dead men. "Give me your Book of Amrath."

He caught Caelwen's eye then, and his friend clearly thought him mad, yet he was true to form, unchanging. He carried his copy of the book everywhere he went, even to his death in the Undercity. *Perhaps especially to that.*

Caelwen reached into his shirt and handed over the tome with a resigned expression, leaving a bloody hand print on the cover. "I hope you know what you're doing."

"They're coming," Ahmed said, as if commenting on the weather.

Both warriors stiffened and closed ranks at the sound of rushing footsteps. Rithard heard as if from a long distance away the ring of metal on metal, and felt himself squeezed as his friends gave and received blows, but his focus was elsewhere.

Quickly, Rithard opened the book and paged to the end. The cryptic, foreign letters swam before his eyes, meaningless symbols. They were indeed the very last things written, as he had remembered.

And before? "Creation. Change. Liberty. Truth. Will. Mysticism. Mastery." *More philosophical drivel.*

The Southlander cried out, though whether in pain or victory, Rithard could not tell. He closed the book and drew the blade Slat had given him. *This end toward the enemy.* He raised it before his face in a halfhearted salute, and froze at what he saw.

Perhaps it was the torchlight that made it visible now. Perhaps, if one looked hard enough, it would have always been visible. Whatever the case, he could see it now clear as day, etched into the metal over and over, all down the blade: the number seven.

Seven means something.

"What does seven mean?" Rithard cried in a strangled voice.

Ahmed cut his eyes briefly in Rithard's direction, not daring to lose focus. The bookish fellow was mad again, eyes bright and burning. He had his weapon ready, though, so at least he would go down fighting.

"What does seven mean?" Rithard shouted again, his voice shrill and demanding.

"I don't—" Ahmed began.

"Numerologically!"

Ahmed blocked an incoming knife strike that would have taken out an eye had it found its mark, and slashed back, but his opponent was wily. The fellow danced back into the darkness, cackling.

We're sitting ducks, here. We're blinded by our own light, and they can choose their moment. And now Rithard wants numerology?

"Truth," he answered. "It means--"

"Yes!" Rithard nearly shrieked. "Mei, it's the damned blade's *name!* How could I have missed that? Creation, change, liberty, those are one, three and five, yes?"

Caelwen grunted as a rock whizzed through the air and caught him in the chest. Ahmed spared Rithard another glance, trying to work out if this was something useful or if the man had simply lost his mind. He *seemed* serious enough, and this look in his eyes had so far indicated he was on to something. "That would be one interpretation, yes."

"I need will, mysticism, and mastery!"

Ahmed wracked his brain as he tried with only half his attention to remember lessons from long ago. "Uh, two, eleven, and twenty two?"

Rithard sheathed his blade and began punching at the key as Wily came again, this time with two friends, one of them bald, the other sporting a patch over one eye. *White wolves, lean, fast, and hungry.* From the corner of his vision, Ahmed saw another four pressing in on Caelwen.

We can do this. He sprung at Wily and slashed hard with his blade while bashing Patch with his shield. Blood flew from Wily's throat, and teeth from Patch's shattered mouth. Before Baldy could react, Ahmed brought his blade swinging upward and sank it seep into the man's gut.

The man's scream of agony almost covered up Rithard's howl of frustration. "Wrong, Southlander!"

Ahmed, gasping for breath, pulled his sword from Baldy and stabbed Wily and Patch to make sure they stayed down as he called back, "Tell me again!"

"What? How can you not—? Mei! Will, mysticism, and mastery!"

Yazid's voice echoed in his mind: *Two is a woman's number, lazy child. Eight is for will.*

"Eight," Ahmed gasped back, staggering for the door as more thugs rushed forward. "It's eight, eleven, twenty two! This is our last chance, Rithard!"

"Oh, fuck off!"

Ahmed raised his shield and placed his back against the door as the wave of attackers charged them. Caelwen, lacking a shield, huddled as close as he could.

It is a good day to die, then.

At first, as he felt himself fall backward, he thought that was indeed what had occurred, that a sword had found its mark and his spirit had left his body. A moment later, he realized the truth: the door was open, and the way behind was clear. He looked to Caelwen, who had also grasped the situation and was now shoulder to shoulder with him. *We can hold it, if there aren't too many, if we don't get too tired.*

But the truth was, he was already tired, and Caelwen was wounded as well. Their position was better, but it was hardly unassailable. As they backed slowly into the open corridor, the number of foes became more clear. At least twenty, and that assumed there were no more outside. *They were taking no chances after this morning. They mean to kill us no matter what cost. They brought the whole gang.*

Ahmed sighed and shrugged his shoulders. He glanced at Caelwen briefly, and saw the Nihlosian knew full well how this would play out. Ahmed nodded and said, "We make them pay dearly for it."

"Oh, pay they will," called a voice from behind. It was clearly not Rithard's voice, because after all, Rithard was busy stammering unintelligibly and quite loudly. *But who, then?* Ahmed shoved the closest attacker with his shield and risked a glance backward.

Rithard was on the floor in a heap, terror in his eyes. The newcomer was tall, lean, and regal, though his dress was nothing spectacular, a simple red robe with black trim. His features were sharp, his cheekbones high, his hair jet-black and pulled tight into a pony tail that ran down his back. He might have been a kindly looking man had his face not been twisted into a cruel sneer. Ahmed focused on him, trying to see more. The air about the man seemed to dance with energy—gray, pulsing light like a pounding, raging heart, stronger than anything Ahmed had ever seen. His aura was nearly blinding. *He might be a god.*

If so, he was not a god of mercy. The stranger raised a hand in the air and clenched it into a fist in a furious gesture. Ahmed turned in horror at the sound of screams and crunching bone, to see the heads of his assailants implode, sending red and gray streamers over the floor, walls, and ceiling.

The bodies collapsed, leaving a single assailant standing, a young man, barely able to grow a beard. His blade fell from his nerveless hand as the blood pooled at his feet.

When the man in red spoke, his voice was like the edge of a knife. "I taught your fathers to stay away from here the same way, you know," he called as he approached the lone survivor, slowly, menacingly, hand still raised. "Human nature is such a sad thing. Every generation needs to learn anew, always crawling back out of the mud and dying, never actually evolving and learning to breathe."

Caelwen sank to a knee and bowed his head as the man passed, and Rithard, likewise, struck a submissive pose. *Ilaweh preserve us, they know him!*

Ahmed's mind raced at this thought, but it did him no good. Whatever knowledge they had, he did not, so for the moment, he had best follow their lead. He knelt as well, from shock as much as from anything else.

The man in red was a Meite. That much Ahmed could guess, and far more powerful than any of the elders he had seen. *He could crush us like bugs, just as he did with these fools.* In truth, Ahmed had no idea why he and his friends had been spared. Only one man was needed to deliver a message.

The Meite unclenched his fist and brushed the cheek of the remaining thug in a gentle caress. "You, perhaps, will evolve this time, yes? You'll remember my name?"

The youth stammered, his trembling so violent that he could barely form the words, but Ahmed could see there was a measure of steel to him, even so. "Tell me, and I will not forget it, by Mei."

"Good," the Meite crooned, as if soothing a terrified child. "You remember the old ways." He said nothing for long moments, drawing out the scene. Ahmed saw the brilliant aura about him grow even brighter, as if the drama of the moment somehow gave him even greater strength. "I am Tasinal. This is *mine*." He swept his arm as if to encompass the world.

More words followed, but Ahmed could not hear them over the roaring in his head.

CHAPTER 16
IMPASSE

AIUL woke with a start, to find himself in near darkness, the silence broken only by the sound of his own breathing and an intermittent dripping. *Of water? Or blood?* He spent a few long seconds disoriented, certain there had been more light, and not understanding why it had gone, before he remembered that it had come from the black pool itself. The blood had been glowing, filling the room with a strange, almost black illumination.

For a moment, panic seized him like a hand compressing his heart. Even without the Torians, Torium was not a place anyone would ever want to be stranded in the darkness. There were plenty of ways to die without being murdered by the occupants, and Aiul did not relish blindly wandering trackless passages until he collapsed from thirst or hunger. He spent a moment to steady himself, breathing deliberately, and found he could in fact see. A dim light still shone from the pool, enough to show Logrus lying where he had fallen, along with the twisted, broken corpse of the Master, still reeking of cooked, rotten meat.

In theory, the thing was dead, but given recent events, death had become a considerably more flexible state to Aiul than it had been previously. He gave the hideous creature a wide berth as he made his way across the cold stone floor toward his traveling companion. The Master's lifeless body did not stir at his passing, and Aiul breathed a sigh of relief.

Logrus could have been taken for a corpse as well, save for the subtle rise and fall of his chest. Aiul checked the several wounds Logrus had received, wishing he had more light, but even the dim illumination was enough to show they needed stitching. Blood still oozed from the rents in Logrus's flesh. *Slower now. Not good.* Aiul raised Logrus's wounded leg and propped it on a stone, tore a strip of cloth from his pants and fashioned it into a tourniquet, then did the same for Logrus's arm. *This isn't good long term, but it should keep you alive while I hunt for light.*

He found his torch lying on the stone floor beside the black pool. There was very little life left in it, and he had his doubts he could even get it to light, but it was something.

His eyes strayed to the pool as if pulled by an invisible force, and suddenly he felt the jagged rage rising in him again. *Why don't you help us? He's dying and you do nothing!*

Aiul remembered clearly the bizarre sensation of his own battered flesh mending, and watching it happen with Logrus as well. Elgar had prevented them from harming one another. He had the power. Why would he not use it now of all times?

Even as he questioned it, he knew the answer. Elgar had mentioned more than once that he was "constrained by the order of things." *Perhaps he can undo the works of his followers, but can't interfere in everything?*

Aiul was not entirely comfortable counting himself amongst Elgar's followers, yet it was difficult to deny, and in any event, was it truly such a bad thing? He had thought so up to now, but excising the Torian cancer had radically changed his perspective. *We have destroyed a great evil, and righted a great wrong. Logrus would seem to have the right of things.*

If so, then he had every right to call upon Elgar, did he not? Aiul held the cold, blackened torch up like a club and shook it at the glass-like surface of the black pool. "We're doing your will! Why don't you help us!"

Aiul felt a response, something akin to wind rustling through his hair. His torch burst into life, brilliant now in the darkness. The surface of the black pool rippled feebly, forming a barely visible face. The lips moved in time with a voice in his mind. *"Weak. Tired. Soon. Wait."*

To his great surprise, Aiul felt a pang of guilt. *Surely, after that display, he might indeed be tired.* Of course, what 'soon' might mean to a god was difficult to say. Aiul wondered if he would starve waiting on 'soon'. At least Elgar had managed to get him some light, which was his most pressing need.

Aiul wedged the torch in a wall sconce and dragged Logrus over to it, then sat next to him to tend the leg wound. It was deep, but mendable. He rifled Logrus's pockets, hoping his companion was as well prepared as he seemed to usually be, and indeed he was. Tucked away in a small bag was a packet containing needle and thread.

He probably did this sort of thing for himself a hundred times, and without the benefit of an anesthetic. Aiul bent to his task and said softly, "Well, my friend, this time you're getting the red-carpet treatment."

It took him a bit, and the task was a bit tricky, but not too much for him. *I would prefer to have some disinfectant, but we can't have you bleeding to death while we wait for it to magically appear.* He followed by stitching Logrus's arm and chest, then removed the tourniquets and considered his handiwork, pleased to see he had plugged at least the most egregious leaks. He put a hand on Logrus's forehead, noting the man was clammy, but decided it didn't really tell him much. *He has a constitution fit for an elephant.* "I prescribe rest, friend. Just keep doing what you're doing."

Aiul leaned against the cold stone of the black pool, wondering what to do next, and reached to his shoulder to examine his own wound, which was surprisingly painless. To his shock, he saw that the wound had vanished entirely. He stared at the spot where the Master had impaled him, finding it difficult to believe, even taking recent events into account. *It must have happened in the black pool.* Again, he felt a pang of guilt for his thoughts. *He would have healed Logrus, too, had he had the power.*

Aiul considered trying to haul Logrus over and toss him into the font, but given that Elgar had just specifically told him to wait, it seemed a bad idea. *So I wait.*

He closed his eyes, not really intending to sleep, but open to it if it came. He had just begun to drift off when he jolted to full alertness at the sound of voices. His belly filled with icy dread. Elgar was sleeping, and Logrus was unconscious. Whoever these intruders were, they would find Aiul helpless and alone.

Not helpless, he corrected himself. *You have killed too many of late to think that way any longer.* Quietly but surely, he reached for his vicious mace, the fist and spikes now familiar and comforting, where once they had horrified him. He rose in silence and hefted the weapon, swinging it experimentally, the dense metal feeling lighter than ever. *I am stronger, faster, better than I was.* Whatever dark power Elgar had given him, it was his now, independent of Elgar. *No, I am far from helpless these days.*

With a jolt, he remembered the ritual book. It still lay where it had fallen from the Master's ruined hand, surrounded by repulsive ichor and cooked flesh, but pristine. No trace of the disgusting creature clung to it at all, which Aiul counted as a grand blessing. Even dead, the creature was horrific, the sort of thing no one in his right mind ever wanted to be near.

Aiul found himself suddenly filled with the terrifying notion that the creature was not in fact dead, but had been feigning all along, waiting for them to be vulnerable. He knew it wasn't true, that surely it had died at Elgar's hand, but he could not resist walking over and prodding at it to be certain before he lifted the book from the stone floor.

The book was heavier than it had any right to be. It was large, yes, and bound in iron, and yet there was a weight, a density to it that seemed almost more than its mere substance. *What is this, that it is so important to him?*

Hearing the voices again, closer now, Aiul decided it was no time to contemplate such. He walked to the black pool and slowly, gingerly touched a finger to the surface, afraid he would perhaps draw back exposed bone, but the liquid felt warm and comforting. He lowered the book into it, feeling certain that it would be safe there. He drew his arms back out, unsurprised to see none of the liquid clung to him.

With a last glance at Logrus, who seemed stable for now, he again hefted his mace and moved to the entrance, hiding in the shadows to one side.

Someone will be very surprised, very briefly.

Aiul peered out at the killing field, still littered with Torian bodies, waiting, when the voices came again, but from *behind* him. He spun, shocked, realizing there must be another entrance to the room, and maddened by the acoustics of the place. *It could be coming from anywhere in this maze!*

He moved back inside the pool room and looked closely at the walls. There were indeed other entrances, one at each of the cardinal directions. *I suppose that's important, for some sort of magical reason.* The other three entrances were more mundane, simple metal doors that could be barred from the inside, but nothing like the massive primary entrance.

He opened the other doors one by one and listened carefully at each, again cursing the acoustics. He finally decided that the voices were coming from the passage directly across from the main entrance, and took up a defensive position just to the side of the entry, ready for battle.

The wait was longer than Aiul had expected. The voices had seemed nearby, and they were clearly growing closer, but they were taking their time. He was fairly certain, from the tone of the voices, that they were actually arguing amongst themselves.

Aiul continued to wait, resolved that the element of surprise was one worth maintaining, but his mind began to play tricks on him. The voices sounded familiar. One, in particular, sounded like—

Mei! Impossible!

As they rounded the corner, he was simultaneously elated and filled with deep dread, because he did indeed recognize them. Maranath and Maklin were surprising, but at least within the realm of possibility. But the third man simply could *not* be there!

He knew he should be wary for a trick in a place like this, but if this were someone else trying to deceive him, how could they possibly have captured the way the three interacted? They groused and carped at one another, stopping and starting to hurl insults or laugh at each other. They *were* exactly who they appeared to be.

Which simply could not be true! Aiul's plan fled from his mind entirely, and he stepped forward into their view. The words burst from his lips like he was a child again. *"Papa?"* he stammered.

The man who couldn't possibly be standing there, and most certainly couldn't look so young, whipped his head toward the sound of Aiul's voice and took a step forward, but Maranath put a hand on his shoulder and called out, "Aiul. Put that damned thing down, son. This has gone too far."

Lothrian (for that was who he was, however insane it might be) glared at Maranath. "Son, is it?"

Maranath looked at Lothrian intently and said with deliberate, slow calm, "This is not the time. Speak to him. This could still end well."

Lothrian nodded, the anger fading from his eyes to something akin to misery or terror as he turned back to Aiul. "Didn't I tell you never to come here, boy?" He offered a shaky chuckle. "I don't understand how it's come to this, Aiul, but it's a very explosive situation. Won't you explain it to me?"

Maklin, pointing to the corpse of the Master, jerked at Maranath's sleeve and muttered, "Mei! What the *fuck* is that?"

Maranath turned on Maklin with a glare, making shushing noises, and Maklin stepped back, looking offended as he muttered under his breath.

Lothrian, however, bent to examine the corpse with a vicious grin. "The Master of Torium, dead as dirt!" he marveled.

Maranath, now interested despite his other concerns, raised an eyebrow at Lothrian. "You knew this…thing?"

Lothrian, still grinning, rose and answered, "Knew him? I should say so. He was key in their overwhelming me before." He turned to Aiul, eyes brimming with curiosity. "He was immensely powerful. How *did* you manage to defeat him, boy?"

Every instinct in Aiul told him to run to his grandfather, embrace him in a hug, and let the elders take him home. So much had passed, so much misery and sorrow, and he had lost so much, but it seemed he could put it all aright if he could just rest a while. Lothrian would fix it.

The jagged thing stabbed at his mind even as he thought of this. *He can't be Papa! Listen to how he is speaking. Papa would command you, not beg. He was never so kind or comforting! This is a trap!*

"We had help," Aiul muttered, slowly backing toward the

black pool, keeping his weapon ready. "As for the rest, what would you hear? That they murdered my wife and unborn child? Or that they threw me in prison to rot?"

Lothrian spun back to Maranath, eyes blazing. "You told me none of this!"

Maranath took a deep breath and let it out. "It's not exactly as he tells it."

Aiul's barking laughter burst from his lips without any real conscious thought, not from amusement, really, just the irony of the situation. "Yes, of course, I imagined it all, my wife bleeding out, the pain of my beatings in prison. And you, Maranath, you let them do it."

Maranath's ire seemed to be growing despite his best efforts to suppress it. "Boy, you conspired with foreigners and attacked the empress! It was all I could do to keep them from killing you!"

"And look at the cost! Even if I had died, my wife and child would live!"

Maranath tugged at his beard a moment, his jaw working. "There is no way any of us could have known how that would play out. We were doing our best to help you."

Aiul's legs bumped against the edge of the black pool. He gave Maranath a sour look. "Like you're trying to help me now, eh?"

"You threw in with the Dead God and stole a piece of the damned Eye! Surely you didn't think we could let that pass?"

Aiul turned to Lothrian without responding. "Papa, are you with them against me?"

Lothrian raised both hands over his head as if in surrender. "Aiul, I am always with you. If this were you doing battle with them, I would choose your side, no matter what the reasons. But this is not just your battle. The Eye of the Lion is reforming, and the end of the world is nigh! Where is the piece you took?"

Aiul shrugged. "I know nothing of this."

Maklin spat on the ground and cried out in a shrill voice, "Liar! It's hanging around your neck! Hand it over at once!"

Aiul pulled the amber sphere from his shirt. "This? Fuck you, old man. It's mine now."

Lothrian burst in, "Is it true you serve the Dead God now?"

Aiul put the sphere back into his shirt and dipped a hand casually into the pool, wondering what any of them would make of the gesture. "And if I do?"

Maranath shook his head vehemently. "You cannot trust him, Aiul!"

Aiul felt the fury rise within him, the jagged thing stabbing at all the soft spots in his mind. "Can't I?" He stepped forward and swept the mace in a vicious arc, the spiked fist passing within inches of Maranath, though the old man didn't even flinch. "Right now, I trust Elgar more than I trust any of you. I've spent weeks with his man Logrus, and he is a better person than me by far. I've just watched Elgar's wrath poured upon the monsters here, *my* wrath, and it was a good thing! It was what he sent us here to do! How is that wrong, eh?" He spat his contempt at them. "The lot of you are selfish and wicked! Why should *anyone* listen to you?"

Lothrian again held his hands aloft, raising and lowering them in a gesture pleading for calm. "Aiul, Elgar is mad! His mind was shattered here in this very place, by the very monsters you speak of! They tried to kill a god and steal his power. You are involved in matters you can't possibly appreciate!"

Aiul grunted at this and glared at Lothrian. "You all still see me as a child. I think you'll find I can appreciate quite a bit now, more than old men and ghosts could guess."

Maklin, red faced, shouted, "Oh for fuck's sake, he's one boy with a stick! I'm pretty sure we can take him without killing him!" He gestured grandly at Aiul, obviously expecting something impressive. Aiul felt what seemed a playful punch to his gut, enough to make him take a step back, but nothing to be concerned with.

"You think so, old man?" he asked with a grin.

Maklin's face fell. "Shit," he muttered, as the others' eyes grew wide.

Furious wind whipped Sadrik's hair about his face as he held his arms overhead, a showman thrilling the crowd and himself with every ounce of drama he could muster. Sparks and flame filled the twilit sky, trailing behind them like the tail of a comet as the last bit of the sun sank behind the trees. *It must be half a mile long. I am damned proud of that!*

Ariano howled in a mixture of glee and frustration from the front of the raft, her hair a fluttering flag in the gale, teeth a-grind and lips parted as if in a rictus grin. Her knuckles had gone white from her death grip on the rail. "More, whelp! Bigger and better! I'm flagging!"

Sadrik felt a brief flutter of panic in his breast. They had been at this for hours, and he was running out of tricks to impress the Southlanders. Being honest, he was fairly impressed himself, not only at his own handiwork, but at Ariano's as well. He had never moved at such speed, and was fairly certain that going much faster would actually strip the flesh from his face. The ground was nothing more than a blur beneath them, a silver, moonlit expanse that seemed more like an ocean than a forest.

Had anyone below been watching, Sadrik and his vessel would surely have seemed a wonder, for the brief moment it was in sight, a flaming raft of logs, bound together with vines and sheer force of will. The very air around them wailed in protest at their violation of nature. *Which is, when you think about it, a fairly excellent thing in and of itself.* Tired as he was, Sadrik felt his face stretching into a mad grin just to think of what they were doing.

It wasn't precisely an abomination, but it was generally considered risky, and their specific application was without a doubt foolhardy. Everyone had emotions, desires, most of them untapped and wasted. In a pinch, and with tremendous focus, a pair of desperate sorcerers could deliberately whip up awe or even terror in a group and turn it into raw fuel, to go further than they could on their own, do more. *And burn up faster, when we fail.*

It worked, for as long as it lasted, at any rate, and assuming the emotions didn't turn against the sorcerers in question, which could prove disastrous. There seemed no danger of their passengers declaring them enemies, and even so, they could hardly be more dead from being spitted on Southlander blades than they would from the ensuing crash. *At this speed, if she folds, at least the end will be mercifully quick.*

Sandilianus shot to his feet and shouted, "There it is!"

Sadrik risked a glance over his shoulder, and felt a chill creep up his spine despite the unnatural warmth. A great, stepped pyramid rose above the jungle, the central piece of a large fortification. Something twisted in his guts and damped his carefully cultivated enthusiasm, leaving him momentarily nauseated. *That is a place of true evil.* It was an odd thought, completely unlike him. *Since when do I believe in good and evil?* He swallowed hard at the growing lump in his throat, the sharp, contrasting angles of the moonlit and shadowed portions of the pyramid seeming like the blade of a knife, the edge of darkness. *Since now, I suppose.*

The sun was completely set now, and, and Sadrik couldn't help but wonder if the Southlanders' god had meant, literally, by sunset, or if there was any wiggle room at all. *It just set! We can be fashionably late, right?*

Their battered craft shuddered and plunged twenty feet,

jarring from his dark musings, before Ariano could right it. She screeched back at him, "Idiot! Focus!"

Sadrik eyed the treetops, now mere feet below, and the terrifying speed at which they were passing. *Mercifully quick, indeed, and then what hope will the world have?* He shuddered again, then forced his mind back where he needed it.

Sadrik raised his hands over his head and cried out with abandon, "Torium! Let the gods mark our passing in blood and flame!" He suppressed a shudder of exhaustion, feeling his own emotion running into his veins like quicksilver, bolstering him, burning along his veins like...

Fire!

The flames burst from his skin, streaming in the wind and joining the fireworks from the raft. The Southlanders leapt to their feet, cheering and waving their weapons in the air.

"For Ilaweh!"

"For Xanthia!"

Sadrik joined them with his own cry. "Mei smiles on us!"

Sandilianus sunk to a knee and jammed the tip of his blade into one of the logs. He hung his head, as if in prayer, but his cry was louder than any of the others. "For the world! *Ilaweh is great!*"

Sadrik felt his knees begin to buckle as the moment drew out, the wild emotion streaming out of him as if his chest had a great hole. The flames would follow soon, and he had nothing left. The Southlanders gave him a bit with their display, but he was fading quickly.

I pray your god is with us as you say, Southlander. One may not be enough this night.

Logrus awoke to the sounds of struggle. The pain hit him immediately, from everywhere at once. It was all he could do not to cry out, but even groggy, he understood that this would be a bad idea. With a supreme effort, he clenched his fists and rode out the wave of agony.

After a bit, it passed, or he became used to it. He wasn't truly certain which was the case, but his mind cleared, and he could sense other things. Darkness. Sharp voices. The smell of blood everywhere, almost certainly his. He saw that Aiul had apparently been kind enough to minister to wounds, but spilled blood stayed spilled. *Is there even any left in me?*

Logrus tried to rise to a sitting position, but his head swam and to his horror, his body simply refused to obey. He tried again, over and over, but weakness permeated his every fiber.

He felt the panic begin in his gut, and crushed it down, refusing to tolerate it. Fear was useless and unnecessary. He began to take inventory, testing one body part and then another. A finger twitched. His eyes could move, and, after a few attempts, so could his head. His arms and legs were like butchered meat, still and numb.

Elgar! My flesh fails me!

"Weak. Come closer."

Logrus cast his eyes toward the black pool. It was perhaps ten feet from him, a seeming eternity. He had no idea how he would reach it, only that he must. He focused all of his will into his right arm. The limb seemed an alien thing, not attached to him at all, someone else's arm. *Move.* Nothing.

He could hear the sounds of struggle more clearly now, curses, grunts, Aiul's voice and others, strangers he didn't recognize. For the moment, it seemed Aiul was holding his own well enough to taunt and prod at them. The others, it seemed, wanted Aiul alive.

Logrus focused on his arm again, summoning every ounce of will he could. To his joy, it moved, just a bit, but it was under his control again. He flexed his fingers and gripped at the floor.

Ten feet.

"We're going down!" Ariano cried.

Sadrik tried desperately to think of something more he could do, some bit of showmanship that could rally his audience, but everyone, himself included, was simply spent. "Can we make the water?"

Ariano hesitated, eyes bulging at the rapidly approaching pyramids, her grin still on her face, though perhaps it was now equal parts fear and elation. "We can damned well try!"

"It's been exhilarating working with you, grandmother!" Sadrik called, and laughed like a loon.

Ariano shot him back a look that was a mixture of fury, gratitude, and terror. "You too, whelp!"

Sadrik was surprised to feel a strong, warm hand on his shoulder. He spun to see Sandilianus. The man offered him a grim smile and extended his hand. Sadrik knew their custom by now. As they grasped forearms, the Southlander said, "Likewise."

Despite the urge to watch the disaster unfold directly, Sadrik held the man's gaze, blue eyes locked with brown in newfound respect, as they passed the wall, descending even more quickly now.

"Brace yourselves!" Ariano cried.

Through the bone jarring impact and the shock of cold water, Sadrik had one last conscious thought. *These are men from the desert. Can they even swim? Because I never learned...*

Blackness rushed in like a wave, and all was quiet.

Just one foot. Were it not for his deep, sincere belief in Elgar, Logrus simply could never have found the strength. It was not possible. It had not been possible when it was ten feet, and it was even less possible now.

Yet, it was *necessary.*

From his new vantage point, Logrus could see his enemies, though they had yet to notice him. Aiul, for all his bravado, was now backed into a corner, swinging his mace furiously at any who approached, the madness in him now fully in control. Logrus couldn't help but wonder what it must be like for the other order, the Knights of Flame, to be driven by rage instead of icy necessity, but he was certain his way was better.

Blood oozed from his torn nails, and he grimaced as he dug his fingers against the stone again, feeling fresh misery lance up his arm. Slowly, he dragged himself forward, inch by agonizing inch, until, at last, he was at the edge of the Black Pool.

It would have been sweet to heave a great sigh, yet he knew he dare not make a sound. Until he could recover, he was nothing but a gnat to these men. He could not literally see their power, but he could feel it, sense it like the sun on his face on a warm day. Likely, they could have killed Aiul by now if that was their intent. They were of his people, pale, lanky, tall, and insufferably arrogant. Perhaps they were related.

One thing was certain: they would have no incentive whatsoever to keep Logrus alive.

He lay in silence and shadow for long moments, slowly catching his breath, listening to the melee. The newcomers sounded reasonable enough, with many cries of, "We don't want to hurt you!" or "Don't make us do this!" Aiul spat and hissed back at them, having none of it.

For a moment, Logrus wondered if perhaps it would be best to let them have him. Elgar's will had been done. Logrus could bring back the book and the blood without help. And what was Aiul to him, really? A nuisance, a disruption of his otherwise orderly life. But also an ally. Logrus thought a moment longer, but finally had to admit the truth. *A friend.*

It was a new concept for Logrus. He understood the word, and had even had 'friendships' when he was young, but the decades since had worn the edges away from such a notion, leaving it shiny and smooth in his mind.

He is not well, though. Logrus felt torn by deep, sincere confusion about what was the right path. If Aiul was a friend, then his welfare was a now a valid concern, and Aiul was very clearly descending ever deeper into misery and madness. Perhaps, if his people were truly there to help, they could heal his agony of soul, mend his mind.

But a stronger part of Logrus said simply: *you do not abandon friends.* Slowly, Logrus reached his hand upward, crawling with his fingers over the rough stone of the pool, and seized the lip. Perhaps Aiul returning with his people *would* be best for him, but that was for him to decide, not them. If it was vengeance he needed to feel whole, then that was what he would have. *Elgar chose him for a reason.*

With the last of his strength, Logrus dragged his numb body upward and plunged a hand into the black pool.

Strength surged through him, furious energy burning along his veins and nerves with such intensity that he felt it blazing from his pores, his eyes, even his hair. His rent leg knitted in a flash as if it had never been torn, and Logrus sprang to his feet, whole and hale and full of fire.

It was only then that he thought to wonder where his weapons had gotten to. No matter. He reached to the floor and took up a stone and a pottery shard left from the battle with the Master. "Stop!" he shouted.

One of the sorcerers was a demon summoner, by the looks of his servants, several creatures that seemed to be composed of thousands of bits of debris. The summoner looked up with a bemused expression and called out to the others, "I presume we can kill this one?"

You can try, old man. Logrus flung the rock. It flew with killing speed, but the old sorcerer was faster than he looked, and managed to dodge well enough to turn what should have been a fatal strike into a merely painful, stunning blow. As the old sorcerer howled in misery, Logrus charged forward, the shard in his hand like a blade.

Maranath felt his calm begin to slip at the sight of the newcomer. *Mei! It never ends!*

He spared Maklin a quick glance. His old friend had a hand clamped to his head, wailing and cursing, as blood trickled down his face. Maranath suppressed a snicker, knowing it might well provoke Maklin into changing his mind about who he was fighting.

In any event, Maranath had more pressing problems. He swept his hands in a grand gesture, imagining the feel of each of the bits of debris as he picked them up with invisible hands, each with its own texture and weight. Rocks, sconces, even a few bits of bone sprung from the floor and arranged themselves into a barrier between him and the stranger, the pieces spinning and weaving in the air. "I don't know who you are, stranger, and you don't know us, so I'll give you this one warning: stay out of it. This is a family matter."

The stranger's gaze seemed to go distant, eyes unfocused and wandering. Too late, Maranath realized the fellow was trying to calculate paths and find a way through. *But that's impossible!*

Nevertheless, the stranger rushed forward, dodging, and leaping. He was on Maranath in the blink of an eye, one hand twisting

Maranath's collar and drawing him close, and the other holding what looked to be a piece from a broken urn to Maranath's throat.

The stranger pressed the shard hard enough to draw a thin bead of blood from Maranath's neck. "I could say the same to you, old man."

Maranath knew he should, by all rights, be afraid, or at least concerned, but the only emotion he could process was cold fury: at his attacker, at Maklin for being caught off guard, and at Lothrian, who seemed to be standing slack jawed and doing nothing useful at all. Maranath looked his enemy in the eye with a piercing glare and muttered, "Then we are at an impasse."

CHAPTER 17
SCHOOLED

CAELWEN knelt in silence for long moments, uncertain if he and his companions were next, or if for the moment, the Great Tyrant's rage was sated. He hazarded a glance at the sorcerer, certain his fear was written all over his face.

Tasinal placed his hands on his hips and rolled his eyes. "Get up, idiot. I have no tolerance for kneelers." He raised an eyebrow imperiously, then lowered it again as his face fell in disappointment. He gestured at Caelwen's face and shoulder wound. "Mei, you're a mess."

Caelwen ground his teeth and clutched at his wound as he rose to his feet, nettled by the barb despite his fear. "Well, you're definitely a Meite."

"Amazing, the wit on you. Have you considered a comedy act?"

Tasinal's gaze wandered to the pile of corpses, his face wrinkling in annoyance. He waved a hand at the offending bodies. Caelwen grimaced at the wet, ripping sound that followed, as the corpses, gore and all, tore themselves from the floor in a large mass and went flying out of the entrance. He bit back a wave of nausea as the door slid silently back into place, leaving the small entryway secure and spotless.

Tasinal seemed to suddenly notice Ahmed. "An Ilawehan," he said, one eyebrow raised high. "Somewhat surprising."

"We call ourselves Xanthians, now," Ahmed volunteered.

Tasinal grunted. "I was not consulted. In my home, you are still Ilawehan."

Ahmed laughed out loud, which seemed to be the correct answer. Tasinal offered him a broad grin, then lowered his gaze to Rithard, who was in process of regaining his feet. "And what is... *this*?"

Rithard scowled and dusted himself off. "Rithard of House Amrath," he groused. "I'm just fine, thank you for asking."

Tasinal's eyebrows rose. "One of Amrath's get, eh? I should have expected it. You're not even a Meite, but here you are tempting fate. So you found the emergency key. How *did* you manage to work out the password?"

"It was a trivial thing."

Tasinal scowled. "Yes, just the sort of thing he would have claimed, and every bit the same audacious lie."

As Rithard opened his mouth, Caelwen prepared for the worst, then sighed with relief as Rithard simply said, "Perhaps."

"You don't look a bit like him, you know, save for that hideous smirk," Tasinal said, his voice considerably more severe than he was able to make his face, as his mouth twitched at the edges. "I suppose that damned key counts as an invitation, so killing the lot of you would be poor form. Come in, have a seat, and please try not to bleed on the furniture, hmm?"

Tasinal led them down what Caelwen now realized was a foyer, and into a large reception room. The place was richly decorated with fine tapestries showing exploits of the founders, and the furniture was exquisitely crafted from a dark wood that Caelwen did not recognize, though it certainly looked expensive.

A great wooden table and chairs, the sort where a king might hold a war council, occupied the center of the room. Light seemed to glow from the ceiling, though he saw no source of flame.

Rithard, medical bag in hand, snapped his fingers in front of Caelwen's face and gestured to the flagstone floor. "Let's plug that leak, shall we?"

Tasinal and Ahmed took seats at the table and looked on with interest as Caelwen lay down on the floor and let Rithard get to his business. Caelwen winced as Rithard poured what felt to be flesh-melting acid into the wound. "Mei, watch it! I'm not a corpse like you're used to working with!"

Rithard frowned as he began threading a needle. "Hold still, ape. No major damage here, but you'll need stitching."

Tasinal turned to Ahmed and asked, "Are they always like this?"

Ahmed chuckled. "Yes."

Caelwen endured both the manhandling from Rithard and the snickering from Tasinal with gritted teeth. Rithard was actually quick about his work, for which Caelwen was thankful, even if it hurt a bit more. *I have no idea how long it will be before our host decides he wants us out of here, so we had best get to business.* He got to his feet quickly and took a chair next to Ahmed.

Tasinal, it seemed, agreed. As soon as Caelwen was settled, the sorcerer clapped his hands together as if to draw the attention of unruly children, and said, "Now that we've shored up the breaches, what was it you wanted?"

Rithard, stowing his gear back into his bag, answered in a sour tone, "Oh, nothing much. Just to save the world from Elgar's wrath."

Tasinal raised an eyebrow. "Oh, my. It's been that long? One loses track of time."

"It must be very difficult for you."

Tasinal's eyebrows knitted together into a tight wedge, and his eyes narrowed with displeasure. "You'll find this conversation even more difficult without your tongue." Tasinal paused a moment, as if to verify that Rithard was sufficiently cowed by his threat, before continuing. "Amrath should have left all we knew in the papers. Mei, you figured out the damned key, so you're no fool. Why disturb me?"

Rithard shot Tasinal an odd look. "How would you know I even have access to them? I thought you'd lost track of time."

Tasinal scowled at Rithard. "It would seem this may take longer than I had hoped, so join us." He gestured toward the table. "As for the rest..." He shrugged. "So I keep my own counsel. That makes two of us. I suspect my reasons for doing so are considerably more thought out than yours."

Rithard took a seat and propped his elbows on the table, a sour look on his face. "Fair enough. Yes, I have the papers, and I see nothing of the sort. I see clues and hints, but key information is missing. I presumed he deliberately created it as a puzzle to discourage meddling."

Tasinal again rolled his eyes. "Imbecile! Why would he do that? 'Oh, my, here's information about the end of the world, let's make it a fucking puzzle to amuse ourselves with. It will be great fun when they fail to work it out!'" Tasinal feigned spitting on the floor. "Idiocy. He left *clear* instructions."

Rithard blinked several times in confusion. "What are you suggesting?"

"Someone removed the information, obviously."

Rithard thought on this a moment, nodding slowly. "I have seen evidence that some things were removed, but I had no way of knowing how much. But surely you can tell us what we need to know, then?"

Tasinal heaved a great sigh. "Hence the emergency plan, but in truth I am not terribly clever like Amrath. Oh, I can crack skulls with the best of them, and I am stubborn, but I have only rudimentary understanding of the forces at work here." He shrugged, looking a little embarrassed. "I didn't need to, you know. I was only 'leader' because Amrath thought I had the most regal features. He said it would play well with the masses."

Caelwen felt his heart sink at this. *If he doesn't know what to do, we're doomed!* But he had questioned many a witness before, and things were not always black and white about knowledge. "Your eminence—"

Tasinal shot him a glare. "*What* did you call me?"

Caelwen felt a chill in his guts. *I have no idea if I am about to die.* He stammered briefly, then managed to blurt out, "I'm sorry. I have no idea of the proper form of address."

Tasinal rapped his knuckles sharply on the table. "That's the trouble with you weaklings. You place so much emphasis on trivia: noble blood, courtly manners, backstabbing and treachery. It's why you make a mess of ruling yourselves, and it's why I eventually threw up my hands at the whole affair."

He leaned forward and beckoned Caelwen closer, as if he were going to impart a secret. "The fact that I once called myself emperor is of no consequence. The fact that I could end your life with a thought is more significant." He focused intently on Caelwen, almost but not quite sneering. "I would be treated as you would treat any other warrior you knew was your superior: directly, without coddling. Am I clear?"

Caelwen stiffened, but found the rebuke actually made him more comfortable. This, he understood. He rose from his chair, offered Tasinal a salute, then shifted to a parade rest stance and continued, "Sir, Rithard is the most clever man I have ever met. He's amazing with his ability to put together disparate pieces of information and solve crimes. You may know more than you think, if he asks the right questions."

Tasinal raised an eyebrow and regarded Caelwen briefly, then turned back to Rithard. "Let's see if he's correct, hmm? Ask your questions, and be quick about it. I do have things to do, you know." He looked back at Caelwen briefly, as if in afterthought, and gestured for Caelwen to sit.

Rithard's lips twitched, and Caelwen suppressed the urge to groan out loud as he took his seat again. Fortunately, Rithard seemed to find the sense to leave it at that, and simply asked, "What was meant by *the blood is more potent than we feared*'?"

Tasinal grinned. "I simply must know what *you* thought it meant before I tell you."

Rithard frowned a moment before answering, "I presumed it had to do with heredity."

Tasinal laughed aloud, and looked about, seeming surprised that he was the only one who got the joke. He turned back to Rithard and grew serious. "It explodes."

Ahmed found himself as confused as Rithard. Rithard stammered briefly, "I'm sorry, I don't—what?"

"The blood. In the Black Pool. It explodes. *Violently.*" He emphasized the point by tapping a finger on the table. "A thimble full of the stuff could take out half the city if properly charged and triggered."

Ilaweh is great! The Black Pool!

Rithard shook his head, still confused, and started to speak again, but Ahmed interrupted. "In Torium."

Tasinal turned quickly to Ahmed, eyes wide in surprise. "Yes! How could you know that?" His surprise turned to a scowl as he gestured at Rithard. "And why spoil my fun toying with this one?"

Ahmed shrugged. "I meant no offense. I only just realized I understood. I have seen it in visions."

Tasinal's eyebrows rose, and he offered a knowing nod. "You have the sight, yes?"

"Aye."

Tasinal paused a moment, drumming his fingers against a table, then seemed to come to a decision. "I have something for you later." He turned back to Rithard. "Go on."

Rithard cleared his throat and asked his next question. "You say 'properly charged and triggered'. What does that mean?"

"Yorn said we would need to reassemble the artifact. It's all one thing, you know: the eyes, the head, and there's a body down there somewhere, too. The Torians used it to suck the power right out of a god." Tasinal reached toward Rithard's chest, then snatched it back and made a slurping sound. "Some in the pool, some in the pieces, some in the body."

Rithard blinked in confusion, but Ahmed groaned softly. "Ilaweh is great. You speak of the Eye of the Lion, yes?"

Tasinal cast a disgusted glance at Rithard. "Why am I even talking to you?" He grinned at Ahmed. "Yes, exactly. You know of it?"

"All too well," Ahmed answered. He reached under his shirt and produced the piece of the eye he carried.

Tasinal's eyes grew wide at the sight of it. "Here?" he gasped. He quickly recovered and reached out his hand. "May I?"

Ahmed gave him a wary glance, then shrugged and lifted the thong from his neck and handed the piece to Tasinal. "I worry, but then, you had this before, I think. It feels of you."

Tasinal examined the small half-head, turning it over in his hands. "I carried it for some time, actually. Until I threw it into the ocean. How did you come by it?"

Ahmed shook his head. "*It* came by *me*. I died. It brought me back."

Tasinal shot Ahmed a piercing look. "Who paid the price?"

"A heathen and blasphemer, who saw the truth in his last moments."

Tasinal handed the piece back, a haggard look on his face. "Live long enough, young ones, and your regrets may come to outweigh your accomplishments."

Ahmed noticed Caelwen eyeing Rithard with concern. The physician was once again looking feverish. Before Ahmed could speak, Caelwen called to his friend, "Rithard?"

Rithard ignored him and turned to Tasinal, eyes blazing and face pale. "How big is the black pool?"

Tasinal gave him an odd look, as if finding the question pointless, but answered anyway. "About ten feet across I should say. Three feet high? That sounds about right."

Rithard, brow furrowed in thought, licked his lips. "Fifteen hundred gallons, or thereabouts, maybe more if it were full to the brim." He swallowed hard, and for a moment, Ahmed thought Rithard would throw up or swoon, but somehow he held it together. "Just over a million thimblefuls, I should wager, depending on the size of the thimble."

Even Tasinal seemed struck dumb at this. For long moments, no one spoke as they absorbed the implications. At last, Ahmed broke the silence, "Ilaweh is great. That is the prophecy."

Tasinal shook his head vehemently. "Are you sure of the math?"

Rithard grunted. "Of course not! I have no idea how much a thimbleful really is, and no idea if it would really level a city." He waved his hands about in excitement and frustration. "Is your estimate high or low? How big of a city are we talking about?" Rithard dropped his hands and gripped the edge of the table hard enough that his knuckles went white. "If you're even close right, it would release an unimaginable amount of energy!"

Caelwen took a deep breath before speaking. "Rithard, are you telling us this thing could blow up the whole world?"

Rithard shrugged. "I have no idea. I doubt it. But anything is possible. This is beyond the scale of any science I ever studied." He paused a moment, lips pressed together in concentration. "It would surely kill a lot of people, maybe even everyone on the continent."

Tasinal cleared his throat, his mouth twisting as if he had eaten something sour. "It is, then, worse than you imagine. Worse than you *can* imagine, I'll wager. Do you understand what ley lines are?"

Caelwen shrugged, and one look at Rithard was enough to see he, too, had no idea. Ahmed nodded, knowing full well what Tasinal meant.

"Well, for the benefit of our two ignorant savages," Tasinal said, "Ley lines are mystical lines of energy that permeate the globe. The structure of the ground itself conforms to them. You can see them if you know what to look for."

Ahmed added, "They are the places where the world fits together."

Tasinal rapped his knuckles on the table, grinning. "Just so!" His features bunched together in an expression of disapproval, as if he smelled something unpleasant. "They are also potent sources and channels for certain schools of magic. It's not something Meites meddle with. It's strictly Torian school, but they can travel and communicate along them, produce effects from one end to the other, all sorts of black arts. I have heard they can create earthquakes, even."

Rithard rubbed at his chin. "And what have they to do with this?"

Tasinal gave him a grim stare. "Torium sits atop the largest conjunction of ley lines on the planet. It's the reason they built the place where they did. They wanted access to them." He looked down at the floor and shook his head. "Releasing that much energy into them would have catastrophic results."

Another long silence followed. Caelwen asked, at last, "So, this could, in fact, blow up the world?"

Tasinal nodded. "Which changes things immensely. Generally, I couldn't care less about what happens to the vast majority of fools and weaklings. They could all die and I would barely notice, much less care. However, I have a vested interest in the existence of the planet." He rose and swept an arm toward them, for the moment seeming the emperor he had once called himself. "If you have preparations, make them. We're going to Torium to settle this, and woe be unto anyone who gets in my way!"

Ahmed realized with a start that he must have nodded off. It was a mad notion, considering the topic, and yet there was no other explanation. Tasinal had been at the head of the table before, and was now standing just to the right of it, yet Ahmed had not seen him move.

Tasinal's mood had changed, too. "After due consideration, perhaps that is not the best course of action."

Rithard clapped both hands to the sides of his head. "*What?*"

Tasinal dismissed him with a wave of his hand. "I'm sure you'll sort it out just fine."

"That's insane! You must be the world's most powerful sorcerer, and you can't be bothered to prevent the planet you live on from blowing up?"

Tasinal's glare was the sort of look one gave his intended victims before giving in fully to mayhem. "There are factors you don't understand. Believe me, I have given this *ample* consideration."

For a moment, Rithard could only stammer. "Do you actually understand the meaning of the word 'ample', or does it just sound interesting to you? You've just contradicted yourself in the space of seconds. There is nothing 'ample' about it!"

Tasinal began rubbing at his temple, as if he were nursing a headache. "As I said, there are things you don't appreciate."

"I *appreciate* the world will explode. How is that not enough?"

Tasinal sat in his chair and buried his face in his hands. "One would think so, wouldn't he?"

Rithard was either out of words or using silence as a stratagem, and Ahmed saw no reason to make himself a target, whichever was the case. He was, therefore, rather surprised to find himself the subject of Tasinal's interest despite his best efforts to avoid it. Tasinal dropped his hands and fixed Ahmed with a piercing stare. "Ilawehan, what did you say your name was?"

Ahmed struggled to remember if he had said at all, and decided that it would be foolish to correct the sorcerer, even if he could remember. "Ahmed Justinius, Master."

"'Master', is it? Are you a slave?"

"I am a your student."

"Then I approve of the term. I have a gift for you."

Rithard could not contain himself, and heaved a huge, disgusted sigh. Caelwen elbowed him in the ribs. Tasinal glanced at them briefly before sighing himself. "There are things you don't understand," he repeated as he rose. "Wait here."

Then it happened again. Ahmed watched Tasinal rise and turn to leave, and then, suddenly, he was on the other side of the room. If it were merely that he had moved, it would have been one thing, but he was also wearing different clothes. Instead of the red and black robe, he now sported tan breeches and a simple white shirt, and he was holding a half-eaten sandwich.

Also, unless Ahmed misunderstood his gestures, Tasinal was shaking his fist and cursing at someone, though Ahmed saw no one else present.

Tasinal turned back to them, a sheepish grin on his face. "As I said, there are things—"

Rithard shouted, "Why are you *toying* with us?"

Tasinal shook his head in denial. "You're being toyed with, indeed, but not by me. I'm a victim, too, just of a different sort. I've been wicked enough to draw unwanted attention."

Rithard looked about, an expression of mock-credulity plastered on his face. "Oh, really? And who might that be, that it's not the all-powerful, annoying sorcerer?"

Tasinal glared at Rithard. "Being honest, I suspect he would stop me from tearing out your tongue, but I am sorely tempted to test that theory."

Ahmed suddenly noticed a weight in his lap, and looked down to see a fine blade lying across his legs. Reflexively, he reached to check his own weapon, but knew even before his hand made contact that it would still be in the scabbard on his belt. This was not his blade *(Brutus's blade*, a small voice in his head reminded him*)*. It was a much finer weapon. In Xanthia, sword making was more science than art, and serviceable weapons were produced in large quantities, but this blade was something else, custom-made with love and devotion, and at considerable expense. It was a no-nonsense weapon, one made for work, not for show. The only concession to pure serviceability was a stylized 'X' graven on both sides of the grip, and a single sphere of amber set into the pommel.

Could this have belonged to... Ahmed banished the idea as childish dreaming. *Surely it could not be so.* But the time period would be correct, and the style matched many of the weapons Ahmed had seen from the Great War. And if this sorcerer were truly Tasinal, there was a chance.

From what seemed like a distance, Rithard and Tasinal were arguing, and Caelwen was simply shaking his head. Ahmed, however, was so focused on the blade that he heard nothing but his own words. He gasped out, in a rasping voice, "How did you get this?"

Tasinal and Rithard stopped their bickering, and the sorcerer raised an eyebrow and grinned. "Husam. He came here after the war, once Xanthius passed away. We all worked together to see the Eye was put asunder and never restored. We failed. But that blade properly belongs to your people. You, since there is no one else here to claim it. Take it home."

Ahmed stared wide-eyed at Tasinal, his mind rebelling at the thought of immortals who knew legends of history, who bore their blades. *Now, I know how it feels when I tell people Ilaweh speaks to me.*

He was about to offer thanks for the blade when he saw from the corner of his eye a vague, human shaped figure. He turned, alarmed, to look at it directly and saw nothing.

Rithard cleared his throat. "So this Husam, he was your code master? You used their language? Why? Weren't you all of the same mind about the Eye?"

"The council was," Tasinal answered. "There were considerably more dabblers then than now. You must understand, those of us on the council saw this all happen. We understood the danger, but for most Meites it was hearsay, and a weapon is something to be seized, an opportunity to be taken. Even I thought so in the beginning."

Ahmed watched the figure with his peripheral vision. It was nothing more than a shimmering, like heat warping the air. It was indeed shaped like a man, yet it seemed something more somehow: deeper, heavier, more real. *I should not be able to see it, but I have the sight.*

Rithard, genuinely curious now, asked, "You used it?"

Tasinal shook his head. "Nay, but I would have, and it would have destroyed me. It was my choice to keep it in this world, and I pay for that decision even still. The long and short of it is that, on this matter, I am extremely limited in my ability to act."

Rithard snorted in derision, but Ahmed spoke up. "No. He speaks truth."

Rithard cast him a sour look. "And you know this how?"

Ahmed shrugged, preferring not to let on to the phantom presence that he had in fact sussed it out. "I just know, Rithard. It is my gift." Ahmed almost laughed as Rithard's features wrinkled in distaste. *No, it is not your logic and science. That makes you uncomfortable.*

Rithard waved a hand. "I suppose I must trust Ahmed. He has a track record." He looked at Tasinal with disapproval. "So do Meites."

Tasinal chuckled. "Oh, indeed. I have told spectacular lies when it suited me. I take no offense. But I *am* telling the truth now. Though, admittedly, I would say that if I were telling a spectacular lie, too." His grin beamed like the sun.

Caelwen nodded sagely. "So you've found some loophole?"

Tasinal looked at him in bemused surprise. "Oh, really, the meathead speaks, *and* he's on target! Why, yes, I *did* find one. How did you know?"

"I've done plenty of interrogations."

"So I'm a criminal sort of mind, am I?"

Caelwen, looking suddenly uncomfortable, shrugged.

Tasinal burst into laughter. "Well, there's really only one way to take that gesture."

If Rithard was happy to play Bad Cop in this scenario, and Ahmed was unwittingly the Good Cop, Caelwen was happy to play Dumb Cop.

Caelwen was well aware that people were less guarded with

you if they thought you weren't very clever. Tasinal was kind enough to leave no doubt of his thoughts. That left Caelwen a lot of time to observe.

The 'blinks' had been quite unnerving the first couple of times. They hadn't really gotten any easier after that, but they had at least become familiar.

Rithard was too busy being angry or smug to notice, but Tasinal seemed, very often, to be looking over his shoulder, or off to the side of the room, as if there were someone else there. Caelwen hadn't been able to understand what was going on until he caught Ahmed doing much the same, watching someone or something with his peripheral vision.

Whatever was there, Caelwen couldn't see it, neither straight on nor from the corner of his eye. The Southlander, though, clearly could, and he had demonstrated some remarkable abilities. Not that it mattered. Caelwen doubted there was anything they could do about it that Tasinal couldn't, but still, it was something to keep an eye on.

Caelwen was fairly certain that, somehow, time was slipping during the 'blinks'. It seemed mad, and yet it was the only thing that made sense. It wasn't just a case of Tasinal moving. He changed clothes. Once, his hair was wet, as if he'd just stepped out of the bath, and now it was dry again.

I would think I was going crazy if the situation weren't already the height of madness. Our ancient, undead emperor just crushed the heads of a couple dozen thugs, then crushed the rest of them into goo, exchanged insults with Rithard, and is presently eating a sandwich he didn't have the last time I looked. Oh, and there's a 'presence' lurking about that only the undead emperor and the holy man can see. I don't know what sanity even means anymore.

Tasinal, done laughing at him for the moment, continued, "The 'loophole', as you put it, is that I can provide you with things you might have gotten in some other way, such as information Amrath put down in the papers. I can answer historical questions. I most definitely cannot fight your enemies."

Caelwen raised an eyebrow. "They would be your enemies, too."

"One would think so, yes, but unfortunately, not everyone agrees."

Caelwen nodded. It seemed, for the moment, he was the one asking questions. "And presumably, you're not allowed to speak of this 'someone', eh?"

"How very astute of you. I, of course, can neither confirm nor deny that, but yes, that's the situation."

Caelwen noticed, to his dismay, another blink. *So he's telling the truth. He's been disciplined during that one, for breaking the rules.* It was rather obvious, once he understood. Tasinal's entire demeanor was a mixture of misery and rage, exactly the sort one would expect of a Meite being forced to knuckle under to a superior.

But who could have that sort of power, and why won't he show himself?

Rithard realized, with a start, that he was late to the party. The others had worked out what was going on some time back, while he had been distracted with anger. *This is what I get for indulging in emotion. Mei, I need a drink!*

"I don't suppose you have any decent vintages hidden away here?" he asked, not really expecting a good response, but Tasinal's face lit up at the mention of alcohol.

"Mei, that's just what we need! But something stronger than wine, assuming your constitution isn't as weak as your wit, eh?"

"You may insult me all you like if the barbs are served with spirits," Rithard told him, offering a slight bow of gratitude.

Tasinal rose, walked to a cabinet, and opened it to reveal an impressive array of liquors. "Go on. Ask your questions," he called, as he busied himself with filling glasses.

"Tell us about charging the blood. How do you even know about this? What must be done, and how will we know it's happening if we need to stop it?"

Tasinal placed a stout drink in front of each of them. Rithard grabbed his at once and knocked it back, as did Tasinal. As the ancient sorcerer moved to refill their glasses, Rithard saw Ahmed take a hesitant sip, as if uncertain what to expect, while he was fairly certain Caelwen merely pressed the glass to his mouth but took nothing from it.

"We captured some of Naritas's notes when we put a stop to his grand experiment. I won't claim to have understood much, but Yorn and Amrath did." Tasinal feigned a yawn. "What I do know is that when all of the pieces of the eye were present, the stuff glowed with a nearly black light, but once any of the pieces were removed, it just looked like oil." He shook a finger at Rithard, his face growing serious. "Mind you, it's still highly volatile, even in that state."

Rithard raised an eyebrow. "How explosive? What if we set it off without the Eye? Perhaps we might solve our problem with a bang, eh?"

Tasinal knocked back another drink, grimaced, and poured a third. *Oh, why not?* Rithard knocked his own back and gestured for a refill as Ahmed and Caelwen looked on with disapproval.

Tasinal swirled liquor in his glass, considering. "It would still be a cataclysmic explosion. I'd expect it would leave a tremendous crater, but without the energy of the Eye behind it, the ley lines would not be threatened. I doubt whoever set it off would survive." He again drained his glass and winked at the group. "Unless they could fly." His expression grew somber, "Or walk ley lines, but that way lies madness. It would be better to die in the explosion."

Rithard pressed on. "How would it be triggered?"

"There is a book in Torium with any number of rituals involving Elgar," Tasinal said, a contemplative look crossing his face. "Or at least there was. Naritas and his toadies had a long tradition of 'publishing', as 'twere. Very jealous sorts, always jockeying for credit." He shrugged and waved a hand in the air dismissively. "We never found it. Presumably it's still down there somewhere." He gave a slight shudder, as if chilled by old memories. "For all I know, so is Naritas. It all became very… fluid after we intervened."

Ahmed, apparently deciding he did like the drink, polished his off and set the glass down with great care. "It is a good plan, if we could get there. I have always doubted we all survive this quest. If there is a chance to stop it, I for one would be happy to die well to see it done."

Tasinal smiled warmly at him. "You remind me very much of Husam."

Ahmed nodded at Tasinal. "A kind thing to say, master, and you give us good knowledge, but it will not help us, I fear. There is little we can do from here, and it all happens tonight."

Rithard stared at Ahmed, aghast. "If you knew this, then why did we even bother with this wild goose chase?"

Ahmed shrugged again. "I did as I was told. I thought perhaps we would discover something we could do here to stop things, or get help from a powerful sorcerer, but with Tasinal bound as he says, it seems things are out of our hands. We cannot possibly arrive in time."

"Indeed," Tasinal said, looking glum and defeated. He poured another drink, and his face suddenly lit with impish glee. "Oh, that's simply too rich!"

Rithard finished his own drink. "What?"

Tasinal giggled like a child at whatever was running through his head. "Yes! Oh, great Mei, the irony is delicious!"

Tasinal rose to his feet, wobbled slightly, raised a finger in the air, and shouted, "I shall teleport you there!"

Ahmed had just enough time to see the shimmering figure surge forward, and then...

CHAPTER 18
ALL THE MARBLES

BLINK, but this time, it was the whole world. Ahmed struggled to keep from heaving up the contents of his last meal as the disorientation sent a wave of nausea through his innards. *And for that matter, when* was *my last meal?* He couldn't remember, though his belly insisted it had been too long. *Better to fight on an empty stomach, though.*

Things were so changed that Ahmed's mind had trouble adjusting to the new circumstances for a moment. They had been inside, and now they were under a dark, star-filled sky. It should have been cold, and yet the gentle breeze felt warm on his skin, though it was tinged with a subtle scent of something foul, like a long-dead corpse.

He realized he was lying, not standing, in a large wooden cart, along with Rithard and Caelwen. The policeman was looking about in wonder and shock, whereas the detective was examining himself, eyes wide and unbelieving.

Rithard was the first to speak. "Impossible."

Caelwen shot him a patronizing look. "Clearly, possible."

Rithard dismissed this with a wave of his hand. "Meites can't do this! They throw things, they set fires, but they don't make things appear or disappear or teleport!"

Caelwen shrugged. "Until now."

"Stop it, dolt! This is important!"

Caelwen hauled himself out of the cart and stretched, shaking his head and chuckling at Rithard. "You're the one denying reality, and I'm the 'dolt'."

Ahmed looked about, trying to get his bearings. Their cart stood in a clear spot that had likely once been a road leading toward a walled city. The road itself was barely visible, nearly overrun with vines, grass, and other wild vegetation, but the walls were clear of any growth, as if living things could not bring themselves to touch it. Eight small ziggurats, defensive structures that would have held archers and other troops in war, were spaced equally about the perimeter. Within, towering above the wall, was an enormous central pyramid, its stepped sides rising over the jungle to near two hundred feet.

Ahmed felt his guts twisting in revulsion as it came clear to him. *This is Torium.* He dropped to a knee, drew his blade, and bowed his head in prayer. To his surprise, Caelwen did likewise.

Ahmed raised an eyebrow. "What god will you pray to?"

Caelwen offered him a thin smile. "Any that will hear me."

Rithard shook his head, the expression on his face leaving no doubt that he was about to say something critical, but it fled him quickly. He hauled himself from the cart and knelt in the dirt with them. "Southlander, we will need your god today, I think. Show me how you pray."

As Ahmed opened his mouth to speak, he was interrupted by an utterly alien sound, a roaring, whooshing noise, and above that, he was certain he could hear shouting voices. As he looked up, a great flaming craft roared overhead, trailing fire and sparks. It cleared the outer defenses of Torium and moments later, as Ahmed and his friends knelt, gaping, they heard it impact, sending a great gout of steam and water into the air, visible above the wall.

Rithard spoke for everyone. "Mei! What *was* that?"

Ahmed leapt to his feet and pointed at the gates. "That was a *sign!* The gods have spoken! With me, quickly!"

Sadrik burst to the surface, his breath ragged, pulse pounding in his ears. The reek immediately assaulted his senses. He gagged, and very nearly vomited before realizing the scent was only mildly unpleasant. He took a great breath as his stomach settled, and tried to take stock as he struggled to tread water, close to panic. *I should have learned to swim, damn it!*

About him, shouts and screams filled the air. At first, he could not understand why. They had landed in water, relatively softly. The raft was still largely intact.

Something cold and slimy wrapped around his foot and pulled, drawing him beneath the surface before he could cry out himself. He caught just a glimpse of a mottled, purplish tentacle before the water closed over him. As the vile liquid filled his mouth, eyes, and nose, Sadrik's stomach again threatened to rebel, and his panic rose almost to an overpowering tenor. He was blind, drowning, and a nightmare creature planned on making a meal of him. It was the end.

No. Just that one thought was enough. A denial, a refusal to accept this fate. The fear fled, and fire took its place. *Time for* you *to scream, beast.* He clamped his searing hand around the tentacle and dug his fingers into the rubbery flesh. The water around him boiled furiously, but from somewhere distant, even through the water in his ears, he heard a monstrous cry of pain and rage.

The beast caught him by surprise with its counter. Something sharp raked across his chest, slashing to the bone, but Sadrik was resolved. He might still die, but not like *that*. In his mind, Sadrik saw the flame cycle from red to yellow to white to searing, devastating blue. *I will take you with me, count on it!* Somewhere, another inhuman scream erupted, and the tentacle released him.

Sadrik struggled to the surface again, gasping, just in time to see Ariano rise above the water and float to the safety of the shore.

"Where are you going?" he cried.

"Time to grow, whelp," she sneered. "Or die. Let's see if you deserve to call yourself a Meite, or if you've just been fooling yourself all along." She turned and began walking toward the central pyramid.

Sadrik screamed in rage at her, "I'll kill you for this, you wrinkled hag!"

Ariano stopped and turned, a bemused look on her face. "You'll have to survive, first." She turned again and walked away, ignoring his curses and threats.

Sadrik's attention was wrenched back to the moat by a shriek of agony. He watched in horror as two tentacles gripped one of the Southlanders and literally tore him limb from limb. Several of the man's fellows hacked at the beast, only to be snatched up themselves and drug beneath the surface.

In stunned silence, Sadrik watched as more tentacles rose to pull down the bloody chunks, and he felt the sickness rising in his throat again. *We can't beat this thing!* "Get out!" he cried, digging frantically at the water, struggling to move himself in the direction Ariano had gone. "There are too many!"

As his head slipped again beneath the surface, he struggled, but he simply could not avoid sinking. Of all the problems he might have encountered, this was by far the most irksome. He considered freezing the water solid, but ending up entombed in ice was no solution, not unless he simply wanted to deprive the beast of its kills out of spite. Even then, it would be far more satisfying if *someone* survived, even if it were not him, just so the tale could be told. *Sadrik the Mad: killed the beast along with his entire party. Not a terrible epitaph, but I could do better.*

His problem was simply that he couldn't find a way to deny his situation. It was too embarrassing, too simple, and perhaps, in his heart of hearts, a secret fear he had always carried with him. Sadrik had always *intended* to learn to swim, chiefly to avoid this exact problem, but he'd never actually gotten around to *doing* it. *I managed to fight off a dread water beast, only to drown like a common rube. What a miserable epitaph that will make. Ariano will thoroughly enjoy writing it.* His frown faded a moment as he realized another simple, pleasant truth. *It won't be Prandil writing my obituary. I outlived that bastard, at least!*

Just as he was returning to the thought of freezing the water, something strong grabbed him around the waist and hauled him upward. For a moment, he fought against it, thinking it was the beast again, but he felt fingers and the mail encasing them, and allowed his rescuer to get on with the rescue.

Shortly, he found himself face down on the shore, hacking up water contaminated with Mei knew what. Sadrik made a point of noting that he was certain it contained nothing permanently harmful.

When he could breathe once again, Sadrik turned to see his rescuer. His first thought was that Caelwen looked quite bizarre in his underwear with mail gloves. His second thought was that he had drowned and the afterlife was indeed a bizarre place. *How could he possibly be here?*

Caelwen dove back in the water and hauled a struggling Southlander to shore. Eleran, too, was dragging an unconscious warrior through the water. Stranger still, Sadrik could see the Southlanders *actual* leader now, the younger, darker colored one that had, supposedly, remained in Nihlos, charging toward them. Sadrik watched as the young man leapt from the shore to the ruins of the raft, skidded briefly, continued to run, and leapt again to the shore right beside Sadrik, gasping for breath.

"Sorcerer!" he wheezed. "What can you do to help?"

It's a good thing we Meites are already mad. Sadrik put the idea of understanding things on hold, and focused on controlling them. He rose to his feet and looked about as he tried to gather his wits, noting a few Southlanders were still in the moat, hacking at what seemed now a hundred tentacles. *Mei!*

"Get out of the water!" Sadrik called in a voice pitched a bit higher and a bit shakier than he had intended, but it carried well enough. "Get out now!" Of course, no one paid him any more attention than they had before.

Sadrik spied Sandilianus in the thick of things, knee deep in the filth and swinging his blade with gusto at a tentacle. The fellow glanced back at him, then backed away from his own fight and shouted Sadrik's message to those who hadn't heard it clearly. "Leave it, fools! Get out of the water!" His shout was loud enough that Sadrik fancied he could actually feel the vibration in his teeth. *Mei, the man has a sorcery all his own with that kind of volume!*

"Remind me of your name, Southlander," Sadrik said to the man standing beside him, his eyes following as the survivors scrambled ashore.

"Ahmed Justinius. Don't worry. I've forgotten yours, too."

"Sadrik Tasinal," Sadrik answered as he sank in a squat and reached for the water. "You'll remember it now, I'll wager."

Rage was temperature. Sometimes, it was a searing, disintegrating blue flame that charred bone and melted flesh. But sometimes...

Sometimes it was cold fury. *It's so strange, how blue can be hot or cold.*

As the last of them cleared the moat, Sadrik put his palms to the toxic water and felt the shock of bone-numbing cold rising from the surface, a freezing fog that had a burn all its own. Sharp reports tore through the air as the ice swelled in the banks and cracked, and from somewhere beneath them came a shrill keening. *We didn't expect that, did we? Die, bastard!*

Sandilianus was of a similar mind. "Finish this damned thing!" he cried. The Southlanders charged across the rapidly spreading ice and began hacking with abandon at the numerous trapped, exposed tentacles, sending putrid, black liquid spraying over the frozen surface. Again, the thing beneath howled in misery, bringing a broad grin to Sadrik's face. Eleran swung a fist at a trapped tentacle with enough force to burst it open, to a round of cheers.

Ahmed shook his head. "This is an indulgence. We waste time."

Caelwen, now dressed again, picked his way gingerly across the ice, trying not to slip.

Sadrik waved and called out, "I don't know how you got here, but I owe you my life."

Caelwen scoffed at this, then grinned. "I'd have left a Meite for last, but Rithard insisted that he owed you."

Sadrik raised an eyebrow, now thoroughly confused. "Rithard of House Amrath? *He's* here, too? But how?"

Caelwen offered him a smirk. "We were teleported here by Tasinal."

Sadrik considered doing something nasty and drastic in response to having his leg pulled so hard, but reminded himself that his intended victim had indeed just saved his life. He settled for a long and luxurious eye roll and a dismissive wave.

Caelwen winced as he checked some sort of wound in his shoulder, then, apparently satisfied, grabbed Ahmed by the arm, his expression urgent. "Ariano is here, too. Be careful."

Ahmed nodded. "We'll have to face her, for good or ill."

Sadrik snickered. "No need to worry. She had it in her head to stop Ahmed from bringing his piece of the Eye here, but…" He shrugged. "Prophesy, eh?" His face grew dark with anger. "At any rate, it's our turn to hunt her, now."

Caelwen frowned at Sadrik, his eyes narrowing. "As I recall, you were with her on that plan."

Sadrik waved Caelwen's point aside, scowling. "You know the rules, Caelwen. Waste not, knuckle under to the stronger. Besides, that was before she left the lot of us to die here."

Sandilianus, having at least dulled the edge of his own rage on the moat beast, slogged out of the water and joined them. "Aye. We have business to settle with her." He sat and began cleaning his blade. "

Sadrik gave him a knowing look. "We'll even the score with that old cunt, believe me."

Sandilianus sighed wistfully. "It will be a glorious battle, when it comes. But we must keep our eye on the prize, eh?"

Ahmed nodded. "No fucking around with personal vendettas until we have done Ilaweh's work."

Sadrik raised an eyebrow. "Patience is not generally a Meite virtue. Of what, pray tell, does Ilaweh's work consist, and why should I care?"

"Saving the world. And because you live here."

"Fair enough. Save the world first. *Then* murder Ariano. One needs to have priorities."

Ahmed gave them each a hard look to drive home his point, then turned to Sandilianus. "I have a gift for you."

Sandilianus's eyebrows rose high on his head. "A gift? *Now?*"

Ahmed grinned at him as he removed Brutus's blade and scabbard from his belt and handed them over.

Sandilianus's shook his head and pushed the sword away, his eyes moist. "Ahmed, no. He gave this to *you.* If he had wanted me to have it, he would have said so."

Ahmed nodded, but continued to offer the blade. "I needed it at the time, but now I have another." He gestured to his new sword, the one Tasinal had given him. "I am certain he would want you to have his blade now. Bring Brutus with us to this last battle. We need him."

Whatever the Southlanders were discussing, it held tremendous power, of that Sadrik was certain. *Only two things move men like that: hate and love, and either will prove invaluable in the coming battle.* "I have no idea of the particulars, but I can feel the strength of the emotion. It will serve us all today."

Sandilianus wiped a tear from his eye with a rough swipe of his arm and took the sword from Ahmed. "Aye, no doubt he is with Ilaweh now, furious at being denied this fight." He held the sword for long moments, gazing at it, his eyes clouded with memories. "I will carry Brutus's blade. But I, too, have a sword already. It was my father's, and he should join us for this battle as well."

Sandilianus gave Ahmed a conspiratorial wink, and shouted at Eleran, "Demon Man Dog! Come here! I have something for you!"

Ariano's shriek of outrage was almost enough to make Maranath forget about the vicious pottery shard poised at his jugular. *"What treachery is this?"* she cried, her voice making the debris on the floor dance in agitation.

Maranath cut his eyes toward his attacker and said, "Go ahead, finish me. You can explain this to her." He grinned at the look of utter confusion that erupted on the man's face.

Lothrian put a palm to his forehead and heaved a deep sigh. Aiul, now pressed against the wall by several of Maklin's junk golems, howled in fury and swiped at them with his mace, but they weren't solid enough to damage. The pieces simply moved back into place once the mace passed, unharmed.

Maklin himself wiped blood from his brow and spat, "Just who we *didn't* need!"

Ariano stood for long moments, chest heaving, eyes bugged, hands clamped to the side of her head.

Maranath's opponent, not relaxing his grip on the shard, muttered, "Is she with you?"

Maranath offered an apologetic shrug. "I told you, it's a family matter."

To Maranath's surprise, the pressure on his neck eased, and the stranger stepped back cautiously, shard still poised to strike, his eyes darting back and forth at everyone. "Can you help him?" he asked, nodding in Aiul's direction.

Maranath rubbed at his neck. "That's why we're here."

The man licked his lips, eyes still nervous. "I cannot read you. I do not know if I can trust you."

Maranath knew just how the man felt. "You're the second person to tell me that, lately. You'll have to do it the old-fashioned way, like the rest of us." He offered a smile, having little else. "Guess."

As the stranger gave Maranath a quizzical look, Lothrian lowered his hand and spoke. "Ariano—"

Her reaction was immediate and furious. "Lothrian wouldn't recognize me!" Her shout was a visible distortion in the air that hurtled at him with breakneck speed. "*What are you?*"

Lothrian's face grew dark and stiff. The wave hit him in the chest, but he held his stance. Even so, he skidded a good three feet backward, but showed no other harm. "I would know you anywhere," he called, his voice cold and imperious. "And you know me, too."

Ariano's eyes grew wider still, then narrowed. "Lothrian is *dead!*"

Lothrian's jaw clenched, and he looked at her as if she were a complete idiot.

Maklin shook a finger at the dark, bearded stranger. "Why don't you do us all a favor throw a damned rock at *her*!"

Maranath shook his head. *How many times do we need to go through this?* "It's him, Ariano."

Ariano looked back and forth between them, near panic, her chest heaving. "How can that *be*?"

Maranath tried desperately to focus her attention, gesturing with his head and eyes toward Aiul. "Couldn't we talk about that later?"

It seemed as if Ariano had only just realized Aiul's presence. The anger drained from her, and she cast a nervous look to Lothrian. He nodded back and mouthed, "Go to him."

Rithard found himself almost running to keep up. Ahead, Sadrik and Sandilianus stalked forward, their eyes filled with vengeful promises. Ahmed was just behind the pair, alternating between cajoling and threatening them to remember why they were here.

Behind Rithard, the remaining Southlanders followed, their numbers much reduced. At least three of them had perished in the moat. Rithard counted eight now. *How tragic to come so far and not see the end.*

He followed the others down an endless flight of stairs and into a huge chamber dominated by a great basin in the center, and suppressed a gasp at what he saw there. *The Black Pool!* To his dismay, the liquid in the pool had begun to glow, shedding a strange, purplish light, unearthly and disturbing. *Mei! It's charged just by the presence of the pieces! We have to find that damned book!*

What his eyes fell on next shattered his analytical calm like a vase dropped from a rooftop. At first, his mind simply refused to accept what it saw. *Mei, what is that?* He tried to categorize it, but it honestly defied description. It was a *thing*, a twisted, mockery of human form, apparently dead on the floor near the pool. *It's huge! How could it even support its own weight?* Rithard was suddenly filled with the mad urge to dash forward and begin dissecting it at once, but knew it would be bad form. *And we have more important matters to attend. But after....*

With some difficulty, he forced his attention away from the bizarre corpse, and back to the practical realm. He looked about, trying to take a lay of the land and form some ideas on where to even begin his search for the book. He saw four exits to the room, each at cardinal points of the compass, one of them enormous. *Presumably, that leads into the rest of the complex.*

Rithard's gut churned as he recognized Aiul, currently pinned against a wall by some of Maklin's sorcerous constructs. Rithard did a doubletake to see Aiul's hair was no longer blond, but bone white. Ariano, her face now sweet and chipper, stood before Aiul, hands clasped, in animated conversation. *I pray you can talk him down, you wicked harridan. I will have to confront my sins if you do, but it's nothing more than I deserve.*

Ariano stiffened as she turned to see them entering. Sadrik cast her a wicked, murderous grin, and Sandilianus's hand tightened on the grip of his sword. Again, Ahmed moved closer and whispered something to them.

Hold it together!

In the last year, Aiul had endured more pain and grief than he knew was possible, and had become quite inured. He was ready to withstand anything except Ariano.

Here I am, surrounded by enemies, and she is somehow here

to save me again. Why? Yet here she was, as always, and with such a simple request: "Let me take you home, Aiul."

Aiul relaxed against the press of the golems and sighed. Suddenly, things seemed...different, the jagged thing in his mind faded, his grief suddenly so much stronger and heavier than his rage.

"You always save me," he croaked. "You treat me better than my own mother."

Ariano looked at him, her eyes filled with a profound sadness that Aiul could not fathom. "Your mother has always taken care of you, Aiul."

The world was too bright and sharp. Aiul closed his eyes, letting the myriad of conflicting thoughts in his mind play out. This had all begun with his family being taken from him, and a part of him still wanted revenge, on everyone and every-thing. *That's a fair thing! Blood calls for blood!* And yet he had only learned that phrase because he had, for reasons he could not fathom, been chosen to understand what it truly meant.

He could still hear the voices of the damned in his mind: their screams of agony and terror as they were made into 'art'; their cries of fury as they took their vengeance on their tormentors. He and Logrus had been instrumental in giving those wretched, broken souls what they needed to overcome their unbearable horror.

Aiul's own pains seemed smaller now, less urgent, just as Logrus had told him. It was not that they were gone. It was just that they were less significant. After seeing the sort of horror and evil that drew Elgar's attention, even the loss of his family dimmed in comparison.

But most of all, he realized he needed to bury his wife and child.

At first, when he opened his eyes, he could not speak. The

emotions in him seemed to fill his throat. He swallowed hard and managed to croak out, "I want to go home."

Ariano, tears in her eyes, nodded and smiled back. "Release him, Maklin."

Maklin looked back and forth at everyone, suspicious. "For the record, this is a bad idea." Finding no supporters, he waved a hand with a resigned air, and his automatons collapsed to the stone floor, lifeless piles of debris. "Don't blame me if he kills anyone."

Aiul nearly collapsed into his Papa's arms. Lothrian swept him up in a hug and reached into Aiul's shirt to remove the silver chain and the amber sphere it held. "You've born this long enough, son. Rest now."

Despite the strong urge to simply collapse in place, Aiul shrugged off the many hands reaching out to help him. It was, as Maranath had said, a family matter, and that included his treacherous cousin. If Aiul was to go home, he needed answers.

To his credit, Rithard met his gaze without flinching, and with a contrite expression, even. Aiul said nothing for long moments, then spoke a single word. "Why?"

"Davron said he would kill me if I didn't. I believed him."

It sounded so simple, so trivial, a contrived lie, and yet Aiul had entertained that very thought, that Rithard had been coerced. He hadn't known for certain until this very moment whether Rithard was even still alive. It *seemed* true, and yet he saw, in Rithard's eyes, something more. "Tell all of it."

Rithard rolled his shoulders as if readying himself for a great task. His throat worked as he tried to find the right phrasing. "I lost another cousin over that whole affair, you know." He stared at his feet, shaking his head.

For a moment, Aiul did not understand, but when it hit him, he felt his rage against Rithard melt away to nothing. *Marissa.*

Mei, he loved her. He talked about her constantly, and I never understood until now.

Rithard looked up again, his eyes glistening. "It had nothing to do with what I did to you. I hadn't even really had a chance to process it. I know it wasn't your fault. It wasn't even Kariana's fault. It's just... hard to let go."

Before Aiul could respond, Sadrik Tasinal stepped forward, a cruel grin on his face. "It was Maralena Prosin's fault, and I settled that score on a permanent basis."

Rithard gestured at Sadrik as if handing him a burden, and stepped aside toward the other Meites. Aiul closed his eyes and let the numbness creep over him as Sadrik told his tale. It was Maralena who wrote the letters, set up the deadly encounter with Lara and Kariana. And it had been his own mother who had sent him down this path to ruin. *No, Ariano, you are wrong. My mother most definitely did* not *take care of me.* And now she was gone, beyond his rage, his grief, even beyond the chance of a simple goodbye.

An unfamiliar and strangely accented voice spoke from behind him, "So you are the one the old man spoke of." Aiul was surprised by the touch of a warm, friendly hand on his shoulder. He turned and looked into the deep brown eyes and alien face of an unknown Southlander. "I see no evil in you," the man said. "Only much pain."

Another of the Southlander's people, older and lighter skinned, with a hard face, stood just behind him. *He was there, in the courtroom.* Aiul couldn't help but smile to realize that somehow or another, the fellow had managed to avoid the death sentence he had been given. *Perhaps he really did beat them all.*

Aiul was just about to respond to the younger man when he caught sight of the sword the older fellow carried. To his shock, he realized he knew the blade. Aiul looked to the weapon and back up. "Sandilianus, yes? Where is Brutus?"

Sandilianus slowly drew the blade and handed to Aiul to inspect. "Brutus is with Ilaweh, now, and no doubt arguing with him over how the world should be managed," he said.

The younger Southlander chuckled, then said, "If you knew Brutus, you knew Yazid, yes? I am Ahmed, Yazid's..." He paused a moment, as if searching for a word before settling on, "...son."

It was almost too much for Aiul to bear, knowing what he had done to this man's father, or rather, what he had helped to do. But he knew enough of their culture to offer the only comfort that could be given. His throat was thick with emotion as he spoke. "I was with him at the end. He died well, as he lived: unbeaten."

Ahmed offered his arm, and Aiul took it, grasping at the forearm. The Southlander's eyes grew moist, and he gripped Aiul's arm with a gentle strength. "Thank you for that. It means more than you could know."

"It's the least I could do for you. I owe you much more."

Logrus, too, was at Aiul's side now, poor, simple Logrus, not stupid but so very naive. He had been a friend to Aiul despite Aiul's terrible treatment. He offered a crooked smile and said, "Elgar has saved you, Aiul. Look at what we accomplished. We eased undying pain. Now, I think, you can heal, too."

Aiul could barely hold back his own tears. It was all too much, and to finally be at the end of it was enough to almost cause him to break down. He nodded his gratitude and managed to choke out, "Imagine that. We saved the world without the battle everyone was expecting."

For a moment, he even believed it. But the look in his Papa's eyes was unsettling, a wild, electric blue that spoke of storms and madness. *That's the look I remember most: the one that said pain was coming.*

Rithard breathed a sigh of relief at having successfully navigated very hazardous terrain. Bragging would keep Sadrik occupied long enough for Rithard to have a discrete word with Maranath and hopefully warn him against the very real possibility that Ariano would be attacked in short order.

As he approached, he realized that he did not recognize one of the people in their group. The blond man, not much older than Aiul, was clearly a Meite. He had the stance, the air, the presence, and seemed familiar, but Rithard couldn't place him. For no reason Rithard could lay his finger on, he felt an intense dislike for the man. *Well, it's hardly unreasonable to dislike Meites.*

Rithard saw with displeasure that the strange Meite had noticed him as well, and was walking over with an extended hand. "You look very familiar. It's not really possible that we could have met, I suppose, but I wonder if I know your father?"

Rithard reluctantly presented his hand and shook. Whatever misgivings Rithard had about the newcomer, he had to admit the man had a warm, firm, confident handshake. "Rithard of House Amrath. I'm afraid—"

The stranger's eyebrows rose in surprise, and he burst into a grin. "Of course! No wonder you seem familiar. I'm Lothrian." He nodded at Rithard's obvious confusion. "It's a long story. Suffice to say I met with some difficulty down here and I've been rescued at long last."

Rithard considered this new information with clinical detachment. It was tempting to dismiss it as an outright lie, and yet the others had heard him say it, and no one was correcting him.

Lothrian pressed on. "And your father?"

Rithard, feeling pinned, answered, "Ah, my father was Barthold."

Lothrian grinned. "Yes, I remember him, a cousin, but he was a very young man when I knew him. You quite favor him, except for the hair, of course. Who is your mother?"

Rithard cleared his throat, looking for an exit. Ariano was looking their way as if she might approach, and from the expression on her face, he would prefer to be elsewhere when she arrived. "Uh, Teretha Prosin."

Lothrian's eyebrows rose as his face fell. "Oh. Ah, I see." He brightened quickly and asked, "And do you hold a title within the house?"

Rithard had been hoping to avoid addressing this. He didn't actually believe this man was Lothrian, but now that the question was asked, Rithard felt certain that the imposter's reaction to the answer would be informative. "As of this morning, I am the Patriarch of the House, sir."

Lothrian's face seemed to simply freeze for a moment, the humor in his eyes fading, making the smile on his lips seem artificial. It, too, faded when he spoke, his slight grin seeming now more a baring of teeth. "Ah, I see. I am not entirely up to speed on events, but I should have thought that spot would have been Aiul's."

"There was a crisis, and an emergency meeting of the council. Aiul was not in a position to be considered."

Lothrian smiled again, but his eyes remained humorless. "Have they given you the Papers, then?"

What a bizarre non-sequitur. Rithard struggled to find words, wishing very much that he was elsewhere with a stiff drink in hand. *Not 'How do you like the job?' or 'What are the biggest issues?' Just straight at The Papers.* Despite the alarm bells ringing in his head, Rithard put the notion aside. There were more pressing matters at the moment. "Indeed."

Lothrian's eyes seemed lit with inner fire now, and he leaned in, uncomfortably close, to almost whisper, "And what brings the Patriarch of House Amrath to the depths of the Pit of Torium?"

I might ask you the same question. Rithard stepped back, more out of reflex than design, and stammered, "There is a doomsday device here. We need to stop it from being triggered. It's the basis of the Dead God's prophecy."

Lothrian's eyebrows again rose, and he grinned back, the old, familiar Meite madness dancing in his eyes like a blue flame. "Is there? I have never heard such a thing."

Rithard tried to keep the contempt he felt from showing in his expression. Lothrian was lying. He was certain of it. But why? *Let's prod you a bit and see where you jump.* "Neither had I, since someone seems to have removed anything about it from the Papers. Fortunately, Tasinal was kind enough to explain it to us before he teleported us here." He watched for a reaction, carefully gauging the man he could only think of now as his opponent.

Lothrian's eyes widened. "Mei, really?" He looked to the side, in Aiul's direction. "Well, then it's a good thing like we've managed to intercept it, eh?" He gave Rithard's arm a friendly squeeze as he walked past, a clearly forced smile on his lips, and called over his shoulder, "Well done, young man! Well done!"

Rithard suppressed an urge to brush at the spot where Lothrian had touched him, so strong was his sense of revulsion for the man. He watched Lothrian walk toward Ahmed, turning over the bizarre reaction in his head. He was certain of it, now. *Mei!* He *took the damned papers!*

There was something more, though, something else that was nagging at him about Lothrian's reaction. *He didn't even flinch when I mentioned Tasinal, or teleportation.* A Meite with no ulterior motive would have argued or mocked such a statement. At the very least, he would have demanded an explanation. He most certainly would *not* have let it stand and walked away, unless he had something to hide.

Or unless he were distracted by something else.

My destiny is so much greater than I had imagined! Lothrian continued to smile at the others, even as the realization that he was on the precipice of greatness swept over him. He took a deep breath, wondering if he were truly committed to the plan that was tearing through his mind, making connections the others would surely call mad if they knew his thoughts.

My daughter is dead. The woman I loved is old and gray, and taken up with my best friend. And my son's mind is shattered beyond hope. My house is now led by an upstart. I have absolutely nothing left to lose, and everything to gain.

His journey had begun humbly enough, with the notion that the pieces of the Eye ought be in more trustworthy hands. What could the founders have been thinking to leave one with the Torians? And to leave a doomsday device in place was simply irresponsible.

At least Amrath had been wise enough to warn about it in the Papers. Once Lothrian had resolved to destroy it, those had become superfluous, a liability, even. Had Maranath or Maklin learned of his plan, they likely would have tried to stop him, and Lothrian had no intention of allowing that to happen, nor any guarantee that the Papers would remain secure while he was on his quest. Once he was finished, the information would be irrelevant. Simple prudence dictated he remove it, and he had never once considered that he might not survive his attempt.

I would have, had I not been betrayed.

Ariano had been more than willing. *In so many ways!* He looked at her, feeling a bit of the old longing, but mostly a deep sadness at what she had become. *Old. Weak. Faded. And treacherous.*

Destiny had spoken, choosing to spare him the ravages of time, to arrive at his appointed moment still full of youthful vigor. Oh, yes, he had begun this second life as a zombie, but it hardly suited him. The hole in his chest had been unsightly, the cold and numbness in his body distracting and unpleasant. They had faded quickly, and no one had even noticed, a fact that both amused and saddened him. People *should* notice beauty and power, and yet, for the moment, it was perhaps best that they were otherwise occupied.

He had not, until the upstart had let the information slip, realized that Tasinal still lived, had somehow managed to overcome death through sheer will. It had, of course, been theorized: sufficient will ought to be able to cheat death. Amrath had spoken against such things in his philosophical works, arguing that to even attempt such a thing was cheating, that the only thing that gave life value was the fact that time was finite.

And what Meite had not, in some dark moment, looked at his situation and imagined killing *everyone*? The doomsday device made that idle, mad thought an actual possibility.

But to realize both were within one's grasp was an altogether different matter, especially when one had certain knowledge men were never meant to possess.

A hundred years past, the Torians had finally overwhelmed him, but not nearly soon enough to stop him from plundering their secrets. Had Ariano's cowardice not overcome her, had she just had a bit of faith, they would have triumphed over the creatures together. Instead, she'd fled, leaving him to die, alone, in that pit of horror and despair.

He had, of course, not simply accepted his fate. He slew the filth as they came at him, desperately trying to use the piece of the Eye the dragon had given him to find his way to the piece the Torians held, to no success. Something was wrong, and whether it was his technique or something else, Lothrian couldn't say, though he suspected it was because he had simply lacked the focus due to his circumstances. Whatever the reason, he had been forced to rely on intuition and garden-variety brutality, at last prying the secret from their much-vaunted Master. Lothrian, pressed for time, had left the fiend to bleed out. *My greatest mistake was not finishing him when I had the chance.*

Lothrian had retrieved the Torian piece, a half-head, along with their Book of the Gods, and torn through it to find the ritual, fully intending to take them all with him, but the counterattack had been bold and well planned. Somehow, the Master had survived and organized them into a final, devastating assault.

Lothrian had made them pay dearly, but in the end, there were simply too many, and he had fallen there, betrayed by the love of his life, alone in the dark, surrounded by monsters. Such a great irony that he had been brought down not by powerful sorcery, but by a simple piling on until he could no longer see, and a mass of wood shoved through his chest. Even then, he had very nearly recovered. Had his heart beaten a few moments more, long enough to retain his mind just a second or two, things would have ended very differently. Lothrian shuddered at the memory and pushed it aside. *Some things are best forgotten.*

The fools had enshrined him as a perfect monster, a beauty so rare that it surpassed all of their work. They had preserved him in every detail, up to and including the partially assembled Eye hanging about his neck. *Did they miss that, or did they know and use me as a display out of spite? Or even admiration?*

Even as the questions ran through his mind, he knew the truth: they sensed his destiny, and they chose not to resist. It was fitting. It was appropriate. It was inevitable. They had prepared him, preserved his flesh, and stood him in a position to ascend to the greatest of heights when at last his moment came.

And my would-be rescuers lacked the presence of mind to even verify things when I told them I didn't have it anymore. So terribly foolish of them. Now, with the piece I took from Aiul, I have three, and the last piece is in this very room.

The crucial point, the information none of the rest understood, was a bit that Naritas and his minions had worked out eons past and written down in the book: the gods themselves were but manifestations of large groups of minds. Men wanted justice, and so a being that stood for justice must exist. Men made war, and so there was a god of war.

That, in and of itself, was no great mystery. Such had been theorized by many a philosopher. But Naritas had worked out the existence of an even greater entity, known as the Sleeper or Dreamer, a vast being that was the sum of *all* minds. It alone was capable of choice, and each living mind had that gift. But because men were almost always at odds, the entity slept, having no specific direction.

The Eye had changed that balance. Suddenly, great swathes of men aligned on the same side, their visions linked together by the ability to communicate in great numbers and mind to mind, without distortion or mistrust. Naritas had indeed created a mighty weapon.

But Naritas had been a small thinker. He had never asked himself the obvious question: what if there were only one man alive? Only one vessel to contain the Sleeper?

That man would be a god of gods.

Ahmed watched the stranger approach, another sorcerer, his intent gray like a madman. Ahmed couldn't help but smile to think that in these interactions, he was forced to live as any normal man might, to judge others not with any special sight but just on experience. *But I have little enough of that to rely on.*

Rithard was running toward him, shouting and gesticulating wildly, and Ahmed understood: there was something terribly wrong with the man standing before him. Ahmed could not see the sorcerer's aura, but he could see the expression on his face, the madness in his eyes, the intent in his gaze.

Ilaweh, guide my hand! He reached for his sword, but it was too late. With a strength and speed Ahmed had never imagined, the smiling sorcerer seized Ahmed about the throat, one hand tightening like an iron band, the other tearing open his shirt and dragging forth the piece of the Eye. Sickly green light poured from the half-head like puss from a gangrenous wound.

The sorcerer held his prize aloft only briefly before turning to the others and sweeping his arm at them in a grand gesture.

Ahmed's eyes closed of their own accord at the brilliant flash that followed, and then he saw nothing at all.

CHAPTER 19

ACTUALLY

IUL awoke to an insistent hand shaking his shoulder. Logrus put a finger to his lips, but it was not necessary. At one time, he might have cried out, but whoever he had been before, he was no longer that fool.

How long was I out? He couldn't say for certain, nor exactly what had happened, but he had a good idea. *This was Papa.*

Logrus sat beside him, fingering a sharp rock like a talisman, his dark eyes full of promises of mayhem, and for once, Aiul found it comforting.

He looked about cautiously, not wanting to alert any enemies. Papa was still on his feet, looking up at the ceiling, and Ariano hovered nearby. He spied Sadrik slumped against a wall, unconscious but breathing. The Southlanders were slowly finding their feet. Aiul did not know the Nihlosian with them, but he, too, was recovering from the blast. Across the room, Caelwen, alert and dutiful as ever, seemed to be checking Rithard's pulse. From the look on the captain's face, Aiul presumed said pulse was found.

The elder Meites were another matter. The blast had been centered on them, and Maklin and Maranath were both face down and not moving at all, covered in blood.

Madness! Damnable Meite madness!

"Papa!" he cried out. "Stop this!"

Lothrian gave Aiul a tired look, waving his left hand dismissively as he reached for the ceiling with his right and jerked downward as if pulling on a rope. Moments later, a massive object came hurtling from the blackness overhead to land with a resounding crash in the middle of the black pool. The liquid within did not splash at all, a fact Aiul found less surprising than he might have. Once things had settled, Aiul could see that it was a large golden statue of a lion, but the head was missing. The surface was so smooth it was difficult to tell if it had been made that way, or cut after the fact.

Aiul turned back to Logrus and met his dark stare with his own. The hunter nodded toward Lothrian and mouthed, "We must stop him."

Aiul nodded back, turned to the Southlanders, and gestured as best he could the swinging of a weapon. *Time to fight.*

Ahmed suppressed the urge to groan as he rose. He was not sure how long he had been out, if at all, but he certainly knew the cause, and was somewhat surprised to find himself still among the living. By rights, he ought be standing before Ilaweh, explaining how he had been so easily ambushed.

Not just me. He looked at the two old men across the way and sighed, feeling anger and grief welling within him. The one they called Maklin was clearly dead, the back of his head torn open. Maranath lay beside him, covered in blood but still breathing, if only just.

Sandilianus growled beside him, "Fucking barbarians and sorcerers! We should never have trusted them!" Eleran, kneeling over Maranath, cast him a glare, but said nothing, and Sandilianus hung his head in chagrin.

From the corner of his eye, Ahmed spotted movement. He turned to see Aiul the Troublemaker gesturing in fairly universal language: *get ready to fight.*

Lothrian, his back to them and busy meddling with something hidden by his body, called out, "Don't be stupid. You're all doomed, but you can still choose an easy or hard death."

Sandilianus leapt to his feet and shouted, "A hard death is fine by me!" He charged at the sorcerer, teeth bared in fury.

Lothrian turned and watched him come, an amused look on his face. As the Southlander neared striking range, Lothrian back-handed the air between them. The empty space seemed to ripple and distort, tiny rainbows visible in the warping, and the air snapped with a cracking sound, sending Sandilianus hurtling against the wall.

"As you wish," Lothrian sneered. "I'll deal with you shortly, when I am finished here." He looked about at the rest of them "Anyone else?"

Ahmed raised a hand to calm the rest of his men as they reflexively went for their weapons. They could not win that fight, not that way. He could not help but smile to see Eleran move quickly to see to Sandilianus. The Nihlosian had become a good friend to them all, but he and Sandilianus had a special bond, even if it wasn't the one Sandilianus would have preferred. It was stronger than that, the bond of men who had shed blood together.

Ahmed spared a glance at Maranath, wondering if Eleran's leaving him meant he, too, had passed. But, no, the old fellow was still breathing, occasionally twitching as if in troubled sleep. *Hold on, old man. We will get to you soon.*

He gripped the sword Tasinal had given him, drawing strength from the knowledge of what it was, and who had once wielded it. If they had any chance at all, it lay with Aiul, Logrus, and whatever they were planning. Ahmed glanced toward the pair and gave them a single, slow nod. *We are allies now, it seems. I will follow your lead.*

Across the room, the wicked sorceress they called Ariano stared at the madman, her eyes narrow with suspicion. "What are you doing, Lothrian?"

Lothrian laughed and spread his arms at her, his face growing bright and animated. "What any of you would have done, had you seen the potential!" His humor fell away as quickly as it had come. He regarded her with a cold, calculated stare. "Are you with me or not?"

Ariano stared at him for long moments, for once, indecisive. "With you for what?"

Lothrian's eyebrows rose, and he smiled again. "Why, *every-thing* my dear!"

"And the cost?"

He grew serious again. "Everyone else."

Ariano stood in silence, her face unreadable, not answering. Lothrian waited a few moments, then gave her a curt nod, as if taking her silence for assent, and turned back to the lion statue in the black pool. He produced the pieces of the eye and began assembling them.

Ahmed's every instinct screamed for him that this was their last chance, to throw caution to the wind and charge with every-thing he had. But he remembered quite clearly his conversation with Maranath outside Nihlos. There would come a moment, and he would know it. *I see no moment. I see only suicide now.*

Lothrian smiled as he pressed a sphere into the eye socket of Ahmed's half of the tiny lion's head, then held the two halves together and with a triumphant grin, applied them to the neck of the lion statue.

His face fell as nothing happened. He tried again, tapping the pieces vigorously against the stump of the neck several times, his face lit from below by the glowing pool, turning his growing fury into something almost demonic.

Slowly, eyes full of menace, he turned to Aiul. "Boy, you think to trick me?" he snarled.

Logrus answered in a dull voice, "We mean to kill you."

Lothrian scoffed, and his humor returned. Holding the pieces of the Eye in an outstretched hand, he began to slowly turn. As he faced Ahmed, he stopped, both eyebrows rising high on his head as his mouth contorted in anger. "Where is the real piece, Southlander?"

Of all the things the sorcerer might have asked of him, this was the one Ahmed least expected. He had no answer prepared, and stammered as he gave the only one that came to mind. "I don't understand."

Ahmed could almost see flame in Lothrian's burning blue eyes. The sorcerer clutched at the air and snatched his hand toward his chest. Ahmed felt invisible, irresistible force seize him and drag him forward, his feet skidding on the cold, damp stone. He came to a stop, arms pinned to his sides, almost nose to nose with Lothrian. The sorcerer's scowl seemed to radiate heat like the sun. "Give it to me!"

Ahmed heard the clatter of blades clearing scabbards, and turned his head, knowing what he would see. His men, Sandilianus at their head, were readying a charge. "Stand down!" he shouted.

With several muttered curses, they obeyed. Ahmed turned away from their reproachful stares and looked Lothrian in the eye. "I do not know what you seek, villain. Kill me if you must. I do not fear death."

Lothrian's face again quickly transformed from utter fury to wry amusement. "You seem sincere." He tapped a finger against his cheek as he considered. "Perhaps you really don't know. Which means I will have to tear you apart to find it. It's nothing personal. You seem a nice enough fellow." He raised a hand high overhead and twisted it into a claw.

Ilaweh, if this is how it ends, if we must fail, give me the strength to die well.

Mei! Why won't these fools simply realize they are beaten?

Lothrian saw movement out of the corner of his eye, and spun in time to see the bearded, dark-skinned assassin leaping through the air at him. The man had told them his name at some point, but Lothrian hadn't bothered to remember it. By all rights he shouldn't even still be alive. None of them should, except the ones he wanted as witnesses to his ascension, but they refused to see the inevitable.

Had there been time to sigh in frustration, Lothrian would have indeed indulged in the pose, but as it was, he had to react too quickly. He reached up and grasped toward the flying fool, stopping him mid-hurtle. He couldn't help but chuckle at the look of confusion and frustration on his would-be assassin's face. "Fools! You are brave, but this is a waste of my time!" He clenched a fist and grinned as his new prisoner howled in agony.

Why do you try to resist a god?

Ahmed realized that, for the moment, they were all forgotten. Aiul had taken the opportunity the Elgarite's distraction had created, and leapt into the black pool. Ahmed was uncertain what the man intended, but it would surely be momentous.

He looked back at his men, and smiled to see Sandilianus had recovered. Ahmed tried to move his arms, but they were still tightly pinned. He caught Sandilianus's eyes and held them a moment, then nodded, praying the man would understand his gesture: *be ready.*

Sandilianus and Eleran, grim faced, nodded back.

Ahmed offered a silent prayer for the Elgarite as well, and for a moment, he thought Ilaweh had indeed intervened. He knew well the feel of a god's touch, the sensations of his work. It had a smell, a taste, a sound, unlike the minor magic's of the Meites. But he quickly realized his error. The sensations were not leather and charred coal, or the ring of steel on steel, but the acrid copper of fresh blood, the reek of freshly opened guts. And the sound—

The sound was a shriek of fury like nothing he had ever heard.

It's come down to this.

Aiul knew he should feel more excited, angry perhaps, betrayed even, but in truth, what he felt was a mixture of deep grief and cool acceptance. *Necessary, like Logrus always says.*

Still, it was a hard thing to do. First Lara and their unborn child, then his mother. And now Papa.

I am just correcting my own mistake.

Logrus wailed in misery. Aiul had no doubt that Papa intended to crush him to death, would have already save that he wanted to draw things out as a demonstration, an object lesson for others that might choose to stand against him instead of meekly going to their doom. *'This is the way you will die if you oppose me!'* he would say. Papa had always been one for object lessons. One was supposed to simply accept it.

No. Not me. Not anymore.

It was a bad idea. Aiul knew it, even as he charged ahead with the plan. *But anything is better than just waiting to die.* Aiul raised both hands over his head and reached out to Elgar. He thought of his despair in prison, his horror at watching Lara and

Kariana fighting, and, ironically, his utter loathing of the very creature he intended to revive.

As he felt the warm embrace of Elgar's fury, the blood flowing up him again like a cloak, he cried out in a voice that shook Torium once again, *"Rise! Rise and remember!"*

Logrus's wail stopped at once, and, to Aiul's great satisfaction, Lothrian turned a near panicked face to him and cried out in high pitched, fearful voice, "What are you *doing* boy?"

Aiul spoke back not in his own voice, but in Elgar's: *"I am Avenger."*

As they all looked on in horror, the blackened, shattered body of the Master of Torium shuddered, then slowly rose, its undead eyes glowing with green malevolence, its razor-filled maw and sword-like claws a hundred pointed promises of painful death.

"Playthings!" it roared, its fetid, wet breath rushing over them all, a fog of putrid, cadaverous gas. "I will rend you *all!*"

As Lothrian's focus shifted to fend off the Master, Logrus fell to the ground. He hit hard and rose quickly, nose gushing from the impact against the stone, but he barely felt anything, so great was the relief from escaping the sorcerer's crushing grip.

The Master charged forward with a mad shriek and snatched Lothrian up by his legs like a doll. "You will *suffer* this time, Monster!" it roared as it swung him like a flail against the floor.

Lothrian hit the stones with a meaty smack, howling in pain and struggling in vain against the Master's grip. The stone beneath him cracked from the force of the blow.

Logrus scrabbled backward on all fours like a spider, desperately trying to avoid the Master's stamping feet and Lothrian's flailing body as the Master pounded his victim against the floor repeatedly.

I must warn the others! From outside, he could already hear the thunderous cries. *Aiul told them to remember!*

Rithard watched it all in vague, undefined horror. As usual, he didn't feel it from within so much as a physical sensation. He noticed with distaste that his muscles were twitching all over his body. It was irksome in general, but the tick at his eye was far and away the most annoying. He rubbed at it as he tried to take stock of things.

Aiul's companion was running toward them, shouting, "Beware! They are hostile!" Outside, shadows stirred as hulking, vaguely man-shaped things lurched to their feet like drunkards rising from a barroom brawl and began to stagger forward.

I should never have come. It seemed a fairly certain thing that he would die here, and if that were to be so, Rithard wanted there to be a reason. He shrugged off Caelwen's ministrations and cast about for his medical bag. "Go. Fight," he said. "I'll do what I can for the rest."

Caelwen gave him a quick wave and drew his blade as Rithard crawled toward the downed Meites. He might have walked, but he saw no reason to draw attention to himself. *If I can get them conscious, they can likely save themselves.*

He held on to that notion like a drowning man would a log, determined to do what he could for as long as he could, until the battle came to him. Caelwen and another Nihlosian Rithard did not know joined the Southlanders and Aiul's companion and rushed to block the entrance from the new threat.

It didn't take long to reach his patients. Behind him the sounds of pitched battle raged. In front of him, the roars and screams of another battle played out.

One look at Maklin was enough to know there was no help for

him. His head had been dashed to a pulp against the floor, its contents scattered. Maranath was little better, his skull clearly fractured, but he clung doggedly to life, drawing slow, shuddering breaths.

Sadrik, however, was relatively whole, save for the hideous gash on his leg that was even now pumping blood over the stone floor. Rithard spared Maranath a final glance and moved to the younger sorcerer. *Hold on, old man. You're next.*

Rithard tore a strip of cloth from Maklin's robe and fashioned a tourniquet for Sadrik's leg. *Simple enough. Now for the dangerous part.* He withdrew a vial of smelling salts from his bag, noting with detached irritation that a bottle of alcohol and several other components had been smashed in the blast.

It was entirely possible that Sadrik had neck injuries that would be worsened, perhaps even kill him if he moved. It was also not out of the realm of possibility that an injured Meite suddenly revived might well lash out at the nearest target.

Rithard had no idea how the battle before him would play out. The beast seemed far stronger, but the fact that Lothrian was still alive after being smashed against the floor and walls spoke well for his resilience. Ariano tried to help, hurling chunks of stone and anything else she could find at the beast, but it simply shrugged off her assault, cackling, and swung Lothrian at her like a club, knocking her flying.

This is not medically sound, Sadrik, but we need you now. He jammed the bottle under the wounded sorcerer's nose and cringed against the myriad possibilities of disaster.

To Rithard's surprise, Sadrik blinked, made a disgusted face, and then looked about, confusion in his eyes. "What happened?"

Rithard grunted. "Lothrian. He betrayed us, and Ariano is with him. Then monsters came. Everyone is killing each other. Confusing enough?"

Sadrik glanced at the elders and raised an eyebrow. Rithard

shook his head. "I'll do what I can for Maranath. There's nothing for Maklin. He's gone."

Sadrik looked almost wistful for a moment, then his face filled with resolve, and he rose, seemingly well, and offered Rithard a wicked grin. "Thank you, my friend. I knew there was a reason I spared your life!"

Rithard couldn't help but chuckle. "Well, we have similar taste in women after all. Let's see if you can eat someone else's lunch, eh?"

"I've arrived late and don't have a score card. Who are *we* killing?"

Rithard looked about at the multiple fights and sighed. *Not my area of expertise, I'm afraid.* "I have no idea."

Sadrik chuckled darkly. "I have several!"

It took Ahmed a moment to realize he was free. Once the *thing* snatched Lothrian up, Ahmed had been able to move his arms, but he had been so busy gawking at the spectacle, his tongue nearly fell from his open mouth. His freedom had only just now sunk in.

To be fair to himself, Ariano, too, had stood stunned for a moment before she could react. Her assault would have killed any normal man or beast, but the *thing* did not look like it could be stopped by anything short of an army.

Of course, it couldn't have chosen a better target. It paused a moment, leering at Ariano, then swung Lothrian against the wall again. The sorcerer cried out, but Ahmed saw no blood.

As Ariano struggled to her feet, Ahmed glanced at Aiul, who was just now climbing back out over the lip of the pool.

Ahmed stepped forward to help him, when a man-shaped object flew across his vision, crashed into the wicked sorceress from behind, and knocked her flat on her backside again. Ahmed cringed a bit to see said man-shaped object was in fact a *man*, a dead one with his head cracked wide open. Ariano struggled out from beneath the bloody corpse, slowly coming to the same realization as she wiped gray matter from her face with a shriek of horror and revulsion.

"That's on you!" Sadrik screamed as he stepped toward her, pointing a finger in accusation, a trail of fiery footprints in his wake. "You treacherous whore! That's at *your* feet!" He followed this up with a sweeping gesture of his arms, and Ariano screamed anew as flames engulfed her.

Ariano recovered quickly. She hurled the dead body aside and scrambled to her feet. "Flame can't harm me, whelp!" The flames licking at her sputtered and died as she stood, cackling, in the smoke.

At Sadrik's gesture, a huge, cracked section of stone worked itself loose from the floor and went hurtling at Ariano. She managed to deflect the brunt of it at the last moment, but it sent her staggering. Sadrik smirked. "The next thing you'll claim is that you're immune to rocks."

It was on, then, the two of them hurling whatever makeshift piece of the environment they could at one another, stones, pottery, sconces, too fast for Ahmed to follow.

Above his head, Lothrian gave a sharp cry as the towering beast smashed him repeatedly against the ceiling, screaming, "Suffer! Rend!" The roar was followed by a brilliant flash and an explosion of energy and sound. Blind and half deaf, Ahmed still heard the grinding of stone on stone well enough to know it for what it was: the roof was collapsing!

Ahmed stood, his vision blank, as the stones rained around him. His fate was in Ilaweh's hands, now.

Caelwen watched the creatures come, feeling his guts turn to jelly. The enemy were smaller versions of the beast Aiul had somehow revived, though the word 'small' was applicable only in comparison. Each stood a full ten feet tall, a twisted, man-shaped nightmare of eyes, teeth, and tentacles.

He spared a brief glance toward the Southlanders, and saw even they were clearly shaken, their jaws clenched and eyes wide, blades and shields quivering with the tension in their arms. And who wouldn't be? *The stranger, I suppose. He looks as if this is routine.* That one stood unflinching, watching the incoming horde, eyes down, a wicked, curved blade in each hand, as if he saw nothing in the world.

The nightmare creatures' voices were like the rumbling of thunder, their approach a coming storm. They were impossibly huge and misshapen, monsters. *We have no chance.*

Davron's voice sprang to mind, mocking, *"Not if you surrender before you've struck a blow. Is that what you intend, coward?"*

Caelwen clenched his jaw and made sure his helmet was secure. He turned to the men to his left and right and exchanged curt nods, assurances of solidarity, no longer finding their dark faces and smoldering eyes shocking or even unusual. These were his brothers in arms. They would all live or die according to the degree they could work together. *What a pity it's taken us so long to learn that lesson.*

As the creatures hit their shield wall, Caelwen heard an explosion behind them, and then the sound of rocks falling. Someone cried, "Ahmed!"

Caelwen stabbed at the mass of writhing teeth and tentacles before him, struggling not to vomit at the reek of the things. Someone else would have to care about the explosion. He had his hands full right here.

At first, Ahmed thought the blow was a falling stone, and that his time had indeed come. A moment later, he registered that it had been far too soft, and it had come from the side, not overhead. Someone had tackled him.

As his vision began to clear, the figure before him slowly resolved itself into the last person he expected. "Logrus? That was your name, yes?"

The Elgarite offered him a crooked smile. "Should I not have?"

Ahmed turned at the sound of Sandilianus's groan, to see his second rising to his feet. Sandilianus clutched at his ribs with one arm as he pointed at Logrus with the other. "He's fast."

Logrus shrugged. "Your man tried, too, but a rock caught him. We are all lucky."

Ahmed suddenly remembered where he was and what was happening. He looked about quickly, at last spying Lothrian on the floor in a heap, slowly trying to rise as the huge creature bore down on him, gnashing its teeth and cackling. It, too, seemed a bit stunned, a little slower.

Aiul was also down and rising to his feet, just outside of the black pool. He quickly retrieved the great black mace he had been using earlier and swung it in a searing arc at Lothrian's head. It rebounded with a sound like a hammer on stone, and Lothrian staggered and fell back to his knees, swooning.

The Torian beast hissed in fury, and shouted at Aiul, "The Dead God's Plaything! Where is my book? I will rend you!"

Aiul quailed and lunged for the black pool, diving into the font with barely a second to spare. The fiend chased him up to the edge and skidded to a stop, howling in rage as Aiul retreated to the far side. *Why will he not enter?*

Before Ahmed had time to give this overmuch thought, one of

the many huge pieces of fallen ceiling streaked through the air and smashed into the creature's knee. The beast gave an almost piteous wail of agony and collapsed to the floor, its shrill, high pitched keening like knives stabbing into Ahmed's ears.

Lothrian turned to Aiul, his face a mask of hatred and fury. "I will deal with you shortly, boy!"

Maranath grimaced in agony as he coughed. Rithard wiped blood from the old man's lips, the only real help he could offer. His bottle of morphine was smashed, and even had it been otherwise, it wasn't the right solution. Maranath needed clarity of mind, and pain could actually serve as a source of fuel for Meites, as near as Rithard could tell. "Easy, old fellow. You're badly injured, even for one of your kind."

Maranath stammered briefly, and Rithard tried to quiet him with a finger over his lips, but injured or not, the man was a Meite. He glared at Rithard a moment, then closed his eyes and took a deep breath. "Can't mend it. Not yet. Need time."

Rithard offered him a sad smile. "We are short of that."

Maranath gasped a moment before speaking. "Ariano is with him, yes?"

Rithard nodded gravely. "I'm sorry."

"*Listen!*" Maranath hissed, his eyes snapping back open, wide and insistent. "There may be a chance to turn her back." His eyes fluttered, then closed as he muttered unintelligible words. All Rithard could make out was "Aiul".

Rithard checked the old sorcerer's pulse. Maranath lived, but whatever secret he held about Aiul was still a mystery.

I pray you can mend yourself soon, old man. We're running out of time.

Ahmed's head was swimming with all of the input from different directions. He forced himself to breathe slowly and focus on each, to avoid being overwhelmed. His moment was coming soon, he was certain of it, and he could not afford to miss it.

Ariano was pressing Sadrik hard now. The younger sorcerer fought valiantly, but he was flagging, slowly giving ground, acquiring wounds from the odd stone or shard he couldn't stop. Ariano pressed in on him, forcing him farther back.

Across the way, Ahmed saw Rithard bending over Maranath. The old sorcerer's lips moved. *He is still alive!* Ahmed could barely contain his elation. He liked the old man, and seeing he still lived gave Ahmed some desperately needed hope. Maranath was powerful indeed, and if he could be brought into the fight, it might change things.

Sandilianus punched Ahmed in the arm. "Why do we wait? We must fight!"

Ahmed turned back to Logrus and Sandilianus, keeping one eye on the several fronts. "Fight *who?*"

Logrus pointed at Lothrian. "Him."

Lothrian had turned from Aiul back to the hideous beast. The monster itself was thrashing about on the floor, screeching and gnashing its teeth, swiping at the sorcerer, but he was careful to stay out of its reach.

Lothrian's rage was so great it seemed his eyes would pop out of his head. He raised both hands above his head in a grand gesture, sending a huge piece of debris zipping into the air, then dropped his hands, crashing it into the head of the wounded creature, over and over. After three times, the whining and thrashing ended, but Lothrian did not stop until there was nothing left of the creature's skull but shattered bone and pink pulp splattered across the floor.

Chest heaving, he spun to Aiul, who was still in the black pool, and shouted, "Now for you, boy!"

He has a hole in his shirt. Ahmed wondered why that would matter to him now of all times, and yet it *did.* Ahmed looked more closely, and saw, peeking through the fabric, one of the half-heads of the Eye.

Ilaweh is great, there is my moment!

There was no time to explain his sudden hunch. He charged forward, knowing it would likely end badly for him. Logrus and Sandilianus both grabbed at his arms in vain as he lunged across the floor and dove, grasping at the piece as he passed and tearing Lothrian's pocket off in the process.

Ahmed landed on his shoulder with a bone jarring crunch, prize in hand, as the other half of the head, eye still in its socket, clattered across the floor. Ignoring the pain, he scrambled forward on all fours and tossed the half he had seized into the black pool.

He felt the Lothrian's boot slam into his belly, and again, he fell into darkness.

Caelwen ground his teeth against the intense pressure, and did his best to keep a grip on his shield. The occasional clawed, putrid hand slipped past their defenses, only to be stabbed repeatedly, but for the most part the entire battle had devolved into a shoving match.

The enemy, due to their sheer size, had Caelwen and his allies at a disadvantage, and their entire entourage of less than a dozen was being steadily driven backward. They had formed two lines, but now they were being collapsed into one as their backs were pressed against the heap of debris from the ceiling.

Could they really crush us against the rocks? Caelwen was uncertain, but it seemed possible, and despite their half-hearted attempts to penetrate the shield wall, it seemed the creatures' primary goal. Certainly, once they were against the stones, the beasts could flank them and take them apart from the ends with surgical accuracy.

He strained as the other side pushed again, and felt his feet slide several inches on the stone, despite his best efforts.

We'll break and take our chances, if it comes to it. He looked to his right, into the grim face and dark eyes of the Southlander who called himself Rashid. *He knows.* "Say when," he hissed through clenched teeth.

Suddenly, from behind them, loud even through tons of stone, came a terrific crash and a screeching so grating that it made him long for the pleasant sound of fingernails on slate. *Mei! What* is *that?*

So unnerving was the sound that it took him a moment to realize that the creatures on the other side of the shield wall had stopped pushing. Before he could think to try to capitalize on it, the screeching was cut off by a thunderous crash that rang the walls and floor like a bell. It was followed by another, and another, like the blows of a giant hammer. Caelwen struggled to stay on his feet. *If they press us now, it's over.*

But no press came, and for a few moments, Caelwen had no real opportunity to wonder why. It was only when the hammering blows ceased and the utter stillness around him settled in that he found a moment to give thought to his surroundings.

Dust filtered from somewhere high overhead, motes twinkling and swirling in the torchlight. Behind, he could hear muffled screams.

But ahead, he heard nothing but silence.

Cautiously, and in conjunction with Rashid, he opened a hole in their wall and almost gasped in surprise.

The creatures were gone.

He and Rashid looked back and forth at each other and the rest of the men as they all lowered their shields in stunned silence.

Eleran broke the silence. "Lot of rocks to haul, guys."

Caelwen looked his way to see Eleran, one hand on his hip, the other on his chin, looking at the heap of rubble, a contemplative expression on his face.

Rashid barked a laugh. "White Wolf must have got hit in the head! He's always last in line for a working party!"

Eleran shook his head as another wail filtered through the rock, his expression grim. "This ain't work. This is still war."

Rithard watched in horror as the sorcerer kicked Ahmed in the gut, sending him careening against the wall with bone-crunching impact. Ahmed slid down, nerveless. *He might have survived.* It was difficult to tell, but there was a chance.

As if he had done nothing more than swat a fly, Lothrian turned back to the pool and plunged his right arm beneath the surface, presumably to retrieve the piece Ahmed had tossed there. His reaction was immediate, an agonized, screeching wail that continued as he jerked back from the pool, staring in horror and disbelief at the charred, smoking ruins. Most of his arm below his shoulder was simply *gone.* Only a small, blackened stump remained.

I hope it's excruciating, you sick *bastard!* Rithard shouted a cry of joy and pumped his fist in the air, but his cheer was short lived. Sadrik hit the ground next to him with a resounding thud. Rithard jumped out of instinct, but quickly recovered his clinical manner and set about checking his wounds. *Broken ribs, burns, and overall crushing trauma. If he weren't a Meite, I'd be worried.*

As it was, he would save his worry for himself. Ariano, grinning ear to ear, madness in her eyes, was headed their way, looking like nothing so much as a cat about to pounce. "You should never have challenged me, whelp!"

Sadrik spat blood at her and scrambled to his feet. "Fuck you, you rotten old cunt! Kill me if you can."

Rithard stepped back, trying to shield Maranath from their wrath. "Why are you doing this?" he shouted at the old sorceress. "Do you really think Lothrian will share ultimate power with you? It's hardly ultimate power if someone else has it too!"

Ariano slammed a palm at the air before her, and Sadrik doubled over, staggered. She turned her mad, green stare on Rithard. "What would you know about power, weakling?" She shook her head in mock sadness. "All that mind, and you can't even defend yourself. All you can do is beg. Pathetic." She raised a fist, and the air around her distorted and warped as if her whole body were a powerful furnace.

Rithard shook his head, feeling hope running out of him like water from a hole in a bucket. *Not much else to do. This is the end, it seems.*

Maranath coughed again and spat more blood. Rithard wiped it away, knowing it was futile. "Look what you've done to him! Was it worth it?"

Ariano's expression was at least a small victory. She broke eye contact, lowered her hand, and turned to the side. When she spoke, it was barely above a whisper "True power is worth anything. Maranath understands that as well as I do."

Maranath coughed and struggled to rise, shaking his head. "No," he rasped. "Not *family.*"

Rithard was about to ask Maranath what great secret he had been trying to communicate earlier, when his mind seemed to surge with a sudden burst of energy. *Something to turn her back. Something about Aiul.* In his mind, he flashed back to his office, saw himself comparing the two birth certificates, side by side.

The knowledge crystalized in his head with the force of a small bomb.

"Why did you leave Lothrian here?" he shouted up at Ariano. "Because he loved power more than he loved you? Or your *son*?"

Ariano turned to look at Rithard, her eyes clouded and distant, but whatever she might have been about to say was lost as Lothrian shouted, "Give me the piece, boy!"

"Why not try again with the other arm?" Aiul shouted back.

Rithard's confusion must have shown on his face. Maranath chuckled and squeezed his arm. "He can't use magic on it," the old man wheezed between pained giggles. "Slides right off. It's not of this world, you know. We might have him!"

Lothrian, furious now, roared, "Last chance, boy! Give me the damned piece!"

Aiul's jaw clenched. "Elgar take you! I—"

His words were cut off as Lothrian extended his one good arm, fury twisting his face into something demonic. Aiul flew from the pool as if he had been snatched up, a look of shock on his face as his weapon fell from his hand and sunk beneath the pool's surface. Lothrian caught him by the throat and held him aloft. "You always did need discipline!" He squeezed, and Aiul began to gasp and struggle.

Ariano stiffened and cried out, "Lothrian! What are you doing?"

Lothrian looked at her, unable to contain his rage. "Did you think I had forgotten?" Aiul's struggles became frantic as Lothrian increased the pressure. "Did you ever once consider what it was like to die down there, alone, with those things tearing at me in the dark?" He bared his teeth at her like a savage animal, for a moment, then shrieked, *"Did you ever even think of me at all?"*

"Stop it!" Ariano screamed. "You can't even do what you intended without the piece in the pool!"

Lothrian looked at Aiul, whose face had grown dark now. "Don't worry, boy! You're sick, and this is your cure!" He voiced a cruel, mocking laugh as Aiul clawed vainly at his grip. "Shh! Rest now. When this is done, I'll have the power to remake you, good as new!"

Aiul's face was purple now, his struggles weaker, as Lothrian turned back to Ariano and cried, "I just need to crush your mother's soul first!"

Lothrian tightened his grip on Aiul's throat still further, the tendons in his neck standing out as he strained.

Aiul's hands tore desperately at Lothrian's grip for a moment, then fell suddenly lifeless to his sides as his neck gave way with a sharp report.

"Forever," Lothrian spat. He effortlessly tossed Aiul's limp corpse into the black pool.

Rithard sat in stunned, horrified silence as Ariano screamed in anguish.

For the third time that day, Ahmed clawed his way back to consciousness. His entire body ached, but some spots ached more. The back of his head felt as if it were on fire. He touched the painful spot with his fingers and felt slick blood and a split in his scalp. His vision blurred and quickly refocused, resolving on a rapidly moving figure: Ariano was charging at Lothrian, screaming an ear piercing, multitone cry that raised the hair along Ahmed's forearms. He could only imagine what it would be like to be in the line of fire of that weapon.

From across the way, Maranath called in a ragged voice, "Southlander, it's now or never!"

Lothrian cackled and extended his good hand in front of him, flat like a shield. "It's definitely never!"

Ariano collided with and rebounded from an invisible barrier between her and Lothrian, as if she had run headlong into a glass wall. She staggered backward, shock on her face, and keeled over in a heap.

Lothrian raised a fist over his head in a gesture of victory, and swept his stump in what would have been a grand, all-encompassing gesture had it still ended in an arm. "Anyone else? Anyone?" He turned back and forth, looking at them all. "No? Very well, let's continue."

Ahmed shook his head. He had no chance but to die well, and that was what he would do. "Sandilianus—" he began, but Logrus interrupted him and pressed something cold and hard into his hand.

Ahmed looked at it, dumbfounded. The amber eye in the half lion's head seemed to wink at him. He looked at Logrus in shock. "How did you get this?"

"He never saw it fall. He is an idiot."

The words sprang to Ahmed's mind almost as if Maranath were speaking them in his ear again. *That thing channels your faith somehow, and it has a strong influence on our abilities. You can help us or hurt us with it, so have a care.*

Ahmed grabbed Logrus's hands in his own. "Pray with me."

Logrus offered him a confused stare. "Pray for what?"

"Strength for our friends. Weakness for our enemies. Victory for the right."

Logrus gave him a wary look. "Would it not be better to fight?"

Ahmed squeezed Logrus's hands tighter against the piece of the Eye. "This *is* our fight! Yours and mine!"

Logrus stared at Ahmed, understanding slowly dawning in his eyes. "Yes. I see it, now!"

Ahmed turned to Sandilianus. "We need just a few moments, I think."

Sandilianus banged a fist against his breast plate and drew his blade as he started toward Lothrian. "Time for you to die, sorcerer."

"Oh, ho!" Lothrian cried. "Such arrogance! You would have made a fine Meite if you had lived, friend."

Sandilianus shrugged. "Kill me, then, dog. If you can."

Ahmed sank to his knees, face to face with Logrus, and the two men began chanting, each in his own way. The Lion's head began to glow with a deep, green light that seemed to bleed over them as it grew brighter and brighter, casting an emerald tint over everything except the black pool.

"Great Ilaweh, I, a humble warrior, call upon you…."

"Elgar, lord of justice, hear my plea…."

Lothrian cast a quick glance at them and shouted. "What are you doing?"

A great piece of stone struck him from behind and knocked him flat. Sadrik swaggered forth, sneering. "Killing *you*, you piece of filth!"

Lothrian leapt to his feet and swung a fist as if throwing a punch at Sadrik. The younger sorcerer grunted and flinched a bit, but kept coming.

Lothrian spat on the ground. "*You*? You couldn't even beat Ariano. You're not strong enough!"

Sandilianus pulled his shield from his back and banged his blade against it as he continued forward. "He is not alone."

Lothrian, scowling, looked back and forth at them, but he began backing up all the same, the green light of the Eye pulsing like a heartbeat. Sadrik slammed his palms forward, sending Lothrian skidding up against the edge of the black pool.

Lothrian's eyes grew wide with shock and anger, and he turned to respond just as Sandilianus charged him. The veteran slammed his shield full-force into the sorcerer and sent him toppling over the edge of the black pool, but not before Lothrian seized him about the neck.

There they froze, Lothrian inches from the surface, nose to nose, their hatred for each other radiating outward like heat on the desert sand. The surface of the black pool rippled with it, as if blown by wind. Weakened as he was, Lothrian was still somehow able to keep himself from toppling into the deadly liquid.

Lothrian clawed at Sandilianus's face, seeking his eyes, his nose, anything to cause pain. Both men's bodies were rigid with strain. "If I go, you go!" Lothrian cried.

Sandilianus hammered a gauntleted fist into Lothrian's face, sending the sorcerer into a brief swoon. "I told you when you started this, I am ready for a hard death!" Sandilianus strained forward, pounding the sorcerer's face again and again. "It is a good day to die!"

Sadrik gestured wildly, to no effect. He turned to Ahmed, eyes wide and helpless, but before he could say anything, Lothrian's will folded under Sandilianus's rain of blows, and he slipped, just an inch or two, but it was enough. As his flesh made contact with the surface, sizzling like meat frying in oil, his face no longer smirking, but pale and taut with stark terror, he found some inner reserve, enough to stop his descent one last time. He stared up at Sandilianus in hate and roared, "No! It does not end like this!"

Sandilianus, nose to nose with him, drew a dagger from his belt. "Yes, it does!" he hissed, and plunged the blade into Lothrian's eye. With a shriek, Lothrian collapsed, and both men toppled into the black pool, leaving not even a ripple on the surface.

Sadrik staggered back, gasping and shaking his head. "I couldn't save him!"

Ahmed released Logrus's hands with a nod and stood, taking a deep breath. "No," he said softly. "We weren't meant to."

Even still, it was not over. The black pool suddenly lit with a brilliant orange flare, and the liquid inside exploded upward toward the ceiling, sending everyone diving for cover.

The light was blinding, but the sounds told their own tale. The liquid struck the ceiling with the ring of a colossal hammer on an anvil, and brought down a huge section in a grinding cacophony. Ahmed once again found himself visionless beneath a hard rain of boulders, with only the will of Ilaweh as shelter.

As the noise faded and the dust settled, Ahmed concluded that Ilaweh did indeed still have plans for him. When his vision returned, he was pleased to see those plans included the rest of his allies as well. The others all stood blinking, save for the wicked sorceress Ariano. She was clawing in vain at the untold tons of fallen debris, as if she might still somehow change what had happened, if only she could clear the stones.

Ahmed Justinius rose to his feet, suddenly feeling a thousand years old. He knew he should be elated at the victory, at having saved the world; he should rejoice for Sandilianus, who had found himself a hero's death if ever there had been one. But there was no joy in his heart. It was all driven out by the wracking sobs of the old woman kneeling at the edge of the black pool, tearing at her hair and calling her dead child's name.

Even the wicked know grief, perhaps they most of all.

It was a lesson he would never forget.

CHAPTER 20
DIVERGENT PATHS

KARIANA stared at her own reflection in her vanity mirror, feeling wholly inadequate for the task at hand. She had put on her face and taken it off three times already, and was slowly coming to the realization that while she had plenty of skill at a seductive look, she had none whatsoever for stately and serious.

In the end, she had called for help. The slave girl had done an admirable job, but it felt somehow artificial. Kariana didn't recognize the person looking back at her from the mirror. This stranger was wise, decisive, a genuine leader, not even remotely close to how Kariana saw herself.

Of course, she's not really me, *when it comes down to it.* The New Empress was a bizarre puppet with Kariana's face and voice, but with someone else's words and thoughts.

Kariana wrinkled her nose in distaste at the changeling staring back at her from the mirror, but she had an official function to lead, and it was necessary. For a brief moment, she was seized by the mad urge to find something, anything really, to take the edge off, but dismissed it. She had endured far too much pain to get free of all of that.

The grief came again, suddenly, like a punch in the gut. Kariana struggled not to ruin her makeup with tears. She hadn't even been able to say goodbye. Sadrik had told her everything, or at least as much as he cared for her to know: Aiul's horrid death, and the Southlander's heroic end. Somehow, the two combined to be bearable. It wasn't how things were supposed to have ended. Yet, she was slowly learning it was how things seemed to go, for the most part.

Sandilianus. His name was Sandilianus, and his god is Ilaweh. It had taken some effort to commit those two names to memory, but since the disaster of a trial where she had first met the man, he had loomed large in her mind, and so had his god. *So much better than Mei. I wonder if I need a church, or if I can just worship him on my own?*

A woman's voice called from behind her, "Have you gone over the speech, Empress?"

Kariana turned to see her new speech writer entering the room without bothering to ask for permission. Thalassa Idlic was tall, thin, and imperious, a thinner, younger Narelki, and full of the same skill and ego as her late uncle, Prandil. She had the same miraculous power to swell men to giants or shrink them to mice with words.

Thalassa raised an eyebrow, her electric-blue eyes accusing, her almost porcelain face sour and disapproving. "I see. Shall we go over it now?" The words carried the proper imperious tone, something Kariana was still working to master, but she at least had a fine example to emulate, thanks to Rithard's suggestion to bring the Idlic woman onboard.

And Rithard himself, well, that had been a rare good decision on Kariana's part. Legend said Tasinal had ever been advised by Amrath. Grief welled in her briefly as she remembered that she had once assumed that would be Aiul, but in truth, sour, gloomy Rithard was far and away a better adviser. Like Sadrik, he did nothing to ingratiate himself. He told her unvarnished truth, and she trusted him. Moreover, he trusted her. Who would have thought that stepping in to save Caelwen's friend would turn out to be such a boon in the long run?

And as for her Captain of the Guard, he, too, seemed a new man. He had, she knew, hated his job for a long time, hated her too, most likely. But now he actually smiled on occasion. Sometimes he even participated in conversations between her and Rithard, when he happened to be present, even occasionally going so far as to pronounce Rithard a drunken idiot for plans he disagreed with. The Stone was flesh and blood now. *Mei, soon he'll be interested in women or some sort of entertainment or comfort!*

Thalassa cleared her throat as she shoved a sheaf of papers at Kariana. With a sigh, Kariana accepted the speech and began reading the words she would pretend were her own, reciting them and being corrected like a child at her intonations.

She couldn't help but grin as she considered how little had changed. They had called her a liar and a whore for years, and now she was the biggest liar and whore possible, a politician. *It's just that I am fucking pretty much everybody at this point, and they actually enjoy it.*

The indignity rankled just a bit, but the power to actually do something worthwhile helped to compensate for that. She had much to make up for, and today would be a great start.

Maybe, just maybe, they would remember her not as Tasinalta the Mad, but as Tasinalta the Wise, or Tasinalta the Peacemaker.

It was good to finally have friends.

The great pavilion in the center of Nihlos was a truly enormous edifice, capable of seating thousands, and arranged in tiers so sound would carry. As an honored guest, Ahmed had been seated at a table right up front with Maranath. About them, more tables were filled with the other house elders and Ahmed's remaining men.

Ahmed shook his head in wonder at the excess. One thing was certain: the Nihlosians had a strong penchant for overdoing things. Victory ought be its own reward, but somehow the Nihlosians felt the need to dress it up with lace, candles, and cakes.

And words. He had not expected their empress to even know so many, and yet somehow she had waxed poetic and philosophical for far too long.

Maranath eyed Ahmed a moment, then said, "I know just how you feel. It's drab, isn't it? You'd think they could have put a little more effort into the celebration." The old man raised an eyebrow and held his deadpan look for a few seconds before a grin broke out across his face, and Ahmed realized he'd been tricked.

Ahmed grinned back at him. "It's not all bad. The monument is a good idea. The dead should be remembered."

Rithard, drink in hand, approached and slid into a seat at their table. "That was actually her idea. Most of the rest was mine, and the words were Thalassa's, but Kariana wanted the monument. A rare good idea from her, I think."

Ahmed reached out a hand to Rithard. "It is good to see you! I would speak with you about our dead."

Rithard grasped forearms with Ahmed in the Xanthian fashion and gave Maranath an apologetic smile. "I'm sorry, I didn't mean to intrude."

Maranath waved the thought aside. "No intrusion. We're just passing the time while we drink."

Rithard raised his glass, offering a toast. "I'll drink to that!"

Maranath clinked his wine against Rithard's hard liquor. "To drinking. That's a fine toast, and I don't think I've ever heard anyone offer it before. You'd think someone would have."

Ahmed, not fully understanding the gesture, followed suit out of politeness. "I would leave our dead here, at this monument your empress will build, alongside your own," he told Rithard. "It will be difficult to preserve the bodies for our voyage, and it seems fitting that they lie with their brothers in arms. Ilaweh approves."

Rithard nodded agreement. "That's easily done. I'll make the arrangements at once. We could hold a small ceremony before you go, if you like."

"I would."

Maranath cleared his throat to draw attention. "If you can bear the whitewashing."

Ahmed shook his head and scowled. "You'll call the mad one a hero, eh?"

Maranath chuckled. "We're all mad, but if you mean Lothrian, yes, that's the general thinking. Died saving the world, side by side with your man, dealing with that monster down there. We'll bully the rest into telling the same tale, assuming you'll play along."

Ahmed laughed out loud. "I will play your game, old man, but I don't understand it. Why not let him be remembered as the villain he was?"

Maranath's voice had a dark edge to it as he spoke. "To be remembered as a wicked, devastatingly powerful sorcerer who returned from the dead, fought us all to a standstill, and damn near destroyed the world? Oh, I suspect he'd be damned proud of that."

Ahmed waited a moment for the punchline before he understood it had already been delivered. He nodded in satisfaction. "Cunning, and cruel."

"I thought so."

Ahmed grew somber. "And the Eye?"

"Well, there's no retrieving half of it. The other half, we'll separate again. Cruentus will get his piece back. As for the half head, honestly, I don't know. I'm leaning toward sending it back with you."

Ahmed slashed a hand through the air. "No. I am a humble soldier and prelate. It was only the intervention of Ilaweh that kept others from taking it by force. It should be with someone strong enough to defend it."

Maranath looked sidelong at Rithard and smiled. "Or someone clever enough to hide it well."

Rithard scowled at them. "I knew I should have sat somewhere else."

Ahmed nodded his approval. "Think of it, Rithard. This time you can make the puzzle for someone else to solve."

Rithard smiled despite himself. "There is that, eh? The game is again afoot."

Ahmed looked back and forth at them, then, satisfied they were all agreed, asked Maranath, "And your woman? Will she go along with all of this?"

Maranath's face grew dark at the mention of Ariano. "It serves her ends. She'll do as she's told, at least for a while. She's on my shit list right now. We're not speaking overmuch."

Rithard looked as if he were about to be ill. "You'll forgive her, won't you?" he said in an accusing tone.

Maranath raised an eyebrow, then shrugged. "Probably. At some point."

Rithard's jaw clenched. "She had the right of you in Torium, eh? You *do* think that way! If you'd had the chance—!"

Maranath waved a hand in derision. "I *didn't* have the chance. That's all that matters."

Rithard turned to Ahmed. "They're a *cancer* here! It's why we deposed them!"

Maranath chuckled. "Oh, give us some credit for saving the world, hmm?"

"You and your kind put all this in motion! Meites are the *cause* of all of it!"

Ahmed put a steady hand on his new friend's shoulder. "No, Rithard. It was all of us. Your people and mine. We all did this. And we all stood together to fix it."

Maranath gave Ahmed a wan smile. "Just so."

Rithard glowered at Ahmed briefly. "They will do it again. Murderers and psychotics and liars, the lot of them!"

Maranath gave Ahmed a shrug. "He's drunk." He looked past Ahmed and rolled his eyes, apparently in response to someone approaching. "And loud."

"He's right," Sadrik added as he joined their group. He, too, put a hand on Rithard's shoulder. "I couldn't help but overhear," he told Rithard with a grin.

Rithard looked suddenly very glum. "Well, I hadn't meant to include you in that assessment, frankly."

"Ah, but you should," Sadrik answered, his tone sharp and bitter. "Or have you forgotten how we met? We all have blood on our hands, and I can't say as any of our sect having passed has done the world a bit of harm."

Ahmed saw something odd in Sadrik's eyes, not the usual Meite madness. He looked hard at the young sorcerer, and saw his normal gray aura seemed off somehow, almost tinted a slight green. *Why are you feeling guilty, Sadrik? And what could that mean for one such as you?*

Maranath grunted. "So you're drunk, too, eh?"

Sadrik gave him a nasty smile and showed them a half empty bottle. "Oh, not nearly drunk *enough*. Come, Rithard, let's put this to proper use. Do you think you can out drink a Meite?"

Rithard smiled despite himself. "It depends on if you cheat."

Sadrik placed an arm around Rithard's shoulders and began to lead him toward a group of young women. As they turned to leave, Maranath called out in a voice a bit more harsh than fit the circumstances, "Sadrik."

Sadrik paused and looked back, and again, Ahmed was struck by his mood. He was hiding it well, but he was angry and full of grief. *Maranath sees it too.*

The old man held Sadrik's gaze with his own smoldering stare a moment, before saying, in a clipped, sharp tone, "Mind yourself."

To Ahmed's surprise, Sadrik gave Maranath an abashed nod before turning again, presumably to drown whatever dark emotions he carried with wine, women, and song.

Maranath watched him leave, then rubbed at his temple as if he had a headache. "I hope there's no trouble."

"What's wrong with him?"

"He's young, and the events of late have unsettled him. Treachery has a way of breaking loose one's moorings until they're accustomed to it."

Ahmed shrugged. "My people deal with traitors differently from yours."

"Yes, yes, I'm sure you do, but then you never have the case of needing to reign in powerful sorcerers with explosive tempers and wild emotions." The old sorcerer scowled at Ahmed's shrug, and continued. "Killing begets reprisals."

"I count only the three of you."

Maranath chuckled. "You don't lie well."

Ahmed almost challenged him before he remembered. "Tasinal," he said softly. "I'd almost forgotten about him."

"He established a clear precedent. Bend the knee, get in line, and rebellions can be forgiven."

Ahmed nodded, remembering his encounter with the great tyrant. I *would not want to get cross with him, if I could avoid it.* "So your woman, she received no punishment at all?"

Maranath grunted. "Oh, I wouldn't say that."

Ariano had drawn the curtains when she returned a week prior, and saw no point in ever opening them again. There was, in truth, nothing outside that she cared to see.

One of the slaves, she had no idea which, was knocking on the door again. They tried to check on her every hour, and they left food, though she took very little. The deep, black depths in her soul left little room for hunger, though she had not taken leave of her senses. *If I wished to die, I'd do it in a more creative way than starving.*

She had expected it to pass, this crushing darkness, and it should have. The only rational explanation was that she didn't really want it to. *Oh, how I misjudged you, Narelki.*

Life had become little more than a loop, the constant reliving of her worst nightmare, watching her child murdered by his own father, and then seeing him, too, brought to his end at the hands of Sadrik, the Southlanders, and the Elgarite.

Worst of all was the recognition that she grieved not just for Aiul, but for Lothrian as well.

It's your fate, for making that damnable bargain in the first place.

They had both been pregnant at the same time, both gone into labor at the same time, and Lothrian had been convinced it was destiny, as he was about everything. *"A child and a grandchild in the same night! That means something!"* As for herself, Ariano had never been quite certain if the child had come at the appropriate time, or if she had subtly willed it, both out of her love for symmetry and her desire to feed Lothrian's ego.

It hardly matters, now. All it had really meant was making an agonizing choice. Narelki's child had been stillborn, and Lothrian was convinced the knowledge would destroy his daughter. *"She's already fragile from what that bastard did to her!"*

Fate had given them an opportunity, and they had seized it. *"We'll still see him every day. We'll still know him and love him. All I am asking is we let Narelki believe he is hers."* It had seemed the right thing at the time, noble even. Help Lothrian's daughter, and conveniently avoid the responsibility of raising the child. *Ever does selfish motivation lead to rationalization.*

In the end, it had all been for nothing. Narelki had still suffered a collapse, and now she and her half-brother were both dead, all of it at Lothrian's feet.

And mine.

It was tempting to wallow in self-pity. Every artist has a weakness for such indulgence, to shut one's self away from the cruel world and pretend it doesn't exist. As grief stricken and shattered as Ariano was, it was simply not in her nature to surrender to such impulses. A part of her did wish she had died in Torium, but more of her still loved life, and hungered to create, as she had always done.

Destruction had been Lothrian's passion, and she had let herself be led down the path by the sheer perversity and madness of it.

To find her way back, she would do as she had always done: create.

If the dragon wants a picture, he'll have one. Let him see how it ended.

She stood, crossed to the window, and pulled the curtains wide. She needed proper light to work. Her easel was next. She dragged it into position and placed a stretched canvas on it. Her palette and brushes were there on a low table beside her.

Ariano sat long moments staring at the empty canvas, deciding on tone. She saw the image clearly in her mind. It had not stopped playing in her head since it had happened.

It should be the color of rust and decay, of pain and loss.

She looked about for a container, frantic to get started now that she had the vision. At last, she located a small tumbler near her palette, along with the small knife she used to trim her brushes.

All good art is, in some way or another, bleeding. For a moment, she considered slashing her wrist, but dismissed it. She had no fear of dying from such a wound, not when she had important work to complete, but it would be too much too fast. She settled for her left thumb, watching in fascination as the sharp blade pushed the flesh down, then bit in and slid to the bone. The pain was excruciating, and yet somehow invigorating as well.

She held her wounded thumb over the tumbler and let the blood flow, humming to herself a lullaby she had sung to the baby on the first and only night he had ever been truly hers.

When Ahmed caught sight of the ship in the distance, he breathed a sigh of relief. He had always known leaving it was a terrible gamble, but what choice had he been given? To see it still where he left it was a minor miracle in and of itself.

He commanded eight men now, less than half of those who had agreed to follow him. It seemed ages ago, now, that gathering on a rocky beach amidst the ruins of their previous ship. Plucky Rashid had had been the only one he could name at the time, and even then only because the man had lost his sword and been mocked for it. Now, he knew all of them, and they him. *But it is easier now. We have lost so many.*

It was not sensible, this pain he felt at the losses, and not just the recent ones, but all of them since he had set out from Xanthia —he paused a moment, counting—*years* ago. *I am nearly twenty now!* So many fallen, and the loss weighed on him: Yazid, Brutus, and even the blasphemous navigator, Tahir, who he now understood had indeed found faith at the end. The man had literally traded his life so that Ahmed could continue his quest. *And the others did likewise, though not with as much understanding as Tahir or Sandilianus of what they were doing.*

No, it was not sensible to mourn men who died well, and yet he did, Sandilianus most of all. *And why not? The greater the hero a man is, the more one wishes he were still with them.*

They had managed to hire a good forty men from the prisons, and their party now resembled a small, ragtag army. Ahmed had some concerns regarding their numbers. If they were to mutiny at sea, it could go badly, but such were the risks of any voyage, in truth. He had chosen men who seemed amiable enough, thieves and drunks mostly, people looking for a fresh start. He smiled to himself, remembering one particularly shocking volunteer: Anthalas, the lone survivor of the mob who had tried to kill him in the Undercity. Apparently, after spreading Tasinal's warning as he'd been ordered to do, he'd been picked up for drunk and disorderly and refused to leave the prison the next morning. He had spoken to no one at all until the Xanthians came looking for men, and he had been at the front of the line. When Ahmed had asked him why, the man had simply said, "I need a new place." Ahmed had understood, and had taken him on.

Caelwen trudged warily alongside their new crew, alert for trouble, and Eleran circulated amongst them, learning who could be trusted and who bore watching. *And likely, who is a good mark.* Rithard, looking suitably dour, swayed in his saddle, clearly not one for horseback riding, especially after having spent most of the previous evening trying to outdrink Sadrik. Ahmed briefly wondered what had become of the young sorcerer. All Rithard would say was that Sadrik didn't want any contact with the elders, and that Sadrik had hinted he had found a new mentor. Ahmed shuddered at that thought, knowing who said mentor was likely to be. *But who could blame either of them, really?*

Aboard the ship, a commotion was brewing as the crew rushed the rails, watching intently as Ahmed and his party approached. Ahmed sighed, knowing this would be difficult. They had left the boat carrying a large sack of left boots, and a crew convinced that shoes were the key to demonic sorcery that would kill them with fire if they disobeyed. What had become of the boots, Ahmed had no idea. They were lost somewhere, likely at the scene of the great battle with the Elgies. There was no telling how the men he had duped with his wild tale would react if their footgear was not returned.

As the party approached within shouting distance, Bendaro, the leader of the old crew, leaned over the railing, his brown, lined face still mottled with the bruises Eleran had given him. "The sorcerer returns! Soon we can go home!" The rest of his men watched intently, terror etched on their faces.

Ahmed called back, "We have a problem." He started to say more, but his tongue froze as his eye caught movement in the sky above the ship. A small dot rapidly grew, becoming man-shaped as it hurtled toward the ship at breakneck speed.

Maranath slammed feet first against the deck with a resounding crash. Bendaro and his men spun as one, eyes wide in horror, as the old sorcerer brushed at his sleeves. "I should damned well say you do!" Maranath shouted.

Eleran cried out in a strangled voice, "The master! He's found us!" He fell to his knees and raised his hands over his head as if to ward off a blow.

Rashid reacted quickest. He hurled himself to the ground and gibbered in mock terror: "Aieee! Please, master, spare us! We were only having fun with the humans!"

Ahmed struggled to keep his face straight as he knelt and

gestured for the rest of his men to do likewise. The new crew looked about, bewildered, as did Caelwen and Rithard.

Maranath seemed to suddenly notice Bendaro and his men, and glared at them briefly. "I believe these belong to you." He unslung the heavy sack from his shoulder and dumped the contents, almost thirty left boots, onto the deck.

For long moments, Bendaro and his men were still and silent, their eyes wide with fear. Maranath glowered at them briefly, then swept his arm at the cringing men. "Take them, fools! I hardly need boots to keep you in line." He gestured at a hanging lantern and balled his hand into a fist. The lantern crumpled, sending shards of glass in all directions as the frame collapsed into a compact ball of twisted metal. "I can crush your skulls any time I like." Maranath opened his hand again, and the metal ball fell to the deck with a thud.

One of Bendaro's men keeled over in a dead faint. The rest rushed for the pile of boots in a single mass and fell immediately to squabbling as they tried to sort the boots amongst themselves.

Maranath scowled down at the group on the shore. "And that goes for you lot as well!" he called, making a point to mug it up for the new crewmembers. Ahmed smiled, knowing full well that Nihlosian commoners feared Meites at least as much as Bendaro and his men feared demons.

As Bendaro and his men scuttled below decks with their boots, Ahmed turned to Eleran and grinned broadly. "You hid them at the battle, eh?"

Eleran grinned back. "Yeah, it's not like I had much else to do. I mentioned it to dad, and he thought it would be a hoot to play along."

Ahmed shook his head and chuckled. "I suppose we did owe them a meeting with a real sorcerer."

Eleran nodded toward the new crew. "Won't hurt keeping this lot in check, either."

"No, it won't."

Caelwen, a disapproving look on his face, proffered a sheaf of documents to Ahmed. "Formalities."

Ahmed looked through the papers without much enthusiasm. "'I do hereby accept custody of these prisoners', bah. This paperwork is the most savage aspect of your culture yet." He shrugged. "I have no ink or quill, at any rate."

Caelwen handed him a long, thin instrument about the length of a hand. "We savages have this covered."

Ahmed turned the thing over in his hands, bewildered, while Rithard snickered quietly. At last, Caelwen had mercy and briefly seized Ahmed's hands to remove a cap from one end of the rod.

Rithard, grinning, explained, "That's the business end. The ink is already inside. We call it a pen."

Ahmed grinned like a child as he understood the workings of the device. He scribbled tentatively on the sheaf of papers, then with more confidence as he saw the device did indeed work as advertised. "Can I keep this?"

Caelwen nodded as he took the paperwork back and began to thumb through it. "I can get another. Expensive, but it's a nice parting gift, I think." His eyes narrowed as he looked at the paperwork. "What sort of chicken scratching is this?"

Rithard, looking over his shoulder, smiled knowingly.

Ahmed tucked the pen into his purse. "That, my friend, is ancient Ilawehan. It seemed appropriate."

Rithard snickered. "Indeed."

Caelwen looked back and forth at them, then shrugged in surrender. "I witnessed the signature. I don't need to be able to read it, I suppose."

Ahmed looked about at his new friends and sighed, feeling wistful. He would truly be sorry to leave, and yet he had duties. "It's time to get these men on board." He turned, for some reason intending to call to Sandilianus, but instead found himself facing

Eleran. The lanky Nihlosian offered a quizzical look, and Ahmed answered with a wry smile. "I seem to be missing a second. What about you, Demon Man Dog? Will you have the job?"

Eleran's face lit with a broad grin. "If you twist my arm."

Maranath, still on the ship, called out, "I heard that, you know!" He pushed off and drifted quickly to the ground in front of Eleran. "So you're going, eh?"

Eleran looked positively sheepish. "That was always the plan, dad."

Maranath scowled at him a moment. "One would presume so, given that you accepted the job. I'm old. Has it occurred to you we might not see each other again?"

Eleran shook his head, grinning. "You're a tough old bird. You just survived the end of the world. I'll see you again."

Ahmed put a hand on Maranath's shoulder and squeezed. "We will meet again, old man. I think you know this, too."

"Aye," Maranath said. "Nothing is over, just delayed." He flashed a mischievous grin. "Which is precisely why I am coming with you, too."

Eleran gaped and stammered, "Since when?"

Maranath shook his head in consternation. "Oh, please. You didn't really think I hauled myself all this way just to pull a prank on some savages, did you?" He pulled at his beard and groused, "What? I'm newly single, and I have in mind to go and do some man things, spend some time with my son. What's wrong with that?" He turned to Ahmed and grew more serious. "Besides, you may need a bit of help controlling those prisoners, considering your losses."

Ahmed nodded at this. "We could use your help, there is no doubt."

Maranath grinned broadly. "Then it's settled."

Eleran, rubbing at his chin, seemed to warm to the idea. "Do you play poker?"

Caelwen and Rithard watched *Ilaweh's Will* recede in the distance, waving until they could no longer identify individual people onboard. Caelwen lowered his arm and turned to Rithard. "Just the two of us now."

Rithard rolled his eyes and trudged toward his horse. "Huzzah! I'm overwhelmed with anticipation of the scintillating conversations we'll have."

Caelwen shrugged and hauled himself atop his own mount. "Sorry, I didn't realize you were in such a hurry to get home to your new girlfriend."

Rithard cast a withering gaze at his friend and said in a deadpan voice, "I *will* stab you."

Caelwen snickered and flicked his reigns, setting his mount moving for home. Rithard, after a moment of confusion, urged his horse to catch up. As Rithard's mount drew abreast, Caelwen continued as if there had been no interruption, "You barely know how to use a blade for anything but cutting your meat."

Rithard scoffed at this and waved a hand dramatically. "I'll have you know I'd make an excellent murderer. I've planned the perfect murder before, in meticulous detail."

Caelwen shook his head, smiling despite his attempt to feign disinterest. "I noticed you only claim you 'planned' it, not that you actually 'committed' it."

"Well, of course not! That would be stupid. It would hardly be the perfect murder if I *confessed* to it."

Caelwen snorted laughter. "Fine, then. *Hypothetically*, if you had actually committed the deed, which case would you be solving by confessing?"

Rithard looked back and forth dramatically, as if verifying they were alone, then, with a grin, answered, "Maralena Prosin."

Caelwen shook his head. "That was clearly a Meite."

Rithard shrugged. "He beat me to it, that's all."

"You're an idiot."

"I would have gotten away with it, too."

"I have little doubt."

"You really don't believe me do you?"

Caelwen sighed. "If I say I do, will you let it go?"

"And then what would we talk about?"

Caelwen laughed out loud. "I guess you have a point."

Sometimes, for the bravest and most valiant of soldiers, Ilaweh grants a final boon before they leave the world of men for good. It was so with Sandilianus, whose name would be sung forever as a true hero.

He asked for one thing only: to look in on the boy he had come to count as a son. Ilaweh had laughed at this and asked if Ahmed would be angry to know Sandilianus still called him boy. Sandilianus had grinned and said he likely would.

It was much like a dream, for in many ways, it *was* a dream. Sandilianus found himself back aboard *Ilaweh's Will,* amazed by simple things. He saw so much more, now. The whole world was frail, an illusion, much like scenery in a play.

But the people, ah, they were deeper, more vibrant, brilliant lights, each unique, and the boy was the brightest of them all. He lit the landscape like the full moon at night, a beacon to all around him.

Sandilianus smiled to hear the boy giving orders to cast off, to set sail for Xanthia. He nodded with appreciation as those orders were obeyed by Xanthian and Nihlosian alike without question, and not out of fear, but out of respect. *He has learned well.*

The pathetic, sham sun set slowly over the artificial ocean, and the bright light of the boy at last entered the skin of the flimsy ship. Sandilianus watched, smiling, as Ahmed prepared for sleep. First, the boy removed his sword and placed it into a cunningly crafted hanger, one that would keep the blade at hand if there were danger, but prevent it from being tossed about in rough waters. Next, he knelt in prayer, and finally, he stripped naked and slung himself in his hammock.

Sandilianus smiled at the sight, glad that the boy did not share his thoughts on women. *We will need more like you, Ahmed. Many more.*

As Ahmed's breathing slowed and became regular, Sandilianus knew it was time for him to go. Even now, Ilaweh had work for him. But his gaze lingered a moment on the boy's new blade.

It was a deadly piece of work. His new eyes could see facets that his old could never have noted. He saw all of the blood it had spilled, and the blood it had spared. He saw its first owner holding it aloft with a battle cry, and wondered if he might meet that proud warrior, now, in the afterlife. *It is time. My work here is done.*

As Sandilianus prepared to depart, his eye was drawn to the sphere of amber in the blade's pommel. For a brief moment, it flared a deep, brilliant emerald. Then it was quiet.

Sandilianus shrugged and smiled. His time for worrying over such things had passed. It was the boy's problem, now.

Sandilianus smiled one last time in the world of the living and corrected himself.

Not boy. Man.

EPILOGUE
BITTER ENDS

LOGRUS promised himself as he slipped away from the others that he would allow himself one month to grieve, and no more. He would begin counting once he reached home. The first morning he woke in his own bed would be day one, and on the thirtieth day, he would let things go and move on.

The cave-in had given him good cover to escape without being seen. He barely knew the others, and even if he had known them better, there would have been far too much talking for his taste. Ahmed, perhaps, would have been good to share words with, but the rest would have been complicated.

The old woman, Aiul's mother, presented a very difficult moral conundrum for Logrus. She was certainly wicked, though not nearly enough to draw Elgar's attention, not under normal circumstances. But she had tried to kill *everyone*, had she not? She *should* be on his list, and yet she was not.

Logrus pondered this as he built a cairn outside Torium for Aiul, a symbolic gesture, but one he had felt the need to express. No one would visit, nor would they know what it signified if they were to stumble on it. Yet, it was some kind of marker.

Logrus found, as he travelled, that he had more interest in

talking with Aiul now that he was dead than he ever had while he was alive. He imagined his friend there, with him, as he piled the stones, and asked him how it could be that it was not a matter of urgency that the old woman be punished. The imaginary Aiul did not know, either, nor did Elgar clarify anything.

Logrus reached home before long and began his vigil of grief. Elgar had not spoken to him since Torium. The last contact Logrus had felt was when he had touched the black pool and been healed. Since then, nothing, and Logrus harbored a growing fear that something terrible had happened to his god. Perhaps the cleansing of Torium had expended so much of his dwindling energy that he had died. *It would explain much.*

So Logrus had grieved for the only two friends he had ever known, hoping against hope that he would receive a sign from Elgar, but knowing the grim truth in his soul: *something* had happened to Elgar. He had known it when he looked at the old woman, knowing she had tried to kill the world, and saw her only as gray. The knowledge had grown within him day by day here as he rose each morning and prayed without any answer.

The Dead God was at long last truly dead. It was the only possible explanation. It had taken him a thousand years to bleed out from his wounds, and he had spent his last breath avenging not just the most wretched, sorrowful people ever to have lived, but himself as well. As much as it pained Logrus to realize that Elgar was no more, it pleased him to know that his oldest friend had found peace at last.

And perhaps, if what gods remained were just, his newest friend Aiul had as well. He had died a hard death, but he had been avenged. Logrus hoped his friend's soul could rest now. If the gods were kind, he would find his wife and child again.

As for himself, Logrus used the time of grieving to think on where he should go and what he should do. For as long as he could remember, he had done what was necessary. And what was necessary was something Elgar had, up to now, defined for him. He still had his book, and even his vision, but seeing the old woman as gray made him doubt it.

How could she have been gray?

As the end of the month approached, Logrus decided that he would need to test his vision. There was but one man he knew for certain would be red, one man whose name he had written in his book, but never crossed off. There had always been something more important, someone who had done even worse evil than to rob a child of his mother.

It almost seemed unfair. What had he done but strangle one woman? He would not be expecting a Knight of Fear to mete out justice.

Logrus shouldered his pack and looked about his humble home one last time, wanting to be certain he had not forgotten anything important. He ticked off the various items he felt necessary, from tinder to sausages to needle and thread. He had what needed.

Logrus thought of his departed friends one last time as he lit a torch and opened his front door. *Is this the rest of my life, hunting men down and slaying them? Is there nothing more for me?* He stood for long moments in the doorframe, wondering if perhaps he should forgive the man who murdered his mother. Perhaps just seeing him would be enough, to know if his vision were still true, or if it had indeed failed him, as the sight of the wicked sorceress suggested.

"Fuck that," he said, and tossed the torch into the house. It landed in the pile of kindling he had prepared, and the flames caught quickly.

As the house began to burn, Logrus opened his book and turned to the only unfinished entry: "It is necessary that Hector Gonzales die for his crimes." Below this, he wrote:

Day 1: Hector last seen in Brust ten years ago. Heading there to look for clues.

From the entrance to his lair, Cruentus watched Ariano rise quickly into the sky, headed... somewhere. Cruentus had never bothered to learn much about short-lived races beyond what he had needed to know to plunder them. At one time, he had found such foolishness the height of entertainment, but it had lost its appeal after the first few thousand years.

Now, he found he treasured beautiful things and stories more than anything else. He looked at the paintings Ariano had brought, payment for her debts, and beside them on the ground, a small, amber sphere.

The first painting was a scene from a nightmare, hideous, misshapen creatures so lifelike Cruentus could almost smell them. *"Monsters. I don't know what to call them. Everywhere,"* he recalled her saying, and here they were. He gazed at the portrait for long moments, then turned to the other. This one depicted simply a woman on her knees, hands over her face as if weeping, as the world about her melted under the intense heat of a bonfire built high enough to touch the sky. On the ground by her side lay a torch, still lit, presumably the very one she had used to start the fire.

"But does she weep because she started the fire, or did she start the fire because she weeps," the dragon wondered aloud.

"Fools damage themselves," came a voice from behind, a sharp, pointed voice Cruentus knew all too well. He turned to see Tasinal, in his preferred red and black, making a rude gesture at the dwindling form of Ariano. "Does it really matter how they view it? It's the harm they cause the rest of us that's of concern."

Cruentus scowled at his uninvited visitor, but stopped short of insult. The others were amusing. This one was dangerous, even to a five-thousand-year-old dragon, and as volatile as any Meite ever was. "You might have put an end to her when Lothrian began his foolishness."

"I might have," Tasinal replied. "But she was much more attractive at the time. She bribed me, as women are wont to do, and I found myself in a forgiving mood."

"She is a good artist," Cruentus said. "This piece moves me."

Tasinal nodded briefly, apparently in agreement, then asked, "Do you think she knew?"

Cruentus ruffled his wings and snorted flame. "About the piece? No." Gingerly, he took the amber sphere from the ground between his two smallest claws, barely able to hold on to such a tiny thing. He held it up to the sun, and looked at it closely. "I was hoping I would get the real one back, but this is the same one Amrath gave me long ago."

"How can you tell?"

"I marked it, of course." Cruentus dropped the sphere and stamped on it, crushing it to dust against the obsidian ground. "She would have been considerably angrier with me if she suspected. I as much as sent her and Lothrian to their deaths in Torium with your Council's little fraud."

Tasinal winked, an almost sheepish grin on his face. "How long have you known?"

"Since the moment Amrath gave it to me. I have a sense for such things. Where is the real piece?"

"Safe," Tasinal said with a cryptic smile. "That's all you need to know. And let's be honest, it all worked out just fine." His smile faded to a sneer. "Lothrian is far and away better off dead."

"And Ariano?"

Tasinal gave this some deep thought for a moment, rubbing at his chin. "She used to be quite the hot little piece of ass back in the day. But yes, she deserves it, too."

Cruentus chuckled. "Fate disagrees with you."

"There's no such thing."

"What's done is done," Cruentus needled.

Tasinal snorted. "I have other thoughts on that, too."

Cruentus eyed the sorcerer warily. Something about that statement felt odd. "What sort of black magic are you up to, sorcerer?"

Tasinal smiled back, an angelic expression of innocence on his face. "None you need concern yourself about."

Aiul did not recognize the afterlife, any more than he had known the place the first time he had visited. He once again lay face down on the charred ground, the scorched wasteland extending to every horizon, stark and barren beneath cold, gray light. Dark clouds boiled overhead, a gathering storm.

He did, however, recognize Elgar. The Dead God, wearing Aiul's own face, stared down at him with black eyes full of pain and rage. His armor seemed even more scored now, the wound in his throat larger, his agony more intense. In his gauntleted hand, he clutched something with a death grip, but Aiul could not make out what it was.

Even as Aiul rose to his feet, the figure before him swooned and staggered. Elgar fell to a knee, using his clenched fist for balance. "It cannot be mended," he whispered. "There is too much evil, too much retribution to mete out."

"Where am I?" Aiul asked.

"Nowhere. A waystation. You will not be here long."

Aiul suddenly felt a terrible chill within as memory poured back into his head like water filling a sinking ship. He remembered Papa's crushing grip, irresistible as fate, inexorable, implacable, just like the man. "Mei!" he gasped.

Elgar, his voice quiet and wispy, managed to chuckle, "No."

Aiul could barely find any words at all, and when he finally forced them from his lips, they came out as a croak. "Am I dead?"

Elgar looked up at Aiul, his black eyes like pits into the deepest void, the very antitheses of existence. "Yes," he said. "For a bit longer." He raised his clenched fist and spoke in his true voice. "*You are the one.*"

As Elgar's voice bored into Aiul's mind like a drill; Aiul could feel his horror slipping away, turning to hatred and rage. In his mind, he saw Papa's mad, electric eyes as he had last seen them, felt the hand tightening about his throat like an iron band and the cold fury of being robbed of life and hope yet again.

Aiul heard the cries of a thousand crows and the roar of flames, felt the flesh melting from his bones as Elgar spoke. "*Do you still want to rest, humble servant?*"

Aiul ground his teeth, despite knowing better. *What does it matter if I crack another? I am dead.*

"No," he answered. "No rest. I would have my revenge on all of them. You promised me!"

"*I am constrained by the order of things.*" Elgar clenched both his hands into fists and raised them before his face. "*You, however, are not.*" Spikes erupted from Elgar's fingers, metal talons now.

Aiul felt he understood, even though he did not. "How long will you suffer here?" he asked in a whisper, as if it were someone else speaking, not him.

"*I have suffered enough.*" Eerie, green light bled through the gauntlet fingers, growing brighter until it was almost blinding as Elgar drove the spikes through his own head.

Aiul stood in stunned silence as Elgar toppled over, dead by his own hand. His fist relaxed as it hit the ground, and Aiul gaped in horror to see what Elgar had been hiding.

A tiny half lion's head rolled from his limp grip and fell to the blasted ground. Even as Aiul recognized the thing for what it was, his vision wavered, and his senses were torn away in a whirlwind.

In the pit of Torium, Tomas rubbed his hands together as his underlings worked at clearing the last of the stone. Already, he could see the black liquid glimmering in the pool beneath, but he could not *reach* it! "Hurry!" he carped, slapping at the backs of multiple heads. "Work harder! Elgar commands!"

Tomas left them to their work and walked back out into the enormous cavern with the massive, spiral staircase. *This is all mine now.* In his mind, he envisioned how he would decorate. He would need a symbol, of course, but what?

Ten long years, he had waited for this moment. From the instant he knew the False Prophet and the Fool had slain the wretched creatures in Torium, that they had cleared a path, Tomas had known it was his destiny. But the leaders of his murder had been visionless cowards, preaching caution as if caution had ever gained Elgar's favor.

No, bold action was required, but to get himself into a position to lead had taken years of patience, slowly advancing to become Javier's right-hand man, and then Eduardo's. Javier had been easy to overcome once Tomas had secured his trust, but Eduardo had been a sly one, sleeping in a different location every night, keeping secrets. Of course, it was only sensible, after what happened to Javier, and it had taken two years to find Eduardo in a weak moment, but Tomas had a head for patterns, and patience eventually paid off.

Once he had presented the rest of the murder with Eduardo's head as proof of his strength, they had accepted him as their new leader. How could they not? He had Elgar's favor. He had the courage to do Elgar's will. He had a destiny, and they were fortunate indeed that he was leading them to glory, allowing them to ride his coattails into history.

When this is done, everyone in the kingdom of Reese will kneel before me or die! For so long, he had endured living as an outsider, hunted and reviled. Once he had the power, he would show them all.

A cry from the workers at the black pool broke Tomas from his dreams of glory. "What?" he shouted, his voice pitched high with excitement. *My ascension is nigh!*

Tomas waited a moment, expecting obedience, but there was no reply, only eerie silence. As he turned to the pool room to see what was the matter, his first thoughts were of the punishment he would inflict on his insolent underlings, but as he approached, he realized he could not see any of his people in the room. He felt a chill run down his spine, any thoughts of vengeance fading to unreasoning fear. He sensed something terribly wrong, something…unspeakable.

A hand, covered in metal, shot from the darkness and seized him about the throat, lifting him as if he were a child, or a toy. He struggled against the merciless grip, and cut his eyes downward to get a glimpse of his attacker. What he saw threatened to tear away what remained of his mind.

It both was and was not Elgar. Tomas had never seen the Dead God himself, only skins he wore, but even the dumbest of the murder knew the tales. The man currently choking the life from Tomas wore Elgar's armor. The skulls, some graven, some embossed, eyes set with obsidian, leered from scored plates. Cruel, gore streaked spikes rose from the attacker's shoulders and wrists, with more skulls at their bases, as if they have been impaled, and the helm he wore suggested a diving crow, wings stretched back, its face another grinning skull.

But the man inside the armor, if he could even be called such, Tomas realized to his horror that he knew. It was Elgar's Scion, the Dark Lord and False Prophet, the very man he had escorted to the Black Tabernacle a decade ago! He had the same white hair, the same deathly pallor, the same hawk face and cruel features. Only his eyes were different. They were now the same black as any that Elgar wore, but only in color. Where the Dead God's eyes had been filled with the cold of the grave, the Dark Lord's stare burned with hate and fury, even as his lips parted in a cruel grin.

"Torch!" the Dark Lord exclaimed, feigning good humor. "I assumed you were dead!" His face fell in brief, mock disappointment, before his mad grin returned. "Aren't you happy to see me?" He held Tomas in his crushing grip a bit longer, showing his power over Tomas's miserable life, before dropping him to the ground.

Tomas landed on the hard stones with a grunt, the fear inside him choking him almost as effectively as the Dark Lord's hand. The Dark Lord looked down on him with those black, burning eyes, his exposed teeth barely visible against his pale skin, and voiced a dark, vicious chuckle. "Don't you wonder what happened to your friends?"

Tomas, still gasping and rubbing at his neck, had no idea what answer would get him killed, or if indeed it would make any difference at all. Trembling, he simply shrugged and awaited a fate that he knew he was powerless to change.

The Dark Lord shook his head, amused by Tomas's fear, and raised a hand overhead. "Come forth, my servants!"

From the black pool came a sick bubbling sound, and Tomas watched in mounting horror as shapes rose from it. At first, he thought them men, but as the black liquid fell from them, leaving no sign of its passing, and exposed their bald heads and twisted faces, he saw that they were men no longer. Their eyes were the same burning black as the Dark Lord's, but there the similarities ended. These creatures were distorted, mockeries of men, with maws full of fangs, sloped foreheads, and hollow depressions where their noses would have been. Vicious talons sprouted from their fingers, like nails of the dead that had kept growing in the grave, but longer, more deadly, surely capable of tearing out a man's throat. Perhaps worst of all was how still they were once they had stood up. They were like statues, unblinking, unbreathing, dead things hungry to end the lives of all those around them once the leash was removed.

The ten workers he had set to clearing the rubble were unrecognizable, but they still wore articles of clothing that let Tomas know who they had been. *He wants me to know this could also be my fate. Perhaps there is hope for me, yet.*

The Dark Lord chuckled again as Tomas absorbed the sight, and said, "I will give you a choice, Torch. Join me," he said, placing a hand on his chest. "Or join them," he offered, gesturing toward the ghouls.

It was not, in Tomas's mind, any sort of choice. He touched his head to the floor and swore, "I live to serve you, Dark Lord."

"Then come with me and witness my ascension." Tomas looked up again, to see a look of intense hatred cross The Dark Lord's face as he ground his teeth. "Unlike my father's, it will be of consequence."

In response to some unheard command, the ghouls leapt from the pool and hunkered at the Dark Lord's feet as he extended a hand to Tomas. "Come."

What else can I do? Tomas took the Dark Lord's hand and rose, his gut telling him that, while he might have been spared, he had agreed to pay a terrible price for his life.

Maybe now, finally, I will gain the power!

The grate at the top of the huge spiral staircase opened silently at

Aiul's touch, allowing him and his minions access to the top of the central pyramid. Aiul walked out of the building and stood in the open on the very top step of Torium, looking out over the courtyard and the jungle beyond. The ghouls were silent, but Aiul could hear Torch's labored breathing, loud both from the climb and, doubtless, sheer terror. *He is but the first of many who will tremble in fear of my coming.*

Mists rose from the jungle, drifting in and out over the face of the fat blood moon hanging overhead, tinting the world below in yellow-orange. Aiul was reminded of Nihlos at night, with its orange light from the cloud cover, though he had never seen the moon there. Despite all of his rage and agony, there was still a part of him that thrilled at seeing the great round light in the sky and the stars around it, the same part that still reveled at snow or rain as small miracles.

He knew, now, where he had been, though he had no idea how long. It had seemed only a little while, mere minutes, yet much had changed. Torch was older, but it was difficult to tell how much time had passed for him. His kind didn't age like humans.

Years. That much is certain. Elgar must have waited for a particular moment, perhaps the right phase of the moon, or maybe it was simpler: he waited until his camp followers cleared the black pool. It didn't really matter. There was nothing and no one to return to, at any rate.

Clearly, Lothrian had failed, and who knew where everyone had gotten off to after that, or who else he took with him. Aiul found he could not bring himself to care. Far more important matters occupied his mind.

His twisted, undead creations followed like dogs, eager to please, anxious to rend flesh and cause destruction.

Destruction was just what Aiul wanted, and just what Elgar had wanted, as well, though he could never quite express it. The world was so full of evil, of hate, of misery and despair. It could never be cleansed. It could only be burned.

As Elgar had tried to explain to everyone long ago, true justice and equality could only be found in one place:

A world of ash.

SPECIAL THANKS TO:

ADAWIA E. ASAD
JENNY AVERY
BARDE PRESS
CALUM BEAULIEU
BEN
BECKY BEWERSDORF
BHAM
TANNER BLOTTER
ALFRED JOSEPH BOHNE IV
CHAD BOWDEN
ERREL BRAUDE
DAMIEN BROUSSARD
CATHERINE BULLINER
JUSTIN BURGESS
MATT BURNS
BERNIE CINKOSKE
MARTIN COOK
ALISTAIR DILWORTH
JAN DRAKE
BRET DULEY
RAY DUNN
ROB EDWARDS
RICHARD EYRES
MARK FERNANDEZ
CHARLES T FINCHER
SYLVIA FOIL
GAZELLE OF CAERBANNOG
DAVID GEARY
MICHEAL GREEN
BRIAN GRIFFIN

EDDIE HALLAHAN
JOSH HAYES
PAT HAYES
BILL HENDERSON
JEFF HOFFMAN
GODFREY HUEN
JOAN QUERALTÓ IBÁÑEZ
JONATHAN JOHNSON
MARCEL DE JONG
KABRINA
PETRI KANERVA
ROBERT KARALASH
VIKTOR KASPERSSON
TESLAN KIERINHAWK
ALEXANDER KIMBALL
JIM KOSMICKI
FRANKLIN KUZENSKI
MEENAZ LODHI
DAVID MACFARLANE
JAMIE MCFARLANE
HENRY MARIN
CRAIG MARTELLE
THOMAS MARTIN
ALAN D. MCDONALD
JAMES MCGLINCHEY
MICHAEL MCMURRAY
CHRISTIAN MEYER
SEBASTIAN MÜLLER
MARK NEWMAN
JULIAN NORTH

KYLE OATHOUT
LILY OMIDI
TROY OSGOOD
GEOFF PARKER
NICHOLAS (BUZ) PENNEY
JASON PENNOCK
THOMAS PETSCHAUER
JENNIFER PRIESTER
RHEL
JODY ROBERTS
JOHN BEAR ROSS
DONNA SANDERS
FABIAN SARAVIA
TERRY SCHOTT
SCOTT
ALLEN SIMMONS
KEVIN MICHAEL STEPHENS
MICHAEL J. SULLIVAN
PAUL SUMMERHAYES
JOHN TREADWELL
CHRISTOPHER J. VALIN
PHILIP VAN ITALLIE
JAAP VAN POELGEEST
FRANCK VAQUIER
VORTEX
DAVID WALTERS JR
MIKE A. WEBER
PAMELA WICKERT
JON WOODALL
BRUCE YOUNG

www.ingramcontent.com/pod-product-compliance
Lightning Source LLC
Chambersburg PA
CBHW031614180726
48284CB00005B/1538